SASSINAK

BAEN BOOKS
by ANNE McCAFFREY

The Planet Pirate Series
Sassinak (with Elizabeth Moon)
The Death of Sleep (with Jody Lynn Nye)
Generation Warriors (with Elizabeth Moon)

SASSINAK

ANNE McCAFFREY
ELIZABETH MOON

Sassinak

This is a work of fiction. All the characters and events portrayed in this book are fictional, and any resemblance to real people or incidents is purely coincidental.

Copyright © 1990 by Bill Fawcett & Associates

A Baen Books Original

Baen Publishing Enterprises
P.O. Box 1403
Riverdale, NY 10471
www.baen.com

ISBN: 978-1-9821-2492-2

Cover art by Bob Eggleton

First printing, March 1990
First trade paperback printing, October 2020

Distributed by Simon & Schuster
1230 Avenue of the Americas
New York, NY 10020

Library of Congress Cataloging-in-Publication Data

Names: McCaffrey, Anne, author. | Moon, Elizabeth, author.
Title: Sassinak / by Anne McCaffrey and Elizabeth Moon.
Description: Riverdale, NY : Baen Books, [2020]
Identifiers: LCCN 2020030405 | ISBN 9781982124922 (trade paperback)
Subjects: GSAFD: Science fiction.
Classification: LCC PS3563.A255 S27 2020 | DDC 813/.54—dc23
LC record available at https://lccn.loc.gov/2020030405

Printed in the United States of America

10 9 8 7 6 5 4 3 2 1

BOOK ONE

Chapter One

By the time anyone noticed that the carrier was overdue, no one cared. Celebrations had started two local days before, when the last crawler train came in from Zeebin. Sassinak, along with the rest of her middle school, had met that train, helped offload the canisters of personal-grade cargo, and then wandered through the crowded streets.

Last year she'd been too young—barely—for such freedom. Even now, she flinched a little from the noise and confusion. The City tripled in population for the week or so of celebration when the orecarriers came in. Every farmer, miner, crawler-train tech or engineer—everyone who possibly could, and some who shouldn't have—came to The City. It almost seemed to deserve the name, with crowds bustling between the rows of one-story prefab buildings that served the young colony as housing, storage, and manufacturing space. Sassinak could pretend she was on the outskirts of a *real* city, and the taller dome and blockhouse of the original settlement, could, with imagination, stand for the great soaring buildings she hoped one day to visit, on the worlds she'd heard about in school.

She caught sight of a school patch ahead of her, and recognized Caris's new (and slightly ridiculous) hairdo. Shoving between two meandering miners, who seemed disposed to slow down at every doorway, Sassinak grabbed her friend's elbow. Caris whirled.

"Don't you—! Oh, Sass, you idiot. I thought you were—"

"A drunken miner. Sure." Arm in arm with Caris, Sassinak felt safer—and slightly more adult. She gave Caris a sidelong look, and

Caris smirked back. They broke into a hip-swaying parody of the lead holovid's "Carin Coldae—Adventurer Extraordinary" and sang a snatch of the theme song. Someone hooted, behind them, and they broke into a run. Across the street, a familiar voice yelled "There go the skeleton twins" and they ran faster.

"Sinder," Caris said a block or so later, when they'd slowed down, "is a planetary snarp."

"Planetary nothing. Stellar snarp." Sassinak glowered at her friend. They were both long and lanky, and they'd heard as much of Sinder's skeleton twin joke as anyone could rightly stand.

"Interstellar." Caris always had to have the last word, Sassinak thought. It might not be right, but it was last.

"We're not going to think about Sinder." Sassinak wormed her fingers through the tangle of things in her jacket pocket and pulled out her credit ring. "We've got money to spend..."

"And you're my friend!" Caris laughed and shoved her gently toward the nearest food booth.

By the next day, the streets were too rowdy for youngsters, Sassinak's parents insisted. She tried to argue that she was no longer a youngster, but got nowhere. She was sure it had something to do with her mother's need for a babysitter, and the adult-only party in the block recreation center. Caris came over, which made it slightly better. Caris got along better with six-year-old Lunzie than Sass did, and that meant Sass could read stories to "the baby": Januk, now just over three. If Januk hadn't managed to spill three-months' worth of sugar ration while they were trying to make cookies from scratch, it might have been a fairly good day after all. Caris scooped most of the sugar back into the canister, but Sass was afraid her mother would notice the brown specks in it.

"It's just spice," Caris said firmly.

"Yes, but—" Sassinak wrinkled her nose. "What's that? Oh... dear." The cookies were not quite burnt, but she was sure they wouldn't make up for the spilled sugar. No hope that Lunzie wouldn't mention it, either—she was at that age, Sass thought, when having finally figured out the difference between telling a story and telling the truth, she wanted to let everyone know. Lunzie prefaced most talebearing with a loud "I'm telling the truth, now: I really am" which Sass found unbearable. It didn't help to be told that she herself had once, at about age five, scolded the Block Coordinator for using a polite euphemism at the table. "The right word is 'castrated,'" was what everyone said she'd said. Sass didn't believe it. She would never, in her entire life, no matter how early, have said something like that right out loud at the table. Now she cleaned up the cookcorner, saving what grains of sugar looked fairly clean, and wondered when she could insist that Lunzie and Januk go to bed.

"Eight days." The captain grinned at the pilot. "Eight days should be enough. For most of it anyway. Aren't we lucky that the carrier's late." They both laughed; it was an old joke for them, and a mystery for everyone else, how they could turn up handily when other ships were "late."

"We don't want to leave witnesses."

"No. But we may want to leave evidence . . . of a sort." The captain grinned, and the pilot nodded. Evidence implicating someone else. "Now—if those fools down there aren't drunk out of their wits, anticipating the carrier's arrival, I'm a shifter. We should be able to fake the contact, unless they speak some outlandish gabble. Let's see . . ." He scrolled through the directory information and shook his head. "No problem. Neo-Gaesh, and that's Orlen's birthtongue."

"He's from here?"

"No, the colonists here are from Innish-Ire, and Orlen's from Innish Outer Station. Same difference; same language and dialect. New colony—they won't have diverged that much."

"But the kids—they'll speak Standard?"

"FSP rules: they have to, by age eight. All colonies provided with tapes and cubes for the creches. We shouldn't have any problem."

Orlen, summoned to the bridge, muttered a string of things the captain hoped were Neo-Gaesh, and opened communications with the planet's main spaceport. For all the captain could tell, the mishmash of syllables coming back was exactly the same, only longer. Hardly a language at all, he thought, smug in his own heritage of properly crisp and tonal Chinese. He spoke Standard as well, and two other related tongues.

"They say they can't match our ID to the files," Orlen said, this time in Standard, interrupting that chain of thought.

"Tell 'em they're drunk and incompetent," said the captain.

"I did. I told them they had the wrong cube in the lock, an out-of-date directory entry, and no more intelligence than a cabbage, and they've gone to try again. But they won't turn on the grid until we match."

The pilot cleared his throat, not quite an interruption, and the captain looked at him. "We could jam our code into their computer..." he offered.

"Not here. Colony's too new; they've got the internal checks. No, we're going down, but keep talking, Orlen. If we can hold them off just a bit too long, we won't have to worry about their serious defenses. Such as they are."

In the assault capsules, the troops waited. Motley armor, stolen from a dozen different captured ships and minor bases, mixed weaponry of all manufactures, they lacked only the romance once associated with the concept of pirate. These were muggers, gangsters, two steps down from mercenaries and well aware of the price of failure. The Federation of Sentient Planets would not torture, rarely executed... but the thought of being whited, mindcleaned, and turned into obedient and useful workers... that was torture enough. So they had discipline, of a sort, and loyalty, of a sort, and were obedient, within limits to those who ruled the ship or hired it. On some worlds they passed as Free Trader's Guards.

Orlen's accusations had not been far wrong. When the last crawler train came in, everyone relaxed until the ore carriers arrived. The Spaceport Senior Technician was supposed to stay alert, on watch, but with the new outer beacon to signal and take care of first contact, why bother? It had been a long, long year, 460 days, and what harm in a little nip of something to warm the heart? One nip led to another. When the inner beacon, unanswered, tripped the relays that set every light in the control rooms blinking in disorienting random patterns, his first thought was that he'd simply missed the outer beacon signal. He'd finally found the combination of control buttons that turned the lights on steady, and shushed the excited (and none too sober) little crowd that had come in to see what happened. And having a friendly voice speaking Neo-Gaesh on the other end of the comm link only added to the confusion. He'd tried to say he could speak Standard well enough (not sure if he'd been too drunk to answer a hail in Standard earlier), but it came out tangled. And so on, and so on, and it was only stubbornness that kept him from turning on the grid when the ship's ID scan didn't match the record books. Damned sobersides spacemen, out there in the stars with nothing to do but sneak up on honest men trying to have a little fun—why should he do them a favor? Let 'em match their own ship up, or come in without the grid beacons on, if that's the game they wanted to play. He put the computer on a search loop, and took another little nip.

The computer's override warning buzz woke him again. The ship was much closer, just over the horizon, low, coming in on a landing pattern . . . and it was red-flagged. Pirate! he thought muzzily. It's a pirate. It can't be . . . but the computer, not fooled, and not having been stopped by the override sequence he was too drunk to key in, turned on full alarms, all over the building and the city. And the speech synthesizer, in a warm, friendly, calm female voice, said, "Attention. Attention. Vessel approaching has been identified as dangerous. Attention. Attention . . ."

But by then it was far too late.

Sassinak and Caris had eaten the last of the overbrowned cookies, and were well into the kind of long-after-midnight conversation they preferred. Lunzie grunted and tossed on her pallet; Januk sprawled bonelessly on his, looking, as Caris said, like something tossed up from the sea. "Little kids aren't human," said Sass, winding a strand of dark hair around her finger. "They're all alien, shapechangers like those Wefts you read about, and then turn human at—" She thought a moment. "Eleven or so."

"Eleven! You were eleven last year; I was. I was human . . ."

"Ha." Sass grinned, and watched Caris. "I wasn't human. I was special. Different—"

"You've always been different." Caris rolled away from Sass's slap. "Don't hit me; you know it. You like it. You would be alien if you could."

"I would be off this planet if I could," said Sass, serious for a moment. "Eight more years before I can even apply—aggh!"

"To do what?"

"Anything. No, not anything. Something—" her hands waved,

describing arcs and whorls of excitement, adventure, marvels in the vast and mysterious distance of time and space.

"Umm. I'll take biotech training and a lifetime spent figuring out how to insert genes for correctly handed proteins in our native fishlife." Caris wrinkled her nose. "You're not going to leave, Sass. This is the frontier. This is where the excitement is. Right here."

"Eating *fish*? Eating lifeforms?"

Caris shrugged. "I'm not devout. Those fins in the ocean aren't sentient, we know that much, and they could give us cheap, easy protein. Personally, I'm tired of gruel and beans, and since we have to fiddle with their genes, too, why not fishlife?"

Sassinak gave her a long look. True, lots of the frontier settlers weren't devout, and didn't find anything but a burdensome rule in the FSP strictures about eating meat. But she herself—she shivered a little, thinking of a finny wriggling in her throat. Something wailed, in the distance, and she shivered again. Then the houselights brightened and dimmed abruptly.

"Storm?" asked Caris. The lights blinked, now quickly, now slow. From the terminal in the other room came an odd sort of voice, something Sass had never heard before.

"Attention. Attention . . ."

The girls stared at each other, shocked for an endless instant into complete stillness. Then Caris leaped for the door, and Sass caught her arm.

"Wait—help me get Lunzie and Januk!"

The younger children were hard to wake, and cranky once roused. Januk demanded "my *big* jar" and Lunzie couldn't find her shoes. Sass, mind racing, dared to use the combination her father had once shown her, and opened her parents' sealed closet.

"What are you *doing*?" asked Caris, now by the door again with the other two. Her eyes widened as Sass pulled down the zipped cases: the military-issue projectile weapons issued to each adult colonist, and the lumpy, awkward part of a larger weapon which should—if they had time—mate with those from adjoining apartments to make something more effective.

Lunzie could just carry one of the long, narrow cases; Sass had to use both arms on the big one, and Caris took the other narrow one, along with Januk's hand. "We should stop at my place," Caris said, but when they got outside, they could see the red and blue lines crossing the sky. A white flare, at a distance. "That was the Spaceport offices," said Caris, still calm.

Other shapes moved in the darkness, converging on the Block Recreation Center; Sass recognized two classmates, both carrying weapons, and one trailing a string of smaller children. They made it to the Block Recreation Center just as adults came boiling out, most unsteady on their feet, and all cursing.

"Sassinak! Bless you—you remembered!" Her father, suddenly looking larger and more dangerous than she had thought for the last year or so, grabbed Lunzie's load and stripped off the green cover. Sass had seen such weapons in class videos; now she watched him strip and load it, hardly aware that her mother had taken the weapon Caris carried. Someone she didn't know yelled for a "PC-8 *base*, dammit!" and Sass's father said, without even looking at her, "Go, Sassy! That's your load!" She carried it across the huge single room of the Center to the cluster of adults assembling some larger weapons, and they snatched it, stripped off the cover, set it down near the door, and began attaching other pieces. An older woman grabbed her arm and demanded, "Class?"

"Six."

"You've had aid class?" When Sass nodded, the woman said "Good—then get over here," *Here* was on the far side of the Center, out of sight of her family, but with a crowd of middle school children, all busily laying out an infirmary area, just like in the teaching tapes.

The Center stank of whiskey fumes, of smoke, of too many bodies, of fear. Children's shrill voices rose above the adults' talking; babies wailed or shrieked. Sass wondered if the ship was down, that pirate ship. How many pirates would there be? What kinds of weapons would they have? What did pirates want, and what did they do? Maybe—for an instant she almost believed this thought—maybe it was just a drill, more realistic than the quarterly drills she'd grown up with, but not real. Perhaps a Fleet ship had chosen to frighten them, just to encourage more frequent practice with the weapons, and the first thing they'd see was a Fleet officer.

She felt more than heard the first concussive explosion, and that hope died. Whoever was out there was hostile. Everything the tapes had said or she'd overheard the adults say about pirates ran through her mind. Colonies disappeared, on some worlds, or survived gutted of needed equipment and supplies, with half their population gone to slavers. Ships taken even during FTL travel, when according to theory no one could say where they were.

Waiting there, unarmed, she realized that the thrice-weekly class in self-defense was going to do her no good at all. If the pirates had bigger guns, if they had weapons better than projectiles, she was going to die ... or be captured.

"Sass." Caris touched her arm; she reached out and gave Caris a quick hug. Around her, the others of her class had gathered in a tight knot. Even in this, Sassinak recognized the familiar. Since she'd started school, the others had looked to her in a crisis. When Berry fell off the crawler train, when Seh Garvis went crazy and attacked the class with an orecutter, everyone expected Sass to know what to do, and do it. Bossy, her mother had called her, more than once, and her father had agreed, but added that bossy plus tact could be very useful indeed. *Tact*, she thought. But what could she say now?

"Who's our triage?" she asked Sinder. He stood back, well away from Sass's friends.

"Gath." He pointed to a youth who had been cleared for off-planet training—medical school, everyone expected. He'd been senior school medic all four years. "I'm low-code this time."

Sass nodded, gave him a smile he returned uneasily, and checked again on each person's assignment. If they had nothing to do now, they could be sure they knew what to do when things happened.

All at once a voice blared outside—a loudhailer, Sass realized, with the speakers distorting the Neo-Gaesh vowels. From this corner of the building, she could pick out only parts of it, but enough to finish off the last bit of her confidence.

"... surrender ... will blow ... resistance ... guns ..."

The adults responded with a growl of defiance that covered the loudhailer's next statements. But Sass could hear something else, a clattering that sounded much like a crawler train, only different somehow. Then a hole appeared in the wall opposite her, as if someone had drawn it on paper and then ripped the center from the circle. She had never known that walls could be so fragile; she had felt so much safer inside. And now she realized that all together inside this building was the very last place anyone should be. Her shoulders felt hot, as if she'd stood in the summer sunlight too long, and she whirled to see the same kind of mark appearing on the wall behind her.

Later, when she had the training to analyze such situations, she knew that everything would have happened in seconds: from the breaching of the wall to the futile resistance of the adults, pitting third-rate projectile weapons against the pirates' stolen armament and much greater skill, to the final capture of the survivors, groggy from the gas grenades the pirates tossed in the building. But at the time, her mind seemed to race faster than time itself, so that she saw, as in a dream, her father swing his weapon to face the armored assault pod that burst through the wall itself. She saw a line of light touch his arm, and his weapon fell with the severed limb. Her mother caught him as he staggered, and they both charged. So did others. A swarm of adults tried to overwhelm the pod with sheer numbers, even as they died, but not before Sass saw what had halted it: her parents had thrown themselves into the tracks to jam them.

And it was not enough. If all the colonists had been there, maybe. But another assault pod followed the first, and another. Sass, screaming like the rest, charged at it, expecting every instant to be killed. Instead, the pods split open, and the troops rolled out, safe in their body armor from the blows and kicks the children could deliver. Then they tossed the gas grenades, and Sass could not breathe. Choking, she slid to the floor along with the rest.

She woke to a worse nightmare. Daylight, dusty and cold, came through the hole in the wall. She was nauseated and her head ached. When she tried to roll over and retch, something choked her, tightening around her throat. A thin collar around her neck, attached to another on either side by a thin cord of what looked like plastic. Sass gagged, terrified. Someone's boot appeared before her face, and bumped her, hard.

"Quit that."

Sassinak held utterly still. That voice had no softness in it, nothing but contempt, and she knew, without even looking up, what she would see. Around her, others stirred; she tried to see, without moving, who they were. Crumpled bodies, all sizes; some moved and some didn't. She heard boots clump on the floor, coming closer, and tried not to shiver.

"Ready?" asked someone.

"These're awake," said someone else. She thought that was the same voice that had told her to quit moving.

"Get'm up, clear this out, and start loading." One set of boots clumped off, the other reappeared in her vision, and a sharp nudge in the ribs made her gasp.

"You eight: get up." Sass tried to move, but found herself stiff and clumsy, and far more impeded by a collar and line than she would have thought. This sort of thing never bothered Carin Coldae, who had once captured a pirate ship by herself. The others in her eight had as much trouble; they staggered into each other, jerking each others' collars helplessly. The pirate, now that she was standing and could see clearly, simply stood there, face invisible behind the body armor's faceplate. She had no idea how big he really was—or even if it might be a woman.

Her gaze wandered. Across the Center, another link of eight struggled up; she saw another already moving under a pirate's direction. A thump in the ribs brought her head around.

"Pay attention! The eight of you are a link; your number is 15. If anyone gives an order for link 15, that's you, and you'd better be sharp about it. You—" the hard black nose of some weapon Sass couldn't name prodded her ribs, already sore. "You're the link leader. Your link gets into trouble, it's your fault. You get punished. Understand?"

Sass nodded. The weapon prodded harder. "You say 'Yessir' when you're asked something!"

She wanted to scream defiance, as Carin Coldae would have done, but heard herself saying "Yessir"—in Standard, no less—instead.

Down the line, the boy on the end said, "I'm thirsty." The weapon swung toward him, as the pirate said, "You're a slave now. You're not thirsty until *I* say you're thirsty." Then the pirate swung the weapon back at Sass, a blow she didn't realize was coming until it staggered her. "Your link's disobedient, 15. Your fault." He waited until she caught her breath, then went on with his instructions. Sass heard the smack of a blow, and a wail of pain, across the building, but didn't look around. "You carry the dead out. Pile 'em on the crawler train outside. You work fast enough, hard enough, you might get water later."

They worked fast enough and hard enough, Sass thought later. Her link of eight were all middle-school age, and they all knew her although only one of them was in her class. It was clear that they didn't want to get her into trouble. With her side making every breath painful, she didn't want trouble right then either. But dragging the dead bodies out, over the blood and mess on the floor . . . people she had known, but could recognize now only by the yellow skirt that Cefa always wore, the bronze medallion on Torry's wrist . . . that was worse than anything she'd imagined. Four or five links, by then, were working on the same thing. Later she realized that the pirates had killed the wounded: later yet she would learn that the same thing had happened all over The City, at other Centers.

When the building was clear of dead, her link and two others were loaded on the crawler train as well; pirates drove it, and sat on the piled corpses—as if they'd been pillows, she thought furiously—to guard the children riding behind. Sass knew they would kill them, wondered why they'd waited this long. The crawler train clanked and rumbled along, turning down the lane to the fisheries research station, where Caris had hoped to work. All its windows were broken, the door smashed in. Sass hadn't seen Caris all day, but she hadn't dared look around much, either. Nor had she seen Lunzie or Januk.

The crawler train rumbled to the end of the lane, near the pier. And there the children had to unload the bodies, drag them out on the pier, and throw them in the restless alien ocean. It was hard to maneuver on the pier; the links tended to tangle. The pirate guards hit anyone they could reach, forcing them to hurry, keep moving, keep working.

Sass had shut her mind off, as well as she could, and tried not to see the faces and bodies she handled. She had Lunzie's in her arms, and was halfway to the end of the pier, when she recognized it. A reflexive jerk, a scream tearing itself from her throat, and Lunzie's corpse slipped away, thumped on the edge of the pier, and splashed into the water. Sass stood rigid, unable to move. Something yanked on her collar; she paid it no heed. She heard someone cry out, say, "That was her *sister*!" and then blackness took her away.

✧　　✧　　✧

The rest of her time on Myriad, those few days of desperate work and struggle, she always shoved down below conscious memory. She had been drugged, then worked to exhaustion, then drugged again. They had loaded the choicest of the ores, the rare gemstones which had paid the planet's assessment in the FSP Development Office, the richest of the transuranics. She was barely conscious of her link's concern, the care they tried to take of her, the gentle brush of a hand in the rare rest periods, the way they kept slack in her collar-lead. But the rest was black terror, grief, and rage. On the ship, after that, her link spent its allotted time in Conditioning, and the rest in the tight and smelly confines of the slavehold. For them, no drugs or coldsleep to ease a long voyage: they had to learn what they were, the pirates informed them with cold superiority. They were cargo, saleable anywhere the FSP couldn't control. As with any cargo, they were divided into like kinds: age groups, sexes, trained specialists. As with any slaves, they soon learned ways to pass information among themselves. So Sass found that Caris was still alive, part of link 18. Januk had been left behind, alive but doomed, since no adults or older children remained to help those too young to travel. Most of The City's adults had died trying to defend it against the pirates; some survived, but none of the children knew how many.

Conditioning was almost welcome, to ease the boredom and misery of the slavehold. Sass knew—at least at first—that this was intentional. But as time passed, she and her link both had trouble remembering what free life had been like. Conditioning also meant a bath of sorts, because the pirate trainers couldn't stand the stench of the slavehold. For that alone it was welcome. The link stood, sat, reached, squatted, turned, all as one, on command. They learned assembly-line work, putting together meaningless combinations some other link had taken apart in a previous session. They learned Harish, a variant of Neo-Gaesh that some of the pirates spoke, and they were introduced to Chinese.

The end of the voyage came unannounced—for, as Sass now expected, slaves had no need for knowledge of the future. The landing was rough, bruisingly rough, but they had learned that complaint brought only more pain. Link by link the pirates—now unarmored—marched them off the ship, and along a wide gray street toward a line of buildings. Sass shivered; they'd been hosed down before leaving the ship, and the wind chilled her. The gravity was too light, as well. The planet smelled strange: dusty and sharp, nothing like Myriad's rich salt smell. She looked up, and realized that they were inside something—a dome? A dome big enough to cover a spaceport and a city?

All the city she could see, in the next months, was slavehold. Block after block of barracks, workshops, factories, five stories high and stretching in all directions. No trees, no grass, nothing living but the human slaves and human masters. Some were huge, far taller than Sass's parents had been, heavily muscled like the thugs that Carin Coldae had overcome in *The Ice-World Dilemma*.

They broke up the links, sending each slave to a testing facility to see what skills might be saleable. Then each was assigned to new links, for work or training or both, clipped and unclipped from one link after another as the masters desired. After all that had happened, Sass was surprised to find that she remembered her studies. As the problems scrolled onto the screen, she could think, immerse herself in the math or chemistry or biology. For days she spent a shift at the test center, and a shift at menial work in the barracks, sweeping floors that were too bare to need sweeping, and cleaning the communal toilets and kitchens. Then a shift at assembly work, which made no more sense to her than it ever had, and a bare six hours of sleep, into which she fell as into a well, eager to drown.

She had no way to keep track of the days, and no reason to. No way to find her old friends, or trace their movements. New friends she made easily, but the constant shifting from link to link made it hard for such friendships to grow. Then, long after her testing was finished, and she was working three full shifts a day, she was unclipped and taken to a building she'd not yet seen. Here, clipped into a long line of slaves, she heard the sibilant chant of an auctioneer and realized she was about to be sold.

By the time she reached the display stand, she had heard the spiel often enough to deaden her mind to the impact. Human female, Gilson stage II physical development, intellectual equivalent grade eight general, grade nine mathematics, height so much, massing so much, planet of origin, genetic stock of origin, native and acquired languages, specific skills ratings, all the rest. She expected the jolt of pain that revealed to the buyers how sensitive she was, how excitable, and managed to do no more than flinch. She had already learned that the buyers rarely looked for beauty—that was easy enough to breed, or surgically sculpt. But talents and skills were chancy, and combined with physical vigor, chancier yet. Hence the reason for taking slaves from relatively young colonies.

The bidding went on, in a currency she didn't know and couldn't guess the value of. Someone finally quit bidding, and someone else pressed a heavy thumb to the terminal ID screen, and someone else—another slave, this time, by the collar—led her away down empty corridors and finally clipped her lead to a ring by a doorway. Through all this Sass managed not to tremble visibly, or cry, although she could feel the screams tearing at her from inside.

"What's your name?" asked the other slave, now stacking boxes beside the door. Sass stared at him. He was much older, a stocky, graying man with scars seaming one arm, and a groove in his skull where no hair grew. He looked at her when she didn't answer, and smiled a gap-toothed smile. "It's all right—you can answer me if you want, or not."

"Sassinak!" She got it out all at once, fast and almost too loud. Her name! She had a name again.

"Easy," he said. "Sassinak, eh? Where from?"

"M-myriad." Her voice trembled, now, and tears sprang to her eyes.

"Speak Neo-Gaesh?" he asked, in that tongue. Sass nodded, too close to tears to speak.

"Take it easy," he said. "You can make it." She took a long breath, shuddering, and then another, more quietly. He nodded his approval. "You've got possibilities, girl. Sassinak. By your scores, you're more than smart. By your bearing, you've got guts to go with it. No tears, no screams. You did jump too much, though."

That criticism, coming on top of the kindness, was too much; her temper flared. "I didn't so much as say ouch!"

He nodded. "I know. But you jumped. You can do better." Still angry, she stared, as he grinned at her. "Sassinak from Myriad, listen to me. Untrained, you didn't let out a squeak... what do you think you could do with training?"

Despite herself, she was caught. "Training? You mean...?"

But down the corridor came the sound of approaching voices.

He shook his head at her, and stood passively beside the stacked cartons, at her side.

"What's *your* name?" she asked very quietly, and very quietly he answered:

"Abervest. They call me Abe." And then so low she could hardly hear it, "I'm Fleet."

Chapter Two

Fleet. Sassinak held to that thought through the journey that followed, crammed as she was into a cargo hauler's front locker with two other newly purchased slaves. She found out afterwards that that had not been punishment, but necessity; the hauler went out of the dome and across the barren, airless surface of the little planet that served as a slave depot. Outside the insulated, pressurized locker—or the control cab, where Abe drove in relative comfort—she would have died.

Their destination was another slave barracks, this one much smaller. Sassinak expected the same sort of routine as before, but instead she was assigned to a training facility. Six hours a day before a terminal, learning to use the math she already knew in mapping, navigation, geology. Learning to perfect her accent in Harish and learning to understand (but never speak) Chinese. Another shift in manual labor, working at whatever jobs needed doing, according to the shift supervisor. She had no regular duties, nothing she could depend on.

One of the most oppressive things was the simple feeling that she could not even *see* out. She had always been able to run outdoors and look at the sky, wander into the hills for an afternoon with friends. Now . . . now some blank ugliness stopped her gaze, as if by physical force, everywhere she looked. Most buildings had no windows: there was nothing outside to see but the wall of another prefab hulk nearby. Trudging the narrow streets from one assignment to another, she learned that looking up brought a quick scolding, or a blow. Besides, she couldn't see anything above but the grayish haze of the dome. She could not tell how large the moon or planet was, how far she'd been taken from the original landing site, even how many buildings formed the complex in which she was trained. Day after day, nothing but the walls of these prefabs, indoors and out, always the same neutral gritty gray. She quit trying to look up, learned to contain herself within herself, and hated herself for making that adjustment.

But one shift a day, amazingly, was free. She could spend it in the language labs, working at the terminal, reading . . . or, as most often, with Abe.

Fleet, she soon learned, was his history and his dream. He had been Fleet, had enlisted as a boy just qualified, and worked his way rating by rating, sometimes slipping back when a good brawl intruded on common sense, but mostly rising steadily through the ranks as a good spacer could. Clever, but without the intellect that would have won him a place at the Academy; strong, but not brutal with it; brave without the brashness of the boy he had been, he had clenched himself around the virtues of the Service as a drowning man might cling to a limb hanging in the water. Slave he might be, in all ways, but yet he was Fleet.

"They're tough," he said to her, soon after they arrived. "Tough as anything but the slavers, and maybe even more. They'll break you if they can, but if they can't. . ." His voice trailed away, and she glanced over to see his eyes glistening. He blinked. "Fleet never forgets," he said. "Never. They may come late, they may come later, but they come. And if it's later, never mind. Your name's on the rolls, it'll be in Fleet's memory, forever."

Over the months that followed, Sassinak began to think of Fleet as something other than the capricious and arrogant arm of power her parents had told her about. Solid, Abe said. Dependable. The same on one ship as on any; the ranks the same, the ratings the same, the specialties the same, barring the difference in a ship's size or weaponry.

He would not say how long he had been a slave, or what had happened, but his faith in the Fleet, in the Fleet's long arm and longer memory, sank into her mind, bit by bit. Her supervisors varied: some quick to anger, some lax. Abe smiled, and pointed out that good commanders were consistent, and good services had good commanders. When she came to their meetings bruised and sore from an undeserved punishment, he told her to remember that: someday she would have power, and she could do better.

She could do better even then, he said one evening, reminding her of their first meeting. "You're ready now," he said. "I've something to show you."

"What?"

"Physical discipline, something you do for yourself. It'll make it easier on you when things get tough, here or anywhere. You don't have to feel the pain, or the hunger—"

"I can't do that!"

"Nonsense. You worked six hours straight at the terminal today—didn't even break for the noonmeal. You were hungry, but you weren't thinking about it. You can learn not to think about it unless you want to."

Sass grinned at him. "I can't do calculus all the time!"

"No, you can't. But you can reach that same core of yourself, no matter what you think of. Now sit straight, and breathe from down here—" He poked her belly.

It was both harder and easier than she'd expected. Easier to slip into a trancelike state of concentration *on* something—a technique she'd learned at home, she thought, studying while Lunzie and Januk played. Harder to withdraw from the world without that specific focus.

"It's in *you*," Abe insisted. "Down inside yourself, that's where you focus. If it's something outside, math or whatever, they can tear it away. But not what's inside." Sass spent one frustrating session after another feeling around inside her head for something—anything—that felt like what Abe described. "It's not in your head," he kept insisting. "Reach deeper. It's way down." She began to think of it as a center of gravity, and Abe nodded when she told him. "That's closer—use that, if it helps."

When she had that part learned, the next was harder. A simple trance wasn't enough, because all she could do was endure passively. She would need, Abe explained, to be able to exert all her strength at will, even the reserves most people never touched. For a long time she made no progress at all, would gladly have quit, but Abe wouldn't let her.

"You're learning too much in your tech classes," he said soberly. "You're almost an apprentice pilot now—and that's very saleable." Sass stared at him, shocked. She had never thought she might be sold again—sent somewhere else, away from Abe. She had almost begun to feel safe. Abe touched her arm gently. "You see, Sass, why you need this, and need it now. You aren't safe: none of us is. I could be sold tomorrow—would have been before now, if I weren't so useful in several tech specialties. They may keep you until you're a fully qualified pilot, but likely not. There's a good market for young pilot apprentices, in the irregular trade." She knew he meant pirates, and shuddered at the thought of being back on a pirate ship. "Besides," he went on, "there's something more you need to know, that I can't tell you until you can do this right. So get back to work."

When she finally achieved something he called adequate, it wasn't much more than her normal strength, and she exhausted it quickly. But Abe nodded his approval, and had her practice almost daily. Along with that practice came the other information he'd promised.

"There's a kind of network," he said, "of pirate victims. Remembering where they came from, who did it, who lived, and how the others died. We keep thinking that if we can ever put it all together, everything we know, well find out who's behind all this piracy. It's not just independents—although I heard that the ship that took Myriad was an independent, or on the outs with its sponsor. There's evidence of some kind of conspiracy at FSP itself. I don't know what, or I'd kill myself to get that to Fleet somehow, but I know there's evidence. And I couldn't put you in touch with them until you could shield your reactions."

"But who—"

"They call themselves Samizdat—an old word, some language I never heard of, supposed to mean underground or something. Maybe it does, maybe not. That doesn't matter. But the name does, and your keeping it quiet does."

Study, work, practice with Abe. When she thought about it— which she did rarely—it was sort of a parody of the life she'd expected at home on Myriad. School, household chores, the tight companionship of her friends. But flunking a test at home had meant a scolding; here it meant a beating. Let Januk spill precious rationed food—her eyes filled, remembering the sugar that last night—and her mother would expostulate bitterly. But if she spilled a keg of seeds, hauling it to the growing frames, her supervisor would cuff her sharply, and probably dock her a meal. And instead of friends her own age, to gossip about schoolmates and families, to share the jokes and dreams, she had Abe. Time passed, time she could not measure save by the subtle changes in her own body: a little taller, she thought. A little wider of hip, more roundness, even though the slave diet kept her lean.

It finally occurred to her to wonder why they were allowed such freedom, when she realized that other slave friendships were broken up intentionally, by the supervisors. Abe grinned mischievously. "I'm valuable; I told you that. And they think I need a lovely young plaything now and then—"

Sass reddened. Here girls younger than she were taught arts of love; but on Myriad, in her family's religion, only those old enough to start a separate family were supposed to know how. Although they'd all complained mildly, life on a pioneer planet kept them too busy to regret. Abe went on.

"I told 'em I'd instruct you myself. Didn't want any of their teachings getting in my way." Sass stared at the floor, furious with him and his amusement. "Don't fluff feathers at me, girl," he said firmly. "I saved you a lot of trouble. You'd never have been assigned that full-time, smart as you are, and saleable as tech-slaves are, but still..."

"All right." It came out in a sulky mutter, and she cleared her throat loudly. "All right. I understand—"

"You don't, really, but you will later." His hand touched her cheek, and turned her face towards his. "Sass, when you're free—and I do believe you'll be free someday—you'll understand what I did and why. Reputation doesn't mean anything here. The truth always does. You're going to be a beauty, my girl, and I hope you enjoy your body in all ways. Which means *you* deciding when and how."

She didn't feel comfortable with him for some time after that. Some days later, he met her with terrifying news.

"You're going to be sold," he said, looking away from her. "Tomorrow, the next day—that soon. This is our last meeting. They only told me because they offered me another—"

"But, Abe—" she finally found her voice, faint and trembling as it was.

"No, Sass." He shook his head. "I can't stop it."

Tears burst from her eyes. "But—but it can't be—"

"Sass, *think*!" His tone commanded her; the tears dried on her cheeks. "Is this what I've taught you, to cry like any silly spoiled brat of a girl when trouble comes?"

Sass stared at him, and then reached for the physical discipline he'd taught her. Breathing slowed, steadied; she quit trembling. Her mind cleared of its first blank terror.

"That's better. Now listen—" Abe talked rapidly, softly, the rhythm of his speech at first strange and then compelling. When he stopped, Sass could hardly recall what he'd said, only that it was important, and she would remember it later. Then he hugged her, for the first time, his strength heartening. She still had her head on his shoulder when the supervisor arrived to take her away.

She passed through the sale barn without really noticing much; this time the buyer had her taken back to the port, to a scarred ship with no visible registration numbers. Inside, her escort handed her collar thong to a lean man with scarlet and gold collar tabs. Sass recalled the rank—senior pilot—from a far-distant shipping consortium. He looked her over, then shook his head.

"Another beginner. Bright stars, you'd think they'd realize I need something more than a pilot apprentice. And a dumb naked girl who probably doesn't even speak the same language." He turned away and poked the bulkhead. With a click and hiss, a locker opened; he rummaged inside and pulled out rumpled tunic and pants, much-mended. "Here. Clothes. You understand?" He mimed dressing, and Sass took the garments, putting them on as he watched. Then he led her along one corridor, then into a pop-tube that shot them to the pilot's "house"—a small cramped compartment lined with vidscreens and control panels. To Sass's relief, her training made sense of the chaos of buttons and toggles and flicking lights. That must be the Insystem computer, and that the FTL toggle, with its own shielded computer flickering, now, in not-quite-normal space. The ship had two Insystem drives, one suitable for atmospheric landings. The pilot tweaked her thong and grinned when she looked at him.

"I can tell you recognize most of this. Have you ever been off-station?" He seemed to have forgotten that she might not speak his language. Luckily, she could.

"No... not since I came."

"Your ratings are high—let's see how you do with this..." He pointed to one of the three seats, and Sass settled down in front of a terminal much like that in training—even the same manufacturer's logo on the rim. He leaned over her, his breath warm on her ear, and entered a problem she remembered working.

"I've done that one before," she said.

"Well, then, do it again." Her fingers flew over the board: codes for origin and destination, equations to calculate the most efficient combination of travel time, fuel cost of Insystem drive, probability flux of FTL... and, finally, the transform equations that set up the FTL path. He nodded when she was done.

"Good enough. Now maximize for travel time, using the maximum allowable FTL flux."

She did that, and glanced back. He was scowling.

"You'd travel a .35 flux path? Where'd you get that max from?" Sass blushed; she'd misplaced a decimal. She placed the errant zero, and accepted the cuff on her head with equanimity. "That's better, girl," he said. "You youngers haven't seen what a high flux means—be careful, or you'll have us spread halfway across some solar system, and you won't be nothin' but a smear of random noise in somebody's radio system. Now—what's your name?"

She blinked at him. Only Abe had used her name. But he stared back, impudent and insistent, and ready to give her a clout. "Sass," she said. He grinned again, and shrugged.

"Suits you," he said. Then he swung into one of the other seats, and cleared her screen. "Now, girl, we go to work."

Life as an indentured apprentice pilot—the senior pilot made it clear they didn't like the word "slave"—was considerably more lax than her training had been. She wore the same collar, but the thong was gone. No one would tell her what the ship's allegiance was—if any—or any more than its immediate next destination, but aside from that she was treated as a crew member, if a junior one. Besides senior pilot Krewe, two junior pilots were aboard: a heavy-set woman named Fersi, and a long, angular man named Zoras. Three at a time worked in the pilothouse when maneuvering from one drive system to another, or when using Insystem drives. Sass worked a standard six hour shift as third pilot under the others. When they were off, one or the other of the pilots gave her instruction daily—ship's day, that is. Aside from that, she had only to keep her own tiny cubicle tidy, and run such minor errands as they found for her. The rest of the time she listened and watched as they talked, argued, and gambled.

"Pilots don't mingle," Fersi warned her, when she would have sought more interaction with the ship's crew. "Captain's due respect, but the rest of 'em are no more spacers than rock is a miner. They'd do the same work groundside: fight or clean or cook or run machinery or whatever. Pilots are the old guild, the first spacers; you're lucky they trained you to that."

History, from the point of view of the pilots, was nothing like she'd learned back on Myriad. No grand pattern of human exploration, meetings with alien races, the formation of alliances and then the Federation of Sentient Planets. Instead, she heard a litany of names that ran back to Old Terra, stories with all the details worn away by time. Lindberg, the Red Baron, Bader, Gunn—names from before spaceflight, they said, all warriors of the sky in some ancient battle, from which none returned. Heinlein and Clarke and Glenn and Aldridge, from the early days in space . . . all the way up to Ankwir, who had just opened a new route halfway across the galaxy, cutting the flux margin below .001.

If she had not missed Abe so much, she might almost have been happy. Ship food that the others complained about she found ample and delicious. She had plenty to learn, and teachers eager to instruct. The pilots had long ago told each other their timeworn stories. But long before she forgot Abe and the slave depot, the raid came.

She was asleep in her webbing when the alarm sounded. The ship trembled around her; beneath her bare feet the deck had the odd uncertain feel that came with transition from one major drive to another.

"Sass! Get in here!" That was Krewe, loud enough to be heard over the racket of the alarm. Sass staggered a little, working her way around to her usual seat. Fersi was already there, intent on the screen. Krewe saw her and pointed to the number two position. "It's not gonna do any good, but we might as well try . . ."

Sass flicked the screen to life, and tried to make sense of the display. Something had snatched them out of FTL space, and dumped them into a blank between solar systems. And something with considerably more mass was far too close behind.

"Fleet heavy cruiser," said Krewe shortly. "Picked us up awhile back, and set a trap—"

"What?" Sass had had no idea that anything could find, let alone capture, a ship in FTL.

He shrugged, hands busy on his board. "Fleet has some new tricks, I guess. And we're about out. Here—" He tossed a strip of embossed plastic over to her. "Stick that in your board, there on the side, when I say."

Sass looked at it curiously: about a finger long, and half that wide, it looked like no data storage device she'd seen. She found the slot it would fit, and waited. Suddenly the captain's voice came over the intercom.

"Krewe—got anything for me? They're demanding to board—"

"Maybe. Hang on." Krewe nodded at Sass, and slid an identical strip into the slot of his board. Sass did the same, as did Fersi. The ship seemed to lurch, as if it had tripped over something, and the lights dimmed. Abruptly Sass realized that she was being pressed into the back of her seat—and as abruptly, the pressure shifted to one side, then the other. Then something made a horrendous noise, all the lights went out, and in the sudden cold dark she heard Krewe cursing steadily.

She woke in a clean bunk in a brightly lit compartment full of quiet bustle. Almost at once she missed a familiar pressure on her neck, and lifted her hand. The slave collar was gone. She glanced around warily.

"Ah...you're awake." A man in a clean white uniform, sleeves striped to the elbow with black and gold, came to her. "And I'll bet you wonder where you are, and what happened, and—do you know what language I'm speaking?"

Sass nodded, too amazed to speak. Fleet. It had to be Fleet. She tried to remember what Abe had told her about stripes on the sleeves; these were wing-shaped, which meant something different from the straight ones.

"Good, then." The man nodded. "You were a slave, right? Taken in the past few years, I daresay, from your age—"

"How do you know my—"

He grinned. He had a nice grin, warm and friendly. "Teeth, among other things. General development." At this point Sass realized that she had on something clean and soft, a single garment that was certainly not the patched tunic and pants she'd worn on the other ship. "Now—do you remember where you came from?"

"My ... my home?" When he nodded, she said, "Myriad." At his blank look, she gave the standard designation she'd been taught in school, so long ago. He nodded again, and she went on to tell him what had happened to the colony.

"And then?" She told of the original transport, the training she'd received as a slave, and then her work on the ship. He sighed. "I suppose you haven't the faintest idea where that depot planet is, do you?"

"No. I—" Her eyes fixed suddenly on the insignia he wore on his left breast. It meant something. It meant ... Abe's face came to her suddenly, very earnest, speaking swiftly and in an odd broken rhythm, something she had never quite remembered, but didn't worry about because someday— And now was someday, and she found herself reciting whatever he had said, just as quickly and accurately. The man stared at her.

"You—! You're too young; you couldn't—!" But now that it was back out, she knew ... knew what knowledge Abe had planted in her (and in how many others, she suddenly wondered, who had been sold away?), hoping that someday, somehow she might catch sight of that insignia (and how had he kept his, hidden it from his owners?) and have the memory wakened. She knew where that planet was, and the FTL course, and the codewords that would get a Fleet vessel past the outer sentinel satellites ... all the tidbits of knowledge that Abe had gleaned in years of slavery, while he pretended obedience.

Her information set off a whirlwind of activity. She herself was bundled into a litter and carried along spotless gleaming corridors, to be set down at last, with utmost gentleness, in a cabin bunk. A luxurious cabin, its tile floor gentled with a brilliant geometric carpet, several comfortable-looking chairs grouped around a low round table. She heard bells in the distance, the scurry of many feet . . . and then the door to the cabin closed, and she heard nothing but the faint hiss of air from the ventilators.

In that silence, she fell asleep again, to be wakened by a gentle cough. This time, the white uniform was decorated with gold stripes on the sleeves, straight ones that went all the way around. *Rings*, she thought vaguely. Four of them. And six little somethings on the shoulders, little silvery blobs. "Stars are tops," Abe had said, "Stars are admirals. But *anything* on the shoulders means officer."

"The Medical Officer says you're well enough," said the person with all that gold and silver. "Can you tell me more about what you remember?" He was tall, thin, gray-haired, and Sass might have been frightened into silence if he hadn't smiled at her, a fatherly sort of smile.

She nodded, and repeated it all again, this time in a more normal tone.

"And who told you this?" he asked.

"Abe. He . . . he was Fleet, he said."

"He must be." The man nodded. "Well, now. The question is, what do we do with you?"

"This—this *is* a Fleet ship, isn't it?"

The man nodded again. "The *Baghir*, a heavy cruiser. Let me brief you a little. The ship you were on—know anything about it?" Sass shook her head. "No—they just stuck you in the pilothouse, I'll bet, and put you to work. Well, it was an independent cargo carrier. Doubles as a slave ship some runs; this time it had maybe twenty young, prime tech-trained slaves and a load of entertainment cubes—if you call that kind of thing entertainment." He didn't explain further, and Sass didn't ask.

"We'd heard a shipment might be coming into a neighboring system, so we had a fluxnet in place. You don't need to know how that works, only it can jerk a ship out of hyperspace when it works right. When it works wrong, there's nothing to pick up. Anyway, it worked, and there your ship was, and there we were, ready to trail and take it. Which we did. The other slaves—and there's two from Myriad, by the way—are being sent back to Sector HQ, where they'll go through Fleet questioning and court procedures to reestablish their identities. They're innocent parties; all we do is make sure they haven't been planted with dangerous hidden personalities. That's happened before with freed slaves; one of them had been trained as an assassin while under drugs. Freed, and back at school, he went berserk and killed fourteen people before he could be subdued." He shook his head, then turned to her.

"You, though. You're our clue to what's really happened, and you know where the slave depot is. You've told us what you know—or what you think you know—but I'm not sure your Fleet friend put all he had to say in one implanted message. If you were willing to come along when we go—"

Sass pushed herself upright. "You're going *there*? Now?"

"Well, not this instant. But soon—in a few shipdays, at the most. The thing is, you're a civilian, and you're underage. I have no right to ask you, and no right to take you. But it would be a help."

Tears filled her eyes; it was too much too soon. She struggled to regain the discipline Abe had taught her, slowing her breathing, and steadying against the strain. The officer watched her, his expression shifting from concern through puzzlement to something she could not define. "I...I want to go," she said. "If...if Abe—"

"If Abe is still alive, we'll find him. Never fear. And now you, young lady, need more sleep."

There had been another implanted message, one that came out under the expert probing of the ship's medical team. This one, Sass realized, gave details of the inner defenses, descriptions of the little planet's surface, and the name of the trading combines which dealt in the slaves...including the one which had purchased and trained her. She came from that session shaken and pale, regaining her normal energy only after another long sleep and two solid meals. For the rest of the journey, she had nothing to do but wait, a waiting made more bearable by the friendly crewwomen who showered her with attention and minor luxuries—real enough for someone who'd been a slave for years. Although the captain would not let her join the landing party, when the cruiser had cleared the skies and sent the marines down, she was on hand when Abe returned to the Fleet. Scarred and battered as he was, wearing the ragged slave tunic, and carrying nothing but his pride, he marched from the shuttle into the docking bay as if on parade. The captain had come to the docking bay himself. Sass hung back, breathless with awe and delight, as they went through the old ritual. When it was over, and Abe came to her, she was suddenly shy of him, half-afraid to touch him. But he hugged her close.

"I'm so *proud* of you, Sass!" He pushed her away, then hugged her again.

"I didn't do much," she began, but he snorted.

"Didn't do much! Well, if that's the way you want to tell the story, it's not mine. Come on, girl—soon's I've changed into decent clothes—" He looked around, to meet the grins of the others in the bay... kind grins, Sass noticed.

One of the men beckoned to him, and he followed. Sass stared after him. He belonged here; she could tell that. Where would she belong? She thought of the captain's comments on the other freed slaves... Fleet questioning and court procedures... hardly an inviting prospect.

"Don't worry," one of the men said to her. "There's enough wealth here to give every one of you a new start—and you most of all, being as you found the place."

Still she worried, waiting for Abe to reappear, and when he did, clad in the crisp uniform and stripes of his rank, she was even more worried. A new start, somewhere else, with strangers... she knew, without asking for details, that none of her family were left.

"Don't worry," he echoed the other man's comment. "You're not going to be lost in the system somewhere. You're my girl, and I'm Fleet, and it's going to be fine."

Chapter Three

By the time Sassinak arrived at Regg with Abe, she was as ready as he to praise the Fleet, and glad to think of herself as almost a Fleet dependent. The only thing better than that was to be Fleet herself. Which, she soon found, was exactly what Abe planned for her.

"You've got the brains," he said soberly, "to make the Academy list and be a Fleet officer. And more than the brains, the guts. You weren't the first I tried to help, Sass, but you were one of only three who didn't fall apart when the time came to leave. And both of those were killed."

"But how?" Sass wanted nothing more than to enter the gleaming white arches of the Academy gates ... but that required recommendations from FSP representatives. How would an orphan from a plundered colony convince someone to recommend her?

"First there's the Fleet prep school. If I formally adopt you, then you're eligible, as the daughter of a Fleet veteran—and no, it doesn't matter that I'm not an officer. Fleet's Fleet."

"But you're—" Sass reddened. Abe had been retired, over his protests; his gimpy arm was past treatment, and wouldn't pass the Medical Board. He had argued, pled, and finally come back to their assigned quarters glum as she'd never seen him before.

"Retired, but still Fleet. Oh, Cousins take it, I knew they'd do it. I knew when the arm didn't heal straight—after six months or so, it's too late. But I thought maybe I could Kipling them into it."

"Kipling?"

"Kipling. Wrote half the songs the Fleet sings, and probably most of the rest. Service slang is, if you're sweet-talking someone into something, 'specially if it's sort of sentimental, that's Kipling. Where you came from, they probably said 'Irish them into it,' and I'll bet you don't know where that came from. But don't worry—I can't be active duty, but disabled vets—" His expression made it clear that he refused to think of himself as disabled. "—we old crips can usually get work in one of the bureaus." Sass asked again about the prep school.

"Three or four years there, 'til you pass the exams—and I don't doubt you will. Don't worry about the letters you need. You impressed the captain more than a little, and he's related to half the FSP reps in this sector."

From there, things went smoothly: the adoption, the entry into the prep school. Although the other students were her age, none had her experience, and they were still young enough to show their awe. Sass found herself ahead of schedule in her math classes, thanks to the slave tech training, while Abe's lessons in physical discipline and concentration helped her regain lost ground in the social sciences. She felt out of place at first in the social life of school—she could not regain the carefree camaraderie of younger years—but she looked forward to the Academy with such singleminded ambition that everyone soon considered her another Academy-bound grind.

Abe's apartment, in a large block of such buildings, was unlike any place Sass had ever lived. Her parents' apartment on Myriad had been a standard prefab, the same floor plan as every other apartment in the colony. Large families had had two or three, as needed, with doors knocked through adjoining walls. None of the living quarters were more than one story high, and few of the other buildings. At the slaver depot, all the buildings were even cheaper prefabs, big ugly buildings designed to hold the maximum cubage. There she had slept in a windowless barracks, in a rack of bunks.

Abe had a second-floor corner apartment, with a bedroom for each of them, a living room, study, and small kitchen. From her room, Sass looked into a central courtyard planted with flowers and one small tree with drooping leaves. From the living room she could see across a wide street to a similar building across from them. It felt amazingly spacious and light; she spent hours, at first, watching people in the street below, or looking out across the city.

For their apartment, like most, stood on one of the low hills that faced the harbor.

Regg itself was a terraformed planet, settled first by the usual colonists, in their case agricultural specialists, and then chosen as Fleet Headquarters because of its position in human-dominated space. Here in its central city, Fleet was the dominant force. Abe took Sassinak touring: to the big blocky buildings of Headquarters itself, all sheathed in white marble, to the riverside parks that ended in the great natural harbor, a wide almost circular bay of deep blue water edged in gray cliffs on the east and west, opening past a small, rocky island to the greater sea beyond. By careful design, the river mouth itself had been left clear, but Sass saw both the Fleet and civilian ports set back on either side. Although FSP regulations forbade the eating of meat, fishing was still done on many human-settled worlds, whose adherence to the code was less than perfect. Ostensibly the excuse was that the code should apply only to warmbloods and *intelligent* (not just sentient) aquatic coldbloods such as the Wefts or Ssli. Sass knew that many of the civilian locals ate fish, though it was never served openly in even the worst dockside joints. The fish, originally of Old Earth origin, had been stocked in Regg's ocean centuries before.

Besides the formal Headquarters complex, there were the associated office buildings, computer centers, technology and research centers...each in a landscaped setting, for Regg was still, after all these years, uncrowded.

"Fleet people do retire here," Abe said, "but they mostly homestead inland, upriver. Maybe someday we can do a river cruise during your holidays, see some of the estates. I've got friends up in the mountains, too."

But the city was exciting enough for a girl reared in a small mining colony town. She realized how silly it had been for the Myriadians to call their one-story collection of prefabs The City. Here government buildings soared ten or twelve stories, offering stunning views of the surrounding country from their windswept observation platforms atop. Busy shops crowded with merchandise from all over the known worlds, streets bustling from dawn until long after dark. Festivals to celebrate seasons and historical figures, theater and music and art...Sass felt drunk on it, for weeks. This was the real world she had dreamed of, on Myriad: this colorful, crowded city connected by Fleet to everywhere else, ships coming and going every day. Although the spaceport was behind the nearest range of hills, protecting the city from the noise, Sass loved to watch the shuttles lifting above forested slopes into an open sky.

In the meantime, she'd had a chance to meet some of the other survivors of Myriad's raid. Caris, now grim and wary, all the playfulness Sass remembered worn away by her captivity. She had found no one like Abe to give her help and hope, and in those few years aged into a bitter older woman.

"I just want a chance to work," she said. "They say I can go to school." Her voice was flat, barely above a whisper, the voice of a slave afraid of discovery.

"You could come here," said Sass, half-hoping Caris would agree. Much as she loved Abe, she missed having a close girlfriend, and her room was big enough for two. And Caris had known her all her life. They could talk about anything; they always had. Her own warmth could bring Caris back to girlhood, rekindle her hopes. But Caris pulled back, refusing Sass's touch.

"No. I don't—Sass, we were friends, and we were happy, and someday maybe I can stand to remember that. Right now I look at you and see—" Her voice broke and she turned away.

"Caris, please!" Sass grabbed her shoulders, but Caris flinched and pulled back.

"It's all over, Sass! I can't—I can't be anyone's friend now. There's nothing left... if I can just have a place to work in peace, alone..."

Sass was crying then, too. "Caris, you're all I have—"

"You don't have me. I'm not here." And with that she ran out of the room. Sass learned later that she'd gone back into the hospital, for more treatment. Later, she went offplanet without even telling Sass, letting her find out from the hospital records that her friend had left forever. For this grief, Abe insisted that work was the only cure—and revenge, someday, against whatever interests lay behind the slave trade. Sass threw herself into her classwork... and by the time the Academy Open Examinations came around, she'd worked off the visible remnants of her grief. She passed those in the top five percent, to Abe's delight. His scarred face creased into a grin as he took her to buy the required gear.

"I knew you could do it, Sass. I knew all along. You just remember what I told you, and in a few years I'll be cheering when you graduate."

But he would not walk her to the great arch that guarded the Academy entrance. He went off to work that morning, as he did every day (she never knew which of the semi-military bureaucracies had found a place for him; he never volunteered the information), leaving her to stare nervously into the mirror, twitching one errant strand of hair into place, until she had to walk fast or risk being late. She made her entrance appointment with time to spare, only to run into a marauding senior on her first trip through the Front Quad. She had carefully memorized the little booklet she'd been sent, and started to answer his challenge in the way it had instructed.

"Sir, Cadet Sassinak, reporting—" Her voice faltered. The cadet officer she had saluted had crossed his eyes and put his tongue out; he had his hands fanned out by his ears. As quickly, his face returned to normal, and his hands to his sides, but the smile on that face was grim.

"Rockhead, didn't anyone ever teach you how to report to a senior?" His voice attempted the cold arrogance of the pirate raiders, and came remarkably close. Sass realized she'd been tricked, fought down the responsive anger, and managed an equable tone in return. Abe hadn't told her they called the entering cadets "rockhead."

"Sir, yes, sir."

"Well, then . . . get on with it."

"Sir, Cadet Sassinak, reporting . . ." This time both eyes slewed outward, his mouth puckered as if he'd bitten a gari fruit, and he scratched vigorously at both armpits. But she wasn't fooled twice, and managed to get through the formal procedure without changing tone or expression, ending with a crisp ". . . sir!"

"Sloppy, slow, and entirely too smug," was the senior cadet's comment. "You're that petty officer's orphan tagalong, aren't you?"

Sass felt her ears burning, started to nod with clenched teeth, and then remembered that she had to answer aloud. "Sir, yes, sir."

"Hmph. Sorry sort of recommendation, letting himself get captured and slaved all those years. Not much like Fleet—" He stopped as Sass opened her mouth, and cocked his head. "Something to say, rockhead? Someone give you permission to speak?"

She didn't wait. "Sir, Abe is worth four of you, *sir!*"

"That's not the point, rockhead. The point is that you—" He tapped her shoulder. "You have to learn how to behave, and I don't think anything in your background's taught you how." Sass stared at him, back in control, furious with herself for taking the bait. "On the other hand, you're loyal. That's something. Not much, but something." He dismissed her, and she set off to find her assigned quarters, careful not to gawk around.

For reasons known only to the architects, the main buildings at the Academy had been constructed in a mix of antique styles, great gray blocks of stone that looked like pictures of ancient buildings on Old Earth. Towers, arches, covered walkways, intricate carvings of ships and battles and sea monsters around windows and doorways, enclosed courtyards paved in smooth slabs of stone. Six of these patriarchal buildings surrounded the Main Quad Parade: Themistocles, Drake, Nelson, Farragut, Velasquez, and the Chapel. Here, where the boldest street urchins could peer through the entrance gates to watch, cadets formed up many times a day to march to class, to mess, to almost every activity. Sass soon learned that the darker gray paving stones, which marked out open squares against a pale background, were slippery in the rain. She learned just where a flash of reflected sunlight from an open window might blind a cadet long enough to blunder into someone else. That meant a mark off, and she wanted no marks off.

Through the great arching salleyport of Velasquez, wide enough for a cadet platoon, were the cadet barracks, these named for the famous dead of Fleet battles. Varrin Hall, Benis, Tarrant, Suige. By the time they had been there a half-year, cadets knew those stories, and many others. Sass, on the third deck of Suige Hall, could recite from memory the entire passage in the history.

Other cadets complained (quietly) about their quarters, but Sass had spent years as Abe's ward. She had never been encouraged to spread her personality around her quarters, "to acquire bad habits" as Abe put it, although he admitted that Fleet officers, once they were up in rank, could and did decorate and personalize their space. But the regulation bunk with its prescribed covers folded just so, the narrow locker for the required uniforms (and nothing else), the single flat box for personal items, the single desk with its computer terminal and straight-backed chair—that was enough for her. She didn't mind sharing, or taking the top bunk, which made her popular with a series of roomies. She felt the neat, clean little cubicles were perfect for someone whose main interest lay elsewhere, and willingly did her share of the floor-polishing and dusting that daily inspections required.

She had actually expected neutral or monotone interiors, but the passages were tinted to copy the color-code used on all Fleet vessels. By the time the cadets graduated, this system would be natural, and they would never have to wonder which deck, or which end of a deck, they were on. Main or Command Deck, anywhere, had white above gray, for instance, and Troop Deck was always green.

Most classes went on in the "front quad" or in the double row of simpler stone-faced buildings that lay uphill from it. History—from Fleet's perspective, which included knowing the history of "important" old Earth navies, all the way back to ships rowed or sailed. Sass could not figure out why they needed to know what different ranks had been called a thousand years ago, but she tucked the information away dutifully, in case it was needed for anything but the quarterly exams. She did wonder why "captain" had ever been both a rank and a position, given the confusion that caused, and was glad someone had finally straightened it out logically. Anyone commanding a ship was a captain, and the rank structure didn't use the term at all. "You think it's logical," the instructor pointed out, "but there was almost a mutiny when the first Fleet officer had to use the rank 'major' and lieutenant commanders and commanders got pushed up a notch." Sass enjoyed far more the analysis of the various navies' tactics, including a tart examination of the effect of politics on warfare, using an ancient text by someone called Tuchman.

Cadets ate together, in a vaulted mess hall that would have been lovely if it hadn't been for the rows and rows of tables, each seating eight stiff cadets. Looking around—up at the carving on the ceiling, for instance—was another way to get marks taken off. Sassinak, with the others, learned to eat quickly and neatly while sitting on the edge of her chair. Students in their last two years supervised each table, insisting on perfect etiquette from the rockheads. At least, thought Sass, the food was adequate.

The Academy was not quite what she'd expected, even with the supposedly inside information she'd had before. From Abe's attitude towards Fleet officers, she'd gotten the idea that the Academy was some sort of semi-mystical place which magically imbued the cadets with honor, justice, and tactical brilliance. He had told her about his own Basic Training, which he described succinctly as four months of unmitigated hell, but that was not the same, he'd often said, as officer training. Sass had found, more or less by accident, a worn copy of an etiquette manual, which had prepared her for elaborate formalities and the fine points of military courtesy—but not for the Academy's approach to freshman cadets.

"We don't have hazing," the cadet commander had announced that first day. "But we do have discipline." The distinction, Sass decided quickly, was a matter of words only. And she quickly realized that she was a likely target for it, whatever it was called: the orphan ward of a retired petty officer, an ex-slave, and far too smart for her own good.

She wished she could consult Abe, but for the first half-year the new cadets were allowed no visitors and no visits home. She had to figure it out for herself. His precepts stood like markers in her mind: never complain, never argue, never start a fight, never boast. Could that be enough?

With the physical and mental discipline he'd taught her, she found, it could. She drew that around her like a tough cloak. Cadet officers who could reduce half the newcomers to red rage or impotent tears found her smooth but unthreatening equanimity boring after a few weeks. There was nothing defiant in that calmness, no challenge to be met, just a quiet, earnest determination to do whatever it was better than anyone else. Pile punishment details on her, and she simply did them, doggedly and well. Scream insults at her, and she stood there listening, able to repeat them on command in a calm voice that made them sound almost as silly as they were.

Abe had been right; they pushed her as hard as the slavers had, and the cadet officers had—she sensed—some of the same capacity for cruelty, but she never lost sight of the goal. *This* struggle would make her stronger, and once she was a Fleet officer, she could pursue the pirates who had destroyed her family and the colony.

That calm reticence might have made her an outcast among her classmates, except that she found herself warming to them. She would be working with them the rest of her life—and she wanted friends—and before the first half-year was over, she found herself once more the center of a circle.

"You know, Sass, we really ought to do something about Dungar's lectures." Pardis, an elegant sprout of the sector aristocracy sprawled inelegantly on the floor of the freshman wardroom, dodged a feinted kick from Genris, another of her friends.

"We have to memorize them; that's enough." Sass made a face, and drained her mug of tea. Dungar managed to make the required study of alien legal systems incredibly dull, and his delivery—in a monotone barely above a whisper—made the class even worse. He would not permit recorders, either; they had to strain to hear every boring word.

"They're so ... so predictable. My brother told me about them, you know, and I'll swear he hasn't changed a word in the past twenty years." Pardis finished that sentence in a copy of Dungar's whisper, and the others chuckled.

"Just what did you have in mind?" Sass grinned down at Pardis. "And you'd better get up, before one of the senior monitors shows up and tags you for unofficerlike posture."

"It's too early for them to be snooping around. I was thinking of something like ... oh ... slipping a little something lively into his notes."

"Dungar's notes? The ones he's read so many times he doesn't really need them?"

"We must show respect for our instructors," said Tadmur. As bulky as most heavyworlders, he took up more than his share of the wardroom, and sat stiffly erect. The others groaned, as they usually did. Sass wondered if he could really be that serious all the time.

"I show respect," said Pardis, rolling his green eyes wickedly. "Just the same as you, every day—"

"You make fun of him for his consistency." Tadmur's Vrelan accent gave his voice even more bite. "Consistency is good."

"Consistency is dull. Consistently wrong is stupid—" Pardis broke off suddenly and sprang to his feet as the door swung open without warning, and the senior monitor's grim face appeared around it. This weekend, the duty monitor was another heavyworlder, from Tadmur's home planet.

"You were lounging on the deck again, Mr. Pardis, weren't you?" The monitor didn't wait for the reply and went on: "The usual for you, and one for each of these for not reminding you of your duty." He scowled at Tadmur. "I'm surprised at *you* most of all."

Tadmur flushed, but said nothing more than the muttered "Sir, yes, sir" that regulations required.

Sassinak even made some progress with Tadmur and Seglawin, the two heavyworlders in her unit. When they finally opened up to her, she began to realize that the heavyworlders felt deep grievances against the other human groups in FSP.

"They want us for our strength," Tadmur said. "They want us to fetch and carry. You look at the records—the transcripts of the Seress expedition, for instance. How often do you think the med staff is assigned heavy duty, eh? But Parrih, not only a physician but a specialist, a surgeon, was expected to do the heavy unloading and loading in addition to her regular medical work."

"They like to think we're stupid and slow." Seglawin took up the complaint. Although not quite as large as Tadmur, she was far from the current standard of beauty, and with her broad forehead drawn down into a scowl looked menacing enough. Sass realized suddenly that she had beautiful hair, a rich wavy brown mass that no one noticed because of the heavy features below it. "Pinheads, they call us, and muscle-bound. I know our heads look little, compared to our bodies, but that's illusion. Look how surprised the Commandant was when I won the freshmen history prize: 'Amazingly sensitive interpretation for someone of your background.' I know what that means. They think we're just big dumb brutes, and we're not."

Sass looked at them, and wondered. Certainly the heavyworlders in the slave center had been sold as cheap heavy labor, and none had been in any of her tech classes. She'd assumed they weren't suited for it, just as everyone said. But in the Academy, perhaps five percent of the cadets were heavyworlders, and they did well enough in classwork. The two heavyworlders looked at each other, and then back at Sass. Seglawin shrugged.

"At least she's listening and not laughing."

"I don't—" Sass began, but Tad interrupted her.

"You do, because you've been taught that. Sass, you're fair-minded, and you've tried to be friendly. But you're a lightweight, and reasonably pretty enough, to your race's standard. You can't know what it's like to be treated as a—a thing, an animal, good for nothing but the work you can do."

It was reasonable, but Sass heard the whine of self-pity under the words and was suddenly enraged. "Oh, yes, I do," she heard herself say. Their faces went blank, the smug blankness that so many associated with heavyworlder arrogance, but she didn't stop to think about it. "I was a slave," she said crisply, biting off the words like so many chunks of steel. "I know *exactly* how it feels to be treated as a thing: I was sold, more than once, and valued on the block for the work I could do."

Seglawin reacted first, blankness then a surging blush. "Sass! I didn't—"

"You didn't know, because I don't want to talk about it." Rage still sang in her veins, lifting her above herself.

"I'm sorry," said Tad, his voice less hard than she'd ever heard it. "But maybe you do understand."

"You weren't slaves," Sass said. "*You* don't understand. They killed my family: my parents, my baby sister. My friends and their parents. And I will *get* them—" Her voice broke, and she swallowed, fighting tears. They waited, silent and immobile but no longer seeming inert. "I will get them," Sass continued finally. "I will end that piracy, that slavery, every chance I get. Whether it's lights or heavies or whoever else. Nothing's worse than that. Nothing." She met their eyes, one and then the other. "And I won't talk about it again. I'm sorry."

To her surprise, they both rose, and gave a little bow and odd gesture with their hands.

"No, it's our fault." Seglawin's voice had a burr in it now, her accent stronger. "We did not know, and we agree: nothing's worse than that. Our people have suffered, but not that. We fear that they might, and that is the source of our anger. You understand; you will be fair, whatever happens." She smiled, as she offered to shake hands, the smile transforming her features into someone Sass hoped very much to have as a friend.

Other times, more relaxed times, followed. Sass learned much about the heavyworlders' beliefs. Some reacted to the initial genetic transformations that made heavy-world adaptation possible with pride, and considered that all heavyworlders should spend as much time as possible on high-gravity planets. Others felt it a degradation, and sought normal-G worlds where they hoped to breed back to normal human standards. All felt estranged from their lighter-boned distant relations, blamed the lightweights—at least in part—for that estrangement, and resented any suggestion that their larger size and heavier build implied less sensitivity or intelligence.

Cadet leave, at the end of that first session, brought her home to Abe's apartment in uniform, shy of his reaction and stiff with pride. He gave her a crisp salute and then a bear hug.

"You're making it fine," he said, not waiting for her to speak. Already, she recognized in herself and in his reactions the relationship they would have later.

"I hope so." She loosened the collar of the uniform and stretched out on the low divan. He took her cap and set it carefully on a shelf.

"Making friends, too?"

"Some." His nod encouraged her, and she told him about the heavyworlders. Abe frowned.

"You want to watch them; they can be devious."

"I know. But—"

"But they're also right. Most normals *do* think of them as big stupid musclemen, and treat them that way. Poor sods. The smart ones resent it, and if they're smart enough they can be real trouble. What you want to do, Sass, is convince 'em you're fair, without giving them a weak point to push on. Their training makes 'em value strength and endurance over anything else."

"But they're not all alike." Sass told him all she'd learned, about the heavyworld cultures. "—and I wonder myself if the heavyworlders are being used by the same bunch who are behind the pirates and slavers," she finished.

Abe had been setting out a cold meal as she talked. Now he stopped, and leaned on the table. "I dunno. Could be. But at least some of the heavyworlders are probably pirates themselves. You be careful." Sass didn't argue; she didn't like the thought that Abe might have his limitations; she needed him to be all-knowing, for a long time yet. On the other hand, she sensed, in her heavyworlder friends, the capacity for honesty and loyalty, and in herself an unusual ability to make friends with people of all backgrounds.

By her third year, she was recognized as a promising young cadet officer, and resistance to her background had nearly disappeared. Colonial stock, yes: but colonial stock included plenty of "good" families, younger sons and daughters who had sought adventure rather than a safe seat in the family corporation. That she never claimed such a connection spoke well of her; others claimed it in her name.

Her own researches into her family were discreet. The psychs had passed her as safely adjusted to the loss of her family. She wasn't sure how they'd react if they found her rummaging through the colonial databases, so she masked her queries carefully. She didn't want anyone to question her fitness for Fleet. When she'd entered everything she could remember, she waited for the computer to spit out the rest.

The first surprise was a living relative (or "supposed alive" the computer had it) some three generations back. Sass blinked at the screen. A great-great-great grandmother (or aunt: she wasn't quite sure of the code symbols) now on Exploration Service. Lunzie . . . so *that* was the famous ancestor her little sister had been named for. Her mother had said no more than that—may not have known more than that, Sass realized. Even as a cadet, she herself had access to more information than most colonists, already. She thought of contacting her distant family members someday . . . someday when she was a successful Fleet officer. Not any time soon, though. Fleet would be her family, and Abe was her father now.

He took his responsibility seriously in more ways than one, she discovered at their next meeting.

"Take the five-year implant, and don't worry about it. You're not going to be a mother anytime soon. Should have had it before now, probably."

"I don't want to be a sopping romantic, either," said Sass, scowling.

Abe grinned at her. "Sass, I'm not telling you to fall in love. I'm telling you that you're grown, and your body knows it. You don't have to do anything you don't want to do, but you're about to want to."

"I am *not*." Sass glared at him.

"You haven't noticed anything?"

Sass opened her mouth to deny it, only to realize that she couldn't. He'd seen her with the others, and he, more than anyone, knew every nuance of her body.

"Take the implant. Do what you want afterwards."

"You're not telling me to be careful," she said, almost petulantly.

"Stars, girl, I only adopted you. I'm not really your father, and even if I were I wouldn't tell you to be careful. Not you, of all people."

"My . . . my real father . . ."

"Was a dirtball colonist. I'm Fleet. You're Fleet now. You don't believe all that stuff you were taught. You're the last woman to stay virginal all your life, Sass, and that's the truth of it. Learn what you need, and see that you get it."

Sass shivered. "Sounds very mechanical, that way."

"Not really." Abe smiled at her, wistful and tender. "Sass, it's a great pleasure, and a great relaxation. For some people, long-term pairing is part of it. Your parents may have been that way. But you aren't that sort. I've watched you now for what? Eight years, is it, or ten? You're an adventurer by nature; you always were, and what happened to you brought it out even stronger. You're passionate, but you don't want to be bothered with long-term relationships."

The five-year implant she requested at Medical raised no eyebrows. When the doctor discovered it was her first, she insisted that Sass read a folder about it " . . . So you'll know nothing's wrong when that patch on your arm changes color. Just come in for another one. It'll be in your records, of course, but sometimes your records aren't with you."

Once she had the implant, she couldn't seem to stop thinking about it. Who would it be? Who would be *first*, she scolded herself, accepting with no more argument Abe's estimate of her character. She watched the other cadets covertly. Bronze-haired Liami, who bounced in and out of beds with the same verve as she gobbled dessert treats on holidays. Cal and Deri, who could have starred in any of the romantic serial tragedies, always in one crisis of emotion or another. How they passed their courses was a constant topic of low-voiced wonder. Suave Abrek, who assumed that any woman he fancied would promptly swoon into his arms—despite frequent rebuffs and snide remarks from all the women cadets.

She wasn't even sure what she wanted. She and Caris, in the old days, watching Carin Coldae re-runs, had planned extravagant sexual adventures: all the handsome men in the galaxy, in all the exotic places, in the midst of saving planets or colonies or catching slavers. Was handsome really better? Liami seemed to have just as much fun with the plain as the handsome. And Abrek, undeniably handsome, but all too aware of it, was no fun at all. What kind of attraction was *that* kind, and not just the ordinary sort that made some people a natural choice for an evening of study or workouts in the gym? Or was the ordinary sort enough?

In the midst of this confusion of mind, she noticed that she was choosing to spend quite a bit of time with Marik Delgaesson, a senior cadet from somewhere on the far side of known space. She hadn't realized that human colonies spread that far, but he looked a lot more human than the heavyworlders. Brown eyes, wavy dark hair, a slightly crooked face that gave his grin a certain off-center appeal. Not really handsome, but good enough. And a superior gymnast, in both freeform and team competitions.

Sass thought about it. He might do. When their festival rotations came up at the same shift, and he asked her to partner him to the open theater production, she decided to ask him. It was hard to get started on the question, so they were halfway back to the Academy, threading their way between brightly decorated foodstalls, when she brought it up. He gave her a startled look and led her into a dark alley behind one of the government buildings.

"Now. What did you say?" In the near dark, she could hardly see his expression.

Her mouth was dry. "I ... I wondered if you'd ... you'd like to spend the night with me."

He shook his head. "Sass, you don't want that with me."

"I don't?" Reading and conversation had not prepared her for *this* reaction to a proposal. She wasn't sure whether she felt insulted or hurt.

"I'm not ... what I seem." He drew his heavy brows down, then lifted them in a gesture that puzzled Sass. People did both, but rarely like that.

"Can you explain that?"

"Well . . . I hate to disillusion you, but—" And suddenly he wasn't there: the tall, almost-handsome, definitely charming cadet senior she'd known for the past two years. Nothing was there—or rather, a peculiar arrangement of visual oddities that had her wondering what he'd spiked her mug with. Stringy bits of this and that, nothing making any sense, until he reassembled suddenly as a very alien shape on the wall. Clinging to the wall.

Sass fought her diaphragm and got her voice back. "You're— you're a Weft!" She felt cold all over: she had wanted to embrace *that*?

Another visual tangle, this time with some parts recognizable as they shifted toward human, and he stood before her, his face already wistful. "Yes. We . . . we usually stay in human form around humans. They prefer it. Though most don't prefer the forms we choose quite as distinctly as you did."

Her training brought her breathing back under full control. "It wasn't your form, exactly."

"No?" He smiled, the crooked smile she'd dreamed about the past nights. "You don't like my other one."

"I liked *you*," Sass said, almost angrily. "Your—your personality—"

"You liked what you thought I was—my human act." Now he sounded angry, too, and for some reason that amused her.

"Well, your human act is better than some who were born that way. Don't blame me because you did a good job."

"You aren't scared of me?"

Sass considered, and he waited in silence. "Not scared, exactly. I was startled, yes: your human act is damn good. I don't think you could do that if you didn't have some of the same characteristics in your own form. I'm not—I don't—"

"You don't want to be kinky and sleep with an alien?"

"No. But I don't want to insult an alien either, not without cause. Which I don't have."

"Mmm. Perceptive and courteous, as usual. If I were a human, Sass, I'd want *you*."

"If you were human, you'd probably get what you wanted."

"Luckily, my human shape has no human emotions attached; I

can enjoy you as a person, Sass, but not wish to couple with you. We mate very differently, and in an act far more...mmm... *biological*...than human mating has become."

Sass shivered; this was entirely too clinical.

"But we do—though rarely—make friends, in the human sense, with humans. I'd like that."

All those books gave her the next line. "I thought I was supposed to say that—no thanks, but can't we just be friends?"

He laughed, seemingly a real laugh. "You only get to say that if you don't make the proposal in the first place."

"Fine." Sass put out her hands. "I have to touch you, Marik; I'm sorry if that upsets you, but I have to. Otherwise I'll never get over being afraid."

"Thank you." They clasped hands for a long moment: his warm, dry hands felt entirely human. She felt the pulse throbbing in his wrist. She saw it in his throat. He shook his head at her. "Don't try to figure it out, Sass. Our own investigators—they're not really much like human scientists—don't understand it either."

"A Weft. I had to fall in love with a damned Weft!" Sass gave him a wicked grin. "And I can't even brag about it!"

"You're not in love with me. You're a young human female with a nearly new five-year implant and a large dose of curiosity."

"Dammit, Marik! How old are you, anyway? You talk like an older brother!"

"Our years are different." And with that she had to be content, for the moment. Later he was willing to say more, a little more, and introduce her to the other Wefts at the Academy. By then she'd spotted two of them, sensitive to some signal she couldn't define. Like Marik, they were all superb gymnasts and very good at unarmed combat. This last, she found, they accomplished by minute shifts of form.

"Say you grab my shoulder," said Marik, and Sass obligingly grabbed his shoulder. Suddenly it wasn't *there*, in her grasp, and yet he'd not shifted to his natural form. He was still right in front of her, only his hand gripped her forearm.

"What did you do?"

"The beginning of the shift changes the surface location and density—and that's what the enemy has hold of, right? We're not where we're supposed to be, and we're not all there, so to speak. In combat, serious combat, we'd have no reason to hold too tightly to the human form anyway."

"Does it...uh...hurt, to stay in human form? Are you more comfortable in your own?"

Marik shrugged. "It's like a tight uniform: not painful, but we like to get out of it now and then." He shifted then and there, and Sass stared, fascinated as always.

"It doesn't bother you?" asked Silui, one of the other Wefts.

"Not any more. I wish I knew how you do it!"

"So do we." Silui shifted, and placed herself beside Marik. <<Can you tell us apart?>> The question echoed in Sass's head. Of course. In their own form they hadn't the apparatus for human speech. But telepathy? She pushed that thought aside and watched as Silui and Marik crawled over and around each other. No more brown eyes and green, although something glittered that might be eyes of another sort. Shapes hard to define, because they were so outlandish...fivefold symmetry? She finally shook her head.

"Not by looking, I can't. Can you?"

"Oh yes." That was Gabril, the Weft who had not shifted. "Silui's got more graceful *sarfin*, and Marik *immles* better."

"That might help if I knew what *sarfin* and *immles* were," said Sass grumpily. Gabril laughed, and pointed out the angled stalklike appendages, and had Marik demonstrate an *immle*.

"Do you ever take heavyworlder shapes?" asked Sass.

"Not often. It's hard enough with you; the whole way of moving is so different. They're too strong; we can make holes in the walls accidentally."

"Can you take *any* shape?"

Silui and Marik reshifted to human, and joined the discussion aloud. "That's an argument we have all the time. Humans, yes, even heavyworlders, though we don't enjoy that. Ryxi is easier than humans, although the biochemistry causes problems. Our natural attention span is even longer than yours, but their brain chemistry interferes. Thek—" Marik looked at the others, as if asking a question.

"Might as well," said Silui. "One of us that we know of shifted to Thek form. A child. He'd meant to shift to a rock, which any of us can do briefly, but a Thek was there and he took that pattern. He never came back. The Thek wouldn't comment."

"Typical." Sass digested that. "So . . . you can take different shapes. How do you decide what kind of human to be? Are you even bisexual, as we are?"

"Video media, for the most part," said Gabril. "All those tapes and disks and cubes of books, plays, holodramas, whatever. We're taught never to choose a star, or anyone well-known, and preferably someone dead a century or so. And then we can make minor changes, of course, within the limits of human variation. I chose a minor character in a primitive adventure film, something about wild tribesmen on Old Earth. At first I wanted blue hair, but my teachers convinced me it wouldn't do. Not for an Academy prospect."

Silui grinned. "I wanted to be Carin Coldae—did you ever see her shows?"

Sass nodded.

"But they said no major performers, so I made my hair yellow and did the teeth different." She bared her perfect teeth, and Sass remembered that Carin Coldae had had a little gap in front. She also noticed that none of them had answered her questions about Weft sexuality, and decided to look it up herself. When she did, she realized why they hadn't tried to explain: *four* sexes, and mating required a rocky seacoast at full tide with an entire colony of Wefts. It produced freeswimming larvae, who returned (the lucky few) to moult into a smaller size of the adult form. Wefts were exquisitely sensitive to certain kinds of radiation, and Wefts who left their homeworlds would never join the mating colony. No wonder Marik wouldn't discuss sex—and had that combination of wistfulness and amused superiority toward eager young humans.

By this time, some of her other friends had realized which cadets were Wefts, and Sass found herself getting sidelong looks from those who disapproved of "messing around with aliens." It was this which led to her worst row in the Academy.

She had never been part of the society crowd, not with her background, but she knew exactly which cadets were. Randolph Neil Paraden, a senior that year, lorded it over all with any social pretensions at all. Teeli Pardis, of her own class, wasn't in the same league with a Paraden, and once tried to explain to Sass how important it was to stay on the right side of that most eminent young man.

"He's a snob," Sass had said, in her first year, when Paraden, then a second-year, had held forth at some length on the ridiculousness of letting the children of non-officers into the Academy. "It's not just me—take Issi. So her father's not commissioned: so what? She's got more Fleet in her little finger than a rich fop like Paraden has in his whole—"

"That's not the point, Sass," Pardis had said. "The point is that you don't cross Paraden Family. No one does, for long. Please...I like you, and I want to be friends, but if you get sour with Neil, I'm— I just *can't*, that's all."

By maintaining a cool courtesy towards everyone that turned his barbs aside, Sass had managed not to involve herself in a row with the Paraden Family's representative—until her friendship with Wefts made it necessary. It began with a series of petty thefts. The first victim was a girl who'd refused to sleep with Paraden, although that didn't come out until later. She thought she'd lost her dress insignia herself, and accepted the rating she got philosophically. Then her best friend's heirloom silver earrings disappeared, and two more thefts on the same corridor (a liu-silk scarf and two entertainment cubes) began to heighten tension unbearably in the last weeks before midterm exams.

Sass, in the next corridor, heard first about the missing cubes. Two days later, Paraden began to spread rumors that the Wefts were responsible. "They can change shape," he said. "Take any shape they want—so of course they could *look* just like the room's proper occupant. You'd never notice."

Issi told Sass about this, mimicking Paraden's accent perfectly. Then she dropped back into her own. "That stinker—he'll do anything to advance himself. Claims he can prove it's Wefts—"

"It's not!" Sass straightened up from the dress boots she'd been polishing. "They won't take the shape of someone alive: it's against their rules."

Issi wrinkled her brow at Sass. "I suppose *you'd* know—and no, I don't hate you for having them as friends. But it's not going to help you now, Sass, not if Randy Paraden has everyone suspecting them."

Worse was to come. Paraden himself called Sass in, claiming that he had been given permission to investigate the thefts. From the way his eyes roamed over her, she decided that theft wasn't all he wanted to investigate. He had the kind of handsome face that is used to being admired, and not only for its money. But he began with compliments for her performance, and patently false praise for her "amazing" ability to fit in despite a deprived childhood.

"I just wish you'd tell me what you know about the Wefts," he said, bringing his gaze back to hers. "Come on—sit down here, and fill me in. You're supposed to be our resident expert, and I hear you're convinced they're not guilty. Explain it to me—maybe I just don't know enough about them..."

Her instinct told her he had no interest whatever in Wefts, but she had to be fair. Didn't she? Reluctantly, she sat and began explaining what she understood of Weft philosophy. He nodded, his lids drooping over brilliant hazel eyes, his perfectly groomed hands relaxed on his knees.

"So you see," she finished, "no Weft would consider taking the form of someone with whom it might be confused: they don't take the forms of famous or living persons."

A smile quirked his mouth, and his eyes opened fully. His voice was still smooth as honey. "They really convinced you, didn't they? I wouldn't have thought you'd be so gullible. Of course, you haven't had a *normal* upbringing—there are so many things beyond your experience..."

Rage swamped her, interfering with coherent speech, and his smile widened to a predatory grin. "You're gorgeous when you're mad, Cadet Sassinak...but I suppose you know that. You're tempting me, you really are...d'you know what happens to girls who tempt me? I'll bet you're good in bed—" Suddenly his hands were no longer relaxed on his knees; he had moved even as he spoke, and the expensive scent he wore (surely that's not regulation! Sass's mind said, focussing on the trivial) was right there in her nose. "Don't fight me, little slave," he said in her ear. "You'll never win, and you'll wish you hadn't...OUCH!"

Despite the ensuing trouble, which went all the way to the Academy Commandant (and probably further than that, considering the Paraden Family), Sass had no happier memory for years than the moment in which she disabled Randolph Neil Paraden with three quick blows and left him grunting in pain on the deck. There was something so satisfying about the *crunch* transmitted up her arm, that it almost frightened her, and she never considered telling Abe, lest he find a reason she should repent. Nor did she confess that part to the Academy staff, though she left Paraden's office and went straight to the Commandant's office to turn herself in.

Paraden's attempt to explain himself, and put the blame for theft on the Wefts, did not work...although Sass wondered if it would have, given more time, or if she had not testified so strongly against him. When the first theft victim found that Paraden was involved, she realized that her "missing" dress insignia might have been stolen instead, and her testimony put the final seal on the case. Paraden had no chance to threaten Sass in person after that, but she was sure she'd earned an important enemy for the future. At least he wouldn't be *in* the Fleet. Paraden's clique, subject to intense scrutiny by the authorities after his dismissal, avoided Sass strictly. Even if one of them had wanted to be friendly, they'd not have risked more trouble.

Sass came out of it with a muted commendation. "You'll not say anything of this to your fellow cadets," the Commandant said severely. "But you showed good judgment. It's too bad you had to resort to physical force—you were justified, I'm not arguing that, but it's always better to think ahead and avoid the need to hit someone, if you can. Other than that, though, you did exactly the right things at the right time, and I'm pleased. The others will be wary of you awhile, and I would be most unhappy to find you using that to your advantage...you understand?"

"Yes, sir." She did, indeed, understand. It had been a narrow scrape, and could have gone badly. What she really wanted was a chance to get back to work and succeed the way Abe would want her to: honestly, on her own merits, without favoritism.

"We may seem to be leaning on you a bit, in the next week or so: don't worry too much."

"Yes, sir."

No one had to lean; she seemed sufficiently subdued, and eager to return to normal, as much as Academy life was ever normal. Her instructors were not surprised, and she would not know for years of the glowing comments in her record.

Chapter Four

Graduation. Sassinak, scoring high on all the exam postings, came into graduation week in the kind of euphoria she had once dreamed of. Honor graduate, with the gold braid and tassels. Cadet commandant: and the two did not often go together. She felt on fire with it, crackling alive a centimeter beyond her fingertips, and from the way the others treated her, that's exactly how she looked. At the final fitting for graduation, she stared into the tailor's mirror and wondered. Was she really *that* perfect, that vision of white and gold? Not a wrinkle, not a rumple, a shape that—she now admitted—was nothing short of terrific, what with all the gymnastics practice. The uniform clung to it, but invested it with dignity, all at once. Nowhere in the mirror could she see a trace of the careless colonial girl, or the ragged slave, or even the rumpled trainee. She looked the way she'd always wanted to look. The mischievous brown eyes in the mirror crinkled... except that she'd never intended to be smug. She hated smug. Laughter fought with youthful dignity, as she struggled to hold perfectly still for the tailor's last stitches. Dare she breathe, in that uniform? She had to.

Abe would be so proud, she thought, leading the formation into the Honor Square for the last time. He was there, but she didn't even think of glancing around to find him. He would see what he had made, what he had saved... for a mood went grim, thinking of the latest bad news, another colony plundered. Every time such news came in, she thought of girls like her, children like Lunzie and Janek, people, real people, murdered and enslaved. But the crisp commands brought her back to the moment. Her own voice rang out in answer, brisk and impersonal.

The ceremony itself, inherited from a dozen military academies in the human tradition, and borrowing bits from all of them and the nonhumans as well, lasted far too long. The planetary governor welcomed everyone, the senior FSP official responded. Ambassadors from all the worlds and races that sent cadets to the Academy had each his or her or its speech to make. Each time the band had the appropriate anthem to play, and the Honor Guard had the appropriate flag to raise, with due care, on the pole beside the FSP banner. Sassinak did not fidget, but without moving a muscle could see that the civilians and guests did exactly that, and more than once. A child wailed, briefly, and was removed. Sunlight glinted suddenly from one of the Marine honor guard's decorations: he'd taken a deep breath of disgust at something a politician said. Sass watched a cloud shadow cross the Yard and splay across Gunnery Hall. Awards: Distinguished teaching award, distinguished research into Fleet history, distinguished (she thought) balderdash. Academic departments had awards, athletic departments had theirs.

Then the diplomas, given one by one, and then—at last—the commissioning, when they all gave their oaths together. And then the cheers, and the hats flying high, and the roar from the watching crowd.

"So—you're going to be on a cruiser, are you?" Abe held up a card, and a waiter came quickly to serve them.

"That's what it said." Sass wished she could be three people: one here with Abe, one out celebrating with her friends, and one already sneaking aboard the cruiser, to find out all about it. Everyone wanted to start on a cruiser, not some tinpot little escort vessel or clumsy Fleet supply ship. Sure, you had to serve on almost everything at least once, but starting on a cruiser meant being, in however junior a way, *real* Fleet. Cruisers were where the action was, real action.

They were having dinner in an expensive place, and Abe had already insisted she order the best. Sass could not imagine what the colorful swirls on her plate had been originally, but the meal was as tasty as it was expensive. The thin slice of jelly to one side she *did* know: crel, the fruiting body of a fungus that grew only on Regg, the world's single most important export...besides Fleet officers. She raised a glass of wine to Abe, and winked at him.

He had aged, in the four years she'd been a cadet. He was almost bald now, and she hadn't missed the wince as when he folded himself into the chair across from her. His knuckles had swollen a little, his wrinkles deepened, but the wicked sparkle in his eye was the same.

"Ah, girl, you do make my heart proud. Not 'girl,' now: you're a woman grown, and a lady at that. Elegant. I knew you were bright, and gutsy, but I didn't know you'd shape into elegant."

"Elegant?" Sass raised an eyebrow, a trick she'd been practicing in front of her mirror, and he copied her.

"Elegant. Don't fight it; it suits you. Smart, sexy, and elegant besides. By the way, how's the nightlife this last term?"

Sass grimaced and shook her head. "Not much, with all we had to do." Her affair with Harmon hadn't lasted past midyear exams, but she looked forward to better on commissioning leave. And surely on a cruiser she'd find more than one likely partner. "You told me the Academy would be tough, but I thought the worst would be over after the first year. I don't see how being a real officer can be harder than being a cadet commander."

"You will." Abe drained his wine, and picked up a roll. "You never had to send those kids out to die."

"Commander Kerif said that's old-fashioned: you don't send people out to die, you send them out to win."

Abe set the roll back on his plate with a little thump. "He does, does he? What kind of 'win' is it when your ship loses a pod in the grid, and you have to send out a repair party? You listen to me, Sass: you don't want to be one of those wet-eared young pups the troops never trust. It's not a game any more, any more than being hauled off by slavers was a game. You're back in the real world now. Real weapons, real wounds, real death. I'm damned proud of you, and that won't change: it's not every girl that could make it like you have. But if you think the Academy was tough, you think back to Sedon-VI and the slave barracks. I daresay you haven't really forgotten, whatever polish they've put on your manners."

"No. I haven't forgotten." Sass stuffed a roll in her mouth before she said too much. He didn't need to know about the Paraden whelp, and all that mess. A shiver ran across her shoulderblades. He must know she hadn't changed that much . . . but he sure seemed nervous about something. As soon as they'd finished eating, he was ready to go, and she knew something more was coming. Outside, in the moist fragrant early-summer night, Sass wished again she could be two or three people. She'd had her invitation to the graduation frolic up in the parked hills behind the Academy square. It was just the night for it, too . . . soft grass, sweet breeze. Mosquito bites where you can't scratch, she reminded herself, and wondered why the geniuses who'd managed to leave the cockroaches back on Old Terra hadn't managed the same thing with mosquitoes.

Abe led her across town, to one of his favorite bars. Sass sighed inwardly. She knew why he came here: senior Fleet NCOs liked the place, and he wanted to show her off to his friends. But it was noisy, and crowded, and smelled, after the cool open air, like the cheap fat they fried their snacks in. She saw a few other graduates, and waved. Donnet: his uncle was a retired mech from a heavy cruiser. Issi, her family's pride: the first officer in seven generations of a huge Fleet family, all noisily telling her how wonderful it was. She shook hands with those Abe introduced: mostly the older ones, tough men and women with the deft precise movements of those used to working in a confined space.

It took them awhile to find a table, in that crowd. Civilian spacers liked the place, too, and Academy graduation brought everyone out to raise a glass for the graduates. Even the hoods, Sass noted, spotting the garish matching jackets of a street gang huddled near the back door. She was surprised they came here, to a Fleet and spacer bar, but a second, smaller gang followed the first in.

"Go get our drinks, Sass," said Abe, once he was down. "I'll just have a word with the Giustins." Issi's family . . . Sass grinned at him. He knew everyone. She took the credit chip he held out and found her way to the bar.

She was halfway back to him with the drinks when it happened. She missed the beginning, never knew who threw the first blow, but suddenly a row of tables erupted into violence. Fists, chains, the flash of blades. Sass dropped the tray and leaped forward, already yelling Abe's name. She couldn't see him, couldn't see anything but a tangled mass of Fleet cadet uniforms, gang jackets, and spacer gray. Her shout brought order to the cadets, or seemed to. At her command they coalesced, becoming a unit; with her they started to clear that end of the room, in a flurry of feints and blows and sudden clutches. From the corner of one eye, as she ducked under someone's knife and then disarmed him with a kick, she saw a move she recognized from one of their opponents. For an instant, she almost recognized that combination of size, shape, and motion.

She had no time to analyze it; there were too many drunken spacers who reacted to any brawl with enthusiasm, too many greenjacketed, masked hoodlums. The fight involved the whole place now, an incredible crashing screaming mass of struggling bodies. She rolled under a table, came up to strike precise blows at a greenjacket about to knife a spacer, ducked the spacer's wild punch, kicked out at someone who clutched her leg. Something raked her arm; the lights went out, then came on in a dazzle of flickering blue. Sirens, whistles, the overloud blare of a bullhorn. Sass managed a glance back toward the entrance, and saw masked Fleet MPs with riot canisters.

"DOWN..." the bullhorn blared. Sass dropped, as all the cadets did, knowing what was coming. Most of the spacers made it down before the MPs fired, but the hoods tried to run for it. A billowing cloud of blue gas filled the room; a thrown canister burst against the back door and felled the hoods who'd headed that way. Sass held her breath. One potato, two potato. Her hand reached automatically to her belt, and her fingernail found the slit for the release. Three potato, four potato. She flicked the membrane mask open, and covered her face with it. Five potato, six potato. Now she had the tube of detox, and smeared it over the nose and mouth portions of the mask. Seven, eight, nine, ten... a cautious breath, smelling of nutmeg from the detox, but no nausea, no pain, and no unconsciousness. Beside her, a spacer already snored heavily. She looked up, eyes protected by the mask. Already the gas had dissipated to a blue haze, still potent enough to knock out anyone without a mask, but barely obscuring vision.

The MPs spread around the room, checking IDs. Several other cadets were clambering to their feet, protected by their masks. Sass pushed herself up, looking for Abe. She wondered if he carried a Fleet emergency mask.

"ID!" It was a big MP in riot gear; Sass didn't argue but pulled out her new Fleet ID and handed it over. He slipped it into his beltcomp, and returned it. "You start this?" he asked. "Or see it start?"

Sass shook her head. "It started over here, though. I was coming across the room—"

"Why didn't you get out and call help?"

"My father—my guardian was over here."

"Name?"

Sass gave Abe's name and ID numbers; the MP waved her out to search. She veered around two fallen tables . . . was it this one, or that? Three limp bodies lay in an untidy pile. Sass shifted the top one; the MP helped. The next wore spacer gray, a long scrawny man with vomit drooling from the corner of his mouth. And there at the bottom lay Abe. Sass nodded at the MP, and he took a charged reviver from his belt and handed it to her; she put it over Abe's gaping mouth. He looked so . . . so *dead*, that way, with his mouth slack. The MP had dragged away the tall spacer, and now helped her roll Abe onto his back.

They saw the neat black hole in his chest the same moment. Sass didn't recognize it at first, reached down to brush off the smudge on the front of his jacket. He'd hate that, dirt on the new jacket he'd bought for her graduation. But the MP caught her wrist. She looked at him.

"He's dead," the MP said. "Someone had a needler."

Even as the room hazed around her, she thought "Shock. That's what's happening." She couldn't think about Abe being dead . . . he wasn't dead. This was another exercise, another test, like the one in the training vessel, when half the students had been made up to look like wounded victims. She remembered the realistic glisten of the fake gut wound, trailing a tangle of intestines across the deck plating. Easier to think about that, about the equally faked amputation, than that silly little black hole in Abe's jacket.

Later she heard, through an open doorway in the station, that she'd acted normally, not drugged, drunk, or irrational. She was sitting on a gray plastic chair, across a cluttered desk from someone who was busy at a computer. The floor had a pattern of random speckles, like every floor she'd seen for the past four years. She turned her head to look out the door, and an MP with his riot headgear under his arm gave her a neutral glance. She was Fleet, she hadn't started it, she hadn't had hysterics when they found Abe's body. Good enough.

It didn't feel good enough. Her mind raced back and forth over that minute or so the fight lasted, playing back minute fragments very slowly, looking for something she couldn't yet guess. Where had it started? Who? She had been carrying the drinks: Abe's square, squatty bottle of Priun brandy, and the footed glass for it, and a special treat for herself: Caprian liqueur. She'd been afraid the tiny cup of silver-washed crystal—the only proper receptacle for Caprian liqueur—would bounce off the tray if someone bumped her, so she hadn't been looking more than one body ahead when the fight started. She'd looked up when . . . was it a sound, or had she seen something, without really recognizing it? She couldn't place it, and went on. She'd dropped the tray, and in her mind it fell in slow-motion, emptying its contents over the shoulders of someone in spacer gray at the table she'd been passing.

Suddenly she had something, or a hint of it. In the midst of that fight, someone to her right had blocked a kick with a move that had to come from Academy training . . . a move that almost had to be learned in low-grav tumbling, although you could use it in normal G. Only it hadn't been one of the graduates, nor . . . her mind focussed on the anomaly . . . nor one of the spacers. It had been someone in purple and orange, with blue sleeves . . . a gang jacket. She'd tried to take a fast look, but like all the second gang, the fighter's face had been painted in geometric patterns that made identification nearly impossible. Eyes . . . darkish. Skin color . . . from the way it took the paint, neither very light nor very dark.

"Ensign." Sass looked up, ready to curse at the interruption until she saw the rank insignia. Not local police; Fleet. And not just any Fleet, but the Academy Vice-Commandant, Commander Derran.

"Sir." She stood, and wished she'd had time to change uniforms. But they hadn't run the scan over all the spots yet, and they'd told her to wait.

"I'm sorry, Ensign," the Commander was saying. "He was a good man, Fleet to the core. And on your graduation night, too."

"Thank you, sir." That much was correct; she couldn't manage much more through a tight throat.

"You're his only listed kin," Derran went on. "I assume you'll want a military funeral?" Sass nodded. "Burial in the Academy grounds, or—"

She had only half-listened when he'd told her, years ago, how he wanted it. "I don't hold with spending Fleet money to send scrap into a star," he'd said. "Space burial's for those who die there. They've earned it. But I'm no landsman, either, to be stuck under a bit of marble on a hillside; I hold by the old code. My life was with Fleet, I had no homeland. Burial at sea, if you can manage it, Sass. The Fleet does it the right way."

"At sea," she said now. "He wanted it that way."

"Ashes, or—?"

"Burial, sir, he said, if it was possible."

"Very well. The Superintendent's told me they'll release the body tomorrow; we'll schedule it for—" He pulled out his handcomp and studied the display. "Two days . . . is that satisfactory? Takes that long to get the arrangements made."

"Yes, sir." She felt stupid, stiff, frozen. This could not be Abe's funeral they discussed: time had to stop, and let her sort things out. But time did not stop. The Commander spoke to the police officer behind the desk, and suddenly they were ready for her in the lab. A long-snouted machine took samples from every stain on her uniform; the technician explained about the analysis of blood and fiber and skin cells to identify those she'd fought.

When she came out of the lab, she found a Lt. Commander Barrin waiting for her, with a change of clothes brought from her quarters, and the same officer escorted her back to Abe's apartment. There, another Fleet officer had already opened the apartment, set up a file to receive and organize visits and notes that required acknowledgment. Already dozens of notes were racked for her notice, and two of her class waited to see her before leaving for their new assignments.

Sass began to realize what kind of support she could draw on. They knew what papers she needed to find, recognized them in Abe's files when she opened the case. They knew what she should pack, and what formalities would face her in the morning and after. Would he be buried from the Academy, or the nearby Fleet base? Would the circumstances qualify him for a formal military service, or some variant? Sass found one or the other knowledgeable about every question that came up. Someone provided meals, sat her in front of a filled plate at intervals, and saw to it that she ate. Someone answered the door, the comm, weeded out those she didn't want to see, and made sure she had a few minutes alone with special friends. Someone reminded her to apply for a short delay in joining her new assignment: she would have to stay on Regg for another week or so of investigation. Her rumpled, stained uniform disappeared, returned spotless and mended. Someone forwarded all required uniforms to her assignment, leaving her only a small bit of packing to do. And all this was handled smoothly, calmly, as if she were someone of infinite importance, not a mere ensign just out of school.

She could never be alone without help, as long as she had Fleet: Abe had said that, drummed it into her, and she'd seen Fleet's help. But now it all came together. No enemy could kill them all. She would lose friends, friends close as family, but she could not lose Fleet.

Yet this feeling of security could not make Abe's funeral easier. The police had offered her the chance to be alone with his body, a chance she refused, concealing the horror she felt. (Touch the body of someone she had loved? For an instant the face of her little sister Lunzie, carried in her arms to the dock, swam before her.) Wrapped in a dark blue shroud, it was taken by Fleet Marines to the Academy mortuary. Sass had no desire to know how a body was prepared for burial; she signed the forms she was handed, and skimmed quickly over the information given.

The body of an NCO, retired or active, could remain on view for one day. That she agreed to: Abe had had many friends who would want to pay their respects. His flag-draped coffin rested on the ritual gun-cradle in a side chapel. A line of men and women, most in uniform, came to shake hands with Sass and walk past it, one by one. Some, she noticed, laid a hand on the flag, patted it a little. Two were Wefts, which surprised her ... Abe had never told her about Weft friends.

The funeral itself, the ancient ritual to honor a fellow warrior, required of Sass only the contained reticence and control that Abe had taught her. She, the bereaved, had only that simple role, and yet it was almost too heavy a burden for her. Others carried his coffin;

she carried her gratitude. Others had lost a friend; she had lost all connection with her past. Again she had to start over, and for this period even Fleet could not comfort her.

But she would not disgrace him. The acceptable tears slid down her cheeks, the acceptable responses came from her mouth. And the old cadences of the funeral service, rhythms old before ever the first human went into space, comforted where no living person could.

"Out of the deep have I called unto thee, O Lord—" The chaplain's voice rang through the chapel, breaking the silence that had followed the entrance hymn, and the congregation answered.

"Lord, hear my voice."

Whatever the original beliefs had been, which brought such words to such occasions, no one in Fleet much cared—but the bond of faith in something beyond individual lives, individual struggles, a bond of faith in love and honesty and loyalty... that they all shared. And phrase by phrase the old ritual continued.

"O let thine ears consider well—"

"The voice of my complaint." Sass thought of the murderer, and for a few moments vengeance routed grief in her heart. Someday— *someday*, she would find out who, and why, and—she stumbled over a phrase about redemption following mercy, having in mind neither.

Readings followed, and a hymn Abe had requested, its mighty refrain "Lest we forget—lest we forget" ringing in her ears through another psalm and reading. Sass sat, stood, knelt, with the others, aware of those who watched her. It seemed a long time before the chaplain reached the commendation; her mind hung on the words "dust to dust..." long after he had gone on, and blessed the congregation. And now the music began again, this time the Fleet Hymn. Sass followed the casket out through the massed voices, determined not to cry.

"Eternal Father, strong to save..." Her throat closed; she could not even mouth the words that had brought tears to her eyes even from the first.

Across the wide paved forecourt of the Academy, the flags in front of the buildings all lowered, a passing squad of junior middies held motionless as the funeral procession went on its way. Out the great arched gates to the broad avenue, where Fleet Marines held the street traffic back, and the archaic hearse, hitched to a team of black horses, waited. Sass concentrated on the horses, the buckles of their harness, the brasses stamped with the Fleet seal . . . surely it was ludicrous that a spacegoing service would maintain a horsedrawn hearse for its funerals.

But as they followed on foot, from the Academy gates to the dock below the town, it did not seem ludicrous. Every step of human foot, every clopping hoofbeat of the horses, felt right. This was respect, to take the time in a bustling, modern setting to do things the old way. As Abe's only listed kin, Sass walked alone behind the hearse; behind her came Abe's friends still in Fleet, enlisted, then officer.

At the quay, the escort commander called the band to march, and they began playing, music Sass had never heard but found instantly appropriate. Strong, severe, yet not dismal, it enforced its own mood on the procession. On all the ships moored nearby, troops and officers stood to attention; ensigns all at half-mast. The *Carly Pierce*, sleek and graceful, Fleet's only fighting ship (a veteran of two battles with river pirates in the early days of Regg's history, before it became the Fleet Headquarters planet). The procession halted; from her position behind the hearse, Sass could barely see the pallbearers forming an aisle up the gangway. Exchange of salutes, exchange of honors: the band gave a warning rattle of drumsticks, and the body bearers slid the casket from the hearse. Sass followed them toward the gangway. Such a little way to go; such a long distance to return . . .

And now they were all on the deck, the body bearers placing the casket on a frame set ready, lifting off the flag, holding it steady despite a brisk sea breeze. Sass stared past it at the water, ruffled into little arcs of silver and blue. She hardly noticed when the ship cast off and slid almost soundlessly through the waves, across the bay and around the jagged island in it. There, in the lee of the island, facing the great cliffs, the ship rested as the chaplain spoke the final words.

"—Rest eternal grant to him, O Lord—" And the other voices joined his, "And let light perpetual shine upon him."

The chaplain stepped aside; the escort commander brought the escort to attention and three loud volleys racketed in ragged echoes from island and cliffs beyond. Birds rose screaming from the cliffs, white wings tangled in the light. Sass clenched her jaw: now it was coming. She tried not to see the tilting frame, the slow inexorable movement of the casket to the waiting sea.

As if from the arc of the sky, a single bugle tolled the notes out, one by one, gently and inexorably. Taps. Sass shivered despite herself. It had ended her days for the past four years—and now it was ending his. It had meant sunset, lights out, another day survived—and now it meant only endings. Her throat closed again; tears burned her eyes. No one had played taps for her parents, for her sister and brother and the others killed or left to die on Myriad. No one had played taps for the slaves who died. She was cold all the way through, realizing, as she had not ever allowed herself to realize, that she might easily have been another dead body on Myriad, or in the slaver's barracks, unknown, unmourned.

All those deaths . . . the last note floated out across the bay, serene despite her pain, pulling it out of her. Here, at least, the dead could find peace, knowing someone noticed, someone mourned. She took a deep, unsteady breath. Abe was safe here, "from rock and tempest, fire and foe," safe in whatever safety death offered, completing his service as he had wished.

She took the flag, when it was boxed and presented, with the dignity Abe deserved.

BOOK TWO

Chapter Five

"Ensign Sassinak requests permission to come aboard, sir." Coming aboard meant crossing a painted stripe on the deck of the station, but the ritual was the same as ever.

"Permission granted." The Officer of the Deck, a young man whose reddish skin and ice-blue eyes indicated a Brinanish origin, had one wide gold ring and a narrow one on his sleeve. He returned her salute, and Sass stepped across the stripe. Slung on her shoulder was the pack containing everything she was permitted to take aboard. Her uniforms (mess dress, working dress, seasonal working, and so on) were already aboard, sent ahead from her quarters before her final interview with the Academy Commandant after Abe's funeral.

Her quarters were minimal: one of two female ensigns (there were five ensigns in all), she had one fold-down bunk in their tiny cubicle, one narrow locker for dress uniforms, three drawers, and a storage bin. Sass knew Mira Witsel only slightly; she had been one of Randolph Neil Paraden's set, a short blonde just over the height limit. Sass hoped she wasn't as arrogant as the others, but counted on her graduation rank to take care of any problems. With the other ensigns, they shared a small study/lounge (three terminals, a round table, five chairs). Quickly, she stowed her gear and took a glance at herself in the mirror strip next to the door. First impressions... reporting to the captain... she grinned at her reflection. Clean and sharp and probably all too eager... but it was going to be a good voyage... she was sure of it.

"Come in!" Through the open hatch, the captain's voice sounded stuffy, like someone not quite easy with protocol. Fargeon. Commander Fargeon—she'd practiced that softened g, typical of his homeworld (a French-influenced version of Neo-Gaesh). Sass took a deep breath, and stepped in.

He answered her formal greeting in the same slightly stuffy voice: not hostile, but standoffish. Tall, angular, he leaned across his cluttered desk to shake her hand as if his back hurt him a little. "Sit down, Ensign," he said, folding himself into his own chair behind his desk, and flicking keys on his desk terminal. "Ah...your record precedes you. Honor graduate." He looked at her, eyes sharp. "You can't expect to start on the top here, Ensign."

"No, sir." Sassinak sat perfectly still, and he finally nodded.

"Good. That's a problem with some top graduates, but if you don't have a swelled head, I don't see why you should run into difficulties. Let me see—" He peered at his terminal screen. "Yes. You are the first ensign aboard, good. I'm putting you on third watch now, but that's not permanent, and it doesn't mean what it does in the Academy. Starting an honor cadet on the third watch just ensures that everyone gets a fair start."

And you don't have to listen to complaints of favoritism, Sassinak thought to herself. She said nothing, just nodded.

"Your first training rotation will be Engineering," Fargeon went on. "The Exec, Lieutenant Dass, will set up the duty roster. Any questions?"

Sass knew the correct answer was no, but her mind teemed with questions. She forced it back and said "No, sir."

The captain nodded, and sent her out to meet Lieutenant Dass. Dass, in contrast to his captain, was a wiry compact man whose dark, fine-featured face was made even more memorable by light green eyes.

"Ensign Sassinak," he drawled, in a tone that reminded her painfully of the senior cadets at the Academy when she'd been a rockhead. "Honor cadet..."

Sassinak met his green gaze, and discovered a glint of mischief in them. "Sir—" she began, but he interrupted.

"Never mind, Ensign. I've seen your record, and I know you can be polite in all circumstances, and probably work quads in your head at the same time. The captain wanted you in Engineering first, because we've installed a new environmental homeostasis system and it's still being tested. You'll be in charge of that, once you've had time to look over the system documentation." He grinned at her expression. "Don't look surprised, Ensign: you're not a cadet in school any more. You're a Fleet officer. We don't have room for deadweights; we have to know right away if you can perform for us. Now. It's probably going to take you all your off-watch time for several days to work your way through the manuals. Feel free to ask the Engineering Chief anything you need to know, or give me a holler. On watch, you'll have the usual standing duties, but you can spend part of most watches with the engineering crew."

"Yes, sir." Sass's mind whirled. She was going to be in charge of testing the new system? A system which could kill them all if she made a serious mistake? This time the flash of memory that brought Abe to mind had no pain. He'd told her Fleet would test her limits.

"Your record says you get along with allies?"

Allies was the Fleet term for allied aliens; Sassinak had never heard it used so openly. "Yes, sir."

"Good. We have a Weft Jig, and several Weft battle crew, and that Weft Ensign: I suppose you knew him at the Academy?" Sassinak nodded. "Oh, and have you ever seen an adult Ssli?"

"No, sir."

"We're Ssli-equipped, of course: all medium and heavy cruisers have been for the past two years." He glanced at the timer. "Come along; we've time enough to show you."

The Ssli habitat was a narrow oval in cross-section: ten meters on the long axis, aligned with the ship's long axis, and only two meters wide. It extended "upward" from the heavily braced keel through five levels: almost twenty meters. The plumbing that maintained its marine environment took up almost the same cubage.

At the moment, the Ssli had grown only some three meters in diameter from its holdfast, and its fan was still almost circular. Two viewing ports allowed visual inspection of the Ssli's environment. The Executive Officer's stubby fingers danced on the keyboard of the terminal outside one viewing port.

"Basic courtesy—always ask before turning on the lights in there."

Sassinak peered over his shoulder. The screen came up, and

displayed both question and answer, the latter affirmative. Dass flipped a toggle, and light glowed in the water inside, illuminating a stunning magenta fan flecked with yellow and white. Sassinak stared. It seemed incredible that this huge, motionless, intricate object could be not only alive, but sentient... sentient enough to pass the FSP entry levels. She could hardly believe that the larval forms she'd seen in the Academy tanks had anything to do with this... this thing.

Somehow the reality was much stranger than just seeing tapes on it. I wonder what it feels like, she thought. How it thinks, and—

"How did they ever figure out...?" she said, before she thought.

"I don't know, really. Thek discovered them, of course, and maybe they're more likely to suspect intelligence in something that looks mineral than we are." Dass looked at her closely. "It bothers some people a lot—how about you?"

"No." Sassinak shook her head, still staring through the viewing port. "It's beautiful, but hard to realize it's sentient. But why not, after all? How do you communicate with it?"

"The usual. Biocomp interface... look, there's the leads." He pointed, and Sassinak could see the carefully shielded wires that linked the Ssli to the computer terminal. "Want an introduction?"

When she nodded, he tapped in her ID code, asked her favorite name-form, and then officer crew: general access.

"That gives it access to the general information in your file. Nothing classified, just what any other officer would be able to find out about you. Age, class rank, sex, general appearance, planet of origin, that kind of thing. If you want to share more, you can offer additional access, either by giving it the information directly, or by opening segments of your file. Now you come up here, and be ready to answer."

On the screen before her, a greeting already topped the space. "Welcome, Ensign Sassinak; my name in Fleet is Hssrho. Have been installed here thirty standard months; you will not remember, but you met me in larval stage in your second year at the Academy."

Sassinak remembered her first introduction to larval Ssli, in the alien communications lab, but she'd never expected to meet the same individual in sessile form. And she hadn't remembered that name. Quickly she tapped in a greeting, and apologies for her forgetfulness.

"Never mind . . . we take new names when we unite with a ship. You could not know. But I remember the cadet who apologized for bumping into my tank."

From the Ssli, Lieutenant Dass led her through a tangle of passages into the Engineering section. Sassinak tried to pay attention to the route, but had to keep ducking under this, and stepping over that. She began to wonder if he was taking a roundabout and difficult way on purpose.

"In case you think I'm leading you by the back alleys," he said over his shoulder, "all this junk is the redundancy we get from having two environmental systems, not just one. As soon as you've got the new one tuned up to Erling's satisfaction—he's the Engineering Chief—we can start dismantling some of this. Most of it's testing gear anyway."

Even after the study of ship types at the Academy, Sass found it took awhile to learn the geography of the big ship. Cruiser architecture was determined by the requirement that the ships not only mount large weapons for battles in space or against planets, but also carry troops and their support equipment, and be able to land them. Cruisers often operated alone, and thus needed a greater variety of weaponry and equipment than any one ship in a battle group. But to retain the ability to land on-planet in many situations, and maneuver (if somewhat clumsily) in atmosphere, cruiser design had settled on a basic ovoid shape. Thanks to the invention of efficient internal artificial gravity, the ships no longer had to spin to produce a pseudo-gravity. The "egg" could be sliced longitudinally into decks much easier to use and build.

In their first few days, all the new ensigns took a required tour of each deck, from the narrow silent passages of Data Deck, where there was little to see but arrays of computer components, to the organized confusion of Flight Two, with the orbital shuttles, drone and manned space fighters, aircraft, and their attendant equipment, all the way down to the lowest level of Environmental, where the great plumbing systems that kept the ship functioning murmured to themselves between throbbing pump stations. Main Deck, with the bridge, nearly centered the ship, as the bridge sector centered Main Deck. Aft of the bridge was Officers' Country, with the higher ranking officers nearer the bridge (and in larger quarters), and the ensigns tucked into their niches near the aft cargo lift that ran vertically through all decks. Lest they think this a handy arrangement, they were reminded that regulations forbade the use of the cargo lift for personnel only: they were supposed to keep fit by running up and down the ladders between decks. Main Deck also held all the administrative offices needed. Between Data Deck and Environmental was Crew, or Troop Deck, which had, in addition to crew quarters, recreation facilities, and mess, the sick bay and medical laboratory. When the ship landed on-planet, a ramp opening from Troop Deck offered access to the planet's surface.

Yet nothing, they were warned, was excess: nothing was mere decoration. Every pipe, every fitting, every electrical line, had its function, and the interruption of a single function could mean the life of the ship in a crisis. So, too, all the petty regulations: the timing of shower privileges, the spacing of the exercise machines in the gyms. It was hard for Sass to believe, but with the stern eye of a senior officer on them all, she nodded with the rest.

Shipboard duty had none of the exotic feel the ensigns had hoped for, once they knew their way around the ship. Mira, away from the social climbers at the Academy, turned out to be a warm, enthusiastic girl, willing to be friends with anyone. Her father, a wealthy merchant captain, had set her sights on a career in space. She frankly admired Sassinak for being "really strong." To Sassinak's surprise, when it came to working out in the gym, Mira was a lot tougher than she seemed.

"We weren't supposed to show it off," said Mira, when Sassinak commented on this. "Mother wanted us to be ladies, not just spacer girls—she said we'd have a lot more fun that way. And then in Neil's bunch at the Academy..." She looked sideways at Sassinak who suddenly realized that Mira really did want to be friends. "They always said there's no use exceeding requirements, 'cause the Wefts'll get all the medals anyway. And Neil—Mother—sent me a whole long tape about it when she found out he was in the same class. She'd have eaten me alive if I'd made an enemy of him without cause." She patted Sassinak on the shoulder, as if she weren't a decimeter shorter. "Sorry, but you weren't cause enough, and it was clear you could deck Neil any time you wanted to."

"You're—" Sass couldn't think of a good term, and shook her

head. Mira grinned. "I'm a typical ambitious, underbred and overfed merchanter brat, who'll never make admiral but plans to spend a long and pleasurable career in Fleet. Incidentally serving FSP quite loyally, since I really do believe it does a lot of good, but not ever rising to flag rank and not really wanting it. Deficient in ambition, that's what they'd grade me."

"Not deficient in anything else," said Sassinak. She caught the wink that Mira tipped her and grinned back. "You devious little stinker—I'll bet you're a good friend, at that."

"I try to be." Mira's voice was suddenly demure, almost dripping honey. "When I have the chance. And when I like someone."

Sassinak thought better of asking, but Mira volunteered.

"I like you, Sass...now. You were pretty stiff in the Academy, and yes, I know you had reasons. But I'd like to be friends, if you would, and I mean friends like my people mean it: fair dealing, back-to-back in a row with outsiders, but if I think you're wrong I'll say it to your face."

"Whoosh. You can speak plain." Sassinak smiled and held out her hand. "Yes, Mira; I'd like that. 'Slong as I get to tell you."

And after that she enjoyed the little free time she had to share impressions with Mira. Meals in the officers' mess were not as formal as those in the Academy, but they knew better than to put themselves forward.

For the first month, Sassinak was on third shift rotation, which meant that she ate with other third shift officers; the captain usually kept a first-shift schedule. From what Mira told her, she wasn't missing much. When she rotated to first-shift watch, and Communications as her primary duty, she found that Mira was right.

Instead of a lively discussion of the latest political scandal from Escalon or Contaigne, with encouragement to join in, the ensigns sat quietly as Captain Fargeon delivered brief, unemotional critiques of the ship's performance. Sassinak grew to dread his quiet "There's a little matter in Engineering..." or whatever section he was about to shred.

The shift to Communications Section gave her some sense of contact with the outside world. Fleet vessels, unlike civilian ships, often stayed in deepspace for a standard year or more. None of the cadets had ever experienced that odd combination of isolation and confinement. Sassinak, remembering the slave barracks and the pirate vessel, found the huge, clean cruiser full of potential friends and allies an easy thing to take, but some did not.

Corfin, the ensign who slipped gradually into depression and then paranoia, had not been a particular friend of hers in the Academy, but when she recognized his withdrawal, she did her best to cheer him up. Nothing worked; finally his supervisor reported to the Medical Officer, and when treatment slowed, but didn't stop, the progression, he was sedated, put in coldsleep, and stored for the duration, to be discharged as medically unfit for shipboard duty when they reached a Fleet facility.

"But why can't they predict that?" asked Sassinak, in the group therapy session the Medical Officer insisted on. "Why can't they pick them out, clear back in the first year, or before—"

Because Corfin had been in the Academy prep school, and had a Fleet medical record going back ten years or more.

"He was told of the possibility," she was told, "it's in his chart. But his father was career Fleet, died in a pod repair accident: the boy wanted to try, and the Board agreed to give him a chance. And it's not wasted time, his or ours either. We have his record, to judge another by, and he'll qualify for a downside Fleet job if he wants it."

Sassinak couldn't imagine anyone wanting it. To be stuck on one planet, or shipped from one to another by coldsleep cabinet? Horrible. Glad she had no such problems herself, she went back to her work eagerly.

It was, in fact, a prized assignment. The communications "shack" was a good-sized room that opened directly onto the bridge. Sassinak could look out and see the bridge crew: the officer of the deck in the command module—or, more often, standing behind it, overlooking the others from the narrow eminence that protruded into the bridge like a low stage. Of course she could not see it all; her own workstation cut off the view of the main screens and the weapons section. But she felt very much at the nerve-center of the cruiser's life. Communications in the newly refitted heavy cruiser were a far sight from anything she'd been taught in the Academy.

Instead of the simple old dual system of sublight radio and FTL link, both useful only when the ship itself was in sublight space, they had five separate systems, each for use in a particular combination of events. Close-comm, used within thirty LM of the receiver, was essentially the same old sublight microwave relay that virtually all technical races developed early on.

Low-link, a low-power FTL link for use when they themselves were not on FTL drive, brought near-instantaneous communications within a single solar system, and short-lag comm to nearby star systems. Two new systems gave the capability for transmissions while in FTL flight: a sublight emergency channel, SOLEC, which allowed a computer-generated message to contact certain mapped nodes, and the high-power FTL link which transmitted to mapped stations. Even newer, still experimental and very secret, was the computer-enhanced FTL link to other Fleet vessels in FTL flight.

For each system, a separate set of protocols and codes determined which messages might be sent where, and by whom . . . and who could or should receive messages.

"One thing is, we don't want the others to know what we've got," said the Communications Chief. "So far, all the commercials in human space are using the old stuff: electromagnetic, lightspeed—radio and stuff like that—and FTL link—really a low-link. Arbetronics is about to come out with a commercial version of the FTL sublight transmitter, but Fleet's got a total lock on the high-link. Our people developed it; all that research was funded in house, and unless someone squeaks, it's our baby. And the Fleet IFTL link even more so. You can see why."

Sassinak certainly could. Until now, Fleet vessels had had to drop into sublight to pick up incoming messages—usually at mapped nodes, which made them entirely too predictable. Her instructors at the Academy had suspected that Fleet messages were being routinely stripped from the holding computers by both Company and unattached pirates. The IFTL link would make them independent of the nodes altogether. "Information," the Comm Chief said. "That's the power out here—who knows what? Now, ordinarily, in any disputed or unsecured sector, all crew messages are held for batch transmission, ordinary sublight radio, to the nearest mail facility. Anything serious—death, discharge, that kind of thing—can be put on the low-link with clearance from the Communications

Officer, who may require the captain to sign off on it. The initiating officer's code goes on each transmission. That means whoever authorized it, not who actually punched the button—right now you're not booked to initiate any signals. The actual operator's code also goes on it; whoever logs onto that system transmitter automatically gets hooked to the transmission. Incoming's always accepted, and automatically dumped in a protected file unless its own security status requires even more. Accepting officer's code— and that's you, if you're on duty right then—goes on it in the file. If it's the usual mail-call batch, check with 'Tenant Cardon; if he says it's clear, then let the computer route it to individuals' E-mail files."

"What about other incoming?"

"Well, if it's not a batch file message, if it's a singleton for one person, you have to get authorization to move it to that individual's file. If it's a low-link message, those are always Fleet official business, and that means route to the captain first, but into his desk file, not his private E-mail file. We don't get any incoming on highlink or SOLEC, so you don't have to worry about them. Now if it's something on the IFTL, that's routed directly to the captain's desk file. Pipe the captain, wherever he is, and no copies at all. Nothing in main computer. Clear?"

"Yes, sir. But do I still patch on my ID code, on an IFTL message?"

"Yes, of course. That's always done."

Some days later, Sassinak came into Communications just as the beeper rang off on the end of an incoming message burst. Cavery, who had already discovered the new ensign could do his job almost as well as he could, pointed at the big display. Sassinak scanned the grid and nodded.

"I'll put it down," she said.

"I've already keyed my code on it. Just the mail run from Stenus, nothing fancy."

Sass flicked a few keys and watched the display. The computer broke each message batch into its component messages, and routed them automatically. The screen flickered far faster than she could read it. She liked the surreal geometries of the display anyway. It hovered on the edge of making sense, like math a little beyond her capability.

Suddenly something tugged at her mind, hard, and she jammed a finger on the controls. The display froze, halfway between signals, showing only the originating codes.

"Whatsit?" asked Cavery, looking over to see why the flickering had stopped.

"I don't know. Something funny."

"Funny! You've been here over six standard months and you're surprised to find something funny?"

"No . . . not really." Her voice softened as she peered at the screen. Then she saw it. Out of eighteen message fragments on the screen, two had the same originator codes, reduplicated four times each. That had made odd blocks of light on the screen, repeating blocks where she'd expected randomness. She looked over at Cavery. "What's a quad duplication of originating blocks for?"

"A quad? Never saw one. Let's take a look—" He called up the reference system on his own screen. "What's the code?"

Sassinak read it off, waited while he punched it in. He whistled. "Code itself is Fleet IG's office . . . who the dickens is getting mail from the IG, I wonder. And quad duplication. That's . . ."

She heard his fingers on the keys, a soft clicking, and then another whistle. "I dunno, Ensign. Some kind of internal code, I'd guess, but it's not in the book. Who're they to?"

Sassinak read off the codes, and he looked them up.

"Huh. 'Tenant Achael and Weapons Systems Officer . . . and that's 'Tenant Achael. Tell you what, Ensign, someone sure wants to have Achael get that signal, whatever it is." He gave her a strange, challenging look. "Want me to put a tag on it?"

"Mmm? No," she said. Then more firmly, as he continued to look at her. "No, just the receiving code tag. It's none of our business, anyway."

Still, she couldn't quite put it out of her mind. It wasn't unknown for the IG to pull a surprise inspection—and not unheard of for a junior officer to be tipped off by a friend ahead of time. Or someone—presumably 'Tenant Achael—might have made a complaint directly to the IG. That also happened. But she couldn't leave it at that. She was responsible, whenever she was on duty, for spotting anything irregular in the Communications Section. Two messages from the IG's office—two messages sent to the same person by different routes, and with an initiating code that wasn't in the book. That was definitely irregular.

"Come in, Ensign," said Commander Fargeon, seated as usual behind his desk. She wished it had been some other officer. "What is it?" he asked.

"An irregularity in incoming signals, sir." Sassinak laid the hardcopy prints on his desk. "This came in with a regular mail batchfile. Two identical strips for Lieutenant Achael, one direct to his E-mail slot, and one to Weapons Officer. The same originating code, in the IG's office, but repeated four times. And it's in code..." She let her voice trail off, seeing that Fargeon's attention was caught. He picked up the prints and looked closely at them.

"Hmm. Did you decode it?"

"No, sir." Sass managed not to sound aggrieved: he knew she knew that was strictly against regulations. She hadn't done anything yet to make him think she was likely to break regs.

"Well." Fargeon sat back, still staring at the prints. "It's probably nothing, Ensign—a friend in the IG's office, wanting to make sure he'd get the message—but you were quite right to bring it to my attention. Quite right." By his tone, he didn't think so—he sounded bored and irritable. Sassinak waited a moment. "And if anything of a similar nature should happen again, you should certainly tell me about it. Dismissed."

Sassinak left his office unsatisfied. Something pricked her mind; she couldn't quite figure it out, but it worried her constantly. Surely Fargeon, the most rigid of captains, couldn't be involved in anything underhanded. And was it underhanded to be receiving messages from the IG? Not really.

She mentioned her inability to feel comfortable with Fargeon's attitude to the Weft ensign, Jrain.

"No, we don't think he's bent," was Jrain's response. "He doesn't like Wefts, but then he doesn't like much of anyone he didn't know in childhood. They're pretty inbred, there on Bretagne. A bit like the Seti, in a way: they have very rigid ideas of right and wrong."

"I thought the Seti were pretty loose," said Sass. "Vandals and hellraisers, always willing to start a fight or gamble it all on one throw."

"They are, but that doesn't mean they don't have their own rules. Did you know Seti won't do any gene engineering?"

"I thought they were primitive in that field."

"They are, but it's because they want to be. They think it's wrong to load the dice—genetic or otherwise. But that's beside the point: what matters is that Fargeon is straight, so far as Wefts can tell. Even though he doesn't like us, Wefts choose to serve on his ship, because he is fair."

Only a few shipdays later, they had their first break in routine since leaving Base. The cruiser had orders to inspect a planet in the system which had generated conflicting reports: an EEC classification of "habitable; possibly suitable for limited colonization" and a more recent free scout's comment of "dead—no hope."

From orbit, the remote survey crews backed up the free scout's report. No life, and no possibility of it without major terraforming. But Fleet apparently wanted a closer investigation, some idea of who had done it—the *Others*, or what? Commander Fargeon himself chose the landing team: Sassinak went as communications officer, along with ten specialists and ten armed guards.

It was her first time since the training cruise at the Academy in full protective gear. This time, a sergeant checked her seals and tanks, instead of an instructor. The air tasted "tanky" as they put it, and she had to remind herself where all the switches were. Carefully, very aware that this was no training exercise, she checked out the main and backup radios she'd be using on the surface, made sure that the recording taps were all open, the computer channels cleared for input.

She didn't see the planet until the shuttle cleared the cruiser's hull. It looked exactly like the teaching tapes of dead planets. Sassinak ignored it after a glance and ran another set of checks on her equipment. Although the planet had once had a breathable oxygen atmosphere, sustained by its biosphere, it had already skewed towards the reducing atmosphere common to unlivable worlds.

Besides, whatever had been used to kill its living component might still be active. They would be on tanks the entire time. She had hardly cleared the shuttle ramp on the surface, and felt the alien grit rasping along her bootsoles, when the landing team commander called a warning.

At first Sassinak could not judge the size or distance of the pyramidal objects that seemed to grow, like the targets in a computer simulation game, from nothing in the upper air. Certainly they didn't follow the trajectories required by normal insystem drives, nor did they slow for the careful landing the shuttle pilot had made. Instead they hovered briefly overhead, then sank apparently straight down to rest firmly on the bare rock.

Sassinak reported this, hardly aware of doing it, so fascinated was she by the display. Half a dozen of the pyramids now sat, or lay, in an irregular array near the shuttle. Theks, the landing party commander had said; apart from teaching tapes, she had never seen a Thek and now she saw many in person, if such designation was accurate for those entities.

Another member of the landing party beeped the LPC and asked, "What do we do about them, sir?"

The LPC snorted, a splatter of sound in the suit com units. "It's more what are they going to do about us. For future reference, this looks to me like the beginnings of a Thek conference. Meanwhile, look your fill. Not many of us ephemerals get a chance to see one forming."

His suit helmet tilted; Sassinak looked up, too. More of the pyramids appeared, sank, and landed nearby.

"If that's what they're doing," LPC said after a brief silence, "we might as well go back in the shuttle and have something to eat. This is going to take longer than we'd planned. Inform the captain, Ensign."

More and more pyramids arrived . . . and then, without sound or warning, the ones already landed rose and joined the others to form a large, interlocking structure of complex geometry.

"That," said the LPC, sounding impressed, "is a Thek cathedral. It's big enough inside for this whole shuttle, and it lasts until they're through. The Xenos think they're linking minds. Humans who have been *in* one don't talk about what happened."

"Humans get drawn into one of those things?" someone asked, clearly unsettled by the notion.

"If a Thek calls, you come," replied the LPC.

"How would you know a Thek wanted you?"

"Oh, there's evidence that the Thek recognize individual humans from time to time . . ."

"Their time?" a wise guy quipped.

"It does look a lot like the Academy Chapel right now," said Sassinak softly. She didn't think this was a time to be clever but people reacted differently to something they couldn't quite understand.

"Most people think that. You're lucky to see one, you know. Just try to keep out of one, if you've got the option. No one says 'no' to one Thek, let alone a whole flotilla."

"Does anyone know more about them than the Academy tapes?"

"Did you take Advanced Alien Cultures? No? Well, it's not that much help anyway. An allied alien race, co-founders of the Federation, we think. Wefts are one of their client races, although I don't know why. They're mineral, and they communicate very... very... slowly... with humans, if at all." Although they were back in the shuttle now, the LPC kept his voice low. "Have a taste for transuranics, and they're supposed to remember everything that ever happened to them, or a distant ancestor. Live a long time, but before they dissolve or harden, or whatever it is they do that corresponds with death, they transmit all their memories somehow. Maybe they're telepathic with each other. For humans they use a computer interface or modulate sound waves. Without, as you can see, any mouth. Don't ask me how; it's not my field, and this is only the second time I've seen a Thek."

Hours later, the Theks abruptly disassembled themselves and flew—or whatever it was—back into the darkening sky. The landing party, now thoroughly bored and stiff, grumbled back into action.

Sass followed them to the outcrop that had been chosen for primary sampling. They set to work as she relayed their results and comments back to the ship. Worklights glared, forming haloes at the edge of her vision as the dust rose, almost like smoke haze in a bar, she thought, watching suited figures shift back and forth. Suddenly she stiffened, wholly alert, her heart racing. One of them—one of the helmeted blurs—she had seen before. Somewhere. Somewhere in a fight.

It came to her: the night of Abe's murder, the night of the brawl in the bar. That same bold geometric pattern on the helmet had then been on the jacket of one of the street gang. That same flicking movement of the arm had—she closed her eyes a moment, now recognizing something she had never quite put together—had aimed something at Abe.

Rage blurred her vision and thought. She opened her mouth to scream into the com unit, but managed to clamp her teeth on the scream. Abe's murderer here? In a Fleet uniform? She didn't know all the landing party, but she could certainly find out whose helmet that was. And somehow, some way, she'd get her revenge.

Through the rest of the time on planet, she worked grimly, determined to hide her reactions until she found out just who that was, and why Abe had been killed. She wondered again about the mysterious duplicated message to 'Tenant Achael. Could that be part of the same problem?

Back on the ship, Sass made no sudden moves. She had had time to think about her options. Going to Fargeon with a complaint that someone on the ship had murdered her guardian would get her a quick trip to the Medical Section for sedation. Querying the personnel files was against regulations, and even if she could get past the computer's security systems, she risked leaving a trace of her search. Whoever it was would know that she was aware of something wrong. Even asking about the helmet's assigned user might be risky, but she felt it was the least risky ... and she had an idea.

Partly because of the Thek arrival and conference, the LPC had permitted more chatter on the circuits than usual, and Sass had already found it hard to tag each transmission with the correct originating code, as required. She had reason, therefore, to ask the rating in charge of the helmets for a list of occupants, "just to check on some of this stuff, and be sure I get the right words with the right person."

The helmet she cared most about belonged to 'Tenant Achael. Gotcha, thought Sass, but kept a bright friendly smile on her face when she called him on the ship's intercom. "Sorry to bother you, sir," she began, "but I needed to check some of these transmissions..."

"Couldn't you have done that at the time?" he asked. He sounded gruff, and slightly wary. Sass tried to project innocent enthusiasm, and pushed all thought of Abe aside.

"Sorry, sir, but I was having trouble with the coded data link while the Theks were there." This was in fact true, and she'd mentioned it to the LPC at the time, which meant she was covered if Achael checked. "The commander said that was more important..."

"Very well, then. What is it?"

"At 1630, ship's time, a conversation on the geo-chemical sulfur cycle and its relation to the fourth stage of re-seeding...was it you, sir, or Specialist Nervin, who said 'But that's only if you consider the contribution of the bacterial substrate to be nominal.' That's just where the originating codes began to get tangled." Just as she spoke, Sass pushed the capture button on her console, diverting Achael's response into a sealed file she'd prepared. Highly illegal, but she would have need of it. And if the shielded tap she'd put together didn't work, he'd hear the warning buzz on her speech first. He should react to it.

"Oh—" He sounded less tense. "That was Nervin—he was telling me about the latest research from Zamroni. Apparently there's some new evidence that shows a much greater contribution from the bacterial substrate in fourth stage. Have you read it?"

"No, sir."

"Really. You were involved in installing the new environmental system, though, weren't you? I'd gotten the idea that biosystems was your field."

"No, sir," said Sassinak firmly, guessing where he wanted to go with this. "I took command course: just general knowledge in the specialty fields. Frankly, sir, I found most of that environmental system over my head, and if it hadn't been for Chief Erling—"

"I see. Well, does that give you enough to go on, or do you need something else?"

Sassinak asked two more questions, each quite reasonable since it involved a period with multiple transmissions at a time when her attention might have been on data relay. He answered freely, seemingly completely relaxed now, and Sassinak kept her own voice easy. He was still willing to chat. Then she cut him off, making herself sound reluctant. Did she want to meet for a drink in the mess next shift indeed!

I'll drink at your funeral, she thought to herself, *and dance on your grave, you murdering blackheart.*

Chapter Six

Sassinak wondered how she could get into the personnel files without being detected. And could she find out anything useful if she did? Certainly Achael wouldn't have "murderer" filling in some blank (secondary specialty?), and since she had no idea who or what had marked Abe for death, she wasn't sure she could recognize anything she found anyway. Still, she had to do something.

"Sassinak, can I ask you something?" Surbar, fellow ensign, was a shy, quiet young man, who nonetheless used his wide dark eyes to good advantage. Sassinak had heard, through Mira, that he was enjoying his recreational hours with a Jig in Weapons Control. Nonetheless, he'd given her some intense looks, and she'd considered responding.

"Sure." Sassinak leaned back, in the relaxed atmosphere of the second watch mess, and ran her hands through her hair. In one corner of her mind, she considered that it was getting a bit too long, and she really ought to go get it trimmed again. Tousled was one thing, but a tangled mass—which is what her hair did every chance it got—was another. The difference between sexy and blowsy.

"D'you know anything about 'Tenant Achael?"

Sassinak barely controlled her reaction. "Achael? Not really—he was on the landing party, but I was too busy with all my stuff to talk to him. Why?"

"Well." Surbar frowned and scratched his nose. "He's been asking about you. Lia wanted to know why, and he said you were too good looking to be running around loose. Thought you might be related to somebody he'd known."

Sassinak made herself chuckle casually. Apparently it worked because Surbar didn't seem to notice anything. "He's one of those, is he? After every new female on the ship?"

Surbar shrugged. "Lia said he made eyes at her, but backed off when she said no. Then he started asking about you—so I guess maybe he is that kind."

"Mmm. Well, then, I'll be sure to stay out of airlocks and closets and other closed spaces if Mr. Lieutenant Achael is around."

"Meaning you're not interested?" Surbar gave her his most melting look.

"Not in *him*," said Sassinak, glancing at the overhead and then letting her glance slide sideways to meet Surbar's. "On the other hand..."

"Lia's coming to play gunna tonight," said Surbar quickly. "Maybe another time?"

Sassinak shrugged. "Give me a call. Thanks, anyway, for the warning about Achael." On her way back to her compartment, she thought about it. Achael had enough seniority to cause her trouble, and as Weapons Officer he had high enough clearance to access most communications files. If he wanted to. If he thought he needed to. She wanted him dead, if he was Abe's killer, or in league with Abe's killer, but she didn't want to ruin herself in the process.

The next shift, Sassinak had her first IFTL message to process. Muttering her way through the protocol, she logged it, stripped the outer codes, and got it into the captain's eyes-only file without help. Cavery nodded. "Good job—you're doing well at that."

"Wonder what it's about."

"Ours not to know—they say your eyes turn to purple jelly and your brain rots if you peek at those things."

Sassinak chuckled; Cavery had turned out to have quite a sense of humor. "I thought ensigns didn't have brains, just vast pools of prediluvian slime—isn't that what I heard you tell Pickett, yesterday?"

"Comes from trying to decode IFTL messages, that's what I just said. Keep your mind, such as it is, on your work. You can't afford to lose more." His grin took all the sting out of it, and Sassinak went on logging in routine communications for the rest of the shift.

That night Fargeon announced in the wardroom that they were

to intercept an EEC craft and pick up reports for forwarding. He spent a long time droning on about the delicate handling necessary to rendezvous in deep space, and Sassinak let her attention wander. Not so far as some, though, for Fargeon's rebuke fell on a Jig from Engineering, who had been doodling idly on her napkin. For some reason, Fargeon chose to interpret this as carelessness with classified information, and by the time he'd finished reaming her out, everyone in the room felt edgy. Of course deep-space rendezvous were tricky, everyone knew that, and of course the EEC pilot couldn't be depended on to arrive at a precise location, as the cruiser would do, but this was no different from any other time, surely. If the EEC ship fouled up badly enough, and they all made a fireworks display that wouldn't be seen anywhere for fifty years or so, too bad.

Since everyone came out of dinner disgruntled, Sassinak didn't pay much attention to her own mood. But the next morning she found that Lieutenant Achael had the bridge: Fargeon, Dass, and Lieutenant Commander Slachek were, he said, in conference. Sassinak glanced around the bridge, and ducked into the communications cubby. It was empty. A scrawled note on the console said that Perry had gone to sickbay: Achael had cleared it. Sassinak frowned, wondering if that's why Cavery was late—perhaps he'd gone with Perry to sickbay. But communications hadn't been uncovered long; the incoming telltales showed nothing in the queue in any system. Odd—they'd been getting regular bursts last shift, relayed position checks on the EEC ship. Sassinak pulled up the last entries in the incoming file, to check the log-in times—if they hadn't had anything coming in for awhile, it might mean trouble with the systems.

She was so intent on the idea of a systems failure that she almost didn't recognize her own initiation code when it flashed on the screen. What? Her nose wrinkled in concentration. She'd just gotten there, and yet her code was time-linked to a file query five minutes before. It couldn't be—unless someone had entered her code by mistake . . . or for some other reason.

"Hey—sorry I'm late." Cavery slid into his seat, took a look at the display, and recoiled. "I thought I told you not to go poking around in the incoming message files."

"You did. I didn't. Somebody used my code."

"What!" After that first explosive word, his voice lowered. "Don't *say* that, Sassinak. Probably every comm posting in the universe has snooped one time or another, but lying doesn't make it better."

"I'm not lying." Sassinak laid her hand over his on the console. "Listen to me. I wasn't here at the time that was logged; I came in right on time, not early as usual. Someone logged my code five minutes before I was here."

"What'd Perry say?"

"He's in sickbay. Nobody was here when I got here, just a note—" She handed it over. Cavery frowned.

"Hardcopy, not on the computer. That's odd. Who's got duty—?" He craned to see around the angle, and snorted. "Oh, great. Achael. Where's Fargeon?"

"In conference, Achael said. But Cavery, the thing is—"

"The thing is, your code's on there, telling the whole world you were snooping in the IFTL files, and if you say you're not either you're a liar, which is one problem, or someone else is, which is another. Damn! All we needed, with the captain the way he is right now, is a Security glitch."

"But I didn't—"

Cavery looked at her, hard, then his mouth relaxed. "No, I don't think you would. But with your code on the file, and—what the dickens is *that*?" He pointed to the realtime display, which was filling with the outgoing batch message for SOLEC transmission. "I don't suppose you put your code on that one either?"

Sassinak looked and saw the other anomaly that Cavery had missed. "Or that quad code for the Inspector General's office, either—it's the same thing we had before, only outgoing, and using my code as originator."

"That one, I will strip." Cavery froze the display, keyed in the ranking codes, and displayed the message itself, along with its initiating and destination sequences. Sassinak noticed that he was copying all this into another file, sealed with his own code. He sat back, clearly baffled by the message.

"Subject unaware; no suspicious activity. Assignment coincidental. Will continue observation."

Cavery looked over at her, brows raised. "Well, Ensign, are you keeping someone under surveillance, or is someone keeping you under surveillance?"

"I—don't know." *Achael,* she thought. *It has to be Achael, but why? And who's behind it?*

"Well, I know one thing, and that's where all this is going: straight to the captain."

"But—" Sassinak stopped herself; if she protested, he'd have reason to think she knew more. Yet she wasn't near ready to accuse Achael of involvement with Abe's death ... how could she? No matter how it came out, she'd lose: ensigns don't get anywhere accusing lieutenants of murder months back and somewhere else.

Cavery waited, his expression clearly daring her to object.

"I know," she said finally, "that Captain Fargeon has to be informed. But he's not on the bridge, and I don't ... really ... want to involve any more officers than necessary."

"I remember whose number was on those quad-coded messages, Ensign Sassinak—" Cavery nodded toward the main bridge area. "You needn't try to be obscure."

"Sorry, sir. I wasn't trying to be obscure, I was just—" She paused, as near waving her hands in confusion as she'd ever been. Then inspiration hit. She saw by Cavery's expression that her own had changed with her idea. "Sir, if all this ties together, right now is a bad time to go charging out of here to the captain, isn't it? And if it doesn't, it would still ... confuse things, wouldn't it?"

Cavery leaned back fractionally, considering. "You have a point." He sighed, and cleared the display. "I can't see that it would hurt to wait until midwatch break, anyway, and maybe later. Depends on the captain's schedule."

Sassinak said nothing more, but settled to her work. Thank whatever gods there were she hadn't meddled with the Personnel files or the message banks: Achael didn't know she suspected anything. Assignment coincidence? What else could it be, when she had no powerful family to pull strings for her ... or had that been Abe's secret, perhaps? More than ever, she needed to see Achael's file, but how was she going to do that?

The shattering clamor of the emergency alarm brought her upright. Fast as she was, Cavery's hand almost covered hers as they shut the console down for normal use and flicked on the emergency systems. After the first blast of noise, the siren warbled up, down, up twice: evacuation drill.

"Stupidest damn drill in the book," grumbled Cavery as he fished under the console for the emergency masks. "Here—put this on. Nobody ever evacuates a cruiser; as long as it takes to get everyone in the shuttles and evac pods, whatever it is will have blown the whole place up. Now remember, Ensign, you close the board when you leave, and that's not until the duty officer clears the bridge." His voice was muffled, now, through the foil and plex hood and mask. Sassinak found that hers cut off all vision to the side and rear. As she fastened the tabs to the shoulders of her uniform, Cavery grunted. "Ah, good: Fargeon's taken the bridge. Soon as this damn drill's over, we can get this other taken care of—" His voice sharpened. "Yes, sir; communications secured, sir."

Although Cavery's acid comments implied that pirates could have boarded the ship and flown it to the far side of the galaxy before their turn came, Sassinak thought it wasn't long at all before she was jogging forward along the main portside corridor from the bridge to the transport bays where the shuttles and evac pods were docked. A stream of hooded figures jogged her way, and another jogged back; once you were logged into your assigned evacuation slot, you had to return to your duty post. It did seem illogical. She looked again at the strip of plastic giving her assigned pod: E-40-A. Here, along a side corridor, through a narrow passage she'd never explored. Bay E: someone in full EVA gear glanced at her assignment strip and waved her to the right; section 40 was the last one at the end. Someone else, also suited up, pointed out Pod A, one of a row of hatches still dogged shut. Sassinak struggled with the hatch lock, checked to see that the telltales were all green, and pulled the heavy lid open. Inside the little brightly lit compartment, she could see the shape of an acceleration couch, shiny fittings, a bank of switches and lights.

She ducked her head to clear the hatch opening. Suddenly a sharp pain jabbed her arm, and when she tried to turn it felt like the weight of the whole cruiser landed on her head. She could do nothing but fall forward into darkness.

Commander Fargeon in a rage was no pleasant sight. His officers, ranged around his desk at attention, had no doubt of his mood. "What I want to know," he said icily, "is *who* dumped that pod. Who sent it out there, and what's that ensign doing in it, and why isn't the beacon functioning, and what's all this nonsense about communications security leaks."

Eyes slid sideways; no one volunteered. Fargeon barked, "Cavery!"

"Sir, Ensign Sassinak had reported an incident of duplicate transmissions with unusual initiation codes—"

"I know about *that*. That's got nothing to do with this, has it?"

Cavery wasn't sure how far to go, yet. "I don't know, sir: I was just starting at the beginning." He took a breath, waited for Fargeon's nod, and went on. "Today she reported that someone had used her initiation code to attempt access to a restricted file—"

"Ensign Sassinak? When?"

"Apparently it happened about five minutes before she came on duty. She reported it to me when I arrived—" Cavery went on to explain what had happened up until the drill alarm went. Fargeon listened without further comment, his face expressionless. Then he turned to another officer.

"Well, Captain Palise: what did you see in E-bay?"

"Sir, we logged Ensign Sassinak into E-bay at 1826.40; she logged off the bridge on evac at 1824.10, and that's just time to go directly to E-bay. As you know, sir, in an evac drill we have personnel constantly shifting about; once someone's logged into the bay, there's no way to keep watch on them until they're into their assigned shuttle or pod. When the hatches are dogged, then they're logged as onboard evac craft, and they're supposed to return to duty as quickly as possible. Within two minutes of Ensign Sassinak's bay log-in, we show fifty-three individuals logging in to the same bay—about what you'd expect. Eight of them were in the wrong bay—and that's about average, too. We had two recording officers in E-bay, but they didn't notice anything until Pod 40-A fired."

"Very well, Captain Palise. Now, Engineering—"

"The pod was live, sir, as they always are for drill. We can't be shutting down the whole system just because somebody might make a mistake—"

"I know that." It had been Fargeon's own policy, in fact, and the Engineering Section had warned more than once that having evac drills with live pods and shuttles while in FTL travel was just asking for trouble. Fargeon glared at his senior engineer, and Erling glared back. Everyone knew that Erling had taken to Sassinak in her first assignment. Whatever had happened, Erling was going to pick Sassinak's side, if he knew which it was.

"Well, sir, activation would be the same as always. If the hatch is properly dogged, inside and out, and the sequence keyed in—"

"From inside?"

"Either. The shuttles have to be operated from inside, but the whole reason behind the pods was safe evacuation of wounded or disabled individuals. Someone in the bay can close it up and send it off just as easy as the occupant."

"I don't think we need to worry about *that*," said Fargeon repressively. "My interest now is in determining if Ensign Sassinak hit the wrong button out of stupidity, or did she intend to desert the ship?"

Into the silence that followed this remark, Lieutenant Achael's words fell with the precision of an artisan's hammer.

"Perhaps I can shed some light on that, sir. But I would prefer to do so in private."

"On the contrary. You will tell me now."

"Sir, it is a matter of some delicacy . . ."

"It is a matter of some urgency, Lieutenant, and I expect a complete report at once."

Achael bowed slightly, a thin smile tightening his lips. "Sir, as you know I have a cousin in the Inspector General's office. As weapons officer, I have particular interest in classified document control, and when that directive came out two months ago, I decided to set up such a test on this ship. You remember that you gave your permission—?" He waited for Commander Fargeon's nod before going on. "Well, I had three hard copies of apparently classified documentation on the new Witherspoon ship-to-ship beam, and— as the directive suggested—I made an opportunity to let all the newly assigned officers know that they existed and where they were."

"Get to the point, Lieutenant."

"The point, sir, is that one of them disappeared, then reappeared one shift later. I determined that three of the ensigns, and two Jigs, had the opportunity to take the copy. I handled the copy with tongs, and put it in the protective sleeve the directive had included, for examination later at a forensic lab. And I reported this, in code, to my cousin, in case anything—ah—happened to me."

"And you have reason to believe that Ensign Sassinak was the person who took the document?"

"She had the opportunity, along with several others. Forensic examination should show whether she handled it. Or rather, it would have."

"Would have?"

"Yes, sir. The document in question, in its protective sleeve, is missing from my personal safe. We have not only a missing pod, and a missing ensign, but a missing document which might have identified someone who had broken security regulations. And a nonfunctioning beacon on the pod. I scarcely think this can be coincidence."

"Not Sassinak!" That was Cavery, furious suddenly. He had had his doubts, but not after the pod ejected. If Sassinak had wanted to escape, she wouldn't have called herself to his attention that very morning.

"As for the outgoing message with her initiation code, I believe she may have been reporting to whomever she—er—worked with."

"The destination code was in the IG's office," said Cavery. "The same code as your incoming message."

"You're sure? Of course, she might have done that to incriminate me—"

"NO!" Erling and Cavery shouted it together.

"Gentlemen." Fargeon's voice was icy, his expression forbidding. "This is a matter too serious for personalities. Ensign Sassinak may have been ejected accidentally. Or, despite her high ratings in the Academy, she may have been less than loyal. There is her background to consider. Of course, Lieutenant Achael, it's one you share."

Achael stiffened. "Sir, I was a prisoner. She was a slave. The difference—"

"Is immaterial. She didn't volunteer for slavery, I'm sure. However, her captors would have had ample time to implant deep conditioning—not really her responsibility. At any rate, Lieutenant, your information only adds to the urgency and confusion of this situation." He took a long breath, but before he could begin the long speech they all knew was coming, Makin, the Weft Jig, spoke up.

"Begging the captain's pardon, but what about retrieval?"

Fargeon became even stiffer, if possible. "Retrieval? Mr. Makin, the pod was ejected during FTL flight, and we are en route to a scheduled rendezvous with an EEC vessel. Either of those conditions alone would make retrieval impossible—"

"Sir, not impossible. Difficult, but—"

"Impossible. The pod was ejected into a probability flux—recall your elementary physics class, Mr. Makin—and would have dropped into sublight velocity at a location describable in cubic light-minutes. With a vector of motion impossible to calculate. Now if the beacon had functioned—which Engineering assures me it did not—we would be getting some sort of distorted signal from it. We might spend the next few weeks tracking it down, if we didn't have this rendezvous to make. But we have no beacon to trace, and we have a rendezvous to make. My question now is what report to make to Fleet Headquarters, and what we should recommend be done about that ensign."

When Fargeon dismissed them, he announced no decision; outside his office, the buzzing conversations began.

"I don't care what that sneak says." Cavery was beyond caution. "I will not believe Sassinak took anything—so much as a leftover muffin—and if she did she'd be standing here saying so."

"I don't know, Cavery." Bullis, of Admin, might not have cared: he argued for the sheer joy of it. "She was intelligent and hardworking, I'll grant you that, but too sharp for her own good. If you follow me."

"Not into that, I won't. I—" He paused, and looked around at Makin, the Weft Jig, who had tapped his arm.

"If I could speak to you a moment, sir?"

Cavery looked at Bullis and shrugged, then followed Makin down the corridor. "Well?"

"Sir, is there any way to convince the captain that we *can* locate that pod, even without a beacon on it?"

"You can? Who? And how?"

"We can because Ensign Sassinak is on it—Wefts, I mean, sir. With Ssli help."

Cavery cocked his head. "*Ssli* help? Wait a minute—you mean the Ssli could locate that little pod, even in normal space, while we're—"

"Together, we could, sir." Cavery had the feeling that the Weft meant something more than he'd said, but excitement overrode his curiosity for the moment.

"But I don't know what I can do about the captain," he murmured, lowering his voice as Achael strolled nearer. "I'm not going to get anywhere arguing."

"Cavery," Achael broke into their conversation. "I know you liked the girl, and she *is* attractive. I'd have spent a night or so with her gladly." Cavery reddened at that insinuation. "But the circumstances are suggestive, even suspicious."

"I suppose you'd suspect any orphan ex-slave?" Cavery meant it to bite, and Achael stiffened.

"I'm not the one who brought up her ancestry," he pointed out.

"No, but you have to admit, if it's a matter of access, you were in the same place at the same time. Maybe someone twisted your mind. Curious you never saw her, hmm?"

Achael glared at him. "You've never been anyone's prisoner, have you? I spent my entire time on that miserable rock locked in a stinking cell with five other members of the *Caleb*'s crew. One of them died, of untreated wounds, and my best friend went permanently insane from the interrogation drugs. I hardly had the leisure to go wandering about the slaveholds looking for little girls, as she must have been then."

"I— I'm sorry," said Cavery, embarrassed. "I didn't know."

"I don't talk about it." Achael had turned away, hiding his face. Now he spun about, pinning Cavery suddenly with a stiffened forefinger. "And I don't expect you, Cavery, to tell everyone in the mess about it, either."

"Of course not." Cavery watched the other man stalk away, and wished he'd never opened his mouth.

"You notice he never answered your question," Makin said. At Cavery's blank look, he went on. "You're right, sir, that during that captivity an enemy had a chance to deep-program Lieutenant Achael . . . and nothing he said makes that less likely. A friend who went insane from interrogation drugs . . . perhaps Achael did not."

"I don't—like to accuse anyone who went through—through something like that—"

"Of course not. But that's what they may have counted on, to cover any lapses. Now, about the pod and Ensign Sassinak—"

✧   ✧   ✧

Sassinak's supporters barely crammed into Cavery's quarters. Wefts, other ensigns, Erling from Engineering. After the first chaos, when everyone assured everyone else that she couldn't have done any of it, they concentrated on ways and means.

"We have to do it soon, because those damn pods don't carry much air. If she's conscious, she'll put herself in coldsleep—and amateurs trying to put themselves in are all too likely to make a fatal mistake."

"Worse than that," said Makin, "we can't track her if she's in coldsleep—it'll be like death. We've got to get her before she does that, or before she dies."

"Which is how long, Erling?" Everyone craned to see the engineer's face. It offered no great amount of hope. He spread his hands.

"Depends on her. If she takes the risk of holding out on the existing air supply as long as she can, or if she opts to go into coldsleep while she's alert. And we don't even know if the person who ejected the pod sabotaged the airtanks or the coldsleep module, as well as the beacon. At an outside, maximum, if she pushes it, hundred-ten to hundred-twenty hours from ejection." Before anyone could ask, he glanced at a clock readout on the wall and went on. "And it's been eight point two. And the captain's determined to make the rendezvous with the EEC ship tomorrow, which eats up another twenty-four to thirty." His glare was a challenge. The Weft ensign Jrain took it up.

"Suppose we can't convince the captain to break the rendezvous— what about going back afterwards? He might be in a more reasonable frame of mind then."

Erling snorted. "He might—and then again he might be hot to go straight to sector command. To go back—hell, how would I know? You tell me you can find her, you and the Ssli, but I sure couldn't calculate a course or transit time. Even if we hit the same drop-point as the ejection—if that's not a ridiculous statement in talking of paralight space—we'd have no guarantee we'd come out with the same vector. They found that out when they tried dropping combat modules out of FTL in the Gerimi System. Scattered to hell all over the place, and it took months to clean up the mess. But again, assume we can use you as guides, we still have to maneuver the ship. Maybe we can, maybe we can't."

"We have to *try*." Mira rumpled her blonde hair as if she wanted to unroot it. "Sassinak isn't guilty, and I'm not going to have her take the blame. She helped others at the Academy—"

"Not *your* bunch," Train pointed out.

"So I grew up," Mira retorted. "My mother pushed me into that friendship; I didn't know better until later. Sassinak is my friend, and she's not going to be left drifting around in a dinky little pod for god knows how long..."

"Well, but what are we going to *do* about it?"

"I think Train had a good idea. Let Fargeon get this rendezvous out of his head, and then try him again. And if he doesn't agree..." Cavery scowled. No one wanted to say mutiny out loud.

Chapter Seven

When Sassinak woke up, to the dim gray light of the evacuation pod, she had a lump on her forehead, another on the back of her head, and the vague feeling that too much time had passed. She couldn't see much, and finally realized that something covered her head. When she reached for it, her arm twinged, and she rubbed a sore place. It felt like an injection site, but... Slowly, clumsily, she pawed the foil hood from her head and looked around. She lay crumpled against the acceleration couch of a standard evac pod; without the hood's interference, she could see everything in the pod. Beneath the cushions of the couch was the tank for coldsleep, if things went wrong. She had the feeling that perhaps things had gone wrong, but she couldn't quite remember.

Slowly, trying to keep her churning stomach from outwitting her, she pushed herself up. It would do no good to panic. Either she was in a functioning pod inside a ship, or she was in a functioning pod in flight: either way, the pod had taken care of her so far, or she wouldn't have wakened. The air smelled normal... but if she'd been there long enough, her nose would have adapted. She tried to look around, to the control console, and her stomach rebelled. She grabbed at the nearest protruding knob, and a steel basin slid from its recess at one end of the couch. Just in time.

She retched until nothing came but clear green bile, then wiped her mouth on her sleeve. What a stink! Her mouth quirked. What a thing to think about at a time like this. She felt cold and shaky, but a little more solid. Aches and twinges began to assert themselves.

She pushed the basin back into its recess, looked for and found the button that should empty and sterilize it (she didn't really want to think about the pod's recycling system, but her mind produced the specs anyway), and turned over, leaning against the couch.

Over the hatch, a digital readout informed her that the pod had been launched eight hours and forty-two minutes before. Launched! She forced herself to look at the rest of the information. Air supply on full; estimated time of exhaustion ninety-two hours fourteen minutes. Water and food supplies: maximum load; estimated exhaustion undetermined. Of course, she hadn't used any yet, and the onboard comp had no data on her consumption. She tried to get onto the couch and almost passed out again. How could she be that weak if she'd only been here eight hours? And besides that, what had happened? Evac pods were intended primarily for the evacuation of injured or otherwise incapable crew. Had there been an emergency; had she been unconscious on a ship or something?

The second try got her onto the bench, with a bank of control switches ready to her hand. She fumbled for the sipwand, and took two long swallows of water. (The recycling couldn't be working *yet*, she told her stomach.) A touch of the finger, and she cut the airflow down 15%. She might not tolerate that, but if she did it would give her more time. Another swallow of water. The taste in her mouth had been worse than terrible. She felt in her uniform pocket for the mints she liked to carry, and at that moment the memory came back.

The drill . . . E-bay . . . ducking to enter her assigned pod . . . and *something* had jabbed her arm, and landed on her head. She rolled up her sleeve, frowning. Sure enough, a little red weal, slightly itchy and sore. She'd been drugged, and slugged, and dumped in a pod and sent off— As suddenly as that first memory, the situation on the cruiser came to her. Mysterious messages, someone using *her* comm code, and her belief that Achael had had something to do with Abe's murder. If she'd had any doubts, they vanished.

With the wave of anger, her mind seemed to clear. Perhaps Achael or his accomplice had thought she'd die of the drug—or maybe they meant to force her into taking coldsleep, and intended the pod to be picked up by confederates.

You have such cheerful thoughts, she told herself, and looked around for distraction.

There, on the control console an arm's length away, a large gray envelope with bright orange stripes across it. *Fleet Security. Classified. Do Not Open Without Proper Authorization.* The pressure seal hadn't quite taken; the opening gaped. Sassinak started to reach for it, then stopped her hand in midair. Whoever had dumped her in here must have left that little gift... which meant she wanted no part of it.

It might even become evidence. She grinned to herself. A proper Carin Coldae setup this was, and no mistake. Now what would Carin do? Figure out a way to catch the villain, without ruffling one hair of her head. Sassinak rumpled her own hair and remembered that she'd been planning to cut it.

Moment by moment she felt better. She'd suspected that something was going on, and she'd been right. She'd felt in danger, and she'd been right. And now she was helplessly locked into an evac pod, which was headed who knows where, and even with the beacon on no one was likely to find her until she'd run out of air... and she was happy. Ridiculous, but she was. A little voice of caution murmured that it might be the drug, and she shouldn't be overconfident. She told the little voice to shut up. But just in case... she found the med kit, and figured out how to lay her arm in the cradle for a venous tap. Take a blood sample, that should do it. If she had been drugged, and the drug proved traceable... the sting of the needle interrupted that thought for a moment. Beacon. She needed to check the beacon.

But as she had already begun to suspect, the beacon wasn't functioning. She looked thoughtfully at the control console. The quickest way to disable the beacon, and the simplest, required a screwdriver and three or four minutes with that console. Lift the top, giving access to the switches and their attached wiring. Then, depending on how obvious you wanted to be, clip or crosswire or remove this and that. She was not surprised to see a screwdriver loose on the "deck" of the pod.

And her first impulse would normally have been to check out the beacon, using that screwdriver to free the console top. After she'd picked up the envelope with *Classified* all over it. Her fingerprints, her body oils, would have been on the tool, the envelope, the console, even the switches underneath, obscuring the work of the person who'd put her here.

Sassinak took another long swallow of water, and rummaged in the med kit for a stimulant tab. This was no time to miss anything.

In the end, the med kit provided most of what she needed. Forceps, with which to lift the screwdriver and put it into a packet that had held headache pills. It occurred to her that while she was unconscious, her assailant might have pressed her fingers against the envelope, or the screwdriver, but she couldn't do anything about that. She found the little pocket scanner that was supposed to be in every evac module, and shot a clip of the envelope as it lay on the console. When she had all the evidence secured, she suddenly wondered how that would help if she were in coldsleep when she was found. Suppose her assailant had confederates, who were supposed to pick her up? They could destroy her careful work, incriminate her even more. That gave her the jitters for awhile, and then she remembered Abe's patient voice saying "What you can't change, don't cry over: put your energy where it works, Sass."

Right now it had to go into prolonging her time before coldsleep.

Which meant, she remembered unhappily, no eating. Digestion used energy, which used oxygen. No exercise, for the same reason. Lie still, breathe slow, think peaceful thoughts. You might as well spend the time in coldsleep, she grumbled to herself, as try to act as if you *were* in coldsleep. But she took the time to clean herself up as well as she could, using the tiny mirror in the med kit. The slightly overlong hair could be tied back neatly, the stains wiped from her uniform. Then she lay down on the couch, pulled up the coverlet, and tried to relax.

She had not been hungry like this since her slave days. Her empty stomach growled, gurgled, and finally settled for sharp nagging pains. She chivvied her mind away from the food fantasies it wanted to indulge in, steering it into mathematics instead. Squares and square roots, cubes and cube roots, visualizing curves from equations, and imagining how, with a shift in values, the curve would shift . . . as a loop of hose shifts with changing water pressure. Finally she slipped into a doze.

She woke in a foul mood, but more clear-headed than before. Elapsed time since ejection was now 25 hours, 16 minutes. Clearly the cruiser hadn't stopped to look for her, or hadn't been able to find her. She wondered if the Ssli could sense such a small distortion in the fields they touched. Or could the Wefts detect her, as a living being they'd known? But that was idle speculation. She gave her arm to the med kit's blood sampler again; she remembered being told that each drug had a characteristic breakdown profile, and that serial blood tests could provide the best information on an unknown drug.

For a moment, the pod seemed to contract around her, crushing her to the couch. Had some unsuspected drive come on, to flatten her with acceleration? But no: the pods had the same artificial gravity as the cruiser itself, to protect injured occupants. She knew that; she knew the walls weren't really closing in... but she suddenly understood just how Ensign Corfin might have felt. She couldn't see out; she had no idea where she was or where she was going; she was trapped in a tiny box with no way *out*. Her breath came fast: too fast. She fought to slow it. So, this was claustrophobia. How interesting. It didn't feel interesting; it felt terrible.

She had to do something. Squares and square roots seemed singularly impractical this time. Could she figure out a way to ensure that the evidence couldn't be faked against her? Any worse than it already was, she reminded herself. That brought another chilling thought: maybe the cruiser hadn't come looking for her because Commander Fargeon was already convinced she was an enemy agent and had absconded with the pod.

Her stomach growled again; she set herself to enter the first stages of control Abe had taught her. Hunger was just hunger; in this case, nothing to worry about. But she did need to worry about her career.

In the long, lonely, silent hours that followed, Sassinak spent much of her time in a near-trance, dozing. The rest she spent doing what she could to make tampering with the evidence as hard as possible. If the pod were picked up by enemies, with plenty of time at their disposal, none of her ploys would work... but if a Fleet vessel, her cruiser or another, came along, it would take more than a few minutes to undo what she'd done and rework it to incriminate her.

When the elapsed-time monitor read 100 hours, and the time to exhaustion of her air supply was less than five hours, she pulled out the instruction manual for the coldsleep cabinet. Evac pods had an automated system, but she didn't trust it: what if the same person who had sabotaged the beacon had fiddled with the medications? She pushed aside the thought that sabotaging the entire coldsleep cabinet wouldn't have been that hard. If it didn't work, she'd never wake up, and that was that. But she had to try it, or die of oxygen starvation . . . and the films they'd been shown at the Academy had made it clear that oxygen starvation was not a pleasant way to go.

She filled the syringes carefully, checking and re-checking labels and dosages. With the mattress off the acceleration couch, she looked the cabinet over as well as she could. Ordinarily, cold sleep required only an enclosed space; she could go into it using the whole pod as the container. But for extra protection in the pods, the reinforced cabinet had been designed, and was strongly recommended. She looked into that blank, shiny interior, and shuddered.

First, the protocol said, program the automatic dispenser, and then have it start an IV. But she wasn't doing that. Her way would mean getting into the cabinet, with the syringes in hand, giving herself the injections, pulling down the lid, turning the cylinder controls, and then . . . then, she hoped, just sleeping away whatever time it took before someone found her.

Nor could she wait until the last moment. Oxygen starvation would make her clumsy and slow, and she might make fatal mistakes. She set the medication alarm in the medkit for one hour before the deadline. The last minutes crept by. Sassinak looked around the pod interior, fighting to stay calm. She dared not put herself in trance, yet there was nothing to do to ease her tension. There was the tape she'd made, her log of this unplanned journey with all her surmises about cause and criminal. In the acceleration couch mattress was a handwritten log, in the hope that redundancy might help.

When the alarm sounded, she snatched the syringe and reached for the alarm release. But it didn't work. Great, she thought, I'll go into coldsleep with that horrible noise in my ears and have nightmares for years. Then she realized it wasn't the same buzzer at all—in fact, it wasn't time for the medalarm—she had fifteen more minutes. She looked wildly around the pod, trying to figure it out, before her mind dredged up the right memory. Proximity alarm: some kind of large mass was nearby, and it might be a ship, and they might even have compatible communications gear.

Only she had carefully set up the console to trap additional evidence while she was in coldsleep, and if she touched it now she'd be confusing her own system.

And what if it wasn't a Fleet vessel? What if it was an ally of her assailant? Or worse, suppose it wasn't a ship at all, and the pod was falling into a star?

In that case, she told herself firmly, you still don't have to worry; you can't stop it, and it'll all be over very quickly. She found the override switch for the proximity alarm, and cut it off. Now it was a matter of deciding whether to ride it out blind, or try to communicate. She decided to save her careful work, and then realized this meant she wouldn't know if whatever it was could rendezvous before her air ran out. It wouldn't take much error, on either side: ten minutes without oxygen would do as well as four days.

Ten minutes left. Five. She had left herself that safe buffer: dare she use it now? Zero. Sassinak looked at the syringe, but didn't pick it up. She'd feel silly if she lost consciousness just as someone came through the door. She'd be flat stupid if she died because she cut it too close. But she could—and did, quickly—tape an addition to her log.

Now she was using her safe margin. Minute by minute went by with no clue from without, of what was happening. She had just picked up the syringe, with a grimace, when something clunked, hard, against the pod. Another thump; a loud clang. Sassinak put the syringe down, lowered the lid of the coldsleep cabinet, and sat on it. She could not—*could not*—miss whatever was going to happen.

What happened first was total silence as the blower in her oxygen system went out. She had a moment to think how stupid she'd been, and then it cut in again; the readout flickered, and shifted to green. "Exterior source" it said now. "Unlimited. Tanks charging." It smelled better, too. Sassinak took a second long breath, and unclenched her fingers from the edge of the cabinet. Other lights flickered on the control console. "Exterior pressure equalized" said one. She didn't trust it enough to open the hatch . . . not yet. "Exterior power source confirmed" said another.

Finally she heard various clicks and bangs from the hatch, and braced herself, not sure what she would do if she found enemies when it opened. But the first face she saw was familiar.

"Ensign Sassinak." Familiar, but not particularly welcoming. The captain himself had chosen to greet her, and behind him she saw both friendly and scowling faces. And a squad of marines, armed. Sassinak stood, saluted, and nearly fell as the hours of inactivity and fasting caught up with her all at once. "Are you hurt?" Fargeon asked when she staggered.

"Just a knock on the head," she said. "Excuse me, sir, but I must warn you—"

"You, Ensign, are the one to be warned," he said stiffly, that momentary warmth gone as if it had never happened. "Charges have been made against you, serious charges, and it is my duty to warn you that anything you say may be used in evidence against you."

Sassinak stared at him, momentarily speechless. Had he really believed Achael's (it must have been Achael's) accusations? Wasn't he going to give her a chance? She caught herself, shook her head, and went on. "Captain, please—it's very important that this pod be sealed, and all contents handled by forensic specialists."

That got his attention. "What? What are you talking about?"

Sassinak waved her hand at the pod's interior. "Sir, I've done my best to secure it, but I really don't know how. Someone knocked me out during evac drill, dumped me in this pod, jettisoned it, and planted it full of items I was supposed to handle, to incriminate myself. I believe those same items may carry traces of the perpetrator—" She nearly stumbled over the word, catching sight of Lieutenant Achael in the group behind the captain. His face was frozen in an expression of distaste. Then it changed to eagerness, and he leaned forward.

"That's exactly what she *would* say, sir. That someone tried to frame her—"

"I can see that for myself, Mr. Achael." Fargeon's expression soured even more.

"I could hardly have planted someone else's fingerprints on the interior of the console while disabling the beacon," Sassinak said crisply. Achael paled; she saw his eyes glance sideways.

"You disabled the beacon?" asked Fargeon, missing the point.

"No, sir. I realized the beacon was disabled, and also realized that if I made an attempt to repair it, I would destroy evidence pointing to the person who *did* disable it. That evidence is intact." She looked straight at Achael as she spoke. He flinched from her gaze, took a step backward.

Fargeon's head tilted minutely; she had surprised him with some of that. "There's a document missing," he said.

Sassinak nodded. "There's a classified document envelope, not quite sealed, in this pod. I found it when I woke—"

"Likely story," said Achael. This time the captain's response was clearly irritated, a quick flip of the hand for silence.

"And did you handle it?" asked the captain.

"No, sir, I did not. Although it's possible that whoever dumped me in there put my fingers on it while I was unconscious."

"I see." The captain pulled himself up. "Well. This is... unexpected. Very well; I'll see to it that the pod is sealed, and the contents examined for evidence of what actually happened. As for you, Ensign, you'll report to Sickbay, and then to your quarters. I'll want a full report—"

"Sir, I taped a report while in the pod. May I bring that tape?"

"You did?" Again this threw him off his stride. "Very good thinking, Ensign. By all means, let me have it now."

Sassinak picked up the tape, and started forward. Her vision blurred, and she nearly hit her head on the hatch rim. A hand came forward, steadied her arm. She ducked under the hatch, and came out into the chilly air of E-bay. It smelled decidedly fresher than the pod. Fargeon peered at her.

"You're very pale—are you sure you're not ill?"

"It's just not eating." The bulkheads seemed to shimmer, then steadied. She was conscious of having to concentrate firmly on the here and now.

"You—but surely there were emergency rations in the pod?"

"Yes, but—to make the air last—" She fought to stay upright, with a soft blackness folding itself around her. "I didn't—trust the coldsleep cabinet—if the same person had tampered with it—"

"Gods!" That was Cavery, she realized as she looked toward the voice. But the blackness rose around her, inescapable, and she felt herself curling into it.

"Don't forget the blood samples," she heard herself say, and then everything disappeared.

✧ ✧ ✧

The medician's face hung over hers, suspended in nothingness. Sassinak blinked, yawned, and found the rest of the compartment in focus again. Sickbay, clearly. An IV line ran from her left hand to a bag; wires trailed across her chest.

"I'm fine," she said helpfully.

"You're lucky," said the medician, pinching back a smile. "You came close to the edge—you can't use Discipline like that and not eat."

"Huh?"

"Don't try to tell me you weren't using it, either—nothing but a crash from it would have sent you that far down. Here—have a mug of this." A flick of the hand, and Sass's couch lifted her so that she could take the mug of thick broth the medician offered.

"What did the blood samples show?" asked Sassinak between sips. She could practically feel the strength flowing back into her.

"You're lucky," the medician said again. "It was a coldsleep prep dose. If you'd hit the tank controls by mistake, you might have been in coldsleep immediately . . . or if you'd chosen to enter coldsleep early, the residual in your blood could have killed you. It didn't completely clear until the third day."

"The cabinet?" She remembered her fear of that featureless interior.

"Nothing: it was normal." The medician looked at her curiously. "You're in remarkably good shape, all things considered. That lump on the back of your head may still hurt, but there's no damage. You're not showing any signs of excessive anxiety—"

Sassinak slurped the last bit of broth and grinned. "I'm safe now. And not hungry. When can I get up?"

Before the medician could answer, a voice from the corridor said, "That's Sass, all right! I can tell from here."

"Not yet," said the medician to Sass. Then, "Do you want visitors? I can easily tell them to let you rest."

But Sassinak could hardly wait to find out what had happened so far. Mira, all trace of fashionable reserve gone, and Jrain, almost visibly shimmering into another shape in his excitement, were only too glad to tell her.

"I knew," Mira began, "that it couldn't have been your fault. You aren't ever careless like that; you wouldn't have hit the wrong button or anything. And of course you, of all people, wouldn't cooperate with slavers or pirates."

"But how did you find me without the beacon?"

Mira nodded at Jrain. "Your Weft friends did it. I don't know if Jrain can explain it—he couldn't to me—but they tracked you, somehow—"

"It was really the Ssli interface," Jrain said. "You know how they can sense other vessels in FTL space—"

"Yes, but I wasn't in FTL space after the pod went off, was I?"

"No, but it turns out they can reach beyond it, somehow. Doesn't make any sense to me, and what Hssro calls the relevant equations I call gibberish. The pod is really too small to sense—like something small too far away to see—but we knew exactly when you'd been dumped, and the Ssli was able to—to do whatever it does in whatever direction that was. Then we Wefts sort of rode that probe, feeling our way toward you."

"But you said—"

"Because you're alive, and we know you. We had to go in our own shapes, of course—" He frowned, and Sassinak tried to imagine the effect on Fargeon of all the crew's Wefts in their own shape, clinging, no doubt, to the bulkheads of the Ssli contact chamber. Or on the bridge? She asked.

"He wasn't pleased with us," said Jrain, a reminiscent smile on his face. "We don't usually clump on him, you know: he doesn't like aliens much, though he tries to be fair. But when it came down to risking the loss of your pod, or giving in to Achael's insinuations—"

"Kirtin *changed* right there in front of the captain," put in Mira. "I thought he was going to choke. Then Basli and Jrain—"

"Ptak first: I was the last one," Jrain put in.

"Whatever." Mira shrugged away the correction and went on. "Can you imagine—this was in the big wardroom, and there they were all over the walls! I'd never seen more than one Weft changed at a time—" She quirked an eyebrow at Sass.

"I have. It's impressive, isn't it?"

"Impressive! It's crowded, is what it is, with these big spiky *things* all over the walls and ceiling." Mira wrinkled her nose at Jrain, who grinned at her. "Not to mention all those eyes glittering out at you.

And you never told me," she said to Jrain, "that you're telepaths in that shape. I thought you'd use a biolink to the computer or something."

"There wasn't time," said Jrain.

"But what about the rendezvous with the EEC ship? Did we miss that?"

"No. What we decided—I mean—" Mira looked sideways. "What the *Wefts* decided, was to let that go on, and then pick you up afterwards. It seemed risky to me—the further we went, the further away you were, the harder to find. It was a real gamble—"

"No," said Jrain firmly and loudly. Mira stared at him, and Sassinak blinked. He took a long breath, and said more quietly, "We don't gamble. We don't ever gamble."

"I didn't mean like a poker game," said Mira sharply. "But it was risky—"

"No." As they looked at him, his form wavered, then steadied again. "I can't explain. But you must not think—" an earnest look at Sassinak "—you must not think we gamble with your life, Sassinak. Never."

"I—oh, all right, Jrain. You don't gamble. But if one of you doesn't get all this in order and tell me *what happened*, and where we are, and where Achael is, I'm going to crawl out of this bed and stuff *you* in a pod."

Jrain, calmer now, sat on the end of her bed. "Achael is dead. That evidence you spoke to the captain about—remember?" Sassinak nodded. "Well, the captain had it put under guard. The pod, and the items removed, like the blood samples. Achael tried to get at it. He did get into the med lab, and destroyed one test printout before he was discovered. Then he broke for the docking bays—I think to steal a pod himself. When the guards spotted him, and he knew he was trapped, he killed himself. Had a poison capsule, apparently. The captain won't *tell* us, not all the details, but we've had our ears open." He patted Sass's foot under the blanket. "At first the captain wanted to think that you and Achael were co-conspirators, but he couldn't ignore the evidence . . . you know, Sass, you really did *cram* that pod with evidence. You did such a good job it was almost suspicious that way."

"Fleet Intelligence is going to get the whole load dumped on them when we get back to Sector HQ," Mira put in. "I heard Fargeon won't even trust the IFTL link."

"We'd better go," said Jrain, suddenly looking nervous. "I think— I think the captain would rather you heard some of this from him . . ." He grabbed Mira's arm and steered her away. Sassinak caught his unspoken thought . . . *And he's had quite enough to put up with from Wefts already this week.*

"Ensign Sassinak." Captain Fargeon's severe face was set in slightly friendlier lines, Sassinak thought. She was, however, immediately conscious of every wrinkle of the bedclothes. Then he smiled. "You had a very narrow escape, Ensign, in more than one way. I understand you've been told about the drug that showed up in the blood samples?" Sassinak nodded, and he went on. "It was very good thinking to take those serial samples. Although normally—mmm—there's nothing to commend in a young officer who manages to get sandbagged and shanghaied, in this case you seem to have acted with unusual intelligence once you woke up. You have nothing to reproach yourself for. I know Lieutenant Cavery looks forward to your return to duty in Communications Section. Good day."

Following that somewhat confusing speech, Sassinak lay quietly, wondering what Fargeon *did* think of her. She had been expecting praise, but realized that to the ship's captain her entire escapade was one big headache. He'd had to leave his intended course to go looking for her, even if the guidance of Wefts and Ssli made that easier than usual. He'd had to worry about her motives, and the presence of unknown saboteurs in his ship; he'd had to assign someone else to cover her work; when they got back to Sector HQ, he was going to have to fill out a lot of forms, and spend a lot of time talking to Fleet Intelligence . . . all in all, she'd caused a lot of trouble by not being quicker in the evacuation drill. If she'd managed to turn and drop Achael with a bit of fancy hand-to-hand, she'd have saved everyone a lot of trouble. She shook her head at her own juvenile imagination. No more Carin Coldae: no more playing games. She'd done a good job with a bad situation, but she hadn't managed to avoid the bad situation. She'd have to do better.

So it was that Fargeon's annual Fitness Report, which he showed her before filing it, startled her.

"Clear-headed, resourceful, good initiative, outstanding self-discipline: this young officer requires only seasoning to develop into an excellent addition to any Fleet operation. Unlike many who rest on past achievements, this officer does not let success go to her head, and can be counted on for continued effort. Recommended for earliest promotion eligibility." Sassinak looked up from this to find Fargeon's face relaxed in a broad smile for the first time in her memory.

"Just as I said the first day, Ensign Sassinak: if you realize that you can't ever start at the top, and if you continue to show your willingness to work, you'll do very well indeed. I'd be glad to have you in my command again, any time."

"Thank you, sir." Sassinak wondered whether to strain this approval by telling him what she suspected about Achael and Abe's death. "Sir, about Lieutenant Achael—"

"All information will go to Fleet Security—do you have something which you did not put in your tape?"

She had included her suspicion that Achael had murdered Abe, but would anyone take it seriously? "It's in there, sir, but—about my guardian, who was killed—"

"Abe, you mean." The captain permitted himself a tight smile. "A good man, Fleet to the bone. Well, this is not for discussion, Ensign, but I would agree with your surmise. Achael was a prisoner on the same slaver base where you and Abe were; the most logical supposition is that Abe knew something about his conduct or treatment there which would have been dangerous to Achael. Perhaps he was deep-conditioned, or something. He killed Abe to keep his secret, and suspected that Abe might have told you something."

"But what might be behind Achael?" asked Sass. But with this question, she had gone too far. The captain's face closed again, although he did not seem angry.

"That's for Security to determine, when they have all the evidence. Myself, I suspect that he was merely protecting himself. Suppose Abe knew he had stolen from other prisoners—that would ruin his Fleet career. I would be willing to wager that the final report will conclude that Achael was acting in his own behalf when he killed Abe and attempted to incriminate you."

Sassinak was not convinced, but knew better than to argue. As Fargeon predicted, Fleet Security agreed with his surmise, and closed the file on the murder. Achael's attacks on Sassinak, and his suicide, made a clear pattern with his years as a prisoner: too clear, Sassinak thought, too simple. When she was older, when she had rank, she promised herself, she'd find out who was *really* responsible for Abe's death, who had set Achael on his trail. For now, she'd honor his memory with her own success.

BOOK THREE

Chapter Eight

The striking, elegant woman in the mirror, Sassinak thought, had come a long way from the young ensign she had been. She had been lucky; she had been born with the good bones, the talent, the innate toughness to survive. She had had more luck along the way. But . . . she winked at herself, then grinned at that egotism. But she had cooperated with her luck, given it all the help she could. Tonight— tonight it was time for celebration. She had made it to Commander, past the dangerous doldrum ranks where the unwanted lodged sullenly until retirement age. She was about to have her own ship again, and this one a cruiser.

She eyed the new gown critically. Once she'd learned that good clothes fully repaid the investment, she'd spent some concentrated time learning what colors and styles suited her best. And then, one by one, she'd accumulated a small but elegant wardrobe. This, now . . . her favorite rich colors glowed, jewellike reds and deep blues and purples, a quilted bodice shaped above a flowing, full skirt of deepest midnight, all in soft silui that caressed her skin with every movement. She slipped her feet into soft black boots, glad that the ridiculous fashion for high heels had once again died out. She was tall enough as it was.

Her comm signal went off as she was putting on the last touches, the silver earrings and simple necklace with its cut crystal star.

"Just because you got the promotion and the cruiser doesn't mean you can make us late," said the voice in her ear, the Lieutenant Commander who'd arranged the party. He'd been her assistant when she was working for Admiral Pael. "Tobaldi's doesn't hold reservations past the hour—"

"I know; I'm coming." With a last look at the mirror, she picked up her wrap and went out. As she'd half-expected, two more of her friends waited in the corridor outside, with flowers and a small wrapped box.

"You put this on *now*," said Mira. Her gold curly hair had faded a little, but not the bright eyes or quick mind. Sassinak took the gift, and untied the silver ribbon carefully.

"I suppose you figured out what I'd be wearing," she said, laughing. Then she had the box open, and caught her breath. When she looked at Mira, the other woman was smug.

"I bought it years ago, that time we were shopping, remember? I saw the way you looked at it, and knew the time would come. Of course, I could have waited until you made admiral—" She ducked Sass's playful blow. "You will, Sass. It's a given. I'll retire in a couple of years, and go back to Dad's shipping company—at least he's agreed to let me take over instead of that bratty cousin.... Anyway, let me fasten it."

Sassinak picked up the intricate silver necklace, a design that combined boldness and grace (and, she recalled, an outrageous price—at least for a junior lieutenant, which she had been then) and let Mira close the fastening. Her star went into the box—for tonight, at least—and the box went back in her room. Whatever she might have said to Mira was forestalled by the arrival of the others, and the six of them were deep into reminiscences by the time they got to Tobaldi's.

Mira—the only one who had been there—had to tell the others all about Sass's first cruise. "They've heard that already," Sassinak kept protesting. Mira shushed her firmly.

"You wouldn't have told them the good parts," she said, and proceeded to give her version of the good parts. Sassinak retaliated with the story of Mira's adventures on—or mostly off—horseback, one leave they'd taken together on Mira's homeworld. "I'm a spacer's brat, not a horsebreeder's daughter," complained Mira.

"You're the one who said we ought to take that horsepacking trip," said Sass. The others laughed, and brought up their own tales.

Sassinak looked around the group—which now numbered

fourteen, since others had arrived to join them. Was there really someone from *every* ship she'd been on? Four were from the *Padalyan Reef*, the cruiser on which she'd been the exec until a month ago. That was touching: they had given her a farewell party then, and she had not expected to see them tonight. But the two young lieutenants, stiffly correct among the higher ranks, would not have missed it—she could see that in their eyes. The other two, off on long home leave between assignments, had probably dropped in just because they enjoyed a party.

Her glance moved on, checking an invisible list. All but the prize she'd been given command of, she thought—and wished for a moment that Ford, wherever he was, could be there, too. Forrest had known her, true, but he'd missed that terrifying interlude, staying on the patrol ship with its original crew. Carew, whom she'd known as a waspish major when she was a lieutenant, on shore duty with Commodore . . . what had her name been? Narros, that was it . . . Carew was now a balding, cheery senior Commander, whose memory had lost its sting. Sassinak almost wondered if he'd ever been difficult, then saw a very junior officer across the room flinch away from his gaze. She shrugged mentally—at least he wasn't causing *her* trouble any more.

Her exec from her first command was there, now a Lieutenant Commander and just as steady as ever, though with gray streaking his thick dark hair. Sassinak blessed the genes that had saved her from premature silver . . . she wanted to wear her silver by choice, not necessity. She didn't need gray hair to lend her authority, she thought to herself. Even back on the *Sunrose*. . . . But he was making a small speech, reminding her—and the others—of the unorthodox solution she had found for a light patrol craft in a particular tactical situation. Her friends enjoyed the story, but she remembered very well that some of the senior officers had not liked her solution at all. Her brows lowered, and Mira poked her in the ribs.

"Wake up, Sass, the battle's over. You don't need to glare at *us* like that."

"Sorry . . . I was remembering Admiral Kurin's comments."

"Well . . . we all know what happened to *him*." And that was true enough. A stickler for the rulebook, he had fallen prey to a foe who was not. But Sassinak knew that his opinion of her had gone on file before that, to influence other seniors. She had seen the doubtful looks, and been subject to careful warnings.

Now, however, two men approached the tables with the absolute assurance that comes only from a lifetime of command, and high rank at the end of it. Bilisics, the specialist in military law from Command and Staff, and Admiral Vannoy, Sector Commandant.

"Commander Sassinak—congratulations." Bilisics had been one of her favorite instructors, anywhere. She had even gone to him for advice on a most private and delicate matter—and so far as she could tell, he had maintained absolute secrecy. His grin to her acknowledged all that. "I must always congratulate an officer who steers a safe course through the dangerous waters of a tour at Fleet Headquarters, who avoids the reefs of political or social ambition, the treacherous tides of intimacy in high places..." He practically winked: they both knew what *that* was about. The others clearly thought it was one of Bilisics's usual mannered pleasantries. As far as she knew, no one had ever suspected her near-engagement to the ambassador from Arion.

"Yes: congratulations, Commander, and welcome to the Sector. You'll like the *Zaid-Dayan*, and I'm sure you'll do well with it." She had worked with Admiral Vannoy before, but not for several years. His newer responsibilities had not aged him; he gave, as always, the impression of energy under firm control.

"Would you join us?" Sassinak asked. But, as she expected, they had other plans, and after a few more minutes drifted off to join a table of very senior officers at the far end of the room.

It hardly needed Tobaldi's excellent dinner, the rare live orchestra playing hauntingly lovely old waltzes, or the wines they ordered lavishly, to make that evening special. She could have had any of several partners to end it with, but chose instead a scandalously early return to her quarters—not long after midnight.

"And I'll wager if we had a spycam in there, we'd find her looking over the specs on her cruiser," said Mira, walking back to a popular dance pavilion with the others. "Fleet to the bone, that's what she is, more than most of us. It's her only family, has been since before the Academy."

Sass, unaware of Mira's shrewd guess, would not have been upset by it—since she was, at that moment, calling up the crew list on her terminal. She would have agreed with all that statement, although she felt an occasional twinge of guilt for her failure to contact any of her remaining biological kin. Yet... what did an orphan, an ex-slave, have in common with ordinary, respectable citizens? Too many people still considered slavery a disgrace to the victim; she didn't want to see that rejection on the faces of her own relatives. Easier to stay away, to stay with the family that had rescued her and still supported her. And that night, warmed by the fellowship and celebration, intent on her new command, she felt nothing but eagerness for the future.

Sassinak always felt that Fleet had lost something in the transition from the days when a captain approached a ship lying at dockside, visible to the naked eye, with a veritable gangplank and the welcoming crew topside, and flags flying in the open air. Now, the new captain of, say, a cruiser, simply walked down one corridor after another of a typical space station, and entered the ship's space by crossing a line on the deck planking. The ceremony of taking command had not changed that much, but the circumstances made such ceremony far less impressive. Yet she could not entirely conceal her delight, that after some twenty years as a Fleet officer, she was now to command her own cruiser.

"Commander Kerif will be sorry to have missed you, Commander Sassinak," said Lieutenant Commander Huron, her Executive Officer, leading the way to her new quarters. "But under the circumstances—"

"Of course," said Sassinak. If your son, graduating from the Academy, is going to marry the heiress of one of the wealthiest mercantile families, you may ask for, and be granted, extra leave: even if it means that the change of command of your cruiser is not quite by the book. She had done her homework, skimming the files on her way over from Sector HQ. Huron, for instance, had not impressed his captain overmuch, by his latest Fitness Report. But considering the secret orders she carried, Sassinak had doubts about all the Fitness Reports on that ship. The man seemed intelligent and capable—not to mention fit and reasonably good-looking. He'd have a fair chance with her.

"He asked me to extend you his warmest congratulations, and

his best wishes for your success with the ship. I can assure you that your officers are eager to make this mission a success."

"Mission? What do you know about it?" Supposedly her orders were secret: but then, one of the points made was that Security breaches were getting worse, much worse.

Huron's forehead wrinkled. "Well...we've been out on patrol, just kind of scouting around the sector. Figured we'd do more of the same."

"Pretty much. I'll brief the senior officers once we're in route; we have two more days of refitting, right?"

"Yes, Commander." He gave her a quizzical look. "With all due respect, ma'am, I guess what they say about you is true."

Sassinak smiled; she knew what they said, and she knew why. "Lieutenant Commander Huron, I'm sure you wouldn't listen to idle gossip...any more than I would listen to gossip about you and your passion for groundcar racing."

It was good to be back on a ship again; good to have the command she'd always wanted. Sassinak glanced down at the four gold rings on her immaculate white sleeve, and on to the gold ring on her finger that gave her Academy class and carried the tiny diamond of the top-ranking graduate. Not bad for an orphan, an ex-slave...not bad at all. Some of her classmates thought she was lucky; some of them, no doubt, thought her ambitions stopped here, with the command of a cruiser in an active sector.

But her dreams went beyond even this. She wanted a star on her shoulder, maybe even two: sector command, command of a battle group. This ship was her beginning.

Already she knew more about the 218 *Zaid-Dayan* than her officers realized. Not merely the plans of the class of vessel, which any officer of her rank would be expected to have seen, but the detailed plans of that particular cruiser, and the records of all its refittings. You cannot know too much, Abe had said. Whatever you know is your wealth.

Hers lay here. Better than gold or jewels, she told herself, was the knowledge that won respect of her officers and crew...something that could not be bought with unlimited credits. Although credits had their uses. She ran her hand lightly along the edge of the desk she'd installed in her office. Real wood, rare, beautifully carved.

She'd discovered in herself a taste for quality, beauty, and indulged it as her pay allowed. A custom desk, a few good pieces of crystal and sculpture, clothes that showed off the beauty she'd grown into. She still thought of all that as luxury, as frills, but no longer felt guilty for enjoying them in moderation.

While the cruiser lay at the refitting dock, Sassinak explored her command, meeting and talking with every member of the crew. About half of them had leave; she met them as they returned. But the onboard crew, a dozen officers and fifty or so enlisted, she made a point of chatting up.

The *Zaid-Dayan* wore the outward shape of most heavy cruisers, a slightly flattened ovoid hull with clusters of drive pods both port and starboard, aft of the largest diameter. Sassinak never saw it from outside, of course; only the refitting crews did that. What she saw were the human-accessible spaces, the "living decks" as they were called, and the crawlways that let a lean service tech into the bowels of the ship's plumbing and electrical circuitry. For the most part, it was much the same as the *Padalyan Reef*, the cruiser she'd just left, with Environmental at the bottom, then Troop Deck, then Data, then Main, then the two Flight Decks atop. But not quite.

In this ship, the standard layouts in Environmental had been modified by the addition of the stealth equipment; Sassinak walked every inch of the system to be sure she understood what pipes now ran where. The crowding below had required rearranging some of the storage areas, so that only Data Deck was exactly the same as standard. Sassinak paid particular attention to the two levels of storage for the many pieces of heavy equipment the *Zaid-Dayan* carried: the shuttles, the pinnace, the light fighter craft, the marines' tracked assault vehicles. Again, she made certain that she knew exactly which craft was stowed in each location, knew without having to check the computers.

Her own quarters were just aft of the bridge, opening onto the port passage, a stateroom large enough for modest entertaining—a low table and several chairs, as well as workstation, sleeping area, and private facilities. Slightly aft and across the passage was the officers' wardroom. Her position as cruiser captain required the capacity to entertain formal visitors, so she also had a large office, forward of the bridge and across the same passage. This she could decorate as she pleased—at least, within the limits of Fleet regulations and her own resources. She chose midnight-blue carpeting to show off the striking grain of her desk; the table was Fleet issue, but refinished to gleaming black. Guest seating, low couches along the walls, was in white synthi-leather. Against the pale-gray bulkheads, this produced a room of simple elegance that suited her perfectly.

Huron, she realized quickly, was an asset in more ways than one. Colony-bred himself, he had more than the usual interest in their safety. Too many Fleet officers considered the newer colonies more trouble than they were worth. As the days passed, she found that Huron's assessment of the junior officers was both fair and leavened by humor. She began to wonder why his previous commander had had so little confidence in him.

That story came out over a game of sho, one evening some days into their patrol. Sassinak had begun delicately probing, to see if he had a grievance of any sort. After the second or third ambiguous question, Huron looked up from the playing board with a smile that sent a sudden jolt through her heart.

"You're wondering if I know why Commander Kerif gave me such a lukewarm report last period?"

Sass, caught off guard as she rarely was, smiled back. "You're quite right—and you don't need to answer. But you've been too knowledgeable and competent since I came to have given habitually poor performance."

Huron's smile widened. "Commander Sassinak, your predecessor was a fine officer and I admire him. However, he had very strong ideas about the dignity of some ... ah ... prominent, old-line, merchant families. He never felt that I had sufficient respect for them, and he attributed a bit of doggerel he heard to me."

"Doggerel?"

Huron actually reddened. "A ... uh ... song. Sort of a song. About his son and that girl he's marrying. I didn't write it, Commander, although I did think it was funny when I heard it. But, you see, I'd quoted some verse in his presence before, and he was sure ..."

Sassinak thought about it. "And do you have proper respect for wealthy merchants?"

Huron pursed his lips. "Proper? I think so. But I am a colony brat."

Sassinak shook her head, smiling. "So am I, as you must already know. Poor Kerif...I suppose it was a very *bad* song." She caught the look in Huron's eye, and chuckled. "If that's the worst you ever did, we'll have no problems at all."

"I don't want any," said Huron, in a tone that conveyed more than one meaning.

Years before, as a cadet, Sassinak had wondered how anyone could combine relationships both private and professional without being unfair to one or the other. Over the years, she had established her own ground rules, and had become a good judge of those likely to share her values and attitudes. Except for that one almost-disastrous (and, in retrospect, funny) engagement to a brilliant and handsome older diplomat, she had never risked anything she could not afford to lose. Now, secure in her own identity, she expected to go on enjoying life with those of her officers who were willing and stable enough not to be threatened—and honest enough not to take advantages she had no intention of releasing.

Huron, she thought to herself, was a distinct possibility. From the glint in his eyes, he thought the same way about her: the first prerequisite.

But her duty came first, and the present circumstances often drove any thought of pleasure from her mind. In the twenty years since her first voyage, Fleet had not been able to assure the safety of the younger and more remote colonies; as well, planets cleared for colonization by one group were too often found to have someone else—legally now the owners—in place when the colonists arrived. Although human slavery was technically illegal, colonies were being raided for slaves—and that meant a market somewhere. "Normal" humans blamed heavyworlders; heavyworlders blamed the "lightweights" as they called them, and the wealthy mercantile families of the inner worlds complained bitterly about the cost of supporting an ever-growing Fleet which didn't seem to save either lives or property.

Their orders, which Sassinak discussed only in part with her officers, required them to make use of a new, supposedly secret, technology for identifying and trailing newer deep-space civilian vessels. It augmented, rather than replaced, the standard IFF devices which had been in use since before Sassinak joined the Fleet. A sealed beacon, installed in the ship's architecture as it was built, could be triggered by Fleet surveillance scans. While passive to detectors in its normal mode, it nonetheless stored information on the ship's movements. The original idea had been to strip these beacons whenever a ship came to port, and thus keep records on its actual travel—as opposed to the log records presented to the portmaster. But still newer technology allowed specially equipped Fleet cruisers to enable such beacons while still in deepspace, even FTL flight—and then to follow with much less chance of detection. Now the plan was for cruisers such as the *Zaid-Dayan* to patrol slowly, in areas away from the normal corridors, and select suspicious "merchants" to follow.

So far as the junior officers were concerned, the cruiser patrolled in the old way; because of warnings from Fleet about security leaks, Sassinak told only four of her senior crew, who had to know to operate the scan. Other modifications to the *Zaid-Dayan*, intended to give it limited stealth capability, were explained as being useful in normal operations.

As the days passed, Sassinak considered the Fleet warnings. "Assume subversives on each ship." Fine, but with no more guidance than that, how was she supposed to find one? Subversives didn't advertise themselves with loud talk of overturning FSP conventions. Besides, it was all guessing. She might have one subversive on her ship, or a dozen, or none at all. She had to admit that if she were planting agents, she'd certainly put them on cruisers, as the most effective and most widespread of the active vessels. But nothing showed in the personnel records she'd run a preliminary screen on— and supposedly Security had checked them all out before.

She knew that many commanders would think first of the heavyworlders on board, but while some of them were certainly involved in subversive organizations, the majority were not. However difficult heavyworlders might be—and some of them, she'd found, had earned their reputation for prickly sullenness—Sassinak had never forgotten the insights gained from her friends at the Academy. She tried to see behind the heavy-boned stolid faces, the overmuscular bodies, to the human person within—and most of the time felt she had succeeded. A few real friendships had come out of this, and many more amiable working relationships... and she found that her reputation as an officer fair to heavyworlders had spread among the officer corps.

Wefts, as aliens, irritated many human commanders, but again Sassinak had the advantage of early friendships. She knew that Wefts had no desire for the worlds humans preferred—in fact, the Wefts who chose space travel were sterile, having given up their chance at procreation for an opportunity to travel and adventure. Nor were they the perfect mental spies so many feared: their telepathic powers were quite limited; they found the average human mind a chaotic mess of emotion and illogic, impossible to follow unless the individual tried hard to convey a message. Sass, with her early training in Discipline, could converse easily with Wefts in their native form, but she knew she was an exception. Besides, if any of the Wefts on board had identified a subversive, she'd already have been told.

After several weeks, she felt completely comfortable with her crew, and could tell that they were settling well together. Huron had proved as inventive a partner as he was a versifier—after hearing a few of his livelier creations in the wardroom one night, she could hardly believe he *hadn't* written the one about the captain's son and the merchant's daughter. He still insisted he was innocent of that one. The weapons officer, a woman only one year behind her at the Academy, turned out to be a regional sho champion—and was clearly delighted to demonstrate by beating Sassinak five games out of seven. It was good for morale, and besides, Sassinak had never minded learning from an expert. One of the cooks was a natural genius—so good that Sassinak caught herself thinking about putting him on her duty shift, permanently. She didn't, but her taste buds argued with her, and more than once she found an excuse to "inspect" the kitchens when he was baking. He always had something for the captain. All this was routine—even finding a homesick and miserable junior engineering tech, just out of training, sobbing hopelessly in a storage locker. But so was the patrol routine... nothing, day after day, but the various lumps of matter that had been mapped in their assigned volume of space. Not so much as a pleasure yacht out for adventure.

She was half-dozing in her cabin, early in third watch, when the bridge com chimed.

"Captain—we've got a ship. Merchant, maybe CR-class for mass, no details yet. Trigger the scan?"

"Wait—I'm coming." She elbowed Huron, who'd already fallen asleep, until he grunted and opened an eye, then whisked into her uniform. When he grunted again and asked what it was, she said, "We've got a ship." At that, both eyes came open, and he sat up. She laughed, and went out; by the time she got to the bridge, he was only a few steps behind her, fully dressed.

"Gotcha!" Huron, leaning over the scanner screen, was as eager as the technician handling the controls. "Look at that..." His fingers flew on his own keyboard, and the ship's data came up on an adjoining screen. "Hu Veron Shipways, forty percent owned by Allied Geochemical, which is wholly owned by the Paraden family. Well, well... previous owner Jakob Iris, no previous criminal record but went into bankruptcy after... hmm... a wager on a horse race. What's that?"

"Horse race," said Sassinak, watching the screen just as intently. "Four-legged mammal, big enough to carry humans. Old Earth origin, imported to four new systems, but they mostly die."

"Kipling's corns, captain, how *do* you know all that?"

"Kipling indeed, Huron. Our schools had a Kipling story about a horse in the required elementary reading list. With a picture. And the Academy kept a team for funerals, and I have seen a tape of a horse race. In fact, I've actually ridden a horse." Her mouth quirked, as she thought of Mira's homeworld and that ill-fated pack trip.

"You would have," said Huron almost vaguely. His attention was already back to his screen. "Look at that—Iris was betting against Luisa Paraden Scofeld. Isn't that the one who was married to a zero-G hockey star, and then to an ambassador to Ryx?"

"Yes, and while he was there she ran off with the landscape architect. But the point is—"

"The point is that the Paradens have laid their hands on that ship *twice!*"

"That we know of." Sassinak straightened up and regarded the back of Huron's head thoughtfully. "I think we'll trail this one, Commander Huron. There are just a few too many coincidences..."

Even as she gave the necessary orders, Sassinak was conscious of fulfilling an old dream—to be in command of her own ship, on the bridge, with a possible pirate in view. She looked around with satisfaction at what might have been any large control room, anything from a reactor station to a manufacturing plant. The physical remnant of millennia of naval history was under her feet, the raised dais that gave her a clear view of everyone and everything in the room. She could sit in the command chair, with her own screens and computer linkages at hand, or stand and observe the horseshoe arrangement of workstations, each with its trio of screens, its banks of toggles and buttons, its quietly competent operator. Angled above were the big screens, and directly below the end of the dais was the remnant of a now outmoded technology that most captains still used to impress visitors: the three-D tank.

Trailing a ship through FTL space was, Sassinak thought, like following a groundcar through thick forest at night without using headlights. The unsuspecting merchant left a disturbed swath of space which the Ssli could follow, but it could not simultaneously sense structural (if that was the word) variations in the space-time fabric... so that they were constantly in danger of jouncing through celestial chugholes or running into unseen gravitational stumps. They had to go fast, to keep the quarry in range of detection, but fast blind travel through an unfamiliar sector was an excellent way to get swallowed by the odd wormhole.

When the quarry dropped out of FTL into normal space, the cruiser followed—or, more properly, anticipated. The computer brought up the local navigation points.

"That's interesting," said Huron, pointing. It was more than interesting. A small star system, with one twenty-year-old colony (in the prime range for a raid) sited over a rich vein of platinum. Despite Fleet's urging, FSP bureaucrats had declined to approve effective planetary defense weaponry for small colonies... and the catalog of this colony's defenses was particularly meager.

"Brotherhood of Metals," said Sass. "That's the colony sponsor; they hold the paper on it. I'm beginning to wonder who *their* stockholders are."

"New contact!" The technician's voice rose. "Excuse me, captain, but I've got a Churi-class vessel out there: could be extremely dangerous—"

"Specs." Sassinak glanced around the bridge, pleased with the alert but unfrantic attitudes she saw. They were already on full stealth routine; upgrading to battle status would cost her stealth. Her weapons officer raised a querying finger; Sassinak shook her head, and he relaxed.

"Old-style IFF—no beacon. Built forty years ago in the Zendi yards, commissioned by the—" He stopped, lowered his voice. "The governor of Diplo, captain."

Oh great, thought Sass. *Just what we needed, a little heavyworlder suspicion to complete our confusion.*

"Bring up the scan and input," she said, without commenting on the heavyworlder connection. One display filled with a computer analysis of the IFF output. Sassinak frowned at it. "That's not right. Look at that carrier wave—"

"Got it." The technician had keyed in a comparison command, and the display broke into colored bands, blue for the correspondence between the standard signal and the one received, and bright pink for the unmatched portions.

"They've diddled with their IFF," said Sass. "We don't know *what* that is, or what it carries—"

"Our passive array says it's about the size of a patrol craft—" offered Huron.

"Which means it could carry all sorts of nice things," said Sass, thinking of them. An illicitly armed patrol craft was not a match for the *Zaid-Dayan*, but it could do them damage. If it noticed them.

Huron was frowning at the displays. "Now...is this a rendezvous, or an ambush?"

"Rendezvous," said Sassinak quickly. His brows rose.

"You're sure?"

"It's the worse possibility for us: it gives us two ships to follow or engage if they notice us. Besides, little colonies like this don't get visits from unscheduled merchants."

Judging by the passive scans, which produced data hours old, the two ships matched trajectories and traveled toward the colony world together—certainly close enough to use a tight-beam communication band. The *Zaid-Dayan* hung in the system's outer debris, watching with every scanning mode it had. Hour by hour, it became clearer that the destination must be the colony. *They're raiders*, Sassinak thought, and Huron said it aloud, adding, "We ought to blow them out of the system!" For an instant, Sassinak let the old fury rise almost out of control, but she forced the memory of her own childhood back. If they blew these two away, they would know nothing about the powers who hired them, protected them, supplied them. She would not let herself wonder if another Fleet commander had made the same decision about her homeworld's raid.

She shook her head. "We're on surveillance patrol; you know that."

"But, captain—our data's a couple of hours old. If they *are* raiders, they could be hitting that colony any time...we have to warn them. We can't let them—" Huron had paled, and she saw a terrible doubt in his eyes.

"Orders." She turned away, not trusting herself to meet his gaze. She had exorcised many demons from her past, in the years since her commissioning: she could dine with admirals and high government officials, make polite conversation with aliens, keep her temper and her wits in nearly all circumstances...but deep in her mind she carried the vision of her parents dying, her sister's body sliding into the water, her best friend changed to a shivering, depressed wreck of the lively girl she'd been. She shook her head, forcing herself to concentrate on the scan. Her voice came out clipped and cold; she could see by their reactions that the bridge crew recognized the strain on her. "We *must* find the source of this— we must. If we destroy these vermin, and never find their master, it will go on and on, and more will suffer. We have to watch, and follow—"

"But they never meant us to let a colony be raided! We're—we're supposed to *protect* them—it's in the Charter!" Huron circled until he faced her again. "You've got discretion, in any situation where FSP citizens are directly threatened—"

"Discretion!" Sassinak clamped her jaw on the rest of that, and glared at him. It must have been a strong glare, for he backed a step. In a lower voice, she went on. "Discretion, Huron, is not questioning your commanding officer's orders on the bridge when you don't know what in flaming gas clouds is going on. Discretion is learning to think before you blow your stack—"

"Did you ever think," said Huron, white-lipped and angrier than

Sassinak had ever seen him, "that someone might have made this decision when *you* were down there?" He jerked his chin toward the navigation display. She waited a long moment, until the others had decided it would be wise to pay active attention to their own work, and the rigidity went out of Huron's expression.

"Yes," she said very quietly. "Yes, I have. I imagine it haunts that person, if someone actually was there, as this is going to haunt me." At that his face relaxed slightly, the color rising to his cheeks. Before he could speak, Sassinak went on. "You think I don't care? You think I haven't imagined myself—some child the age I was, some innocent girl or boy who's thinking of tomorrow's test in school? You think I don't *remember*, Huron?" She glanced around, seeing that everyone was at least pretending to give them privacy. "You've seen my nightmares, Huron; you know I haven't forgotten."

His face was as red as it had been pale. "I know. I know that, but how *can* you—"

"I want them all." It came out flat, emotionless, but with the power of an impending avalanche . . . as yet no sound, no excitement . . . but inexorable movement accelerating to some dread ending. "I want them all, Huron: the ones who do it because it's fun, the ones who do it because it's profitable, the ones who do it because it's easier than hiring honest labor . . . and above all the ones who do it without thinking about why . . . who just do it because that's how it's done. I want them *all*." She turned to him with a smile that just missed pleasantry to become the toothy grin of the striking predator. "And there's only one way to get them all, and to *that* I commit this ship, and my command, and any other resource . . . including, with all regret, those colonists who will die before we can rescue them—"

"But we're going to try—?"

"Try, hell. I'm going to do it." The silence on the bridge was eloquent; this time when she turned away from Huron he did not follow.

The scans told the pitiable story of the next hours. The colonists, more alert than Myriad's, managed to set off their obsolete missiles, which the illicit patrol craft promptly detonated at a safe distance.

"Now we know they've got an LDsl4, or equivalent," said Huron without emphasis. Sassinak glanced at him but made no comment. They had not met, as usual, after dinner, to talk over the day's work.

Huron had explained stiffly that he wanted to review for his next promotion exam, and Sassinak let him go. The ugly thought ran through her mind that a subversive would be just as happy to have the evidence blown to bits. But surely not Huron—from a small colony himself, surely he'd have more sympathy with them . . . and besides, she was sure she knew him better than any psych profile. Just as he knew her.

Meanwhile, having exhausted the planetary defenses, the two raiders dropped shuttles to the surface. Sassinak shivered, remembering the tough, disciplined (if irregular) troops the raiders had landed on her world. The colonists wouldn't stand a chance. She found she was breathing faster, and looked up to find Huron watching her. So were the others, though less obviously; she caught more than one quick sideways glance.

Yet she had to wait. Through the agonizing hours, she stayed on the bridge, pushing aside the food and drink that someone handed her. She had to wait, but she could not relax, eat, drink, even talk, while those innocent people were being killed . . . and captured . . . and tied into links (did *all* slavers use links of eight, she wondered suddenly). The two ships orbited the planet, and when this orbit took them out of LOS, the *Zaid-Dayan* eased closer, its advanced technology allowing minute hops of FTL flight with minimal disturbance to the fields.

Their scan delay was less than a half-hour, and the raiders had shown no sign of noticing their presence in the system. Now they could track the shuttles rising—all to the transport, Sassinak noted— and then descending and rising again. Once more, and then the raiders boosted away from the planet, on a course that brought them within easy range of the *Zaid-Dayan*. Huron only looked at Sass; she shook her head, and caught her weapons officer's eye as well. Hold on, she told the self she imagined lying helpless in the transport's belly. We're here: we're going to come after you. But she knew her thoughts did those children no good at all—and nothing could wipe out the harm already done.

Chapter Nine

All too quickly the transport and its escort showed that they were preparing to leave the system. Powerful boosters shoved them up through the planet's gravity well—a system cheap and certain, if inelegant. Sassinak wondered if the transport that had carried her had had an escort—or if Fleet activities in the past twenty years or so had had that much effect. Considering the cost of each ship, crew, weaponry... if Fleet had made escorts necessary... then either the profit margin of slavers should be much narrower, or the slave trade brought even more money than anyone had guessed. And why?

"Commander Sassinak—" This mode of address, perfectly correct but slightly more formal than usual to a ship's captain on board, made it clear to her just how upset her bridge crew were. She glanced at Arly, senior weapons officer, who was pointing at her own display. "We finally got a good readout on their weapons systems... that's one more hot ship."

Sassinak welcomed the diversion, and leaned over the display. Since the escort vessel had tampered with its own IFF transmission, they had had to use other detection methods to figure out its class and armament... methods which were supposed to be undetectable, although they'd not yet been tested against any but Fleet vessels. Now she'd find out—in the fabric of her own ship if the designers were wrong—just how accurate and undetectable they were.

"Patrol class: way too big and too hot for anyone but Fleet to have legally," Arly went on, pointing out the obvious. "Probably modified and refitted from a legal insystem escort or patrol vessel... although it might be a pirated hull from something consigned to scrap."

"I hope not," said Sass. "If there's a hole in our scrap and recycling operation, we could find ourselves facing a pirated battle platform—"

"Best fit of hull and structure is to a Vannoy Combine insystem escort. Then if they retrofitted an FTL drive component—" The weapons officer's fingers danced over the controls, and the display split, one vertical half showing a schematic with the changes she proposed. "—and beefed up the interior a good bit—they'd lose crew space, but gain the reinforcement they need to mount *these*." A final flick of the finger, and the armament that the *Zaid-Dayan*'s detectors and computer had come up with came up as a list.

"On *that*!?" Sassinak stared at it. A vessel only one third the mass of her own was carrying nearly identical weaponry, with a nice mix of projectile, beam, and explosives.

"Just as well we didn't sail in to take an easy kill," said the weapons officer quietly. Her expression was completely neutral. "Could have been messy."

"It's going to be messy," said Sassinak, just as quietly. "When we catch them."

"We *are* following—" It was not quite a question.

"Oh, yes. And as soon as we have their destination coordinates, we'll be calling in the whole bloody Fleet."

But it was not that easy. The two ships moved away from the planet they'd raided, boosting toward a safe range for FTL flight. Sassinak would like to have checked the planet itself for survivors (unlikely though she knew that to be) and evidence, but she could not risk losing the ships when they left normal space. She waited as the ships built speed, until their own scans must be nearly blind as they approached their insertion velocity. The Ssli had queried twice when she finally gave the order to shift position and pursue. Just before they entered FTL flight, she had a burst sent to Sector HQ by lowlink, explaining what happened to the colony and her plan of pursuit.

Then it was the same blind chase as they had had following the transport in the first place. Sassinak could only imagine how it must seem to the Ssli on whose ability to sense the trace they all depended. Their lives were hostage to the realities of such travel ... the Ssli concentrated so on the traces of their quarry that it could not warn them of potentially fatal anomalies in their path.

With the Ssli controlling the ship's movement through its computer link, the crew had all too little to do. Sassinak spent some time on the bridge each shift, and much of the rest prowling the ship wondering how she was going to find her subversives—without driving the perfectly loyal and honorable crew up the walls in the process. Dhrossh, their link to their quarry, would not initiate an IFTL link without her direct command, but someone still might loose a message by SOLEC or highlink, not to warn the raiders, but their allies. That would require knowing the coordinates of either a mapped Fleet node or receiving station, but an agent might. She considered sending regular reports to Fleet by the same means, and decided against it. Better to have some conclusion to report, after that disaster at the colony.

Sassinak worked out a duty schedule that involved keeping a Weft on the bridge constantly—at least they could contact her, instantly, if something happened, and they were exceptionally able in reading the minute behaviors of humans. She had to hope that her human crew would not guess her reasons.

She was acutely aware of the crew's reaction to her decision not to engage the raiders before they attacked the colony, or during the attack. She imagined their comments... "Is the captain losing it? Has someone bought her off?" Volume 8 of the massive *Rules of Engagement* managed to be lying around the senior officers' wardroom more than once, although she never caught anyone reading the critical article. Some of the crew sided with her, and she heard some of that. "Pretty sharp, figuring out we were outgunned before we'd come in close-scan range," one of the biotechs was saying one day as Sassinak passed quietly along on a routine inspection of the environmental system. "I wouldn't have guessed that the initial readouts were wrong... whoever heard of someone fooling with an IFF?" Sassinak smiled grimly: that wasn't a new trick, and bridge crew all knew it. But it was nice to have credit somewhere. Too bad that she discovered a minor leak in the detox input filter line, and had to file a report on the very tech who'd been defending her.

The environmental system was, in fact, a nagging worry. Among the modifications made on station, a rerouting of most of the main lines had meant shifting them into cramped, hard-to-inspect compartments rather than out in the open where inspection was easy. Sassinak remembered her first cruise, and the awkwardness of it. Supposedly the equipment now mounted in midline was worth it, in the protection it gave from enemy surveillance, but if the environmental system failed, they would have a miserable trip back—if they survived. Sassinak glared at the big gray cylinders that lay in recesses originally meant for pipelines. They'd *better* work. In the meantime, either because of the less efficient layout, with its more variable line pressures, or because the line was harder to inspect, minor leaks repeatedly developed in one or another subsystem.

Of course, it could be sabotage. That's why she walked the lines herself, struggling to relearn the details of the system so that she knew what she was looking for. But in any complicated system of tubing and pumps, a thousand opportunities exist for subtle acts of sabotage, and she didn't expect to find anything obvious. She was right.

As the ship's days passed in pursuit, with the Ssli certain that it had a lock on the ships ahead, Huron finally came around. Literally, as he appeared at her cabin door with a peace offering: wine and pastries. Sassinak had not realized how much she'd missed his support until she saw the old grin on his face.

"Peace offering," he said. Typically, he wasn't trying to pretend they'd had no quarrel. Sassinak nodded, and waved him in. He set the basket of hot, sugary treats on her desk, and opened the wine. They settled down in comfortable chairs, one on either side of the pastry basket, and munched in harmony for a few minutes.

"I was afraid they'd split up, or we'd lose them," he said with a sideways glance. "And then when we got the final scan on the escort—that it might have been fatal to take it on—I knew you were right, but I just couldn't—"

"Never mind." Sassinak leaned back against the padded chair. Just to have someone to talk with, to relax with—it wasn't over, and it was going to get worse before it got better, but if Huron could accept her decision . . .

"I wish we knew *where* they're going!" He bit into his pastry so hard that flaky bits showered across his lap. He muttered a curse through the mouthful of food, and Sassinak chuckled. Problems and all, life was more fun with Huron in her cabin some nights.

"Huh. Don't we all! And I don't dare send anything back to Sector HQ in case something intercepts it. . ."

"Remember when Ssli and the IFTL system were new, and we were *sure* no one else had them?" He was still swiping crumbs from his lap, and looked up at her with the mischievous lift of eyebrow she'd come to love.

"Sure do." Sassinak ran her hands through her dark hair, and flipped the ends toward him. His eyes widened, then narrowed again.

"One track mind." He shook his head at her.

"You're any different?" Sassinak pointed to the now-empty pastry basket and the bottle of wine. "Think I can't recognize bait when I see it?"

"Brains with your beauty—and a few other things . . ." His eyes finished what she had started, and they were more than halfway undressed when Sassinak remembered to switch the intercom to alert-only. The bridge crew knew what that meant, she thought with satisfaction, before dragging the big brilliantly rainbowed comforter over the pair of them.

"And what I still don't understand," said Huron, far more awake than usual for 0200, "is how they could mount all that on a hull that size. Are they crewing it with midgets, or what?"

Sassinak had taken a short nap, and wakened to find Huron tracing elaborate curlicues on her back while he stared at the readout on the overhead display. She yawned, pushed back a thick tangle of hair, and reached up to switch the display off. "Later . . ."

He switched it back on. "No, seriously—"

"Seriously, I'm sleepy. Turn it off, or go look at it somewhere else."

He glowered at her. "Some Fleet captain *you* are, lazing around like someone's lapcat after a dish of cream."

Sassinak purred loudly, yawned again, and realized she was going to wake all the way up, like it or not. "Big weapons, small hull. Reminds me of something." Huron blushed, extensively, and Sassinak snapped her teeth at him. "Call your captain a cat, and you deserve to get bit, chum. If we're going to go back to work, I'm getting dressed." She felt a lot better, relaxed and alert all at once.

Now that she was awake, she realized that she had not followed through on the analysis of the escort vessel as carefully as she could have. She'd been thinking too much about her main decision and its implications. Together she and Huron ran the figures several times, and then adjourned to the main wardroom. She called in both Arly and Hollister. They arrived blinking and yawning: as main shift crew, they were normally asleep at this hour. After a cup of stimulant and some food, they came fully awake.

"The question is, are we sure of our data, even that last? Is that thing built on a patrol-class hull, and if so does it really carry those weapons, and if so what's their crew size and how are they staying alive?" Sassinak took the last spiced bun off the platter the night cook had brought in.

Hollister shrugged. "That new detection system isn't really my specialty, but if that's the size we think—dimensional and mass— then it'll depend on weaponry. With up-to-date environmental, guidance, and drive systems, they'd need a crew of fifty to work normal shifts—plus weapons specialists. Say, sixty to seventy altogether. If they work long shifts, maybe fifty altogether, but they'd chance fatigue errors—"

"But they don't expect to need top efficiency for long," Sassinak said. "They come in, rout a colony, escort the transport to their base, wherever that is... and most times they never see trouble."

"Fifty, then. That means... mmm..." He ran some figures into the nearest terminal. "'Bout what I thought. Look—" A ship schematic came up on the main screen at the end of the table. "Fifty crew, here's the calories and water needs... best guess at system efficiency... and that means they'll need eight standard filtration units, eight sets of re-op converters, plus the UV trays—" As he talked, the schematic filled with green lines and blocks, the standard representation of environmental system units. "This is assuming their FTL route doesn't take more than twenty-five standard days, and they've got the same kind of oxygen recharge system we do. Most surveyed routes come in under twenty days, as you know. Now if we add the probable drives: we know they have insystem chem boosters as well as insystem mains, and FTL—" The drive components came up in blue. "And minimum crew space: access and living—" That was yellow. "Weapons?"

Arly took over, and the schematic suddenly bled with red weapons symbols. "This is what we got off the scans, captain. Their IFF was a real nutcase: no sense at all. But the passives showed two distinct patterns of radiation leakage: here, and there. And we saw how they knocked out those ground-space missiles . . . they do have optical weapons."

"And it doesn't fit," said Huron, sounding entirely too smug. "Look." Sure enough, the display had a blinking symbol in one corner: excess volume specified.

Arly looked stubborn. "I could not ignore the scan data—"

"Of course not." Sassinak held up her hand for silence when both mouths opened. "Look, Huron, both the scans and this schematic come in part from assumptions we made about those criminals. *If* they crew their ship to a level we think safe, *if* they aren't stressing their environmental system, *if* a few extra particles means that they've got a neutron bomb . . . all if."

"We have to make some assumptions!"

"Yes. I do. I'm assuming they sacrifice everything else to speed and firepower. They want no witnesses: they want to be sure they can blow anything—up to a battle platform, lets say—into nothing, before it can call in help. They want to be able to escape any pursuit. They're not out on patrol as long as we normally are: they sacrifice comfort, and some levels of efficiency. I will bet you that they're undercrewed and carry every scrap of armament our scans found."

"Less crew means they could have a smaller environmental system," said Hollister.

"And with any luck less crew means they're a little less alert to a tail."

"I wish I knew how good their fire-control systems were," said Arly, running a finger along the edge of the console. "If they've got anything like the Gamma system, we could be in trouble with them."

"Are you advising me not to engage?" asked Sass. Arly's face darkened a little. A senior weapons officer could give such advice, but under all the circumstances, it meant taking sides in the earlier argument: something Arly had refused to do.

"Not precisely . . . no. But they've got almost as much as we have, on a smaller hull with different movement capability. Normally I don't have to worry about something that size—with all its mobility, it still can't take us. But this—" She tapped the display. "This *could* breach us, if they got lucky . . . and their speed and mobility increase the danger. Call it even odds, or a shade to their favor. I'd be glad to engage them, captain, but you need to be aware of all the factors."

"I am." Sassinak stretched, then shook the tension out of her hands. "And you'll no doubt have a chance to test our ideas before long. If they're short-crewed and short on environmental supplies, surely they'll have a short FTL route picked out . . . it's been eighteen days, now."

"Speaking of environmental systems," said Hollister gruffly. "That number nine scrubber's leaking again. I could take it down and repack it, but that'd mean tying up a whole shift crew—"

Sassinak glanced at Huron. "Nav got any guesses on their destination?"

"Not a clue. Dhrossh is downright testy about queries, and about half the equation solutions don't fit anything in the books."

"Just keep an eye on the scrubber, then. We don't want Engineering tied up if we're suddenly on insystem drive with combat coming up."

Another standard day passed, and another. None of the crew did anything but what she expected. No saboteur or subversive stood up to expound a doctrine of slavery and planet piracy. At least her relationship with Huron was better, and the other hotheads in the crew seemed to follow his lead. She was squatting on her heels beside the number nine scrubber, with Hollister, looking at a thin line of greasy liquid that had trickled down the outer casing, when the ship lurched slightly as the Ssli-controlled drive computers dropped them out of FTL.

Chapter Ten

By the time Sassinak reached the bridge, Huron had their location on the big display.

"Unmapped," said Sassinak sourly.

"Officially unmapped," agreed Huron. "Sector margins—you can see that both the nearest surveys don't quite meet."

"By a whole lot of useful distance," said Sassinak. Five stars over *that* way, the Fleet survey codes were pink. Eight stars the other, the Fleet survey codes were light green. And nothing showed in the other vectors.

"Diverging cones don't fill space," said Huron. She glowered at him; she'd hit her head on the input connector of the scrubber when the call came in, and besides, she'd wanted to be on the bridge when they came into normal space.

"They could have, if those survey crews had been paying attention. This is one *large* survey anomaly out here." Then it came to her. "I wonder, Huron, if this was *missed*, or left out on purpose." He looked blank, and she went on. "By the same people who found it so handy to have an uncharted system to hide out in."

"Who assigns survey sectors?" asked Arly.

"I don't know, but I intend to find out." Huron had already put the cruiser on full stealth mode; Sassinak now tapped her own board into the Ssli biolink. Two more screens of data came up in front of her, highlighted for easy recognition. "But after we deal with this— and without getting killed. I have the feeling that their detection systems out here will be very, very good."

The ships they pursued had dropped out of FTL in the borders of a small star system: only five planets. The star itself was a nondescript little blip on the classification screen: small, dim, and, as Huron said, "as little there as a star can be." In that first few minutes, their instruments revealed three large clusters of mass on "this" side of the star—presumably planets or planet-systems toward one of which their quarry moved.

They were still days from any of them. Sassinak insisted that their first concern had to be the detection systems the slavers used. "They wouldn't assume anything: they'll have some way to detect ships that happen to blunder in here."

Huron frowned thoughtfully at the main display screen, now a shifting pattern of pale blues and greens as the *Zaid-Dayan*'s passive scans searched for any signs of data transmission. "We can't hang around out here forever hunting for it—"

"No, we're going in. But I want to surprise them." Suddenly she grinned. "I think I know—did you ever live on a free-water world, Huron? Skip stones on water?"

"Yes, but—"

"Everyone sees the splash of the skips—and then the rock sinks, and disappears. We'll make sure they see us—and then they don't— and if we're lucky it'll look like someone in transit with a malfunctioning FTL drive, blipping in and out of normal space."

"They'll see *that*—"

"Yes. But with our special capabilities, they're unlikely to spot us when we're drifting. Suppose we get in really close to whatever planet they're using—"

"It'd help if it had a moon, and if we knew which it was." As the hours passed, and their tracking computers reworked the incoming data, it became clear where the others were going. A planet somewhat larger than Old Earth Standard, with several small moons and a ringbelt.

"The gods are with us this time," said Sass. "Bless the luck of a complicated universe—that's as unlikely a combination as I've seen, but perfect for creating unmappable chunks of debris..."

"Into which we can crunch," pointed out Huron.

"Getting cautious in your old age, Lieutenant Commander?" Her question had a little bite to it, and he reddened.

"No, captain—but I'd prefer to take them with us."

"I'd prefer to take them, and come home whole. That's what we have Ssli assistance for."

After careful calculation, Sassinak's plan took them "through" the outer reaches of the system in a series of minute FTL skips, a route that taxed both the computers and the Ssli. With a last gut-wrenching hop, the *Zaid-Dayan* came to apparent rest, drifting within a few kilometers of a large chunk of debris in the ring, its velocity not quite matched, as would be true of most chunks. Their scans began to pick up transmissions from the surface, apparently intended for the incoming slaver ships. At first, some kind of alarm message, about the skip-traces noted . . . but as the hours passed, it became clear that the surface base had not detected them, and had decided precisely what Sassinak had hoped: something had come through the system with a bad FTL drive, and was now somewhere else. In the meantime, the alarm message had activated beacons and outer defenses: Sassinak now knew exactly where the enemy's watchers watched.

One of the moons had a small base, on the side that faced away from the planet, and a repeated station placed to relay communications to and from the surface. A single communications satellite circling the planet indicated that all settlement was confined to one hemisphere—and by the scans, to one small region.

"A *big* base," was Arly's comment, as scans also picked up weapon emplacements on the surface. "Their surface-to-space missiles we can handle. But those little ships are going to cause us trouble; they've got only one or two optical weapons each, but—"

"Estimated time to launch and engagement?" Sassinak looked at Hollister.

"If they're really battle-ready, they can launch in an hour, maybe two. Nobody keeps those babies really ready-to-launch: you boil off too much propellant. Most of the time they like to fight from a high orbit, or satellite transit path, in systems like this with moons. I'd say a minimum of ninety standard minutes, from the alarm . . . but will we pick up their signals?"

"We'd better. What about larger ships?"

"There's something like the slaver escort, but it's cold . . . no signs of activity at all. More than two hours to launch—at least five, I'd say. But it's still twenty-three standard hours before the incoming ships arrive, if they hold their same trajectory and use the most economical deceleration schedule. We may see more activity as they get closer."

But except for brief transmissions every four hours, between the incoming ships and the base, little happened that they could detect from space. Sassinak insisted on regular shift changes, and rest for those off-duty. She followed her own orders to the extent of taking a couple of four-hour naps.

Then the ships neared. For the first time, they drifted apart; the escort, Sassinak realized, was taking up an orbit around the outermost moon, alert for anything following them or entering the system. The slave-carrying trader began braking in a long descending spiral.

Taking the chance that the attention of the base below would be fixed on the incoming slaver, and the attention of the escort ship above on anything "behind" them, Sassinak ordered the *Zaid-Dayan*'s insystem drive into action: they would ease out of the ring-belt, and intercept the slaver on the blind side of the planet, out of sight/detection of the escort.

All stations were manned with backup crews standing by. Sassinak glanced around the bridge, seeing the same determination on every face.

One of the lights on Arly's panel suddenly flashed red, and a shrill piping overrode conversation. She slammed a fist down on the panel, and shot a furious glance around her section, then to Sass.

"It's a missile—Captain, I didn't launch that!"

"Then who—?" But the faces that stared back at her, now taut and pale, had no answer. *Yes, we do have a saboteur on board*, Sassinak thought, then automatically gave the orders that responded to this new threat. All firing systems locked into bridge control, automatic partitioning of the ship, computer control of all access to bridge . . . and the fastest maneuver possible, to remove them from the backtrail of that missile.

"They know something's here, and they know it's armed—so if we want to save those kids on the slaver, we'd better do it *fast*."

Red lights winked on displays around the bridge, scans picking up enemy activity, from communications to missile launch.

"Oh, brillig! Of course they saw it, and just what we need—!"

Huron gave her an uneasy glance, and she grinned at him. "But life is risky, eh? If we go for their armed ships, we'll lose the kids for sure, and if that slaver has any sense and a peashooter, it could plug us in the rear. So—" The *Zaid-Dayan* surged, suddenly freed of its stealth constraints, and closed on the slaver. They were just over the limb, out of line-of-sight from both the escort and the base below, although the missiles launched would be a factor in a few minutes. The slaver vessel, cut off from radio communication with its base, could have chosen to boost away from the planet, or try a faster descent . . . but whether in confusion or resignation did neither. Nor did it fire on them.

"Huron!" He looked up from his own console, when Sassinak called. "You take the boarding party—get that ship out of here, safely into the next sector. I'll give you Parrsit: he's good in a row, and Currald's sending half our ground contingent—" She quickly named the other boarding party members. Huron frowned when she named the two Wefts.

"Captain—"

"Don't argue now, Huron. Wait 'til they've shown you—you need both the heavy-world muscle *and* Weft ability. Get ready—" Huron saluted, and left the bridge. Sassinak waited for the boarding party's report: the marines had already donned their battle armor, but the crew that would take the trader on had to get into EVA suits and armor. Seconds passed; the ships closed. When the forward docking bay signalled green, Sassinak nodded to the helmsman. "Screens open to code, tractor field on—" Now the screen showed a computer-enhanced visual of the fat-bellied trader vessel, within easy EVA range. It attempted a belated burn, but the shields absorbed the energy, and the tractor field held it, dragged it nearer. The boarding party, clustered in assault pods whose nav codes overrode the tractor, blew an airlock and started in.

The fight for the slaver was short and bitter: once inside the lock, the boarding party found well-armed and desperate slavers who fought hand-to-hand in the passages, between decks, and finally on the bridge. The marines lost five, when a passage they thought they'd cleared erupted behind them in a last desperate flurry of fighting. Sassinak followed the marine officer's comments on her headset, wincing at the losses. Slavers were dangerous: they knew they faced mindwipe if they were taken alive. You had to check *every* hole and corner. But she could do nothing from the *Zaid-Dayan*, and she could not leave her ship. The last thing the marines needed was her scolding them over the radio. Deck by deck the marines reported the ship safe; in the background Sassinak could hear hysterical screams which she assumed must be the prisoners.

Finally a very out-of-breath Huron called to report success, and admitted that the Wefts were "more than impressive." The trader had, he said, adequate fuel, air, and supplies for a shortest-route journey to the nearest plotted station, but he wouldn't be able to use the ship's maximum insystem capabilities because of the captives, some seven to eight hundred of them.

"They're not in good shape, and they're half-wild with panic and excitement. They don't know a thing about ship discipline; there aren't any acceleration barriers, and this thing doesn't have a zero-inertia converter. I'd pile 'em all up along the bulkheads like fruit in a dropped crate—"

"All right. We'll shield you. Just get out as quick as you can, and if you *do* jink, be sure we know ahead of time."

"I can't jink in this junk," said Huron, quick-tongued as ever, even in a crisis. "I'll be lucky to jump in it. And the nav computer is a joke."

"That we can help," she said. "What's your cleanest com link?" When he told her, she had her communications specialists patch a direct line from the *Zaid-Dayan*'s navigation computer to the slaver's. Now Huron could keep track of the various incoming threats, and have a chance to evade them.

"Take care," she said. She wished she'd said it before he left; she wished they'd had time for a real farewell. His face in the vidscreen already looked different, the face of a fellow captain . . . she saw him turn as one of his crew—no longer hers—asked a question.

"You, too," he said, his expression showing that his thoughts ran with hers, as they did so often. She wanted to touch his hand, his shoulder, wanted a last feel of his body against hers. But it was too late: he was captain of a very vulnerable ship, and she was captain of a Fleet cruiser—and even if they met again, it would be a different meeting.

Sassinak looked around the bridge at a very sober crew. Fighting off a single enemy was one problem—keeping several enemies from blowing an unarmed transport with limited maneuvering capability was another. They all realized that the pirates would be perfectly happy to lose that ship—the evidence of their crimes. Now that lost ship would include loss of Fleet personnel as well—their own friends and shipmates.

But there was little time to think about it. Already the missiles from the surface were within range, homing (as Sassinak had suspected they might) on the transport. Arly took out this first assault easily, dumping the data generated by their explosion into a primary bank for analysis later. If there was a later. For the escort vessel, boosting at its maximum acceleration, would all too soon round the planet's limb on their trail. Already Huron had boosted the transport into an outward trajectory; Sassinak let the *Zaid-Dayan* fall behind and inward, where she could more easily intercept the surface-launched missiles. Behind them, she knew, would be the manned craft: the little one-man killerships, and the larger escort. Their only chance to protect the transport, and save themselves, lay in using every scrap of cover the complex system offered.

The main display screen now showed a moire pattern of red, yellow, and green: safe zones, when both transport and cruiser were hidden from all known enemy bases and ships, zones when one or the other were exposed, and maximum danger zones when both were exposed. On this pattern their current and extrapolated courses showed in two shades of blue—and the display shifted every time another factor came into play.

"If that tub had any performance capabilities at all," Sassinak muttered angrily, punching buttons, "Huron could use that inner moon as a swingpoint, and head back out picking up another swing from the middle one—and that'd take him safely over the ring, too. But I'll bet that thing won't take it—" Sure enough the return from Huron's ship showed unacceptable acceleration that way. But she had performance to spare, plenty of it, if she guessed right about how the slaver escort would choose to come in.

"Swingpoint off the second moon gives 'em the best angle," said Arly, hands busy on her console as she checked out the systems again.

"No—fastest is the deep slot, using the planet itself. They'll come by like blown smoke—maybe get a lucky shot, and for sure see what they're up against. They can use the maneuver Huron can't—it's a high-G trick, but they'll save fuel, really, and it gives them a reverse run in less than two hours."

"So?"

"So we go up and meet them. Outside."

The *Zaid-Dayan* barely vibrated as the most versatile insystem drive known lifted her poleward and away from the planet. Sassinak held to the edge of their own green zone, making sure that they could blow any missile sent after the transport with their LOS optical weaponry. Ahead, the transport lumbered along, slow and graceless. Sassinak tried not to think of the children on board, and hoped that Huron had enough sedative packs along.

"Captain—got a ripple." The faint disturbance ahead of the escort's high speed movement showed on one screen. Sassinak tapped her own console, while nodding a commendation to the Helm tech. "Good eyes, good handling. Yes—here she comes. Arly, see what you can do—"

Arly chose an EM beam, lethal to unshielded ships, and temporarily blinding to the sensors of most others. Sassinak followed the green line of its path on the monitor; the beam itself was invisible. Something flared out there, and Arly grunted. "Thought they'd have shields. But it may have glared out their scan." In the meantime, a flick of pale blue sparkled into brilliant rainbows: the escort had fired back, but their own shields held easily. Sassinak watched another line score with bright orange the yellow zone near them on the monitor—a clear miss, but remarkably good aim for a ship that had just been lashed by an EM beam. The *Zaid-Dayan* shifted in one of the computer-controlled jinks, covering the transport's stern just as the escort vessel fired at it. Again the cruiser's shields held.

The escort, on the course Sassinak had predicted, was now in rapid transit between them and the planet. Arly lay a barrage of missiles near its expected path. At the same time, the scans showed the telltale white blips of missiles boosting from the escort.

"Those are targeted to the transport," Arly said. "They've got all its signature." Even as she spoke, she had their own optical weapons locking on. But although two of the missiles burst suddenly into silent clouds of light, another had jinked wildly and continued. Arly swore, and reset her system. "If that sucker gets too close to Huron, I can't use these—" Again the missile seemed to buck in its course, and continued, now clearly aiming up the transport's stern.

Sassinak opened the channel to Huron on the transport. "Huron—dump the bucket!" The only defenses they'd been able to give him had all been passive, and this one depended on a fairly stupid self-guidance system.

The "bucket" was a small container of metal foil strips, armed with explosive to disperse them and make a hot spot of itself. It could be launched from a docking bay or airlock. If heat, light, and a cloud of metal fragments could confuse it, they'd be safe. If not, Sassinak would have to try to "grab" the missile with the cruiser's tractor field, a technique dismissed in the *Fleet Ordinance Manual* as "unnecessarily risky."

She watched tensely as the monitor showed the "bucket" being launched on a course that fell behind and below the transport. When it exploded, the missile shifted course, and headed for that bait. So— they had stupid missiles. Now if Huron had enough buckets...

But in the meantime, the escort passing "beneath" them had gained on the transport, improving its firing angle. It had detonated or avoided the missiles Arly had sent to its expected position. Helm countered with a shift that again brought the cruiser between the worst threat and the helpless transport. The cruiser's shields sparkled as unseen beam weapons lashed at her. Arly's return attack met adequate shielding; the deflected beams glowed eerily as they met the planet's atmosphere below.

Unfortunately, the best solution was narrowing rapidly, as all three vessels were approaching the terminator. Beyond that, too quickly, the base's own missiles and scoutships would be rising to join the fray. Sassinak could not keep the cruiser between the transport and everything else. *There are no easy answers*, she thought, and opened the channel to Huron again.

"If your ship will take it, get on out of here," she said. "I know you'll have casualties, but we can't hold them all off for long."

"I know," he said. "We can't afford another close transit—I've done what I can for 'em." She saw by the monitor that the transport had increased its acceleration, climbing more steeply now.

"Can you make the swingpoint for that inner moon?" she asked.

"Not... quite. Here's the solution—" And her right-hand screen came up with it: far from the ideal trajectory, but much better than before. It would lengthen the attack interval from below and the manned moonlet would be on the far side of the planet when they passed its orbit. Best of all, surface-launched missiles wouldn't have the fuel to catch it. Only the escort already engaged was a serious threat. And that, committed as it was to its own high-speed path, could not maneuver fast enough to follow, after the next few minutes. Not without going into FTL—*if* it had the capability to do that so near a large mass.

"Good luck, then." She would not think of the children crushed in the slaveholds, the terrified ones who found themselves pressed flat on the deck, or against a bulkhead, unable to scream or move. They would be no better off if a missile got them, or one of the optical beams.

The configuration of the three ships had now changed radically. The *Zaid-Dayan* had fallen below the transport, keeping between it and the escort, which was now approaching its turnover if it was intending to use the inner moon as a swingpoint. Its course so far made that likely. All she had to do, Sassinak thought, was keep it from blowing the transport before the transport was out of LOS around the planet's limb.

She had just opened her mouth to explain her plan to Arly when the lights darkened, and the *Zaid-Dayan* seemed to stumble on something, as if space itself had turned solid. Red lights flared around the bridge: power outage. Before anyone could react, a flare of light burned out the port exterior visuals, and a gravity flux turned Sass's stomach. A simple grab for the console turned into a wild flailing of arms, and then a thump as normal-G returned. Someone hit the floor, hard, and stifled a cry; voices burst into a wild gabble of alarm.

Sassinak took a deep breath and bellowed through the noise. Silence returned. The lights flickered, then steadied. An ominous block of red telltales glowed from Helm's console, red lights blinked on others. The main screen was down, blank and dark, but to one side a starboard exterior visual showed some kind of beam weapon flickering harmlessly against the shields.

"Report," said Sass, more calmly than she expected. Her mind raced: another act of sabotage? But what, and how, and why hadn't the ship blown? She couldn't tell anything by the expressions of those around her. They all looked shaken and unnatural.

"Ssli..." came the speech synthesizer, from the Ssli's biolink. Sassinak frowned. The Ssli usually communicated by screen or console, not by speech. For one frantic instant she feared the Ssli might be her unknown saboteur—and the cruiser depended, absolutely, on its Ssli—but its words reassured her. "Pardon, captain, for that unwarned maneuver. The enemy ship went into FTL, to catch the transport—no time to explain. Used full power to extend tractor, and grab enemy. This lost power to the shields, and enemy shot blew the portside pods." From relief she fell into instant rage: how *dared* the Ssli act without orders, or warning, and put her ship in danger. She fought that down, and managed a tight-lipped question.

"The transport?"

"Safe for now."

"The escort?" This time, instead of speech, the graphics came up on her monitor: the escort had decelerated, braking away from its original course to attempt to match their course. Well—she'd wanted the transport safe, and she'd hoped to get the escort into a one-to-one with the *Zaid-Dayan*. However unorthodox its means, the Ssli had accomplished that...and she was hardly the person to complain of unorthodoxy in tactical matters. If it worked. Her temper passed as quickly as it had risen. Sassinak glanced up at the worried faces on the bridge, and grinned. "Shirty devils...they think they can take us hand-to-hand!" An uncertain chuckle followed that. "Never mind: they won't. Thanks to our Ssli, they didn't get the transport, and they aren't going to get us, either. Now, let's hear the rest: report."

Section by section, the report came in. Portside pods out— probably repairable, but it could take days. Most of their stealth systems were still operative—fortunate, since they couldn't get into FTL flight without at least half the portside pods. Internal damage was minimal: minor injuries from the gravity flux, and loss of the portside visual monitors. All their weapons systems were functional, but detection and tracking units mounted on the pods were blown.

And where, Sassinak wondered, *do I find a nice, quiet little place to sit tight and do repairs?* She listened to the final reports with half her mind, the other half busy on the larger problem. Then it came to her. Unorthodox, yes, and even outrageous, but it would certainly keep all the enemy occupied, their minds off that transport.

Everyone looked startled when she gave the orders, but as she explained further, they started grinning. With a click and a buzz, the main monitor warmed again and showed where they were going—boosting toward the course Sassinak had originally plotted for the escort.

The *Zaid-Dayan* had lost considerable maneuvering ability with the portside pods, but Sassinak had insisted that they make her disability look worse than it was. Having lost the transport, surely the escort would go after the "crippled" cruiser—and what a prize, could it only capture one! As if the cruiser could not detect the escort, now nearly in its path, it wallowed on. Such damage would have blinded any ship without a Ssli on board . . . and apparently the escort didn't suspect anything. Sassinak watched as the escort corrected its own course, adjusting to the cruiser's new one. They would think she was trying to hide behind the moonlet . . . and they would be right, but not completely.

Comm picked up transmissions from the escort to the planet's single communications satellite, and routed them to her station. Sassinak didn't know the language, but she could guess the content. "Come on up and help us capture a cruiser!" they'd be saying.

If they were smart, they'd go for the crippled side: try to blow the portside docking bay. So far they'd been smart enough; she hoped they'd find the approach just obvious enough. Would they know that was normally a troophold bay? Probably not, although it shouldn't matter if they did. Handy for the marines, thought Sass.

"ETA twenty-four point six minutes," said Bures, Navigation Chief. Sassinak nodded.

"Everyone into armor," she said. That made it official, and obvious. Bridge crew never wore EVA and armor, except during drills—but this was no drill. The enemy would be on their ship—on board the cruiser itself—and might penetrate this far. If they were unlucky. If they were extremely unlucky. The marines, already clustering near the troop docking bay below, were of course already in battle armor, and had been for hours. Sassinak clambered into her own white plasmesh suit, hooking up its various tubes and wires. Once the helmet was locked, her crew would know her by the suit itself—the only all-white suit, the four yellow rings on each arm. But for now, she laid the helmet aside, having checked that all the electronic links to communications and computers worked.

The one advantage of suits was that you didn't have to find a closet when you needed one; the suit could handle that, and much more. She saw by the relaxation on several faces that hers hadn't been the only full bladder. Minutes lurched past in uneven procession—time seemed to crawl, then leap, then crawl again. From the Ssli's input, they knew that the escort was sliding in on their supposedly blind side. If it had external visuals, Sassinak thought, it probably had a good view of the damage—and blown pods would look impressively damaged. She'd seen one once, like the seedpod of some plant that expels its seeds with a wrenching destruction of the once-protective covering.

Closer it came, and closer. Sassinak had given all the necessary orders: now there was nothing to do but wait. The Ssli reported contact an instant before Sassinak felt a very faint jar in her bootsoles. She nodded to Arly, who poured all remaining power to their tractor field. Whatever happened now, the escort and cruiser were not coming apart until one of them was overpowered. With any luck the escort wouldn't notice the tractor field, since it wasn't trying to escape right now anyway.

Interior visuals showed the docking bay where she expected the attack to come. Sure enough, the exterior bay lock blew in, a cloud of fragments obscuring the view for a moment, and then clearing as the vacuum outside sucked them free. A tracked assault pod straight out of her childhood nightmare bounced crazily from the escort's docking bay and its artificial gravity, to the cruiser's, landing so hard that Sassinak winced in sympathy with its contents, enemies though they were.

"Bad grav match," said Helm thoughtfully. "That'll shake 'em up."

"More coming," Arly pointed out. She was hunched over her console, clearly itching to do *something*, although none of her weaponry functioned inside the ship. Sassinak watched as two more assault pods came out of the escort to jounce heavily on the cruiser's docking bay deck. How many more? She wanted them all, but the docking bay was getting crowded: they'd have to move on soon. A thin voice—someone's suit radio—came over the intercom at her ear.

"—Can see another two pods, at least, Sarge. Plus some guys in suits—"

That clicked off, to be replaced by Major Currald, the marines' commanding officer. "Captain—you heard that?" Sassinak acknowledged, and he went on. "We think they'll stack the pods in here, and then blow their way in. We've bled the whole quadrant, and everyone's in position; if they can fit all the pods in here we'll take them then, and if they can't we'll wait until they unload the last one."

"As you will; fire when ready." Sassinak looked around the bridge again, meeting no happy faces. Letting an enemy blow open your docking bay doors was not standard Fleet procedure, and if she got out of this alive, she might be facing a court martial. At the very least she could be accused of allowing ruinous damage to Fleet property, and risking the capture of a major hull. That, at least, was false: the *Zaid-Dayan* would not be captured; she had had the explosives planted to prevent that, by Wefts she knew were trustworthy.

Two more pods came into the docking bay: now six of them waited to crawl like poisonous vermin through her ship. Sassinak shuddered, and fought it down. She saw on the screen an enemy in grayish suit armor walk up to the inner lock controls and attach something, then back away. A blown door control was easier to fix than a blown door. The white flare of a small explosion, and the inner lock doors slid apart. One pod clanked forward, its tracks making a palpable rumbling on the deck, steel grating on steel.

"Three more waiting, captain," said the voice in her ear.

"Snarks in a *bucket*," said someone on the bridge. Sassinak paid no attention. One by one the assault pods entered the ship, now picked up on the corridor monitors. Here the corridor was wide, offering easy access for the marines' own assault vehicles when these were being loaded.

"They can do one *hell* of a lot of damage," said Arly, breathing fast as she watched.

"They're going to take one hell of a lot of damage," said Sass. The first pod came to a corner, and split open, disgorging a dozen armored troops who flattened themselves to the bulkhead on either side. Now the escort's last pods were entering the docking bay. "And any time now they'll start wondering why no one seems to have noticed—"

A wild clangor drowned out her words, until Communications damped it. The enemy should take it that the damaged sensors were finally reacting, and that the *Zaid-Dayan*'s unsuspecting crew were only now realizing the invasion. On the monitor, the first assault pod, its troop hatch now shut, trundled around the corner and loosed a shot down the corridor to the right. That shot reflected from the barrage mirrors placed for such occasion, and shattered the pod's turret. Its tracks kept moving, but as they passed over a mark on the deck a hatch opened from below and a shaped explosive charge blew a hole in its belly. Sassinak could see, on the screen, its troop hatch come partway open, and a tangle of armored limbs as the remaining men inside fought to get free. One by one they were picked off by marine snipers shooting from loopholes into the corridor. By now the second and third pods were open, unloading some of their troops. The second one then lumbered to the corner, and around to the left.

"Stupid," commented Arly, looking a little less pale. "They ought to realize we'd cover both ends."

"Not that stupid." Sassinak pointed. The enemy assault pod, moving at higher speed and without firing, was making a run for the end of the corridor. With enough momentum, it might trigger several traps, and open a path for those behind. Sure enough, the first shaped charge slowed, but did not stop it, and even after the second blew off one track, it still crabbed slowly down the passage toward the barrage mirror. This slid aside to reveal one of the marines' own assault vehicles, which blew the turret off the invader before it could react to the mirror's disappearance. Another shot smashed it nearly flat.

"That's the last time I'll complain about the extra mass on troop deck," said the Helm Officer. "I always thought it was a stupid waste, but then I never thought we'd have a shooting war inside."

"It's not over yet," said Sass, who'd been watching the monitor covering the docking bay itself. Three more assault pods had entered, and now the foremost started toward the inner hatch. "We're going to lose some tonnage before this is done." Even as she spoke, high access ports in the docking bay bulkheads slid aside to reveal the batteries that provided fire support in hostile landings. The weapons had been hastily remounted to fire down into the docking bay, with charges calculated to blow the docking bay contents—but not that quadrant of the cruiser. Even so, they could all feel the shocks through their bootsoles, as the big guns chewed the attackers' pods to bits. None of the troops in five of the pods escaped, but the foremost one managed to unload some into the corridor beyond, where they joined the remnants from the first three pods.

With frightening speed, that group split into teams and disappeared from the monitor's view. Sassinak flicked through the quadrant monitors, picking up stray visuals: gray battle armor jogging here, flashes from weapons there, Fleet marine green armor sprawled gracelessly across a hatchway—she noted the location, and keyed it to the marine commander.

The computer, faster than any human, displayed a red tag for each invader, moving through the schematics of the cruiser. Marines were green tags, forming a cordon around the docking bay, and a backup cordon of ship's crew, blue tags, closed off the quadrant.

Almost. Someone—Sassinak had no time then to think what someone—had left a cargo lift open on Troop Deck. Five red tags went in . . . and the computer abruptly offered a split screen image, half of troop deck, and half of the schematic of the cargo lift destination. The lift paused, airing up as it passed from the vacuum of the evacuated section to the pressurized levels. But it was headed for Main!

In one fluid motion, Sassinak slammed her helmet on and locked it, scooped her weapons off the console, and ran out the door. She tongued the biolink into place just under her right back molar, and felt/saw/heard the five who followed her out: two Wefts and two humans. Fury and exultation boiled in her veins.

The cargo lift opened onto the outer corridor, aft of the bridge and behind the galleys that served the officers' mess. Instead of going forward to the cross corridor, and then aft, Sassinak led her party through the wardroom, and the galley behind it. Through the exterior pickup, she could hear the invaders clomping noisily out of the lift, and in her helmet radio she could hear the marine commander even more noisily cursing the boneheaded son of a Ryxi egglayer who left the lift down and unlocked. Forward, the nearest guardpost on Main was in the angle near the forward docking bay. Aft, the same. Main Deck had not been built to be defended; it was never supposed to be subject to attack.

They heard the invaders heading aft; Sass's computer link said all five were together. Cautiously, she eased the hatch open, and a blast of fire nearly took it apart and her hand with it. They were all together, but some of them were facing each way. Too late for surprise—and the standing guard might walk into this in a moment. Sassinak dove out the door and across the corridor, trusting her armor; she came to rest in the cargo lift itself, with a hotspot on her shoulder, but no real damage—and a good firing position. Behind her, the two Wefts went high, grabbing the overhead and skittering toward the enemy like giant crabs. The other humans stayed low.

Everyone fired: bolts of light and stunner buzzes and old fashioned projectiles that tore chunks from the bulkheads and deck. That was one of the enemy, and whatever it was fired rapidly, if none too accurately, knocking one of the Wefts off the bulkhead in pieces, and smashing a human into a bloody pulp. The other was wounded, huddled in the scant cover of the galley hatch. His weapon had been hit by projectiles, and the bent metal had skidded five meters or so down the corridor. One of the enemy went down, headless, but another one apparently recognized Sassinak by her white armor.

"That's the captain," she heard on the exterior speaker of her helmet. "Get him, and we've got the ship."

You've got the wrong sex, Sassinak thought to herself, *and you're not about to get me or my ship.* She braced her wrist and fired carefully. A smoking hole appeared in one gray-armored chest.

"He's armed," said a surprised voice. "Captains don't carry—" This time she checked her computer link first, and her needler burned a hole in the speaker's helmet. Three down—and where was that Weft?

He was flattened to the overhead, trying to position a Security riot net over the two remaining, but they edged away aft, firing almost random shots at Sassinak and the Weft.

"Forget capture," Sassinak said into her helmet intercom. "Just get 'em."

The Weft made a sound no human could, and *shifted*, impossibly fast, onto one of the enemy. Sassinak heard the terrified shriek over her speakers, but concentrated on shooting the last one. She lay there a moment, breathless, then hauled herself up and locked the cargo lift's controls to a voice-only, bridge-crew only command. The forward guard peeked cautiously around the curve of the corridor, weapon ready. Sassinak waved, and spoke on the intercom.

"Got this bunch—you take over; I'm going back to the bridge." The Weft clinging to the dead enemy let go—reluctantly, Sassinak thought—and *shifted* back to human form. Inside his armor—a neat trick.

"I'll call Med," he said. On the way back through the galley and wardroom, Sassinak queried the situation below. No other group had broken out; in fact, none had reached the outer cordon, and the marines had lost only five to the twenty-nine enemy dead. Two of the enemy had thrown plasma grenades, damaging the inner hull slightly, but Engineering was on it. The marine assault team was about to enter the escort, and someone on it had signalled a desire to surrender. "And I trust that like I'd trust a gambler's dice," the marine commander said grimly.

Sassinak came back onto the bridge to find everyone helmeted and armed and as much in cover as the bridge allowed. She nodded, popped her helmet, and grinned at them, suddenly elated and ready to take on anything. Other helmets came off, the faces behind them smiling, too, but some still uncertain. Most of the consoles had red lights somewhere, blinking or steady . . . too many steady.

"Report," she said, and the reports began. With portable visual scanners, Engineering had finally gotten a view of the portside pod cluster.

"Not much left to work with," was the gruff comment. "We'll have to use the replacement stores, and we may still be one or two short."

"But we can shift again?"

"Oh, aye, if that's all you want. I wouldn't go on another chase in FTL, though, not if you want to live to see your star. It'll get us home, that's about it. And that's assuming you find us a quiet place to work. From what I hear, they're in short supply. We'll need three to five days, and that's for the pods alone. What you did to the portside docking bay is something else."

Sassinak shook her head. Engineering always thought the ship counted for more than anything else. "I didn't blow that hole," she said, well aware that a court martial might think she'd been responsible anyway.

Fire Control was next, reporting that their external shields were still operative: to normal levels except in the damaged quadrant, where they would hold off minor weapons, and offer partial protection from larger ones. Their own distance weapons were in good shape, although the detection and ranging systems on the port side were not. "Soon as we can get someone outside, we can rig something on the midship vanes, and link it to the portside battle computers—except the one that got holed, of course."

Nav reported that they were almost out of LOS of the oncoming ships from the planet. "They only had a two minute window, and apparently were afraid of hitting their own ship: they didn't fire, and they won't be in position for the next five hours." Sassinak grimaced. Five hours wasn't enough for any of the repairs, except—maybe—rigging the detector lines. And she still didn't know how the fight for the escort was coming.

Just then the marine commander came on line, overriding another report. "Got it," he said. "And they didn't get word off, either: we had to blow a hole in the bow, and they're all dead—nobody to question—" Sassinak didn't really care about that, not now. She didn't want to worry about prisoners on board. "You wouldn't believe this ship," he went on. "Damn thing's stuffed with weaponry and assault gear: like a miniature battle platform. Most of the crew travels in coldsleep: that's how they did it."

"Anything we need?" she asked, interrupting his recital. "Never mind—I'll patch you to Engineering and Damage Control: if they've got components we can use, take 'em . . . then clear the ship. Twenty minutes."

"Aye, captain." Med was next: eighteen wounded, including the man who'd been with Sass, and the Weft she'd thought was dead. Its central ring and one limb were still together, and Med announced smugly that Wefts could regenerate from that. Minor ring damage, but they'd sewn it up and put the whole thing in the freezer. Sassinak shivered, and glanced around to see if the other Weft had come back in yet. No. She looked at the bridge chronometer, and stared in disbelief. All that in less than fifteen minutes?

Chapter Eleven

By the grace of whatever gods ruled this section of space, they had a brief respite, and Sassinak intended to make the most of it. She had the grain of an idea that might work to buy them still more time. Now, however, her crew labored to dismantle the escort's docking bay hatch—although not as large as their own, it could form part of the repair far more quickly than Engineering could fabricate a complete replacement. Another working party picked its way along the *Zaid-Dayan*'s outer hull, rigging detector wires and dishes to replace the damaged portside detectors. Inside the cruiser, the marines hauled away the battered remains of the enemy assault pods, and stacked the corpses near the docking bay. That entire quadrant remained in vacuum.

Red lights began to wink off on consoles in the bridge. A spare targeting computer came online to replace the one destroyed by a chance shot, a minor leak in Environmental Systems was repaired without incident, and Engineering even found that a single portside pod could deliver power—it had merely lost its electrical connection when the others blew. One pod wasn't enough to do much with, but everyone felt better nonetheless.

One hour into the safe period, Sassinak confirmed that the escort vessel had been stripped of everything Engineering thought they might need, and was empty, held to the cruiser by their tractor field.

"This is what I want to do," she explained to her senior officers.

"It'll stretch our maneuvering capability," said Hollister, frowning. "Especially with that hole in the hull—"

165

"The moon's airless—there's not going to be any pressure problem," said Sass. "What I want to know is, have we got the power to decelerate, and has anyone seen a good place to go in?"

Bures, the senior Navigation Officer, shrugged. "If you wanted a rugged little moon to hide on, this one's ideal. Getting away again without being spotted is going to be a chore—it's open to surveillance from the ground and that other moon—but as long as we don't move, and our stealth gear works?" Sassinak glanced at Hollister.

"*That's* all right—and it's the first time I've been happy with it where it is."

"—Then I can offer any patch of it," said Bures. "—the only thing regular about it is how irregular it is. And yes, before you ask, our surface systems are all functional."

The next half hour or so was frantic, as working parties moved the enemy corpses and attack pods into the escort—along with escape modules from the cruiser, a Fleet distress beacon and every bit of spare junk they had time to shift. Not all would fit back in, and cursing crewmen lashed nets of the stuff to the escort's hull. Deep in the escort's hull and among the wreckage in its docking bay, they placed powerful explosive charges. Last, and most important, the fuses, over whose timing and placement Arly fussed busily. Finally it was all done, and the cruiser's tractor field turned off. The *Zaid-Dayan*'s insystem drive caught hold again, easing the cruiser away from the other ship, now a floating bomb continuing on the trajectory both ships had shared. The cruiser decelerated still more, pushing its margin of safety to get to the moonlet's surface before any of the pursuit could come in sight.

It was only then that Sassinak remembered that Huron's navigational computer, on the transport, was still slaved to the *Zaid-Dayan*'s. She dared not contact him—had no way to warn him that the violent explosion about to occur was not the mutual destruction of two warships. The Fleet beacon would convince him—and he was not equipped to detect that the *Zaid-Dayan*'s tiny IFF was not in the wreckage—only a Fleet ship could enable that. She looked at the navigational display—there, still boosting safely away, was the transport. She tapped the Nav code, and said, "Break Huron's link."

A startled face looked back at her. "Omigod. I forgot." Bures's thumb went down on the console and the coded tag for Huron's ship went from Fleet blue to black neutral.

"I know. So did I—and he's going to think the worst, unless it occurs to him that the link went quiet a while first."

On the main screen, the situation plot showed the cruiser's rapid descent to the moon's surface. Navigation were all busy, muttering cryptic comments to one another and the computer; Helm stared silently at the steering display, with Engineering codes popping up along its edges: yellow, orange, and occasionally red. Sassinak called up a visual, and swallowed hard. She'd wanted broken ground, and that's exactly what she saw. At least the radar data said it was solid, and the IR scan said it had no internal heat sources.

They were down, squeezed tight as a tick between two jagged slabs on the floor of a small crater, within eight seconds of Nav's first estimate. Given the irregularity of the moon, this was remarkable, and Sassinak gave Nav a grin and thumbs-up. Ten seconds later, the escort blew, a vast pulse of EM, explosion of light, fountains of debris of every sort. And on the outward track, the Fleet distress beacon, screaming for help in every wavelength the designers could cram into it.

"That had me worried," Hollister admitted, grinning, as he watched it. "If that damn thing had blown this way, they might have decided to come get it and shut it off. I had it wired to the far side, but still—"

"The gods love us," said Sass. She looked around, meeting all their eyes. "All right, people, we've done it so far: now we'll be hiding out *silently* for awhile, until they're convinced. Then repairs. Then I suppose we'd better explain to Fleet that we weren't actually blown away." They looked good, on the whole, she thought: still tense, but not too stressed, and confident. "Full stealth," she said, and they moved to comply, switching off nonessential systems, and powering up the big gray canisters amidships to do whatever they did however they did it.

There was still the matter of the person who caused the first disturbance, and Sassinak wondered why more trouble hadn't surfaced during the fight. Surely that would have been the perfect time . . . unless she'd sent the subversive off with Huron, part of the boarding party. Her heart contracted. If she had—if he didn't know, if he were killed because—she shook her head. No time for that. Huron had his own ship; he'd deal with it. She had to believe he could do it—and besides, she hadn't any choice. Here, though—what about that cargo lift?

She called Major Currald, the marine commander, and asked who had been assigned to secure the cargo lift when they cordoned the area.

"Captain, it's my fault. I didn't give specific orders—"

She looked at his broad face in the monitor. Subversive? Saboteur? She couldn't believe it, not with his record and the way he'd handled the rest of the engagement. If he'd slipped much, the enemy would have won. "Very well," she said finally. "I'm holding a briefing in my quarters after the overpass—probably about four hours—we're going to need your input, too."

So. The cargo lift could be pure accident, or "Once is accident, twice is coincidence, and three times is enemy action." That reminded her to take it off bridge voice command, now that the fight was over. Once could be enemy action, too.

Sassinak had taken what precautions she could to ensure that only a few senior officers had access to controls for exterior systems. If her bridge crew wanted to sabotage her, there was really no way to prevent it. Now, with the ship on full stealth routine, all they could do was wait as the enemy's ships appeared, and see if they accepted the evidence of a fierce and fatal struggle. Every kind of debris they might expect to find was there, and surely none of them had any idea what, precisely, the *Zaid-Dayan* was. They would not know what total mass to expect. Besides, that Fleet beacon screeching its electronic head off was not the sort of thing a live captain wanted reporting on his or her actions. She winced, thinking of what would happen when its signal finally reached a Fleet relay station, if she hadn't managed to get word through on a sublight link earlier. She had better have a whole ship, and a live crew, and a good story to tell.

In the meantime, they had another hour and a bit to wait until the first of the enemy ships came into scan. Miserable as it was, they should stay in their protective gear until it was obvious that the enemy had accepted the scam. Not that a suit would really keep anyone alive long on that moonlet, but—

"Coffee, captain?" Sassinak glanced around, and smiled at the steward with a tray of mugs. She was, she realized, feeling the letdown after battle. She waved him toward the rest of the bridge crew. They could all use something. But she had something better than coffee... a private vice, as Abe had called her leftover sweet tooth. She always kept some in her emergency gear, and this was just the time for it... chocolate, rare and expensive. And addictive, the medical teams said, but no worse than coffee. She left her mug cooling on the edge of her console as the thin brown wedge went into her mouth. Much better. As they waited, the crew settled again to routine tasks, and Sassinak assessed their mood. They had gained confidence—she liked the calm but determined expressions, the clear eyes and steady voices. Most of the bridge crew made an excuse to speak to her; she sensed their approval and trust.

The first enemy vessel appeared on scan, high and fast, a streak across their narrow wedge of vision. It continued with no visible sign of burn or course change; the computer confirmed. Another, lower, from the other side, followed within an hour. This one flooded the moonlet with targeting radar impulses... which the *Zaid-Dayan* passively absorbed, analyzed, and reflected as if it were just another big rock. Over the next couple of hours, three more of the small ships crossed their scan; none of them changed course or showed any interest in the moon.

"I don't expect any of them carrying the fuel to hang around and search," said Hollister. "If they were going to, they'd have to get into a stable orbit—which this thing doesn't encourage."

"And I'm glad of it." Sassinak stretched. "Gah! I can't believe I'm stiff after that little bit of running—"

"And getting shot at. Did you know your back armor's nearly melted through?"

So that had been the hotspot she'd felt. "Is it? And I thought they'd missed. Now—do you suppose that other escort is going to show up—and if it is, do they have it crammed with as much armament?"

"Yes, and yes, but probably not for another couple of hours. The little ships will have told them about the explosion. Wish we could pick up their transmissions."

"Me, too. Unfortunately, they don't all speak Standard, or anything close to it."

Finally, the steward came again to pick up the dirty mugs, and gave Sassinak a worried look. "Anything wrong, captain?"

"No—thanks for the thought. I just indulged my taste for chocolate instead. Tell you what—I'm briefing the senior officers in my office in—" she looked at the chronometer, "—about fifteen minutes. Why don't you bring a pot of coffee in there, and something to eat, too. We'll be there awhile." The steward nodded and left. Sassinak turned to the others. "Bridge crew, you can get out of armor, if you want: have your reliefs stand by in case. Terrell—" This to her new Executive Officer, a round-faced young man.

"Yes, captain?"

"Take the bridge, and tell the cooks to serve the crew coffee or some other stimulant at their duty stations. As soon as we're sure that cruiser isn't onto us, we'll stand down and give everyone a rest, but not quite yet. I'll be in my office, but I'm going to the cabin first." Sassinak went aft to her cabin, got out of the armored suit, and saw that the beam had charred a streak across her uniform under it. Grimacing, she worked it off her shoulder, and peered at the damage in her mirror. A red streak, maybe a couple of blisters; she'd peel a little, that was all. It didn't hurt, really, although it was stiffening up. She grinned at her reflection: not bad for forty-six, not bad at all. Not a silver strand in that night-dark hair, no wrinkles around the eyes—or anywhere else, for that matter. Not for the first time she shook her head at her own vanity, ducked into the stall, and let the fine spray wash away sweat and fatigue. A clean, unmarked uniform, a quick brush to her curly hair, and she was ready to face the officers again.

In her office, her senior officers waited; she saw by their faces that they appreciated this effort: nothing could be too wrong if the captain appeared freshly groomed and serenely elegant. Two stewards had brought a large pot of coffee and tray of food: pastries and sandwiches. Sassinak dismissed the stewards, with thanks, and left the food on the warmer.

"Well, now," she said, slipping into her chair behind the broad fonwood desk, "we've solved several problems today—"

"Created a few, too. Who let off that firecracker, d'you know?"

"No, I don't. That's a problem, and it's part of another one I'll mention later. First, though, I want to commend all of you: you and your people."

"Sorry about that cargo lift—" began Major Currald.

"And I'm sorry about your casualties, Major. Those here and those on the transport both. But we wouldn't have had much chance without you. I want to thank you, in particular, for recommending that we split the marines between us as we did. What I really want to do, though, is let you all in on a classified portion of our mission." She tapped the desk console to seal the room to intrusive devices, and nodded as eyebrows went up around the room. "Yes, it's important, and yes, it has a bearing on what happened today. Fleet advised me—has advised all captains, I understand—of something we've all known or suspected for some time. Security's compromised, and Fleet no longer considers its personnel background screening reliable. We were told that we should expect at least one hostile agent on each ship—to look for them, neutralize their activities, if we could, and *not* report them back through normal channels." She let that sink in a moment. When Hollister lifted his hand she nodded.

"Did you get any kind of guidance at all, captain? Were they suspecting enlisted? Officers?" His eye traveled on to Currald, whose bulk dwarfed the rest of them, but he didn't say it.

Sassinak shook her head. "None. We were to suspect everyone—any personnel file might have been tampered with, and any apparent political group might be involved. They specifically stated that Fleet Security believes most heavyworlders in Fleet are loyal, that Wefts have never shown any hint of disloyalty, and that religious minorities, apart from political movements, are considered unlikely candidates. But aside from that, everyone from the sailor swabbing a latrine to my Executive Officer."

"But you're telling us," said Arly, head cocked.

"Yes. I'm telling you because, first of all, I trust you. We just came through a fairly stiff engagement; we all know it could have ended another way. I believe you're all loyal to Fleet, and through Fleet to the FSP. Besides, if my bridge crew and senior officers are, singly or together, disloyal, then I'm unlikely to be able to counter it. You have too much autonomy; you *have* to have it. And there we were, right where you could have sabotaged me and the whole mission, and instead you performed brilliantly: I'm not going to distrust that. We need to trust each other, and I'm starting here."

"Do you have any ideas?" asked Danyan, one of the Wefts who had been in the firing party. "Any clues at all?"

"Not yet. Today we had two incidents: the firing of an unauthorized missile which gave away our position, and the cargo lift being left unlocked in an area which could easily be penetrated. The first I must assume was intentional: in twenty years as a Fleet officer, I have never known anyone to fire a missile accidentally once out of training. The second could have been accidental or intentional. Major Currald takes responsibility for it, and thinks it was an accident; I'll accept that for now. But the first... Arly, who could have fired that thing?"

The younger woman frowned thoughtfully. "I've been trying to think, but haven't really had time—things kept happening—"

"Try now."

"Well—I could, but I didn't. My two techs on the bridge could have, but I think I'd have seen them do it—I can't swear to that, but I'm used to their movements, and it'd take five or six strokes. At that time, the quadrant weaponry was on local control—at least partly. Ordinarily, in stealth mode, I have a tech at each station. That's partly to keep crew away, so that accidents won't happen. That went out of quad three, and there were two techs on station. Adis and Veron, both advanced-second. Beyond that, though, someone could have activated an individual missile with any of several control panels, if they'd had previous access to it, to change its response frequency."

"What would they know about the status of any engagement?" asked Sass.

"What I'd said today was that we were insystem with those slavers, trying to lie low and trap them. Keep a low profile, but be ready to respond instantly if the captain needed us, because we probably would get in a row, and it would happen fast. I'd have expected them to be onstation, but not prepped: several keystrokes from a launch, though not more than a five second delay."

"The whole crew knew we were trailing slavers, captain," said Nav. "I expect the marines, too—?" The marine commander nodded. "So they'd know when we came out of FTL that we were reasonably close. Full-stealth-mode's a shipwide announcement... easy enough for an agent to realize that's just when you don't want a missile launched."

"Arly, I'll need the names of those on duty, the likeliest to have access." She had already keyed in Adis and Veron, and their personnel records were up on her left-hand screen. Nothing obvious—but she'd already been over all the records looking for something obvious. "And, when you've time, a complete report on alternate access methods: if an exterior device was used, what would it look like, and so on." Sassinak turned to Major Currald. "I know you consider that cargo lift your fault, but in ordinary circumstances, who would have locked it off?"

"Oh . . . Sergeant Pardy, most likely. He had troop deck watch, and when the galley's secured, he usually does it. But I'd snagged him to supervise the mounting of those barrage mirrors, because Carston was already working on the artillery. That would have left . . . let's see . . . Corporal Turner, but she went with the boarding party, because we needed to send two people with extra medical training. I really think, captain, that it was a simple accident, and my responsibility. I didn't stop to realize that Pardy's usual team had been split, when the boarding party left, and that left no one particular assigned to it."

Sassinak nodded. From what he said, she thought herself that it was most likely an accident—almost a fatal one, but not intentional. And even if it had been—even if one of the marines now dead had told another to do it, in all that confusion she would find no proof.

"What I'm planning to do now," she told them all, "is sit here quietly until the fuss clears, then do our repairs as best we can, and then continue our quiet surveillance until something else happens. If the slavers decide to evacuate that base, I'd like to know where they go. Even if they don't leave, we can log traffic in and out of the system. Huron's taking that transport to the nearest station—a minimum of several weeks. If something happens to him, our beacon is . . . mmm . . . telling the world just where the *Zaid-Dayan* was. It'll be years before anyone picks it up, probably, but they will. If we see something interesting enough to tell, we will; otherwise, we'll wait to see if Huron brings a flotilla in after us."

"Won't he think we're destroyed?" asked Arly.

"He might. Then again, he might think of the trick we used—we both read about a similar trick used in water-world navies, long ago. Either way, though, he knows the base is here, and I'm sure he'll report it." Sassinak paused, her throat dry. "Anyone for coffee? Food?" Several of them nodded. Nav and Helm rose to serve it. Sassinak took two of her favorite pastries, and sipped from her full mug. Her nose wrinkled involuntarily. Coffee wasn't her favorite drink, but this had a strange undertaste. Major Currald, who'd taken a big gulp of his, grimaced.

"Somebody didn't scrub the pot," he said. He took another swallow, frowning. The others sniffed theirs, and put them down. Nav sipped, and shook his head. Helm shrugged, and went to fill the water pitcher at the corner sink.

Sassinak had taken a bite of pastry to cover the unpleasant taste when Currald gagged, and turned an unlovely shade of bluish gray. His eyes rolled up under slack lids. Hollister, beside him, quickly rolled him out of the seat onto the floor, where the commander sprawled heavily, his breathing harsh and uneven. "Heart attack," he said. "Probably the stress today—" But as he reached for the emergency kit stowed along the wall, Sassinak felt an odd numbness spread across her own tongue, and saw the frightened expression of those who had taken a sip of coffee.

"Poison," she managed to say. Her tongue felt huge in her mouth, clumsy. "Don't drink—" Her vision blurred, and her stomach roiled. Suddenly she doubled up, helplessly spewing out the little she'd had. So was Bures, and now Currald, apparently unconscious, vomited copiously, gagging on it. Someone was up, calling for Med on the intercom. Someone's arm reached into her line of sight, wiping up the mess, and then her face. She nodded, acknowledging the help but still not able to speak.

When she looked again, Hollister was trying to keep the commander's airway open, and Bures was still hunched over, wild-eyed and miserable. She expected she herself didn't look much better. A last violent cramp seized her and bent her around clenched arms. Then it eased. Her vision was clearer: she could see that Arly was trying to open the door for Med, and realized that it was still on voice-only lock. She cleared her throat, and managed an audible command. The door slid aside. While the med team went to work, she put the room ventilation on high to get rid of the terrible stench, and rinsed her mouth with water from the little sink. This was not what she'd had in mind when she'd insisted on running a water line into this office, but it was certainly handy. The med team had Currald tubed and on oxygen before they spoke to her, and then they wanted her to come straight back to sickbay.

"Not now." She was able to speak clearly now, though she suspected the poison was still affecting her. "I'm fine now—"

"Captain, with all due respect, if it's a multiple poison there may be delayed effects."

"I know that. But later. You can take Bures, keep an eye on him. Now listen: we think it's the coffee, in here—" She pointed to the pot. "I don't want panic, and I don't want the whole ship knowing that someone tried to poison the officers: clear?"

"Clear, captain, but—"

"But you have to find out. I know that. If we're the only victims, that's one thing, but you'll want to protect the others—I recommend the sudden discovery that those invaders may have put something in the galley up here, and you need to see if they contaminated the galley on Troop Deck."

"Right away, captain."

"Lieutenant Gelory will help you." Gelory, a Weft, smiled quietly; she was the assistant quartermaster, so this was a logical choice.

The movement of a litter with an unconscious Major Currald aboard couldn't be concealed. Sassinak quickly elaborated her cover story about the invaders having somehow contaminated the galley for the officers' mess. The bridge crew were angry and worried—so was she—but she had to leave them briefly to get out of her stinking uniform. Her face in the mirror seemed almost ten years older, but after another shower her color had come back, and she felt almost normal—just hungry.

Bures and the others who had sipped the coffee were also better, and had taken the opportunity to get into clean uniforms. That was good: if they cared about appearance, they were going to be fine. She settled into her seat and thought about it. Poisoning, an open cargo lift through the cordons, and a missile launch . . . ? Three times enemy action: that was the old rule, and a lot better than most old rules. But it didn't feel right. It didn't feel like the same *kind* of enemy. If someone wanted the ship to reveal itself to the slavers—and that was the only reason for a missile launch—what was the poison supposed to do? If they all died of it, retching their guts out on the decks, the whole crew together wouldn't make enough noise to be noticed. So the subversive could take over the ship? No one person could: a cruiser was too complicated for any one individual to launch. Was it pique because the earlier sabotage hadn't done its work? Then why not put poison in something where it couldn't be tasted? The poison was, in fact, a stupid person's plot—she leaned forward to put Medical on a private line and picked up her headset.

"Yes?"

"Yes, poison in the coffee: a very dangerous alkaloid. Yes, more cases, although so far only one is dead." Dr. Mayerd's usually business-like tone had an extra bite in it.

Dead. Tears stung her eyes. Bad enough to lose them in combat, bad enough to have her ship blown open . . . but for someone *in* the crew to poison fellow crew! "Go on," she said.

"Major Currald's alive, and we think he'll make it, though he's pretty bad. He'll be out for at least three days. Two more have had their stomachs pumped; those who just sipped it heaved it all up again, as you did. So far everyone's buying the idea of the invaders having dumped poison in the nearest canister in the galleys—that would almost fit, because the coffee tins were sitting out, ready to brew. Apparently it wasn't in all the coffee—or didn't you drink that first batch sent to the bridge?"

"I didn't, but some others did, with no effect. What else?"

"The concentration was wildly different in the different containers we found—as if someone had just scooped a measure or so, carelessly, into the big kettles, and not all of those. Altogether we've had eleven report in here, and reports of another nine or ten who didn't feel bad enough to come in once they quit vomiting— I'm tracking those. More important: captain, if you experience any color change in your vision—if things start looking strange—report here at once. Some people have a late reaction to this; it has to do with the way some people's livers break down the original poison. Some of the metabolites undergo secondary degradation and lose the hydroxy—"

Sassinak interrupted what was about to be an enthusiastic description of the biochemistry of the poison, with, "Right—if things change color, I'll come down. Talk to you later." She found herself smiling at the slightly miffed snort that came down the line before she clicked it off. Mayerd would get over it; she should have known the captain wouldn't want a lecture on biochemical pathways.

So someone had tried to poison not only the more senior officers, but also the crew—or some of the crew. She wondered just how random the poisoning had been . . . had the kettles which hadn't been poisoned been chosen to save friends? Poisoning still made little sense in terms of helping the slavers. Unless this person planned to kill everyone, and somehow rig a message to them . . . but only one of the Communications specialists would be likely to have the skills for that. Sassinak was careful not to turn and look suspiciously at the Com cubicle. Morale was going to be bad enough.

Her intercom beeped, and she put the headset back on. "Sassinak here."

It was the Med officer again. "Captain, it's not only an alkaloid, it's an alkaloid from a plant native to Diplo."

She opened her mouth to say "So?" and then realized what that meant. "Diplo. Oh . . . dear." A heavy-world system. As far as some were concerned, the most troublesome heavy-world political unit, outspoken to the point of rudeness about the duties of the lightweights to their stronger cousins. "Are you sure?"

"Very." Mayerd sounded almost smug, and deserved to be. "Captain, this is one of the reference poisons in our databank—because it's rare, and its structure can be used to deduce others, when we run them through the machines. It is precisely that one—and I know you don't want to hear the name, because you didn't even want to hear about the hydroxy-group cleavage—" Sassinak winced at her sarcasm, but let it pass. "—And I can confirm that it did *not* come from medical stores: someone brought it aboard as private duffel." A longish pause, and then, "Someone from Diplo, I would think. Or with friends there."

"Currald nearly died," said Sass, remembering that the Med officer had had more than one sharp thing to say about heavyworlders and their medical demands on her resources.

"And might still. I'm not accusing Currald; I know that not every heavyworlder is a boneheaded fanatic. But it is a poison from a plant native to an aggressively heavyworlder planet, and that's a fact you can't ignore. Excuse me, they're calling me." And with the age-old arrogance of the surgeon, she clicked off her intercom and left Sassinak sitting there.

A heavyworlder poison. To the Med officer, that clearly meant a heavyworlder poisoner. But was that too easy? Sassinak thought of Currald's hard, almost sullen face, the resigned tone in which he claimed responsibility for the open cargo lift. He'd expected to be blamed; he'd been ready for trouble. She knew her attitude had surprised him—and his congratulations on her own success in the battle had also been a bit surprised. A lightweight, a woman, and the captain—had put on armor, dived across a corridor, exchanged fire with the enemy? She wished he were conscious, able to talk...for of all the heavyworlders now on the ship, she trusted him most.

If not a heavyworlder, her thoughts ran on, then who? Who wanted to foment strife between the types of humans? Who would gain by it? *A medical reference poison*, she reminded herself...and the medical staff had their own unique opportunities for access to food supplies.

"Captain?" That was her new Exec, to her eye far too young and timid to be what she needed. She certainly couldn't get any comfort from him. She nodded coolly, and he went on. "That other escort's coming across."

Sassinak looked at the main screen, now giving a computer enhanced version of the passive scans. This vessel's motion was relatively slower; its course would take it through the thickest part of the expanding debris cloud.

"Its specs are pretty close to the other one," he offered, eyeing her with a nervous expression that made her irritable. She did not, after all, have horns and a spiked tail.

"Any communications we can pick up?"

"No, captain. Not so far. It's probably beaming them to that relay satellite—" He paused as the Communications Watch Officer raised a hand and waved it. Sassinak nodded to her.

"Speaks atrocious Neo-Gaesh," the Com officer said. "I can barely follow it."

"Put it on my set," said Sass. "It's my native tongue—or was." She had kept up practice in Neo-Gaesh, over the years, just in case. If they had even the simplest code, though, she'd be unlikely to follow it.

They didn't. In plain, if accented, Neo-Gaesh, the individual on the escort vessel was reporting their observation of the debris. "—And a steel waste disposal unit, definitely not ours. A . . . a cube reader, I think, and a cube file. Stenciled with Fleet insignia and some numbers." Sassinak could not hear whatever reply had come, but in a few seconds the first speaker said, "Take too long. We've already picked up Fleet items you can check. I'll tag it, though." Another long pause, and then, "Couldn't have been too big—one of their heavily armed scouts, the new ones. They're supposed to be damned near invisible to everything, until they attack, and almost as heavily armed as a cruiser." Another pause, then, "Yes: verified Fleet casualties, some in evac pods, and some in ship clothes, uniforms." That had been hardest, convincing herself to sacrifice their dead with scant honor, their bodies as well as their lives given to the enemy, to make a convincing display of destruction.

When the escort passed from detection range, Sassinak relaxed. They'd done it, so far. The slavers didn't know they were there, alive. Huron and his pitiful cargo were safely away. One lot of slavers were dead—and she didn't regret the death of any of them.

But in the long night watch that followed, when she thought of the Fleet dead snagged by an enemy's robot arm to be "verified" as a casualty, she regretted very much that Huron had gone with the trader, and she had no one to comfort her.

Chapter Twelve

Repairs, as always, ran overtime. Sassinak didn't mind that much: they had time, right then, more than enough of it. Engineers, in her experience, were never satisfied to replace a malfunctioning part: they always wanted to redesign it. So mounting replacement pods involved rebuilding the pod mounts, and changing the conformation of them, all to reconcile the portside pod cluster with the other portside repairs. Hollister quoted centers of mass and acceleration, filling her screen with math that she normally found interesting . . . but at the moment it was a tangle of symbols that would not make sense. Neither did the greater problem of ship sabotage. If someone hadn't blown their cover, they might have gotten away without that great gaping hole in the side of her ship, or the fouled pods. Or the deaths. This was not, by any means, the first time she'd been in combat, or seen death . . . but Abe had been right, all those years ago: it was different when it was her command that sent them, not a command transmitted from above.

Finally they were done, the engineers and their working parties, and as the pressure came up in the damaged sector, and the little leaks whistled until they were patched, Sassinak could see that the ship itself was sound. It needed time in the refitting yards, but it was sound. Marine troops moved back into their quarters when the pressure stabilized, to the great relief of the Fleet crew who'd been double-bunking, and not liking it. Seven days, not three or four or five, but it was done, and they were back to normal.

Currald was out of sick bay, just barely in time to move his troops back into their own territory. Sassinak had visited him daily once he regained consciousness, but he'd been too sick for much talk. He'd lost nearly ten kilos, and looked haggard.

She was in the gym, working out with Gelory in unarmed combat, when Currald came in for the first time. His eyes widened when he saw the shiny pink streak across her shoulder.

"When did that—?"

"One of the pirates nearly got me—the five that got up to Main." She answered without pausing, dodging one of Gelory's standing kicks, and throwing a punch she blocked easily.

"I didn't know you'd been hurt." His expression flickered through surprise, concern, and settled into his normal impassivity. Sassinak handsigned Gelory to break for a moment.

"It wasn't bad," she said. "Are you supposed to be working out yet?"

He reddened. "I'm supposed to be taking it easy, but you know the problem—"

"Yeah, your calcium shifts too readily in low-grav. I could have Engineering rig your quarters for high-grav..."

His brows raised; Sassinak gave herself a point for having gotten through his mask again. "You'd do that? It takes power, and we're on stealth—"

"I'd do that rather than have you blow an artery working out here before you're ready. I know you're tough, Major, but poisoning doesn't favor your kind of strength."

"They said I could use the treadmill, but not the weight harness yet." That was an admission; the treadmill wasn't even in the gym proper. Currald gave her the most human look she'd had yet, and finally grinned. "I guess you aren't going to think I'm a weakling even when I look like one..."

"Weaklings don't survive that kind of poisoning, and weaklings aren't majors in the marines." She delivered that crisply, almost barked it, and was glad to see the respectful glint in his eye. "Now— if you and Med think that a high-grav environment would help you get back to normal, tell me. We can't take the power to do more than your quarters, without risking exposure, but we can do that much, I have no idea if that's enough to do any good. In the meantime, I'd appreciate it if you'd follow Med's advice—you don't want them telling you how to handle troops, and they know a bit more about poisoning than either of us."

"Yes, captain," he said. This time with neither resentment, defensiveness, nor guilt.

"I'll expect you for the staff conference at 1500," Sassinak went on. "Now, I've got another fifteen minutes of Gelory's expertise to absorb."

"May I watch?"

"If you want to see your captain dumped on the gym floor a dozen times, certainly." She nodded to Gelory, who instantly attacked, a move so fast she was sure it must have been half shapechange. Something that felt almost boneless at first stiffened into a leg over which she was flipped—but she coiled in midair, managed to hang onto a wrist, and flipped Gelory in her turn. But this was the only change that Gelory pulled on her for the rest of the session. Instead they sparred as near-equals, and she hit the floor only once. She could not ask, in front of Currald, but suspected the Weft of making her look good in front of the heavyworlder.

Staff meeting that day found almost the same group in her office as on the day of the poisoning. Sassinak noted with amusement that suddenly no one went near the coffee service—although until Currald's return, the coffee fiends had been drinking at their normal rate.

"I'm fairly sure *this* coffee is safe," she said, and watched their faces as they realized their unconscious behaviors. When everyone was settled, and had taken the first cautious sips, she brought Currald up to date, outlining the repairs, the few changes necessary for the marines on Troop Deck, and the discreet hunt for the poisoner. The chief medical officer had already told him the poison was from Diplo, she knew, and she outlined what they had discovered since.

"It's obvious that any saboteur, as we discussed before, would want to foment trouble between factions. My first thought was that having a heavyworld poison pointed to someone who wanted to put heavyworlders in a bind, and knew that I had a reputation for trusting them. But we had to take a look at the possibility that a heavyworlder had, in fact, done the poisoning. It had to be someone with access to the galleys—preferably both, although it's just barely possible that some of the coffee from Main made it down to Troop Deck. Since we were serving all over the ship, it's hard to trace the source of everyone's drink... particularly if one or more of the stewards was involved."

"You no longer believe that the intruders poisoned open canisters?"

"No. There'd have been no reason for them to do so: they thought they were taking the ship. They'd have used our supplies. And remember, we have that other sabotage to consider, the missile."

"Have you figured it out, captain?"

"No. Frankly, Major, I wanted you well before we went further. I do have a list of suspects... and one of them is a young woman from an ambiguous background." She paused; no one said anything, and Sassinak went on. "She was a medical evacuee from Diplo—an unadapted infant who did not respond to treatment. Reared on Palun—"

"That's an intermediate world," said Currald slowly. Sassinak nodded.

"Right. She lived there until she was thirteen, with a heavyworlder family related to her birth family. Applied for light-G transfer on her own, as soon as she could, and joined Fleet as a recruit after finishing school."

"But you're not sure—"

"No, if I were sure she'd be in the brig. She had access, but so did at least four other stewards and the cooks. Thing is, she's the only one with a close link to Diplo—not just any heavy-world planet, but Diplo. She's actually visited twice, as an adult, in protective gear. We don't know anything about it, of course. And anyone who wanted to incriminate a heavyworlder could hardly have found a better way than to use a Diplo poison."

"Could she have popped the missile?" Currald glanced at Arly, who quickly shook her head.

"No—we checked that, of course, right away. Particularly when both my techs in that quadrant came up sick. But they were well when the missile went off, and unless they're in it together they clear each other. I think myself it was a handheld pulse shot, probably from a service hatch down the corridor, that triggered the missile."

"You remember that Fleet Intelligence warned each captain to expect at least one agent . . . they didn't say *only* one," said Sass. "I think the character of the missile launch and the poisoning are so different as to point to two different individuals with two different goals. But what I can't figure out for sure is what someone hoped to gain by random poisoning. Unless the poisoner had a group of supporters to take over the ship . . ."

Currald sighed, and laced his fingers together. Even gaunt from his illness, he outweighed everyone else at the table, and his somber face looked dangerous. "Captain, you have the reputation of being fair . . ." He stopped, clearly unhappy with that beginning and started over. "Look: I'm just the marine commander; I don't mingle with your ship's crew that much. But I know you all believe heavyworlders clump together, and to some extent that's true. I think I'd know if you had any sort of conspiracy among them on your side of the ship, and I hope you'll believe that I'd have told you."

Sassinak smiled at his attempt to avoid the usual heavyworlder paranoia, but gave him a serious response. "I told you before, Major, that I trust you completely. I don't think there was a conspiracy, because nothing happened while the poisonings were being discovered. But I am concerned that if this steward is the source, and *if* I arrest her, you and other heavyworlders will see that as a hasty and unthinking response to the Diplo poison. And I'd be very interested in what you thought such a person could hope to gain by it. What I know of heavyworlder politics and religion doesn't suggest that poisoning would be the usual approach."

"No, it's not." Currald sighed again. "Though if I had to guess, I'd bet her birth family—and her relations on Palun—were strict Separationists. She couldn't be, because she couldn't handle the physical strain. Some of those Separationists are pretty harsh on throwback babies. A few even kill them outright—unfit, they say." He ignored the sharp intakes of breath, the sidelong glances, and went on. "If she's been unable to adjust to being a lightweight, or if she thinks she has to make up for being unadapted, she might do something rash just to make the point." He glanced around, then looked back at Sass. "You don't have any heavyworlder officers, then?"

"I did, but I sent them with Huron on the prize ship." At his sharp look, Sassinak shrugged. "It just worked out that way: they had the right skills, and the seniority."

Something in that had pleased him, for he had relaxed a little. "So you might like a heavyworlder officer to have a few words with this young woman?"

"If you think you might find out whether she did it, and why."

"And you do trust me for that." It was not a question, but a statement tinged with surprise. "All right, captain; I'll see what I can do."

The rest of the meeting involved the results of their surveillance. For the first few days after the landing, they'd recorded no traffic in the system except for a shuttle from the planet to the occupied moon. But only a few hours before, a fast ship had lifted, headed outsystem by its trajectory.

"Going to tell the boss what happened," said Bures.

"So why'd they wait this long?" asked Sass. She could think of several reasons, none of them pleasant. No one answered her; she hadn't expected them to. She wondered how long it would be before the big transports came, to dismantle the base and move it. The enemy would know the specs on the ship Huron had taken; they'd know how long they had before Fleet could return. A more dangerous possibility involved the enemy attempting to defend the base, trapping a skimpy Fleet expedition with more overweaponed ships like the little escort she had fought.

"So what we can do," she summed up for them at the end of the meeting, "is trail one of the ships that leaves, and hope we're following one that goes somewhere informative, *or* sit where we are and monitor everything that goes on, to report it to Fleet later, *or* try to disrupt the evacuation once it starts. I wish we knew where that scumbucket was headed."

Two hours later, Currald called and asked for a conference. Sassinak agreed, and although he'd said nothing over the intercom, she was not surprised to see the steward under suspicion precede him into her office.

The story was much as Currald had suggested. Seles, born without the heavyworlder's adaptations to high-G, had nearly died in the first month of life. Her grandfather, she said, had told her mother to kill her, but her mother had lost two children in a habitat accident, and wanted to give her a chance. The medical postbirth treatments hadn't worked, and she'd been evacuated as a two-month-old infant, sent to her mother's younger sister on Palun. Even there, she had been the weakling, teased by her cousins when she broke an ankle falling from a tree, when she couldn't climb and run as well as they could. At ten, on her only childhood visit to Diplo, she had needed the adaptive suits that lightweights wore... and she had had to listen to her grandfather's ranting. She had ruined them, he said: not only the cost of her treatment, and her travel to Palun, but the simple fact that a throwback had been born in their family. They had lost honor; it would have been better if she had died at birth. Her father had glanced past her and refused to speak; her mother now had two "normal" children, husky boys who knocked her down and sat on the chest of her pressure suit until her mother called them away—clearly annoyed that Seles was such a problem.

In school on Palun, she had been taught by several active Separationists, who used her weakness as an example of why the heavyworlders should avoid contact with lightweights and the FSP. One of them, though, had told her of the only way in which throwbacks could justify their existence... by proving themselves true to heavyworlder interests, and serving as a spy within the dominant lightweight culture.

In that hope she had requested medical evacuation to a normal-G world, a request quickly granted. She'd been declared a ward of the state, and put into boarding school on Casey's World.

Sassinak realized that Seles must have gone to that strange boarding school at about the same age she herself had come to the Fleet prep school—within a year or so anyway. But Seles had had no Abe, no mentor to guide her. Bigger than average, stronger than usual (though weak to heavyworlders), she already believed she was an outcast. Had anyone tried to befriend her? Sassinak couldn't tell; certainly Seles would not have noticed. Even now her slightly heavy-featured face was not ugly—it was her expression, the fixed, stolid, slightly sullen expression, that made her look more the heavyworlder, and more stupid, than she was. She had been in trouble once or twice for fighting, she admitted, but it wasn't her fault. People picked on her; they hated heavyworlders and they hadn't trusted her. Sassinak heard the self-pitying whine in her voice and mentally shook her head, though she made no answer. No one likes the whiner, no one trusts the sullen.

So Seles had come from school still convinced that the world was unfair, and still burning to justify herself to her heavyworld relatives. In that mood, she had joined Fleet—and in her first leave after basic training, had gone back to Diplo. Her family had been contemptuous, refused to believe that she really meant to be an agent for the heavyworlders. If she'd had any ability, they told her, she'd have been recruited by one of the regular intelligence services. What could she do alone? Useless weakling, her grandfather stormed, and this time even her mother nodded, as her younger brothers smirked. Prove yourself first, he said, and then come asking favors.

On her way back to the spaceport, she had bought a kilo of poison—since its use on Diplo was unregulated, she had assumed that the heavyworlders were immune to it. She was going to kill all the lightweight crew of whatever ship she was on, turn the whole thing over to heavyworlders, and that would prove—

"Exactly *nothing!*" snapped Major Currald, who had held his tongue with difficulty through this emotional recitation. "Did you *want* the lightweights to think we're all stupid or crazy? Didn't it occur to you that some of us *know* our best hope is inside FSP, alongside the lightweights?"

The girl's face was red, and her hands shook as she laid a rumpled, much-folded piece of paper on Sass's desk. "I—I know how it is. I know you're going to kill me. But—but I want to be buried on Diplo—or at least my ashes—and it says in regulations you have to do that—and send this message."

It was as pitiful and incoherent as the rest of her story. "In the Name of Justice and Our Righteous Cause—" it began, and wandered around through bits of bad history (the Gelway Riots had not been caused by prejudice against heavyworlders—the heavyworlders hadn't been involved at all, except for one squad of riot police) and dubious theology (at least Sassinak had never heard of Darwin's God before) to justify the poisoning of the innocent, including other heavyworlders as "an Act of Pure Defiance that shall light a Beacon across the Galaxy." It ended with a plea that her family permit the burial of her remains on their land, that "even this Weak and Hopeless Relic of a Great Race can give something back to the Land which nurtured her."

Sassinak looked at Currald, who at the moment looked the very personification of heavyworlder brutality. She had the distinct feeling that he'd like to pound Seles into mush. She herself had the same desires toward Seles' family. Perhaps the girl wasn't too bright, but she could have done well if they hadn't convinced her that she was a hopeless blot on the family name. She picked up the paper, refolded it, and laid it in the folder that held the notes of the investigation. Then she looked back at Seles. Could anything good come out of this? Well, she could try.

Briskly, holding Seles' gaze with hers, she said, "You're quite right, that a captain operating in a state of emergency has the right to execute any person on board who is deemed to represent a threat to the security of the vessel. Yes, I could kill you, here and now, with no further discussion. But I'm not going to." Seles' mouth fell open, and her hands shook even more. Currald's face had hardened into disgust. "You don't deserve a quick death and this—" she slapped the folder, "sort of thing, these *spurious* heroics. The Fleet's spent a lot of money training you—considerably more than your family did treating you and shipping you around and yelling at you. You owe us that, and you owe your shipmates an apology for damn near killing them. Including Major Currald."

"I—I didn't *know* it would hurt heavyworlders—" pleaded Seles.

"Be quiet." Currald's tone shut her mouth with a snap; Sassinak hoped he'd never speak to *her* like that, although she was sure she could survive it. "You didn't think to try it on yourself, did you?"

"But I'm not pure—"

"Nor holy," said Sass, breaking into that before Currald went too far. "That's the point, Seles. You had a bad childhood: so did lots of us. People were mean to you: same with lots of us. That's no reason to go around poisoning people who haven't done you any harm. If you really want to poison someone, why not your family? They're the ones who hurt you."

"But I'm—but they're—"

"Your birth family, yes. And Fleet has tried to be—and could have been—your *life* family. Now you've done something we can't ignore; you've *killed* someone, Seles, and not bravely, in a fight, but sneakily. Court martial, when we get back, maybe psychiatric evaluation—"

"I'm not crazy!"

"No? You try to please those who hurt you, and poison those who befriend you; that sounds crazy to me. And you *are* guilty, but if I punish you then other heavyworlders may think I did so because of your genes, not your deeds."

"Heavyworlders should get out of FSP, and take care of themselves," muttered Seles stubbornly. "It never helped *us.*"

Sassinak looked at Currald, whose mask of contempt and disgust had softened a little. She nodded slightly. "I think, Major Currald, that we have a combined medical and legal problem here. Under the circumstances, we don't have the best situation for psychiatric intervention . . . and I don't want to convene a court on this young lady until there's been a full evaluation."

"You think it's enough for—"

"For mitigation, and perhaps for a full plea of incompetence. But that's outside my sphere; my concern now is to minimize the damage she's done, in all areas, and preserve the evidence."

Seles looked back and forth between them, clearly puzzled and frightened. "But I—I demand—!"

Sassinak shook her head. "Seles, if a court martial later calls for your execution, I will see that your statement is returned to your family. But at the moment, I see no alternative to protective confinement." She opened a channel to Sickbay, and spoke briefly to the Medical Officer. "Major Currald, I can have Security take her down, or—"

"I'll do it," he said. Sassinak could sense that pity had finally replaced disgust.

"Thank you. I think she'll be calmer with you." For several reasons, Sassinak thought to herself. Currald had the size and confident bearing of a full-adapted heavyworlder, trained for battle . . . Seles would not be likely to try escape, and under his gaze would be unwilling to have hysterics.

Less than an hour later, the Medical Officer called back, to report that he considered Seles at serious risk of suicide or other violent action. "She's hanging on by a thread," she said. "That note—that's the sort of thing the Gelway terrorists used. She could go any minute, and locked in the brig she'd be likely to do it sooner rather than later. I want to put her under, medical necessity."

"Fine with me. Send it up for my seal, when you've done the paperwork, and let's be very careful that nothing happens to *that* coldsleep tank. I don't want any suspicions whatever about our proceedings."

Now that was settled. Sassinak leaned back in her seat, wondering why she felt such sympathy for this girl. She'd never liked whiners herself, the girl had killed one of her crew—but the bewildered pain in those eyes, the shaky alliance of courage and stark fear—that got to her. Currald said much the same thing, when he got back up to Main Deck.

"I'm an Inclusionist," he said, "but I've always believed we should test our youngsters on high-g worlds. We've got something worth preserving, something *extra*, not just something missing. I've even supported those who want to withhold special treatment from newborn throwbacks. There's enough lightweights in the universe, I've said, breeding fast enough: why spend money and time raising another weakling? At first glance, this kid is just the point of my argument. Her family spent all that money and worry and time, FSP spent all that money on her boarding school, Fleet spent money and time on her in training, and all they got out of it was an incompetent, fairly stupid poisoner. But—I don't know—I want to stomp her into the ground, and at the same time I'm sorry for her. She's not good for anything, but she *could* have been." He gave Sassinak another, far more human, glance. "I hate to admit it, but the very things I believe in probably turned her into that wet mess."

"I hope something can be salvaged." Sassinak pushed a filled mug across her desk, and he took it. "But what I told her is perfectly true: many of us have had difficult childhoods, many of us have been hurt one way or another. I expect you've faced prejudice on account of your background—" He nodded, and she went on. "—But you didn't decide to poison the innocent to get back at those who hurt you." Sassinak took a long swallow from her own mug—not coffee, but broth. "Thing is, humans of all sorts are under pressure. There've been questions asked in Council about the supposed human domination of Fleet."

"What!" Clearly he hadn't heard that before.

"It's not general knowledge, but a couple of races are pushing for mandatory quotas at the Academy. Even the Ryxi—"

"Those featherdusters!"

"I know. But you're Fleet, Currald: you know humans need to stick together. Heavyworlders have a useful adaptation, but they couldn't take on the rest of FSP alone." He nodded, somber again. Sassinak wondered what went on behind those opaque brown eyes. Yet he was trustworthy: had to be, after the past week. Anything less, and they'd not have survived.

Her next visitor was Hollister, with a report on the extended repairs and probable performance limits of the ship until it went in for refitting. Even though the portside pods had not been as badly damaged as they'd originally thought, he insisted that the ship would not stand another long FTL chase. "One hop, two—a clear course into Sector—that we can manage. But the kind of maneuvering that the Ssli has to call for in a chase, no. You've no idea what load that puts on the pods—"

Sassinak scowled. "That means we can't find out where they go when they leave?"

"Right. We'd be as likely to end up here as there, and most likely to be spread in between. I'd have to log a protest."

"Which would hardly be read if we did splatter. No, never mind. I won't do that. But there must be something more than sitting here. If only we could tag their ships, somehow..."

"Well, now, that's another story." He'd been prepared to argue harder, Sassinak realized, as he sat back, brow furrowed. "Let's see...you're assuming that someone'll come along to evacuate, and you'd like to know where it goes, and we can't follow, so..." His voice trailed off; Sassinak waited a moment, but he said nothing. Finally he shook himself, and handed her another data cube. "I'll think about it, but in the meantime, we've got another problem. Remember the trouble we were having with the scrubbers in Environmental?"

"Yes." Sassinak inserted the cube, wondering why he'd brought a hardcopy up here instead of just switching an output to her terminal. Then she focussed on the display and bit back an oath. When she glanced at him, he nodded.

"It's worse." It was much worse. Day by day, the recycling efficiency had dropped, and the contaminant fraction had risen. Figures that she'd skimmed over earlier came back to her now: reaction equilibrium constants, rates of algal growth. "One thing that went wrong," Hollister went on, pointing to the supporting data, "is that somehow an overflow valve stuck, and we backflushed from the 'ponics into the supply lines. We've got green crud growing all along here—" He pointed to the schematic. "Cleaned it out of the crosslines by yesterday, but that's nutrient-rich flow, and the stuff loves it. We can't kill it off without killing off the main 'ponics tanks, and that would mean going on backup oxygen, and we lost twenty percent of our backup oxygen in the row with that ship."

Sassinak winced. She'd forgotten about the oxygen spares damaged or blown in that fight.

"Ordinarily," Hollister went on, "it'd help that we have a smaller crew, with the prize crew gone. But because we weren't sure of the biosystems on that transport, I'm short of biosystems crew. Very short. What we need to do is flush the whole system, and replant—but it'd be a lot safer to do that somewhere we could get aired up. In the meantime, we're going to be working twice as hard to get somewhat less output, and that's if nothing else goes wrong."

"Could it be sabotage?" asked Sass.

Hollister shrugged. "Could be. Of course it could be. But it could just as easily be ordinary glitches."

Chapter Thirteen

Day by day the biosystems monitors showed continued system failure. Sassinak forced herself to outward calmness, though she raged inwardly: to be so close, to have found a slaver base, and perhaps a line to its supporters, and then—not to be able to pursue. Hollister's daily reports reinforced the data on her screens: they had no reserves for pursuit, and they could not hold station much longer.

She hung on, nonetheless, hoping for another few ships to show up, anything to give her something to show for this expedition. Or, if Huron's relief expedition arrived, they could take over surveillance. She spent some time each day digging through the personnel files, checking every person who should have been in the quadrant from which the missile came, and who might have had access to a signalling device. There were forty or fifty of them, and she worked her way from Aariefa to Kelly, hoping to be interrupted by insystem traffic. Finally a single ship appeared at the edge of her scanning range, just entering the system. Its IFF signal appeared to be undamaged, giving its mass/volume characteristics straightforwardly.

"Hmm." Sassinak frowned over the display. "If that's right, it should have the new beacon system installed."

"Can we trip it?"

"We can try." The new system functioned as planned, revealing that the ship in question had come from Courcy-DeLan: before that it had hauled "mixed liquids" on the Valri-Palin-Terehalt circuit for eighteen months. "Mixed liquids" came in ten-liter carboys, whatever that meant. Fuels? Drugs? Chemicals for some kind of synthetic process? It could be anything from concentrated acids to vitamin supplements for the slaves' diet. Not that it was important right then, but Sassinak wished she could get a look at the ship's manifest.

Two more transports entered the system, and cautiously made their way down to the planet surface. The *Zaid-Dayan*'s sensitive detectors were able to pinpoint the ships' locations on the surface, confirming that they had both settled onto the original contact site. Then a huge ship appeared, this one clearly unable to land on-planet. A Hall-Kir hull, designed for orbital station docking, settled into a low orbit. Now Sassinak was sure they were going to evacuate the base. A Hall-Kir could handle an enormous load of machinery and equipment. But the ship was at least twelve years old, and lacked the new beacon; nor could Sassinak figure out a way to tag it for future surveillance. Its IFF revealed only that it was leased from General Systems Freight Lines, a firm that had nothing on its records. Since the IFF reported only serial owners, Sassinak could not tell who had it under lease, or if it had been leased to doubtful clients before.

"Fleet signal!" Sassinak woke from her restless doze at the squawk in her ear, and thumbed down the intercom volume control.

"What is it?"

"Fleet signal—inbound light attack group, Commodore Verstan commanding. It's on a tight beam, coded—but they're sure to have noticed—"

"I'm on my way." Sassinak shook her head, wondering if the slight headache was an artifact of worry, or really a problem with the air quality. Into the shower, fresh uniform, then onto the bridge, where alertness replaced the slightly jaded look of the past few days.

"It was aimed for this planet's local system," said the Com officer. "They must know we're—"

Sassinak shook her head. "They're hoping—they don't know for sure."

"Well, aren't you going to send a return signal?"

"What's our window?"

"Oh. That's right." Shoulders sagged. "We just barely picked it up, and now that miserable planet's in the way."

"And their moon station should have intercepted it, right?"

"Yes, but—"

"So we lie low a little longer," said Sass. "Give me a plot to the nearest Fleet position, and your best guess at its course."

That came up in light blue on the system graphics. Sassinak tried to think what she'd heard about Commodore Verstan. Would he ease cautiously into the system on the slower but very accurate insystem drives, or would he take FTL chunks across, as she had? How many were in his battle group—would he send a scoutship or escort vessel ahead? Surely Huron would have warned him about the falsified IFF signals, and he'd be ready for trouble ... but some flag officers tended to downplay the warnings of juniors.

She called Hollister up to the bridge, to ask about their capabilities. It would be lovely if they could spring a trap on the pirates—although how to arrange that without revealing their existence was a bit tricky.

Far sooner than she expected, they intercepted another Fleet signal—evidently the Commodore *had* elected to come in fast, leapfrogging his smaller vessels ahead of the cruisers. The *Scratch*, an escort-class ship, was now sunward of them, scanning the entire "back" side of the planet system for any activity. Sassinak put a single coded message burst onto the tightest focus she could manage, and then waited. With any luck, the pirates wouldn't have anything around to notice that transmission.

Within seconds, she had a reply, and then a relayed link to Commodore Verstan. He wanted a rendezvous, and insisted that she move the *Zaid-Dayan* from its hidden location. Her suggestion that they arrange a trap, in which her concealed ship could suddenly intercept ships fleeing from his more obvious attack force was denied.

There was nothing to do but comply. The outside crew retrieved the sensors and nets it had deployed on nearby chunks of rock, and when they were all back inside, Hollister gave the various drive components a last check. Then they waited over two hours, to clear the pirate surveillance.

"I may have to give up a good observation post," said Sass, "but I'm not about to jump out in front of them and say 'Boo.' We might be able to sneak away without their knowing we existed."

Carefully, delicately, the pilots extricated the *Zaid-Dayan* from the rocky cleft in which it had been hidden, and boosted away from the moonlet. Once free of it, Sassinak took a deep breath. Although it had given them safety at a critical time, a moon's surface was not her ship's natural home, and she felt irrationally safer in free flight. Besides, they could now "see" all around them, no longer confined to the narrowed angle of vision imposed by the moon and its rugged surface.

As the ship came up to speed, all systems functioned perfectly— no red lights flared on the bridge to warn of imminent disaster. If she had not known about the damaged pods, and the patched hole in the port side docking bay, Sassinak would have thought the ship in perfect condition.

Navigating through the planet's cluttered space required all her concentration for the next few hours. By the time they were outside all the satellites and rings, the Fleet attack force was only a couple of light minutes away. She elected not to hop it, but continued on the insystem main drives, spending the hours of approach to ensure that her ship and its crew were ready for inspection. A couple of minutes with the personnel files had reminded her that Commodore Verstan had a reputation for being finicky. She had a feeling he would have plenty to say about the appearance of her ship.

Meanwhile, she noted that his approach to the pirate base followed precisely the recommendations of the Rules of Engagement. Two escort-class vessels, *Scratch* and *Darkwatch*, were positioned sunward of the planet, no doubt "to catch strays." The command cruiser, *Seb Harr*, and the two light cruisers formed a wedge; three patrol craft were positioned one on either flank and one trailing. They held these positions as the *Zaid-Dayan* approached, rather than closing with the planet system.

Sassinak brought the *Zaid-Dayan* neatly into place behind the *Seb Harr*, and opened the tightly shielded link to Commodore Verstan. He looked just like his holo in the Flag Officer Directory, a lean, pink-faced man with thick gray hair and bright blue eyes. Behind him, she could see Huron watching the screen anxiously.

"Commander Sassinak," said Verstan, formally. "We received signals from a Fleet distress beacon."

Sassinak's heart sank. If he was going to take *that* approach...

"But I see that was some kind of... misunderstanding." She started to speak but he was going on without waiting. "Lieutenant Commander Huron had suggested the possibility that the apparent explosion of your ship was *staged* somehow, though I believe... uh... tradition favors disabling the beacon if this is done..."

"Sir, in this instance the beacon's signal was necessary to fool the pirates—"

"Ah, yes. The pirates. And how many armed ships were you facing, Commander?"

Sassinak gritted her teeth. There would be a court of inquiry; there was always a court of inquiry in circumstances like these, and *that* was the place for these questions.

"The first armed ship," she said, "was escorting the slaver transport. We did not know at that time if the slaver were armed—"

"But it wasn't. You had the IFF signal—"

"We knew the IFF of the escort had been falsified, and weren't sure of the transport. Some of them are: you will recall the *Cles Prel* loss, when a supposedly unarmed transport blew a light cruiser away—" That was a low blow, she knew: the captain of the *Cles Prel* had been Verstan's classmate at the Academy. His face stiffened, then she saw dawning respect in his eyes: he was a stickler for protocol, but he liked people with gumption.

"You said 'the first armed ship,'" he went on. "Was there another?"

Sassinak explained about the well-defended base, and the ships that had boosted off to join the battle. She knew Huron would have told him about the weaponry on the first ship—if he'd listened. Then, before he could ask details of the battle, she told him about the traffic in the system since.

"They've had three Gourney-class transports land in the past few days, and there's a Hall-Kir in low orbit. One of the Gourney-class is definitely from a heavyworlder system, and it's made unclassified trips before. I think they're planning to evacuate the base; we monitored considerable shuttle activity up to the orbital ship."

"Any idea how big the base is?"

"Not really. We were on the back side of that moonlet, with only a small sensor net deployed for line of sight to the planet. The thermal profile is consistent with anything from one thousand to fifteen thousand, depending on associated activities. If we knew for sure what they were doing, we could come closer to a figure. I can dump the data for you—"

"Please do."

Sassinak matched channels, and sent the data. "If their turnaround is typical, Commodore, they could be loaded and ready to lift in another couple of days."

"I see. Do you think they'll do it with our force here?"

"Probably—they won't gain anything by waiting for you to put them under siege. Oh—that outer moon—did Huron tell you about their detection profile?"

"Yes. I know they know we've entered the system—we also stripped their outer warning beacon. But that's exactly what I'm hoping for. Three medium transports, one Hall-Kir hull...we should be able to trail several of them, if we can tag them. If we wait another week, we may have more in the net when we attack. How about you?"

She wanted to join the hunt more than anything in years, but Hollister was shaking his head at her. "Sir, my environmental system is overloaded, and my portside pods sustained considerable damage... the engineers tell me we can't do another long chase."

"Humph. Can you give us a visual? Maybe we have something you can use for repairs?"

Apparently one of the other cruisers had a visual on them, for before Sassinak could reply, she saw a picture come up on the screen behind Commodore Verstan. One of his bridge officers pointed it out to him, and he turned—then swung back to face Sassinak with a startled expression.

"What the devil happened to you? It looks like your portside loading bay—"

"Was breached. Yes, but it's tight now. Looks pretty bad, I know—"

"And you're short at least two portside pods...you're either lucky or crazy, Commander, and I'm not sure which."

"Lucky, I hope," said Sassinak, not displeased with his reaction. "By the way, is Lieutenant Commander Huron attached to your command, now, or are you bringing him back to me?"

Verstan smiled, and waved Huron forward. "We weren't sure

you were here, after all—but if you're in need I'm sure he'll be willing to transfer over."

Huron had aged in those few weeks, a stern expression replacing the amiable (but competent) one he had usually worn. Sassinak wondered if he felt the same about her—would he even want to come back? She shook herself mentally—he was telling her about his trip with the slaver transport, the horrible conditions they'd found, the impossibility of comforting all those helpless children, orphaned and torn from their homes. Her eyes filled with tears, as much anger and frustration at not having been able to stop it as grief from her own past. His ship had been short of rations—since it had been inbound, at the end of a planned voyage—and to the other miseries of the passengers hunger and thirst had been added. Now he wanted to be in the assault team; as he had no regular assignment on the flagship, he had requested permission to land with the marines.

"I'll come back, of course, if you need me," he said, not quite meeting her eyes. Sassinak sighed. Clearly his experience haunted him; he would not be content until he'd had slavers in his gunsight...or gotten himself killed, she thought irritably. He wasn't a marine; he wasn't trained in ground assault; he ought to have more sense. In the long run he'd be better off if she ordered him back to the *Zaid-Dayan*, and kept him safe.

"Huron—" She stopped when he looked straight at her. Captain to captain, that gaze went—he was no longer the compliant lover, the competent executive officer whose loyalty was first to her. She could order him back, and he would come—but without the self-respect, the pride, that she had learned to love. She could order him to her bed, no doubt, and he would come—but it would not be the Huron she wanted. He would have to fight his own battles awhile first, and later—if they had a later—they could discover each other again. She felt an almost physical pain in her chest, a wave of longing and apprehension combined. If something happened to him—if he were killed—she would have to bear the knowledge that she *could* have kept him out of it. But if she forced him to safety now, she'd have to bear the knowledge that he resented her.

"Be careful," she said at last. "And get some of the bastards for me."

His eyes brightened, and he gave her a genuine smile. "Thank you, Commander Sassinak. I'm glad you understand."

Whatever she did, the battle would be over by the time she got back to Fleet Sector Headquarters for refitting. Sassinak hoped her answering smile was as open and honest as his: she felt none of his elation.

In fact, the trip back to Sector Headquarters was one of the most depressing of her life. She, like Huron, had itched to blow away some pirates and slavers . . . and yet she'd had to run along home, like an incompetent civilian. She found herself grumbling at Hollister—and it wasn't *his* fault.

Her new executive officer seemed even less capable after that short conversation with Huron . . . she knew she criticized him too sharply, but she couldn't help it. She kept seeing Huron's face, kept imagining how it would have been to have him there. For distraction, such as it was, she kept digging at the personnel records, looking over every single one which could possibly have had access to the right area of the ship when the missile was fired. After Kelly came Kelland, and from there she plowed through another dozen, all the way to Prosser. Prosser's ID in his records had an expression she didn't like, a thin-lipped, self-righteous sort of smirk, and she found herself glaring at it. Too much of this, and she'd come to hate every member of the crew. They couldn't all be guilty. Prosser didn't look that bad in person (she made a reason to check casually); it was just the general depression she felt. And she knew she'd face a Board of Inquiry, if not a court martial, back at Sector.

Sector Headquarters meant long sessions with administrative officers who wanted to know *exactly* how each bit of damage to the ship had occurred, exactly why she'd chosen to do each thing she'd done, why she hadn't done something else instead. As the senior engineers shook their heads and tut-tutted over the damage, critiquing Hollister's emergency repairs, Sassinak found herself increasingly tart with her inquisitors. She had, after all, come back with a whole ship and relatively few casualties, *and* rescued a shipload of youngsters, when she might have been blown into fragments if she'd followed a rigid interpretation of the Rules of Engagement. But the desk-bound investigators could not believe that a cruiser like the *Zaid-Dayan* might be out-gunned by a "tacky little pirate ship" as one of them put it. Sassinak handed over the data cubes detailing the escort's profile, and they sniffed and put them aside. Was she *sure* that the data were accurate?

Furthermore, there was the matter of practically *inviting* a hostile force to breach her ship and board. "Absolutely irresponsible!" sniffed one commander, whom Sassinak knew from the Directory hadn't been on a ship in years, and never on one in combat. "Could have been disastrous," said another. Only one of the Board, a one-legged commander who'd been marooned in coldsleep in a survival pod on his first voyage, asked the kinds of questions Sassinak herself would have asked. The chair of the Board of Inquiry, a two-star admiral, said nothing one way or the other, merely taking notes.

She came out of one session ready to feed them all to the recycling bins, and found Arly waiting for her.

"Now what?" asked Sass.

Arly took her arm. "You need a drink—I can tell. Let's go to Gino's before the evening rush."

"I feel trouble in the air," said Sass, giving her a hard look. "If you've got more bad news, just tell me."

"Not here—those paperhangers don't deserve to hear things first. Come on."

Sassinak followed her, frowning. Arly was rarely pushy, and as far as Sassinak knew avoided dockside bars. Whatever had come unstuck had bothered her, too.

Gino's was the favorite casual place for senior ship officers that season. For a moment, Sassinak considered the change in her taste in bar decor. Ensigns liked tough exotic places that let them feel adventurous and mature; Jigs and Tenants were much the same, although some of them preferred a touch of elegance, a preference that increased with rank. Until, Sassinak had discovered, the senior Lieutenant Commanders and Commanders felt secure enough in their rank to choose more casual, even shabby, places to meet. Such as Gino's, which had the worn but scrubbed look of the traditional diner. Gino's also had live, human help to bring drinks and food to the tables, and rumor suggested a live, human cook in the kitchen.

Arly led her to a corner table in the back. Sassinak settled herself with a sigh, and prodded the service pad until its light came on. After they'd ordered, she gave Arly a sidelong look.

"Well?"

"An IFTL message. For you." Arly handed her the hardcopy slip. Sassinak knew instantly, before she opened it, what it had to be. An IFTL for a captain in refitting? That could only be an official death notice, and she knew only one person who might... she unfolded the slip, and glanced at it, trying to read it without really looking at it, as if this magic might protect her from the pain. Official language left the facts bald and clear: Huron was dead, killed "in the line of duty" while assaulting the pirate base. She blinked back the tears that came to her eyes and gave Arly another look.

"You knew." It wasn't a question.

"I... guessed. An IFTL message, after all... why else?"

"Well. He's dead, I suppose you guessed that, too. Damn *fool!*" Rage and grief choked her, contending hopelessly in her heart and mind. If only he hadn't—if only she had—if only some miserable pirate had had a shaky hand...

"I'm sorry, Sass. Commander." Arly stumbled over her name, uncertain. Sassinak dragged herself back to the present.

"He was... a good man." It was not enough; it was the worst trite stupid remark, but it was also true. He had been a good man, and being a good man had gotten himself killed, probably unnecessarily, probably very bravely, and she would never see him again. Never *feel* him again. Sassinak shivered, swallowed, and reached for the drink that had just been delivered. She sipped, swallowed, sipped again. "He wanted to go," she said, as much to herself as to Arly.

"He was headed for that before you ever got the *Zaid-Dayan*," said Arly, surprisingly. Sassinak stared at her, surprised to be surprised. Arly gulped half her own drink and went on. "I know you... he... you two were close, Commander, and that's fine, but you never did know him before. I served with him six years, and he was good... you're right. He was also wild—a lot wilder before you came aboard, but still wild."

"Huron?" It was all she could think of to say, to keep Arly talking so that she could slowly come to grips with her own feelings.

Arly nodded. "It's not in his record, because he was careful, too, in his own way, but he used to get in fights—people would say things, you know, about colonials, and he'd react. Political stuff, a lot of it. He wouldn't ever have gotten his own ship—he told me that, one time, when he'd been in a row. He'd said too many things about the big families, in the wrong places, for someone with no more backing than he had."

"But he was a good exec..." She had trouble thinking of Huron as a hothead causing trouble.

"Oh, he was. He liked you, too, and that helped, although he was pretty upset when you didn't go in and fight for that colony."

"Yeah...he was." Sassinak let herself remember their painful arguments, his chilly withdrawal.

"I—I thought you ought to know," said Arly, tracing some design with her finger on the tabletop. "He really did like you, and he'd have wanted you to know...it's nothing you did, to make him insist on going in. He'd have managed, some way, to get into more and more rows until he died. No captain could have been bold enough for him."

Despite Arly's well-meant talk, Sassinak found that her grief lasted longer than anyone would approve. She had lost other lovers, casual relationships that had blossomed and withered leaving only a faint perfume...and when the lover disappeared, or died, a year or so later, she had felt grief...but not like this grief. She could not shake it off; she could not just go on as if Huron had been another casual affair.

She was not even sure why Huron had meant so much. He had been no more handsome or skilled in love, no more intelligent or sensitive than many men she'd shared her time with. When more details of the raid came in, she found that Arly's guess had been right: Huron had insisted on joining the landing party, had thrown himself into danger in blatant disregard of basic precautions, and been blown away, instantly and messily, in the assault on the pirate's headquarters complex. Sassinak overheard what her own crew were too thoughtful to tell her: the troops he'd gone in with considered him half-crazy or a gloryhound, they weren't sure which. But the more official reports were that he'd distinguished himself with "extreme bravery" and his posthumous rating was "outstanding." Still, this evidence of his instability didn't make her feel any better. She *should* have been able to influence him, in their months together, should have seen something like this coming and headed it off—it was such a waste of talent. She argued with herself, in the long nights, and carefully did not take a consoling drink.

Meanwhile the ship's repairs neared completion. The environmental system had had to be completely dismantled and refitted, filling the two lower decks with a terrible stench for several days. Apparently the sulfur bacteria had overgrown the backflow sludge, and coupled with the fungal contamination from the downstream scrubbers created a disgusting mix of smells. Worse than that, the insides of the main lines had become slightly pitted, providing a vast surface for the contaminants to grow on. So every meter of piping had to be replaced, as well as all valves, pumps, scrubbers, and filters.

Hollister still could not tell whether the problems were inherent in the new layout, or had resulted from deliberate sabotage. Attempts to model the failures on computer, and backtrack to a cause, led to six or seven different possible routes to trouble. Two of them would have involved a single component failure very early in the voyage—highly unlikely to be tampering, in Hollister's opinion. The others required multiple failures, and one clearly favored sabotage, with eight or ten minor misadjustments in remote compartments. But which of these was the *real* sequence of events, no one could now determine. In trying to correct the problems once they developed, Hollister and his most trusted technicians had handled virtually every exposed millimeter of the system.

Sassinak grimaced at Hollister's presentation. "So you can't tell me anything solid?"

"No, captain. I think myself sabotage was involved—things could have gone a lot worse, as the simulations show, and someone wanted to save his or her own life—but I can't prove it. Worse than that, I can't prevent it happening next time, either. If I request entirely new personnel, who's to say *they're* all loyal? And it needn't be an engineering specialist, although that's a good guess. Everyone knows some of the basics of environmental systems: they have to, in case of disaster. An agent could have been provided specialist knowledge, if it comes to that—Fleet's environmental systems use the same standard components as everyone else's."

"What about the other repairs?" Hollister nodded, and brought her up to date on those. The structural damage had required more dismantling of the portside than Sassinak expected; Hollister explained that was nearly always true. But repairs on that were complete, and on the portside pods as well. To his personal satisfaction, mounting the newest issue of pods there meant replacing half the starboard pods to match them...he had been worried, he confided, that their prolonged FTL flight on unbalanced pods, with the starboard pods taking the strain, might have caused hidden damage in them. None of the stealth gear had taken damage, and all the computer sections out of service had been replaced. It was just the environmental systems holding them up, and he calculated it would be another two weeks before it was done.

Sassinak began to wonder if the *Zaid-Dayan* would still be in refitting when Verstan's battle group returned with Huron's body. By now everyone had seen reports of the successful assault on the pirate base, holos of shattered domes and blasted prefab buildings. Sassinak stared at them, wondering if the base where she'd lived for her years as a slave had looked anything like this. At least her action had saved those children from being imprisoned in those domes. She visited the hospital once or twice, chatting with youngsters who were now orphans, as she had been. They were less damaged psychologically, if "less" meant anything. Looking at some of them, mute anguished survivors of inexplicable disaster, she almost cursed herself for not intervening before the colony was raided. But some had already bounced back, and some had relatives already coming to take them into known families.

The Board of Inquiry wound down, and turned in a preliminary report—subject to further analysis, the chair explained to her. She was commended for saving the children from the colony, and mildly scolded for not having saved the colony itself—although a dissenting comment argued that any such attempt would have been an unnecessary and reckless risk to her ship. She was commended for the outcome of the battle, but not for the methods she'd chosen. Entirely too risky, and not a good example for other commanders— but effective, and perhaps justified by circumstances. The structural damage to the *Zaid-Dayan* certainly resulted from her decision to allow the enemy too close, but the environmental system damage might well have been sabotage, or simply bad engineering in the first place. They approved of her handling of the suspected poisoner: "a deft manipulation of a politically explosive situation." Sassinak thought of the girl, now in the hands of the psychiatric ward of the

Sector military hospital—could she ever be rehabilitated? Could she ever find a way to respect herself? Fleet wouldn't take another chance on her, that was certain. On the whole, the Board chair said, recapturing her full attention, they found that she had acted in the best interests of the service, although they could not give an unqualified approval.

Under the circumstances, that was the best she could hope for. Admiral Vannoy, Sector Commandant, would make his own decision about how this Board report would affect her future. She had worked with him several years before, and expected better from him than from the Board. He liked officers with initiative and boldness. Sure enough, when he called her in, he waved the report at her, then slapped it on his desk.

"The vultures gathered, eh?"

Sassinak cocked her head a little. "I think they were fair," she said.

"Within their limits, I hear under your words. So they were— some Boards would have landed on you a lot harder for coming in with damage like that. And for having a Fleet distress beacon telling the universe that a Fleet cruiser had bumped its nose on something painful. Bad for our reputation. But I'm satisfied: you got back a load of kids—frightened out of their wits, some of them hurt, but still alive and free. And you defeated one of their little surprise packages—which, by the way, have caused more than one cruiser to come to grief. You're the first survivor to come out with a good profile of them and the specifics of their faked IFF signals: that's worth all the rest, to my mind. And then you managed to stick tight, undiscovered, and pick up quite a bit of useful information. Now we know how well the stealth technologies work in real life. All in all, I'm pleased, Commander, as you probably expected. After all—you know my prejudices. We're going to put you back out on the same kind of patrol, in another part of the sector, and hope you catch another odd fish."

"Sir, there is one thing—"

"Yes?"

"I'd like to have more options free in case of another encounter."

"Such as?"

"Last time my orders specified that surveillance was my primary mission—and on that basis, I did nothing when the colony was attacked. My crew and I both had problems with that . . . and I'd like to be free to act if we should face another such situation."

The admiral's eyes fell. "Commander, you have an excellent record, but isn't it possible that in this case your own experience is affecting your judgment? We've tried direct, immediate confrontation before, and repeatedly the perpetrators, or some of them, have been able to escape, and strike again. Tracking them to their source must be more important—"

"In the long term, yes, sir. But for the people who die, who are orphaned or enslaved—have you been to the hospital, sir, and talked to any of the kids Huron brought in?"

"Well, no . . . no, I haven't."

"All they want to know is why Fleet couldn't prevent the attack—why their parents died—and what's going to happen to them now. And it's not just my own feeling, sir. Lieutenant Commander Huron, my exec, was very upset about my decision not to intervene—and, as you know, he insisted on joining the attack force, and then the landing party, and he died. Other officers and crew have expressed the same feelings—"

"Openly? To you?" Sassinak could tell he did not entirely approve of such openness.

She nodded. "Some of them. Others in conversations I overheard. They don't like to think of themselves—of Fleet—as standing by idly, in safety, while helpless civilians get killed and captured."

"I see. Hmm. I still feel, Commander, that surveillance must be your primary mission, but under the circumstances . . . and considering your crew's most recent experience . . . yes, if you find it absolutely necessary to engage a hostile force, to save innocent lives . . . yes. And I'll amend your orders to make that discretion explicit." He looked closely at her. "But I'm not going to take kindly to any shoot-'em-up action you get into that's not absolutely necessary, is that clear? You've damn near bankrupted our sector repair budget for the next eighteen standard months, with that bucket of bent bolts you brought into the yard, so take better care of it. And call for help if you need it—don't wait until you're shot to pieces."

"Yes, sir!" She left his office with a lighter heart. No, she would not get into an unnecessary fight—but she wouldn't have to go through the misery of standing by while others suffered, either.

In the meantime, she would be busy checking in additional crew. Some were those who had been assigned to the prize vessel, but had not gone back out with the battle group. Others were newly assigned to replace casualties or transfers out.

BOOK FOUR

Chapter Fourteen

"Commander Sassinak . . ." The voice was vaguely familiar; Sassinak pulled her attention out of an engineering report and glanced up. Incredulous joy engulfed her.

"Ford!" She could hardly believe it, and then wondered why she hadn't already known. Surely the name would have been on the roster of incoming officers—

"Lieutenant Commander Hakrar broke a leg and two ribs in a waterboat race . . . and they offered it to me, so—" His broad grin was the same as ever, but now he subdued it. "Lieutenant Commander Fordeliton reporting for duty, captain." He held out his order chip, and she took it, feeding it into the reader. Her side screen came up with a list.

"There're just a few chores waiting for you, as you can see—"

"Mmm. Maybe I should have stopped for a drink before I reported aboard." He leaned over to take a look at the screen, and feigned shock. "Good grief, Commander, hasn't anyone done any work on this ship since you docked?"

Sassinak found herself grinning. "Did you see the holos of the damage we came in with?"

"No—but I heard rumors of a Board of Inquiry. Bad fight?"

"Fairly stiff. I'll tell you later. For now—" She looked him up and down. The same dark bronze face, the same lean body that could slouch carelessly in a dockside bar or dance elegantly at a diplomatic reception, the same tone of voice, wordlessly offering support without challenge. If she had had her pick of all the possible executive officers, he would have been the one. And yet—she wasn't ready for anything more, not yet. Would he understand? "Just get yourself settled, and we'll have a briefing at 1500. Need any help?"

"No, Commander, thank you. I met your Weapons Officer on the way to the dock, and she's helped me find my way around."

Sassinak leaned back, after he'd gone, and let herself remember that crazy trip as prize crew on a captured illicit trader, something more than ten years before. She'd been exec on a patrol-class vessel, *Lily of Serai*, and they'd caught a trader carrying illegal and unmarked cargo. So her captain had put her and five others aboard, as a prize crew to bring the trader to Sector HQ; she'd had command, and Fordeliton, then a Jig, had been her exec. She'd hardly known him before, but it was the kind of trip that made solid relationships. For the trader crew had tried to take the ship back, and they'd killed two of the marines—and almost killed Ford, but she had led the other two in a desperate hand-to-hand fight through the main deck corridors. If Huron had seen *that*, she told herself, he'd never have doubted her will to fight. In the end they'd won—though they'd had to space most of the trader's original crew—and she had brought the ship in whole. When Ford recovered from his injuries, they'd become lovers—and in the years since, whenever they chanced to meet, they had enjoyed each other's company. Nothing intense, nothing painful—but she could count on his quiet, generous support.

Another incoming officer brought her much less content. Fleet Security, apparently impressed by her conviction that she had yet another agent on board, decided to assign a Security officer to the ship. Sassinak frowned over his dossier: a Lieutenant Commander (in Security, a very high rank) from Bretagne. All she'd wanted was a deeper scrutiny of her personnel records, and instead she got this . . . she looked at his holo. Slim, dark hair and eyes, somehow conveying even in that official pose a certain dapper quality.

In person, when he reported for duty, he lived up to his holo: suave, courteous, almost elegant. His voice had the little lilt she remembered from Bretagne natives, and he used it to compliment her on her ship, her office decor, her reputation. Sassinak considered biting his head off, but it was never wise to alienate Security. She gave him courtesy for courtesy, alluding to her first ship service under a Bretagnan captain, and he became even sleeker, if possible. When he'd gone to his quarters, Sassinak took a long breath and blew it out.

Security! Why couldn't they do the job right in the first place, and prevent hostiles from getting into Fleet, instead of sending people like this to harass honest officers and interfere with their work?

But Dupaynil turned out better than his first impression. He got along well with the other officers, and had a strong technical background that made him useful in both Engineering and Weaponry. His witty conversation, which skirted but never quite slid into malicious gossip about the prominent and wealthy among whom he'd worked, livened their meals. And he was more than a quick wit, Sassinak found out, when they discussed the matter of planet piracy and slave trading.

"You haven't been at Headquarters for several years," he said. "I'm sure you remember that speculation about certain families had begun even ten years ago..."

"Yes, of course."

"Our problem has been not in finding out who, but in proving how—with persons of such rank, we cannot simply accuse them of complicity. And they've been very, very clever in covering their tracks, and making their accounts clean for inspection. That ship you captured, for instance—"

"I was thinking Paraden," said Sass.

"Precisely. But you noted, I'm sure, that although there were apparent links to Paraden family enterprises, there was no direct, traceable proof..."

"No. I'd hoped the traces on those transports coming into the pirate base would be helpful."

"Oh, they were. Commodore Verstan forwarded all available data—and we're now sure of some kind of complicity between the Paradens and at least one group of political activists from Diplo."

"That's what I don't understand," said Sass. "The Paradens I've met were all prejudiced against any of the human variants—I'd think they'd be the last people to consort with heavyworlders."

"The Paraden family stronghold maintains a body of heavyworlder troops. That's not widely known, but we have—had, I should say—an agent that had infiltrated them just so far. It would be within their philosophy to use the heavyworlders that way—and to gain exclusive access to chosen worlds."

"That young woman who went crazy and tried to poison us all

was born on Diplo. But I thought she was too irrational to be anyone's agent—"

"You're undoubtedly right. No, if you have a saboteur on your ship, Commander, it's someone more subtle than that. And quite possibly not a heavyworlder. There's a growing sentiment that Fleet demands too much and delivers too little protection . . . that it's used to keep colony planets subdued, or to prevent the opening of suitable worlds for colonies. Exploration has shifted a lot of blame to Fleet, over the past decade or so—and that concerns us, too. Why are we blamed when Exploration chooses to classify a world as unsuited for colonization? Why is Fleet responsible when the alien vote in the FSP puts a system off-limits for humans? Because we enforce the edicts, apparently . . . but who is emphasizing that, and why?"

"And you have no idea if any of this crew is such an agent?"

Dupaynil shook his head. "No—the records all seem clear, and that's what you'd expect from a professional. They're not going to do anything stupid, like use a fake name or background. We can check too easily on that sort of thing these days—the Genetic Index gives us the references for each planet-of-origin. If I said I was from Grantly-IV, for instance, you could look it up in the Index and find out that I should be blue-eyed and a foot taller."

"But surely most planets have a variety of genomes—"

"A variety, yes, but not the entire range of human possibilities. Much of the time it doesn't tell us precisely where someone is from—although with tissue samples for analysis it does much better—but it certainly tells *me* what questions to ask, and what to look for. Anyone from Bretagne, my home world, has experienced double moonlight, and knows about the Imperial Rose Gardens. You're from Myriad—you lived in its one city—and so I know you experienced a seacoast with mountains inland, and you must have seen at least one gorbnari."

Sassinak had an instant memory of the gorbnari, the wide-winged flyers of Myriad, who preyed on its native sealife. Not birds, not fishes—exactly—but gorbnari swooping down for krissi.

"So if I asked you," Dupaynil went on, "whether gorbnari were gray or brown, you'd know—"

"That they were pale yellow on top and white underneath, with a red crest on the males . . . I see what you mean."

"Since the Myriad colony was wiped out, and not replanted, the references to native wildlife are pretty vague. In fact, the only comment on gorbnari gives their color as 'mid-to-light brown, lighter below' because it's taken from the first scoutship report—and that ship sampled on the other continent, where they *are* that color."

"So you're going to mingle with the crew, and check that sort of thing, stuff that doesn't come up in the records at all?"

"Right. And of course, I'll fill you in on whatever I find."

Dupaynil was the last incoming crewman—when Sassinak thought about it, the perfect arrangement, since anyone transferring out so late would be noticed. The orders came through for them to leave, and soon they were on their way to their assigned position. Sassinak wasn't sure whether to be glad or sorry that she had no chance to attend Huron's funeral. Soon she was far too busy to brood about it.

For one thing, she had to supervise the continuing education of five newly "hatched" ensigns, fresh from the Academy, and eager to prove themselves capable young officers. Fordeliton handled their assignment slots, but she had an interview with each one, and chaired the regular evaluation sessions. It was a very mixed group. Claas, one of the largest heavyworlder women Sassinak had ever seen, came with a special recommendation from Sass's old friend Seglawin at the Academy. ("I can trust you," she'd written, "to perceive the sensitivity and generosity of this ensign—she's bright, of course, and reasonably aggressive, but still too easily hurt. Toughen her, if you can, without sending her straight into the Separationists.") Sassinak looked up—and up—at the broad face with its heavy brow and cheekbones, and mentally shook her head. If this girl was still oversensitive, after four years in the Academy, she had small chance of curing it.

Timran, stocky and just above the minimum height, had a low rank in the graduating class, and an air of suppressed glee. Clearly he was thrilled (surprised, even?) to have made it through commissioning, and equally delighted to have such a good assignment—and such a commanding officer. Sassinak was used to male appreciation, but his wide-eyed admiration almost embarrassed her. She wondered if she'd really been that callow herself. His only redeeming characteristic, according to the file, was "luck." As his pilot instructor said, "Under normal circumstances, this cadet is adequate at best, and too often careless or rash. But in emergencies, everything seems to come together, and he will do five wrong things that add up to the best combination. If he continues to show this flair in active duty, he may be worth training as a scoutship pilot, or a junior gunnery officer."

Gori, on the other hand, was a quiet, studious, almost prim young man who had ranked high in academics and sports, but only average in initiative. "The born supply officer," his report said. "Meticulous, precise, will do exactly what he is told, but does not react well in chaotic situations. He should do well in a large crew, and ultimately onstation in a noncombat capacity. Note that this is not lack of courage; he does not panic in danger—but he does not exceed his orders even when this is desirable."

Kayli and Perran were more "average," in that their abilities seemed to be all on one level. Physically they were something else. Kayli was a stunning diminutive brunette, who could have had a new partner every night if she'd wanted it. What she wanted, apparently, was Gori. Sassinak was not surprised to find that they were already engaged, and planned to marry at the end of their first cruise. What did surprise her was Kayli's continuing disinterest in the other men—very few people were exclusive in their relationships. But despite all suggestions, Kayli spent her off-duty time with Gori, much of it in the junior officers' mess with books spread all over the table. Perran, not at all as overtly attractive as Kayli, turned out to be the vamp of the group. She had an insatiable interest in electronics . . . and men. Ford's description of her stalk of the senior communications tech gave Sassinak her first relaxed laugh in weeks.

As the trip progressed, Claas seemed content enough, if quiet, and Sassinak noted that she seemed to spend some free time with Perran. It seemed like an odd combination, but Sassinak knew better than to interfere with what worked. Timran got into one scrape after another, always apologetic but undaunted as he discovered the inexorable laws of nature all over again. Sassinak wondered if he'd ever grow up—it didn't seem likely at this point. Only her experience with other such youngsters, who surprisingly grew into competent adults if given the chance and a few years, reassured her. Gori and Kayli occupied each other, and Perran, having caught her first man, soon started looking for another. Sassinak felt a twinge of sympathy for the unlucky quarry; Perran was none too gentle in her disposal of the former lover.

Dupaynil turned up evidence of several anomalies in the crew. He said quite frankly that most of them were probably innocent errors—data entered wrong in the computer, or misunderstandings of one sort or another. But sorting them out meant hours of painstaking work, correlating all the data and holding more interviews to recheck vital facts.

"I had no idea that the personnel files were this sloppy," grumbled Sass. "Surely most of these must mean *something*." They were back to Prosser, and Sassinak was careful to say nothing about her earlier reaction to his holo in the files. His eyes weren't quite as close together as she'd thought earlier. Dupaynil passed over the file with a shrug—nothing wrong with it at all.

"Have you ever really looked at your own file?" asked Dupaynil with a sly smile.

"Well, no—not carefully." She had never wanted to brood over the truncated past it would have revealed.

"Look." He called up her file onscreen, and ran it through his expanded database backups. "According to this, you had two different grades in advanced analytic geometry in prep school ... and you never turned in your final project in social history ... and you were involved in a subversive organization back on Myriad—"

"What!" Sassinak peered at it. "I wasn't in anything—"

"A club called *Ironmaids*?" Dupaynil grinned.

"Oh." She had forgotten completely about *Ironmaids*, the local Carin Coldae fan club that she and Caris had founded in their last year of elementary school. She and Caris and—who was that other girl? Glya?—had chosen the name, and written to the address on the bottom of the Carin Coldae posters. And almost a year later a packet had come for them: a club charter, replica Carin Coldae pocket lasers, and eight copies of the newest poster. Her parents wouldn't let her put it up where anyone could see it, so she'd had it on the inside of her closet door. "But it wasn't *subversive*," she said to Dupaynil. "It was just a kids' club, a fan club."

"Affiliated with the Carin Coldae cult, right?"

"Cult? We weren't a cult." Even her parents, conservative as they were, had not objected to the club . . . although they'd insisted that a life-size poster of Carin Coldae, in snug silver bodysuit with a blazing laser in each hand, was not the perfect living room decoration.

Dupaynil laughed aloud. "You see, captain, how easy it is for someone to be caught up in something without realizing it? I suppose you didn't know that Carin Coldae's vast earnings went into the foundation and maintenance of a terrorist organization?"

"They did?"

"Oh yes. All you little girls—and boys, too, I must admit—who sent in your bits of change and proofs of purchase were actually funding the Sector XI resurgents, as nasty a bunch of racist bullies as you could hope to find. The Iron Chain, they called themselves. Carin herself, I understand, found them romantic—or one of them, anyway. She was convinced they were misunderstood freedom fighters, and of course they encouraged that view. So your little Ironmaids club, in which I presume you all felt brave and grownup, was a front for terrorists . . . and you had your brush with subversive activity."

Sassinak thought back to their six months of meetings, before they got tired of the routine. The little charter and handbook, which had them elect officers and discuss "old business" and "new business" according to strict rules. The cookies they'd made and served from a Carin Coldae plate, and the fruit juice they'd drunk from special glasses. If that was subversive activity, how did anyone keep doing it without suffering terminal boredom? She remembered the day they'd disbanded—not to quit watching Carin Coldae films, of course, but because the club itself bored them stiff. They'd gone back to climbing in the nearby hills, where they could pretend that villains were hiding behind the rocks.

"I think the most subversive thing we did," she said finally, "was decide that our school principal looked exactly like the villain in *White Rims*. I still have trouble believing—"

Dupaynil shrugged. "It doesn't really matter. Security knows that nearly all the kids in those clubs were innocent. But some of them went on to another level of membership, and a few of those ended up joining the Iron Chain . . . and *those* have been a continuing problem."

"I remember...maybe a year after we quit holding meetings, we got another mailout, suggesting that we form a senior club. But we'd lost interest, and anyway that was just before the colony was taken."

"Right. Now—can you explain the two grades in analytic geometry? Or the uncompleted social history project?"

Sassinak frowned, trying to remember. "As far as I know, I always got top grades in math...what are those? Oh...sure...they were trying a pass/fail system, and gave all of us dual grades in math that semester. It's not two grades, really; it's the same grade expressed two ways. As for social history—I can't remember anything."

"You see? Three little things, and you can't clear up all of them. And yet it's not important. If we had a pattern—if you seemed to have incompletes in all your social science classes—it might matter. But this is nothing, and most of the odd things in your crew's records are nothing. Still, we must look into all of it, even so silly a thing as a child's fan club."

Among the odd bits Dupaynil turned up in the next week were a young man who'd chosen to use his matrilineal name rather than his far more prominent patrilineal title, and yet another person of heavyworlder genetic background posing as a normal human. Sassinak came in on the interviews of both of these, but neither had the unstable personality of the poisoner. The young man insisted that he'd joined Fleet to get away from his father's influence—he'd been pushed to enter the diplomatic service, but preferred to work with his hands. The heavyworlder said frankly that heavyworlders looked down on him, but that he had found acceptance and even friendships among the lightweights. "If they know I'm from a heavyworld family, they're afraid of my strength—I can tell by the way they hold back. But I can pass as a strong normal, and that suits me just fine. No, I wouldn't help heavyworlders expand their influence—why should I? They're snobs—they teased me and threw me out for being a weakling, as if they really were superior. They're not. Let 'em stay on their worlds, and let me go where I fit in."

Dupaynil, Sassinak noticed, seemed far more sympathetic to the young man escaping a pushy father than to the heavyworlder. She herself found both convincing.

They had been on-station a month when their detectors picked up a ship off the normal FTL paths. Its IFF and passive beam gave its ownership as General Freight (again! thought Sass), but from the passive beam they could strip its origin code...and that was a heavyworld system.

Once more the *Zaid-Dayan* took up the chase, guided by its Ssli perception of the quarry's disturbance of space. And once more it soon became clear that the quarry was headed for someplace unusual.

Chapter Fifteen

"And just what is *this*?" No one answered the navigation officer's murmur; Sassinak leaned over to see what identification data were coming up on the screen. Nav went on. "Mapped...hmm...on the EEC survey, Ryxi on the fifth planet, which is on this side of the system, and a human team dropped to do some exploration on the fourth, called Ireta. Wonder why it's got a name, if it doesn't have a colony and this was the first exploration team. Something about mesozoic fauna, whatever *that* means."

"New contact: ship on insystem drive boosting out of the fifth planet's system—" That went up on the main screen, where they could all see it. "No leech beacon—d'you want to try its IFF, captain?"

"No—if they're what I think, another pirate escort, they'll notice that," said Sass. "But...Ryxi?"

"Dropped here some forty years ago—colonial permit—"

"No one's *ever* suggested Ryxi were involved in this kind of thing," said Dupaynil, looking as confused as Sassinak felt. "Certainly not in anything with heavyworlders. They hate them worse than they do normal humans."

The *Zaid-Dayan* crept cautiously after the other two ships, which now seemed to be making for Ireta, a journey of some days on insystem drive. Sassinak wondered what someone might be planning—another "accidental" missile release? Some other dangerous accident? Dupaynil had come up with nothing definite, and although she had moved both the most likely suspects away from their usual duties, that didn't make her feel any safer. She made sure that none of the same people were assigned duty in the quadrant missile rooms, that the stewards' duties were rotated differently. What else could she do? Nothing, really.

Day by day the two target ships arced toward the distant fifth planet. Sassinak had time to look it up in the Index for herself, and check out the reference to "mesozoic." One of her new Jigs, a biology enthusiast, rattled on to everyone about the possibilities. Huge reptilian beasts from prehuman history on old Terra, superficially similar to some races of reptiloid aliens, but really quite stupid... Sassinak grinned to herself. Had she ever had that kind of enthusiasm, and been so unaware of everyone else's lack of interest? She thought not, but indulged him when he showed her his favorite slides from his files.

Fordeliton happened into the middle of this, and turned out to be another enthusiast, though more restrained. "Dinosaurs!" he said. "Old Terran, or near enough—"

"Pirates," said Sassinak firmly. "Dangerous, or near enough."

By the time they were close enough to be sure the quarry was intending to land, Sassinak had to worry what the other ship was doing. This could not be a colony raid, as on Myriad—there was no colony to raid. The ship that had come up from the Ryxi world was not holding a particularly good position for an escort—in fact, it almost seemed to be unaware of the transport. Could it be accidental? A ship on regular movement between planets?

The transport began to decelerate, dropping toward the planet. Behind, the second vessel seemed to be heading for a stable orbit. So far neither had detected the *Zaid-Dayan* in its stealth mode. But she could not take the cruiser to the surface leaving a possible enemy up in orbit... yet she wanted to be sure just what the transport was up to. She needed two ships... and there was a way....

"Take a shuttle down, and see where they're going. This world doesn't have a landing grid, that we know of—hard to believe they're actually going to land, but what else could they be doing? Stay in their dead zone, until they're committed to a site, and then if you can possibly get away unseen, do it. Stay below and behind, until their landing pattern—"

"What about a landing party?" Timran's dark eyes flashed.

"Ensign, I just said I wanted you to observe and return without alarming them—you don't *need* a landing party. Just stay behind 'em, low and fast, and once they're down get back here. If I give you a troop of marines, you'll try to find a use for 'em."

Ford shook his head as they watched the ensigns clamber into the shuttle hatch. "You know Timran would try to take on that entire transport by himself—"

"Yes, that's why I wanted Gori with him. Gori's got sense, besides being a good shuttle pilot. I just hope they follow orders."

"Oh, they will. You've got 'em scared proper." The docking bay alarm hooted, and the load crew scurried for airlocks. The docking hatch opened, flowerlike, and the shuttle elevator lifted it level with the ship's outer hull. Sassinak watched the flight deck officer signal the shuttle to start engines, and then boost away from the *Zaid-Dayan.*

The shuttle made an uneventful approach to the transport, and on their screens appeared to be snugged into the transport's blind spot. From high orbit, the *Zaid-Dayan*'s technicians observed the next few descending circuits of the planet. Nothing indicated that the transport had realized it had a tail. Nor did any signal come from the ground. Then Com picked up a landing beacon, and radio signals from below.

"There's the grid ... weird ... it's on the edge of that plateau."

"City? Town?"

"Nothing. Well ... some infrared indication of cleared fields, plantings ... but nothing big enough to put in a grid like that."

"We can take *that* out easily enough," said Arly. "One lousy transport and landing grid—"

"But what are they after? There's no colony to raid for slaves, nothing to raid for minerals or other goods. Why's there a grid here, and what are they doing here?"

"Wait a minute—that's got to be artificial—" Onto the main screen went a shot of something that looked like a working open-pit mine. "I haven't seen anything like that without someone nearby. A mine? Iron? Copper?"

Sassinak looked at the puzzled faces around her, and grinned. It had to be important. And this time she had a degree of freedom to act. "A landing grid, a beacon, an open pit mine, and no city—on a world supposedly not open for colonization. I think it's time we stripped our friend's IFF."

"Right, captain." The Com officer flipped a switch, and then came back on line, sounding puzzled. "Captain, it's a colony supply hauler, on contract to that Ryxi colony."

"And I'm a rich ambassador's wife. Try again." A screen came up at her right hand as the Com officer insisted. "Nothing wrong with the IFF signal, captain, I'd swear it. Look."

It looked clean. *Mazer Star*, captained by one Argemon Godheir, owned by Kirman, Vini & Godheir, Ltd., registration numbers, crew size, mass cargo and volume...every detail crisp and unmistakable. Com had already queried the database: *Mazer Star* was a thirty-seven year old hull from a respectable shipyard, refitted twice at the normal intervals, ownership as given, and no mysterious disappearances or changes in use.

"So what is it doing *here*?" asked Sass, voicing everyone's confusion. She looked back at the Com section, and the Com watch all shrugged. "Well. They're acting as if we don't exist, so let's see how close we can get."

Whatever *Mazer Star* was doing, it was not looking for a cruiser in its area; Sassinak began to feel a wholly irrational glee at how close they were able to come. Either their stealth gear was better than even she had supposed, or the stubby little insystem trader had virtually no detection gear (or the most incompetent radar operator in seven systems). Finally they were within tractor distance, and Sassinak ordered the shields full on and stealth gear off. And a transmission by tight-beam radio, although she felt she could almost have shouted across the space between ships. Certainly could have, in an atmosphere.

"*Mazer Star, Mazer Star*! FSP Cruiser *Zaid-Dayan* to *Mazer Star*—"

"What the—who the formative novations are *you*! Get off our tail or we'll—" That voice was quickly replaced by another, and a screen image of a stocky man in a captain's uniform.

"*Mazer Star*, Godheir commanding, to Federation ship *Zaid-Dayan*...where did you come from? Did you receive the same distress message?"

Distress message? What was he talking about? Sassinak took over from the Com officer, and spoke to him herself.

"Captain Godheir, this is Commander Sassinak of the *Zaid-Dayan*. We're tracking pirates, captain. What do you mean, distress beacon? Can you explain your presence in company with a heavyworlder transport?"

"Heavyworlder transport? Where?" On the screen, his face looked both ways as if he expected one to come bursting through his bulkheads.

"Below—it's going in to land. Now what's this about a distress beacon? And what kind of range and detection gear do you have?"

His answers, if a bit disorganized, quickly made sense out of the past several days. On long-term contract to supply the Ryxi colony, he'd recently returned to the system from a Ryxi relay-point. "You know they prefer to hire human crews," he said with a twinkle. "Routine flying's too boring for them, or something like that. We'd picked up some incoming specialists, and the supplies. Unloaded over there—" He waved in a way that Sassinak interpreted as meaning the planet in question. "Then we heard about some kind of problem here, a human exploration team that needed help, maybe a mutiny situation. So we came over—we can land without a grid, you see—But if you're here instead, then I guess we're not needed. You certainly gave us a start, Commander, that you did—"

"You may be needed yet," said Sass. "How were you supposed to find this missing team?" Godheir gave her the reference numbers, and said he'd detected a faint beacon signal from near the coast. While they were talking, Com suddenly waved wildly.

Timran, piloting the number one shuttle of the *Zaid-Dayan*, felt for the first time since coming on active duty like a *real* Fleet officer. On the track of slavers or pirates or something, in command of his own ship, however small. Actually it was better small—more of an adventure. Gori, hunched in the copilot's seat, was actually pale.

"This is really it," Timran said, with another quick sideways glance. He had said it before.

"Don't look at me, Tim—keep an eye on your sensors."

"We're doing just fine." In his mind's eye, he saw himself

reporting back to Commander Sassinak, telling her exactly what she needed to know, saw her smiling at him, praising him . . .

"Tim! You're sliding up on him!"

"It's all right." It wasn't, quite, but he eased back on the power, and settled the shuttle into the center of the transport's blind cone, where turbulence from its drive prevented its sensors from detecting them. It was harder than he'd thought, keeping the shuttle in the safe zone. But he could do it, and he'd follow it down to the bottom of the sea, if he had to. Too bad he didn't have enough armament to take it himself. He toyed with the idea of enabling the little tractor beam that the shuttles used around space stations, what the engineering chief called the "parking brake," but realized it wouldn't have much effect on something the mass of that transport.

"This is what I thought about during finals," he said, hoping to get some kind of reaction from Gori.

"Huh. No wonder you came in only twelfth from the bottom."

"Somebody has to be on the bottom. If they didn't think I could do the work, they wouldn't have let me graduate. And the captain gave me this job—"

"To get you out of her hair while she deals with that escort or whatever it is. Krims, Tim, you spend too much time daydreaming about glory, and not enough—look *out*!"

Reflexively, Tim yanked on the controls, and the shuttle skimmed over a jagged peak, its drive whining at the sudden load. "She said stay low," he said, but Gori snorted.

"You could let me fly. I can keep my mind on my work."

"She gave it to me!" In that brief interval, the transport had pulled ahead. "And I've got better ratings as a shuttle pilot."

Gori said nothing more, which suited Timran fine right then. He *had* cut it a little close—although he was certainly low enough for fine-detail on the tapes. Now he concentrated on the landscape ahead, wild and rough as it was, and tried to anticipate where the transport would land. There—that plateau. "Look at that," he breathed. "A landing grid. A monster—" The transport sank toward it, seeming even larger now that it was leaving its own element and coming to rest.

He barely saw the movement—something small, but clearly *made*, not natural—when a bolt of colored light from the transport reached out to it. "Look out!" he yelled at Gori, and slammed his hand on the tractor beam control. The shuttle lurched, as the badly aimed beam grabbed for anything in its way. Tim's hands raced over the controls, bringing the shuttle to a near hover, and catching the distant falling object in the tractor beam just before it hit a low cliff.

"An *airsled*!" breathed Gori. "Oh gods, Tim, what have you *done*!"

"Did you see those murderers?" His teeth were clenched as he worked the beam to set the airsled down as gently as possible. "Those dirty, rotten, slimy—"

"Tim! That's not the point! We're supposed to be invisible!"

All the latent romanticism burst free. "We're Fleet! We just saved lives, that's what we're supposed to do."

"That's not what the captain *ordered* us to do. Tim, you just told everyone, from the transport to whoever they're meeting, that we're here. That *Fleet's* here."

"So ... so we'll just ... mmm ... we'll just tell them they're under arrest, for ... uh ... attempting to ... uh ..."

"Illegal use of proscribed weaponry in a proscribed system is one charge you're looking for." Gori was punching buttons on his console. "Kipling's copper corns! The captain's going to be furious, and I've heard about her being furious. She's going to eat us alive, buddy, and it's all your fault."

"She'd want us to save lives ..." Tim didn't sound quite so certain now. For one thing, that transport had lifted, and then settled itself firmly on the grid. He sent the shuttle forward again, slowly, and wondered whether to stand guard over the airsled or threaten the transport, or what. It had seemed so simple at the time ...

The voice in his earplug left him in no doubt. "I told you," the captain's crisp voice said, "to follow that transport down *cautiously*, with particular care not to be noticed. Did you understand that order?"

"Yes, ma'am, but—"

"Yet I find that you have engaged a possibly hostile vessel, making sure that you would be noticed; you may have damaged Federation citizens—" That wasn't fair at all; it was the crash that damaged them, and he hadn't caused the crash ... at least, he hadn't shot the airsled, although his handling of the tractor beam had been

less than deft. "Moreover, you've made it necessary for me to act—
or abandon *you*, and if you were alone that would be a distinct
temptation!" Gori smirked at this; he was getting the same tirade in
his own earplug. "Now that you've started a riot, young man, you'd
better stay in control of things until I get there."

"But how—?" Tim began, but the com cut off. He was breathing
fast, and felt cold. He looked over at Gori, no longer smirking.
"What do we do now?"

Gori, predictably, had a reference. "Fleet Landing Force
Directives, Chapter 17, paragraph 34.2—"

"I don't care where it *is*—what does it say?"

Gori went on, pale but determined, with his quotation. "It says if
the landing party—which is us—is outnumbered or outgunned, and
Fleet personnel are in danger of capture or injury—"

"They're civilians," said Timran. As he said it he wondered—but
surely anyone on planet had to be civilians, or they would have
known Fleet was down here.

"Really? Those look like Fleet duty uniforms to me." Gori had a
magnifier to his eye. "Shipboard working...Anyway, when
personnel are in danger of capture or injury, and the landing party
is outnumbered, then the decision to withdraw must be made by the
commander of the orbiting ship, unless such ship—"

"She told us to stay here and stay in charge—"

"So that's paragraph 34.3: In cases where rescue or protection of
the Fleet personnel is deemed possible or of paramount importance,
the pilot of the landing party shuttle will remain with the craft at all
times, and the copilot will lead the rescue party—"

"That's backwards!" said Tim, thinking of Gori's character.

"That's regulations," said Gori. "Besides, if we just hover here we
can keep anyone from bothering them. By the way, d'you have the
shields up?"

He hadn't thought of it, and thumbed the control just as the
transport's single turret angled their way. Gori was watching the
plateau now, and commented on the people clumped near the ship.
"Native? This planet's not supposed to be inhabited at all, but—"

"They might shoot, Gori," Tim pointed out. He was glad to hear
that his voice was steady, though his hands trembled slightly. He'd
never expected that the mere sight of a blast cannon muzzle aimed

his way would be so disturbing. Were shuttle shields strong enough, at this distance, to hold against a blast cannon?

Time passed. Down below still figures slumped in an airsled crumpled against the rocky face of the plateau. Above, the transport's blast cannon continued to point directly at them. With only two of them aboard, Tim couldn't see asking Gori to go out and check on the injured (dead? He hoped not) sled passengers. Should he hail the transport? Command them to send medical aid? What if they didn't? What if they fired? Gori maintained a prudent silence, broken only by observations on activity around the transport. It felt like years before the com unit burped, and put the Navigation Senior Officer on the line. "Not long," Bures said. "We've got a fix on you and the transport. How's it going?"

Tim swallowed hard. "Oh . . . nothing much. We're just hovering above the sled—"

"Don't move," Bures advised. "We're coming in *very* fast, and if you move we could run right over you."

"Where are you going to land?" But no one answered that question; the line had cut off. Gori and Tim exchanged anxious glances before settling to their watch again. Tim let his eyes stray to the clock—surely it had been longer than *that*.

Even through the shields they heard and felt the shockwaves of the *Zaid-Dayan*'s precipitous descent. "Krims!" said Gori. "She's using the emergency insystem—" Another powerful blast of wind and noise, and the great cruiser hung above the plateau, its Fleet and Federation insignia defining the bow. Clouds of dust roiled away from it, temporarily blinding Tim even in the shuttle; when it cleared, Tim could see the transport shudder at its berth. "—drive," finished Gori, paler than before. Tim, for once, said nothing.

"The only good thing about all this," said Sassinak, when they were back aboard, "is that I know you can't be a saboteur, because you weren't on board when the sabotage occurred, and it would have required immediate access. Of course you might be in collusion. . . ."

Tim tried to swallow, unsuccessfully. It wasn't that she bellowed, or turned red, the way some of his instructors had when he had been particularly difficult. She looked perfectly calm, if you didn't notice the pale rim around her mouth, or the muscles bunched along her jaw. Her voice was no louder than usual. But he had the feeling that his bones were exposed to her gaze, not to mention the daydreams in his skull . . . and they seemed a lot less glamorous right then. Even, as she said, stupid, shortsighted, rash, and unjustified. She had left them hovering where they were until the locals (whoever they were) had extricated the injured and moved them into the cruiser. Then the cruiser's own tractor beam had flicked out and towed them in as if the shuttle were powerless and pilotless. Once in the shuttle bay, they'd been ordered to their quarters until "the captain's ready for you." Gori had said nothing while they waited, and Tim had imagined himself cashiered and stranded on this malodorous lump of unsteady rock.

"I'll expect you to recite the relevant sections of regulations, Ensign, the next time you see me. I'm sure your cohort can give you the references." That was her only dig at Gori, who had after all been innocent. "You may return to your quarters, and report for duty at shift-change." He didn't ask where: it would be posted in his file. He and Gori saluted, and retired without tripping over anything—at that point Tim was mildly surprised to find out his body worked as usual.

Curiosity returned on the way to their quarters. He looked sideways at Gori. No help there. But who were the husky, skin-clad indigenes? They had to be human, unless everything he'd been told about evolution was wrong. Why had someone built a landing grid on an uncharted planet? Who were the people in the Fleet uniforms, if they weren't from this ship?

Alone with Gori in their quarters, he had no one to ask. Gori said nothing, simply called up the *Fleet Regulations: XXIII Edition* on screen, and highlighted the passages the captain had mentioned. The computer spat out a hardcopy, and Gori handed it to Tim. Duties, obligations, penalties . . . he tried not to let it sink in, but it got past his defenses anyway. Disobeying a captain's direct order in the presence of a hostile (or presumed hostile) force was grounds for anything the captain chose to do about it, including summary execution. She *could* have left him there, left both of them there, including innocent Gori, if she'd wanted to, and no one in Fleet would have had a quibble.

For the first time, Tim thought about the stories he'd heard . . . *why* the ship was so long in the repair yard, what kind of engagement that had been. A colony plundered, while Sassinak did nothing, in hopes of catching more pirates later. More than two or three people had died there; she had let them die, to save others. He didn't like that a bit. Did she? The ones who'd talked about it said not, but ... if she really cared, how could she? Men and women, children, people of all sorts—rich, poor, in between—had died because she didn't do what he had done—she didn't come tearing in to save them.

Gradually, in the hollow silence between his bunk and Gori's, Tim began to build a new vision of what the Fleet really was, and what his captain had intended. What he had messed up, with his romantic and gallant nonsense. Those people in the colony had died, so that Sassinak could trace their attackers to powers behind them. Some of her crew had died, trying to save the children, and then destroy a pirate base. This very voyage probably had something to do with the same kind of trouble, and saving two lives just didn't mean that much. If he himself had been killed before his rash act—and for the first time he really faced that chilling possibility of not-being— it would have done Fleet no harm, and possibly his captain some good.

When the chime rang for duty, Tim set off for his new job (cleaning sludge from the filters) with an entirely new attitude. He fully intended to become the reformed young officer the Fleet so needed, and for several hours worked diligently. No more jokes, no more wild notions: sober reality. He recited the regulations under his breath, just in case the captain should appear in this smelly little hole.

In this mood of determined obedience to nature and nature's god in the person of his captain, he didn't even smile when Jig Turner, partner in several earlier escapades, appeared in the hatchway.

"I guess you know," said Turner.

"I know if I don't finish these filters, we'll be breathing this stink."

"This isn't bad—you should smell the planet's atmosphere." Turner lounged against the bulkhead, patently idle, with the air of someone who desperately wants to tell a secret.

"You've been out?" Despite himself, Tim couldn't fail to ask that.

"Well, no. Not *out* exactly, but we all smelled it when they brought the injuries in. Worse than this ... like organic lab." Turner leaned closer. "Listen, Tim—did you really fire on that transport?"

"No! I put a tractor on the airsled, that's all."

"I wish you *had* blown it."

"I didn't have anything to blow it with. But why? The captain's mad enough that I caught the sled."

"D'you know what that transport was?" Of course he didn't, and he shook his head. Turner went on, lowering her voice. "Heavyworlders."

"So?"

"So *think*, Tim. Heavyworlders, meatheads, in a transport—tried to tell the captain they were answering a distress beacon, but it scans like a colony ship. To a proscribed planet...which has heavyworlders on it *already*."

"Huh?" He couldn't follow this. "The ones in the airsled?"

"No. The ones on the ground...near the transport, and getting the victims out...you *must* have been watching, Tim, even you."

"I saw them, but they didn't look like heavyworlders...exactly." Now he came to think of it, they had been big and well-muscled.

"It's a heavyworlder *plot*," Turner went on quickly. "They wanted the planet—there was a mutiny, I heard, in a scouting expedition, and the heavyworlders started eating raw meat, and killed the others and ate them—"

"I don't believe it!" But he would, if he let himself think about it. Eating one sentient being had to be the same as eating another: that's why the prohibition. He'd had an aunt who wouldn't eat anything synthesized from perennial plants, on the grounds that shrubs and trees might be sentient.

"The thing is, if one heavyworlder can mutiny, why not all? There's already this bunch of them living free out there, eating meat and wearing skins—what's to stop the ones on this ship from going crazy, too? Maybe it's the smell in the air, or something. But a lot of us think the captain should put 'em all under guard. Think of the heavyworld marines...we wouldn't stand a chance if they mutinied."

Tim thought about it a moment, while screwing the access port back on the filter he'd just cleaned, and shook his head. "No—I can't see anyone from this ship turning on the captain—"

"But they could. They could be planning something right now, and if we don't warn her—"

Tim grinned. "I don't think, Turner, that the captain needs our warning to know where danger is."

"You mean you won't sign the petition? Or come with us to talk to her?"

"No. And frankly I think you're nuts to bother her with this."

"I'm glad you think so." Commander Sassinak, Tim saw, looked as immaculate as usual, though she must have gone through the same narrow passages that had smudged his uniform. She gave him a frosty smile, which vanished as she met Turner's eyes. "Tell me, Lieutenant Turner, did you ever happen to read the regulations on shipboard conspiracy?"

"No, captain, but—"

"No. Nor were you serving on this ship when heavyworlder marines—the very ones you're so afraid of—saved the ship and my life. Had they been inclined to mutiny, Lieutenant, they'd have had more than one opportunity. You exhibit a regrettable prejudice, and an even more regrettable tendency to faulty logic. The actions of heavyworlders on an exploration team more than four decades ago say nothing about the loyalty of my crew. I trust them a long sight more than I trust you—they've given me reason. I don't want to hear any more of this, or that you've been spreading such rumors. Is that clear?"

"Yes, captain." At Sass's nod, Turner hurried away. Tim stood at attention, entirely too aware of his smelly, stained hands and messy uniform. The captain's lips quirked: not a smile, but something that required control not to be.

"Learned anything, Ensign Timran?"

"Yes, captain. I ... uh ... memorized the regulations—"

"About time. As it happens, and I don't want you getting a swelled head about this, things have worked out very well. From this point on, consider that you acted under orders at all times: is that clear?"

It wasn't clear at all, but he tried to conceal his confusion. His captain sighed, obviously noticing the signs, and explained. "The other ship, Tim, the one that appeared from the Ryxi planet, was not a pirate: it was a legal transport, on contract to supply the Ryxi, replying to a distress signal."

"Yes, captain." That was always safe, even though the rest of it made no sense at all.

"For political reasons, which you will no doubt hear discussed later, your rash intervention has turned out to benefit Fleet and the FSP. It is necessary that those outside this ship believe your actions were on my orders. Therefore, you are not to mention, ever, to anyone, at any time, in any place, that your actions in the shuttle were your own bright idea. You did what I told you to do—is that clear now?"

Slightly clearer, and from the tone in her voice he had better understand, with no more questions.

"I've also told Gori, and all previous comments in the files have been wiped." Which meant it was *serious* ... but also that he wasn't going to have that around his neck forever. Dawning hope must have shown on his face, for hers softened slightly. "Timran, listen to me, and pay attention. You've got natural good luck, and it's priceless ... but *don't* depend on it. It takes more than good luck to make admiral."

"Yes, captain. Uh—if I may—are the people all right? The ones in the airsled?"

"Yes. They're quite well, and you may even meet them someday. Just remember what I said."

"Yes, captain."

"And clean up before mess." With that she was gone, a vision of grace and authority that haunted his life for years.

Chapter Sixteen

Sassinak returned to the bridge by way of Troop Deck, as she wanted to manage a casual encounter with the marine commander. She had already realized that the combination of events might alarm some of the crew, and inflame suspicion of heavyworlders.

She found Major Currald inspecting a rack of weapons; he gave her a somewhat abstracted nod. "Captain—if you've a moment, there's something—"

"Certainly, Major." He led the way to his office, and Sass noticed that he had seating for both heavyworlders and smaller frames. She chose neither, instead turning to look at the holos on the wall across from his desk. A team of futbal players in clean uniforms posed in neat rows, action shots of the same players splattered with mud, a much younger Currald rappelling down a cliff, two young marine officers (one of them Currald? She couldn't tell) in camouflage facepaint and assault rifles. A promotion ceremony; Currald getting his "tracks." Someone not Currald, the holo in a black frame.

"My best friend," said Currald, as her eyes fixed on that one. She turned to face him; he was looking at the holo himself. "He was killed at Jerma, in the first wave, while I was still on a down shuttle. He'd named his son after me." He cleared his throat, a bass rasp. "That wasn't what I asked to speak to you about, captain. I hesitated to come up to Main Deck and bother you, but—" He cleared his throat again. "I'm sorry to say I expect some trouble."

Sass nodded. "So do I, and I wanted to tell you first what I'm going to do." His face stiffened, the traditional heavyworlder

237

response to any threat. "Major Currald, I know you're a loyal officer; if you'd wanted to advance heavyworlder interests at my expense, you'd have done it long before. We've discussed politics before; you know where I stand. Your troops have earned my trust, earned it in battle, where it counts. Whoever that saboteur is, I'm convinced it's not one of your people, and I'm not about to let anyone pressure me into thinking so."

He was surprised; she was a little annoyed that he had not trusted her trust. "But I know a lot of the crew think—"

"A lot of the crew *don't* think," she interrupted crisply. "They worry, or they react, but they don't think. Kipling's bunions! The heavyworlder mutiny here was forty-three years ago: before you were born, and I was only a toddler on Myriad. None of your marines are old enough to have had anything to do with that. Those greedyguts would-be colonists set out months ago—probably while we were chasing that first ship. But scared people put two and two together and get the Annual Revised Budget Request—" At that he actually grinned, and began to chuckle. Sass grinned back at him. "I trust you, Major, and I trust you to know if your troops are loyal. You'll hear, I'm sure, that people have asked me to 'do something'— throw you all in the brig or something equally ridiculous—and I want you to know right now, before the rumors take off, that I'm not even thinking about that. Clear?"

"Very clear, captain. And thank you. I thought...I thought perhaps you'd feel you had to make some concession. And I'd talked to my troops, the heavyworlders, and we'd agreed to cooperate with any request."

Sass felt tears sting her eyes...and there were some who thought heavyworlders were always selfish, never able to think of the greater good. How many of *them* would have made such an offer, had they been innocent suspects? "You tell your troops, Major, that I am deeply moved by that offer—I respect you, and them, and appreciate your concern. But if no other good comes out of this, the rest of this crew is going to learn that we're *all* Fleet: light, heavy, and in-between. And thank you."

"Thank *you*, captain."

Sassinak found the expected delegation waiting outside the bridge when she got back to the main deck. Their spokesman,

'Tenant Varhes, supervised the enlisted mess, she recalled. Their concern, he explained in a reedy tenor, was for the welfare of the ship. After all, a heavyworlder had already poisoned officers and crew. . . .

"A mentally imbalanced person," said Sassinak coldly, "who happened to also be a heavyworlder, poisoned officers—including the marine commander, who happens to be a heavyworlder—and crew, including some heavyworlders. Or have you forgotten that?"

"But if they should mutiny. The heavyworlders on this planet mutinied—"

"Over forty years ago, when your father was a toddler, and Major Currald hadn't been born. Are you suggesting that heavyworlders have telepathic links to unborn heavyworlders?" That wasn't logical, but neither were they, and she enjoyed the puzzlement on their faces as they worked their way through it. Before Varhes could start up again, she tried a tone of reasonableness, and saw it affect most of them. "Look here: the heavyworlders on this ship are *Fleet*—not renegades, like those who mutinied here, or those who want to colonize a closed world. They're our companions, they've fought beside us, saved our lives. They could have killed us many times over, if that's what they had in mind. You think they're involved in sabotage on the ship—I'm quite sure they're not. But even so, we're taking precautions against sabotage. If it should be a heavyworlder, that individual will be charged and tried and punished. But that doesn't make the others guilty. Suppose it's someone from Gian-IV—" a hit at Varhes, whose home world it was, "would that make Varhes guilty?"

"But it's not the same," came a voice from the back of the group. "Everybody knows heavyworlders are planet pirates, and now we've found them in action—"

"*Some* planet pirates are heavyworlders, we suspect, and some are not—some are even Ryxi." That got a nervous laugh, "Or consider the Seti." A louder laugh. Sassinak let her voice harden. "But this is enough of this. I don't want to hear any more unfounded charges against loyal members of Fleet, people who've put their lives on the line more than once. I've already told one ensign to review the regulations on conspiracy, and I commend them to each of you. We have real hostiles out there, people: real would-be planet pirates, who may have allies behind them. We can't afford finger-pointing and petty prejudices among ourselves. Is that quite clear?" It was; the little group melted away, most of them shamefaced and clearly regretting their impetuous actions. Sass hoped they'd continue to feel that way.

Back on the bridge, Sass reviewed the status of the various parties involved. The heavyworld transport's captain had entered a formal protest against her action in "interfering with the attempt to respond to a distress beacon." Her eyebrows rose. The only distress beacon in the story so far had been at the Ryxi planet, the beacon that had sent *Mazer Star* on its way here. The heavyworlder transport had run past there like a grass fire in a windstorm. Now what kind of story could he have concocted, and what kind of faked evidence would be brought out to support it? She grinned to herself; this was becoming even more interesting than before.

The "native" heavyworlders, descendants of the original survey and exploration team . . . or at least of the mutineers of that team . . . were mulling over the situation but keeping their distance from the cruiser. The transport's captain had kept in contact with them by radio, however.

The *Mazer Star,* supply ship for the Ryxi colony, had managed to contact the survivors who'd been in cold-sleep. So far their statements confirmed everything on the distress beacon, with plenty of supporting detail. A mixed exploration team, set down to survey geological and biological resources—including children from the EEC survey vessel, the ARCT-10, that had carried them, highly unusual. Reversion of the heavyworlder team members to carnivory—their subsequent mutiny—murder, torture of adults and children—their attempt to kill all the lightweights by stampeding wildlife into the camp. The lightweights' successful escape in a lifeboat to a seacliff cave, and their decision to go into coldsleep and await the ARCT-10's return.

Sass ran through the computer file Captain Godheir had transferred, explaining everything from the original mixup that had led the Ryxi to think the human team had been picked up by the ARCT-10, to the *Mazer Star*'s own involvement, after a Thek intrusion. Thek! Sass shook her head over that; this had been complicated enough before; Thek were a major complication in themselves. Godheir's story, unlike that of the heavyworlder Captain Cruss, made perfect (if ironic) sense, and his records checked out clean with her onboard databanks. *Mazer Star* was in fact listed as one of three shuttle-supply ships on contract to a Ryxi colony in this system. She frowned at the personnel list Godheir had transferred, of the expedition members stranded after the mutiny. Lunzie? It couldn't be, she thought—and yet it wasn't a common name. She'd never run into another Lunzie. Medic, age 36 elapsed—and what did *that* mean? Then she saw the date of birth, and her breath quickened. By date of birth this woman was ancient—impossibly old—and yet— Sass fed the ID data into the computer, and told Com to ready a lowlink to Fleet Sector Headquarters. About time the Admiral knew what had happened, and she was going to need a *lot* of information. Starting with this.

"Captain?" That was Borander, on the pinnace, with a report of the airsled victims' condition.

"Go ahead."

"The woman is conscious now; the medics have cleared her for transport. The man is still out, and they want to package him first."

"Have you had a contact from their base?"

"No, captain."

"You may find them confused, remember, and not just by a knock on the head. Don't argue with them; try to keep them calm until you get a call from their base, or our medical crew gets to them." The message relayed from Godheir was that both crew were barriered by an Adept, and thought they were members of a Fleet cruiser's crew. They'd be more than a little surprised to find themselves in a different cruiser, Sass thought, particularly if the barriers had been set with any skill.

And one of these was the team co-leader—essentially the civilian authority of the entire planet. Governor? Sass wondered what she was like, and decided she'd better be set up for a formal interview just in case. Some of these scientist types didn't think highly of Fleet. She signalled for an escort, then went to her office, and brought up all the screens. One showed the pinnace just landing, and when she plugged in her earpiece, Borander told her that a message had just come from the survivors' base for the woman. Sass approved a transfer, and watched on the screen as Borander and his pilot emerged to give their passenger privacy. She presumed that the unconscious man was in the rear compartment, with a medic.

When the woman—Varian, Sass reminded herself—came out, she seemed to be a vigorous, competent sort. She was certainly used to having her own way, for she took one look around and began to argue with Borander about something. Sass wished she'd insisted on an open channel between them, but she hadn't expected that anything much would happen. Now she watched as the argument progressed, with handwaving and headshaking and—by the expressions—raised voices. She pressed a button, linking her to the bridge, and said "Com, get me an audio of channel three."

"—Nothing to do with Aygar and anyone in his generation or even his parents'." The woman's voice would have been rich and melodic if she hadn't been angry—or stressed by the crash, Sass reminded herself. She followed the argument with interest. Borander let himself be overwhelmed—first by the woman's vehemence, and then by her claim of precedence as planetary governor. Not, Sass was sorry to notice, by her chain of logic, which was quite reasonable. She shook her head at the screen, disappointed—she'd thought Borander had more backbone. Of course the woman was right: the descendants of mutineers were not themselves guilty, and he should have seen that for himself. He should also have foreseen her claim of authority, and avoided the direct confrontation with it. Most of all, Fleet officers shouldn't be so visibly nervous about their captains' opinion—acting that way in a bar, as an excuse not to get into a row, was one thing, but here it made him look weak—never a good idea. How could she help him learn that, without losing all his confidence—because he didn't seem to have much.

So, Co-leader Varian wanted to bring both those young heavyworlders into her office and argue their case right away, did she? She was no doubt primed for an argument with a boneheaded Fleet battleaxe...Sass grinned to herself. Varian might be a planetary governor, of sorts, but she didn't know much about tactics. Not that she planned to be an enemy.

She followed their progress up the ramp and through the ship, but by the time they appeared outside her office, she was waiting to greet them. As she stood and shook hands with Varian, she saw the younger woman's eyes widen slightly. Whatever she'd thought a cruiser captain was like, this was clearly not it... *Not the old battleaxe you expected, hmm?* thought Sass. *Nor the office you expected?* For Varian's eyes had lingered on the crystal sculpture, the oiled wood desk with its stunning pattern of dark red and black graining, the rich blue carpet and white seating. Sass gave the two young heavyworlders a polite greeting. One of them—Winral?—seemed almost dazed by his surroundings, very much the country cousin lost in a world of high technology. The other, poised between hostility and intelligent curiosity, was a very different order of being indeed. *If there were wild humans,* Sass thought, *as there are wild and domestic kinds of some animals, this would be a wild one. All the intelligence, but untamed.* On top of that, he was handsome, in a rough-cut way.

She continued with pleasantries, offering a little information, feeling out the three of them. Varian relaxed quickly once she realized Sassinak intended no harm to the innocent descendants of the mutineers. Clearly she felt at home in civilized surroundings and had not gone native. Varian wanted to know the location of the ARCT-10, of course.

"That's another good question to which I have no answer," Sass told her, and explained that she'd initiated a query. It hadn't been listed as destroyed, and no distress beacon had shown up, but it might take days to figure out what might have happened. Then she turned to Aygar, and asked for his personal identification—which he gave as a pedigree. Typical, she thought, for the planetborn: you are who your parents were. Fleet personnel gave ship and service history; scientists, she'd heard, gave university affiliation and publications. Winral's pedigree, when he gave it, contained some of the same names... and after all the mutineers had been few. They'd probably worked to avoid inbreeding, especially if they weren't sure how long it would be before a colony ship joined them. Or if one would come at all.

When she began to review the legal status of the younger heavyworlders, Varian interrupted to insist that the planet did, indeed, have a developing sentient species. Sass let her face show surprise, but what she really felt was consternation. Things had been complicated enough before, with the contending claims of mutiny, mining rights, developmental rights derived from successful settlement—and the Theks' intervention. But all rules changed when a planet had a sentient or developing sentient native species. She was well-read in space law—all senior officers were—but this was more than a minor complication—and one she could not ignore.

Avian, too, Varian told her. Sass thought of the Ryxi, volatile and vain, and decided to keep all mention of Varian's flyers off the common communication links. At least the Ryxi weren't as curious as they were touchy—they wouldn't come winging by just to see what the excitement was all about.

Aygar, meanwhile, wanted to insist that the heavyworlders at the settlement owned the entire planet—and could grant parts of it to the colonists in that transport if they wanted to. Sassinak found herself enjoying his resistance, though she made it clear that under Federation law his people could not claim anything but what they had developed: the mine, the fields, the landing grid. And she strongly advised him to have nothing more to do with the heavyworlder transport, if he wanted to avoid suspicion of a conspiracy.

When she offered him her hand, at the conclusion of the interview, she wondered if he'd try to overwhelm her. If he was as smart as he looked—as he must be to have accomplished what the reports said—he would restrain himself. And so he did. His grip on her hand was only slightly stronger than hers on his, and he released her hand without attempting a throw. She smiled at him, well-pleased by his manner, and made a mental note to try recruiting him for Fleet duty. He'd make a terrific marine, if he could discipline himself like that. She explained that she'd be sending over data cubes on FSP law, standard rights and responsibilities of citizenship, the sections on colony law, and so on, and that she'd supply certain items from the ship's stores under the shipwreck statutes. Then the two heavyworlders were gone, with an escort back to the outside, and she turned her attention back to Varian.

Varian would clearly rather have left with the heavyworlders, and Sass wondered about that. Why was she being so protective? Most people in her position would, Sass thought, have been more ready to see all the heavyworlders in irons. Had she formed some kind of attachment? She watched the younger woman's face as she settled into one of the chairs. "A rather remarkable specimen, that Aygar. Are there more like him?" She let her voice carry more than a hint of sensuality, and watched a flush spread across Varian's cheek. So...did she really think older women had no such interests, or was it jealousy?

"I've only encountered a few of his generation—"

"Yes, generation." Sassinak decided to probe a little deeper. "You're now forty-three years behind your own. Will you need counseling? For yourself or the others?" She knew they would, but saw Varian push that possibility away. Did she not realize the truth, or was she unwilling to show weakness in front of a stranger?

"I'll know when I get back to them," Varian was saying. "The phenomenon hasn't caught up with me yet."

Sassinak thought it had, at least in part, but admired the woman for denying it. And what was this going to do to Lunzie? Somehow she wasn't nearly as worried about *her*. Varian asked again about the ARCT-10, as if Sassinak would have lied in the first place. A civilian response, Sass thought: she never lied without a good reason, and usually managed without needing to. Someone came in to report that Varian's sled had been repaired, and Sass brought the interview to a close. Supplies—of course, a planetary governor could requisition anything she required—just contact Ford. Sass knew he would be glad for a chance to get off the plateau and see some of the exotic wildlife. But now...

"Your medic's name *is* Lunzie, isn't it?" she asked. Varian, slightly puzzled, nodded. Sass let her grin widen, enjoying the bombshell she was about to drop. "I suppose it was inevitable that one of us would encounter her. A celebration is in order. Will you convey my deepest respects to Lunzie?" Varian's expression now almost made her burst out laughing: total confusion and disbelief. "I cannot miss the chance to meet Lunzie," Sass finished up. "It isn't often one gets the chance to entertain one's great-great-great grandmother." Varian's mouth hung slightly open, and her eyes were glazed. *Gotcha*, thought Sass wickedly, and in the gentlest possible tones asked one of the junior officers to escort Varian to her sled.

Nothing wrong with that young woman that seasoning wouldn't

cure, *but*—Sass chuckled to herself—it was fun to outwit a planetary governor. Even one who'd had a concussion. She followed Varian's progress through the ship, and was pleased to note that shock or not, she remembered to check on her crewmate. When Med queried, with a discreet push of buttons, Sass acknowledged and approved his leaving with Varian. Varian, she suspected, never considered that he might have been held.

Ford appeared, and shook his head at her expression. "Captain, you look entirely too pleased about something."

"I may be. But compared to the last cruise, things are going extremely well, complications and all. Of course we don't know why the Thek are here, or what they're going to do, or if that heavyworlder transport has allies following after—"

Ford shook his head. "I doubt that. A hull that size could carry colony seedstock, machinery and all—"

"True. That's what I'm hoping—but you notice I put a relay satellite in orbit, and left a streaker net out. Just in case. Oh yes—you're interested in the sort of wildlife they've got here, aren't you?"

"Sure—it was kind of a hobby of mine, and when I was on the staff at Sector III, they had this big museum just down the hill—"

"Good. Are you willing to take on a fairly dangerous outside job? And do some acting in the meantime?"

"Of course." He blanked all the expression off his face and faked a Diplo accent. "I could pretend to be a heavyworlder if you want, but I'm afraid they'd notice something..."

Sass shook her head at him. "Be serious. I need to know more about this world—direct data, not interpreted by those survivors, no matter how expert they are in their fields. Varian, the co-leader who came today, is entirely too eager to claim sentient status for an avian species. It may be justified, or it may not, but I want independent data. There's something odd about her reactions to the Iretan-born heavyworlders, too. She ought to be furious, still—she's less than a tenday out of coldsleep; she witnessed a murder; the initial indictment filed with Godheir spoke of intentional injury to both co-leaders. That's all fresh in her mind, or should be. Her reasoning's correct: the grandchildren of mutineers are not responsible. But it's just not normal for her to think that clearly when her friends and colleagues have suffered. I've seen this kind of idealism backfire—this determination to save every living thing can be carried too far. She's very dedicated, and very spirited, but I'm not sure how stable she is. With a tribunal coming up to determine the fate of this planet and those people, I need something solid."

"I see your point, captain, but what do you want me to do?"

"Well—I'd guess she'd fall for unconditional enthusiasm. Boyish gush, if you can manage it—and I know you can." She let her eyes caress him, and he laughed aloud. "Yes—exactly that. Be dinosaur-crazy, act as if you'd do anything for a mere glimpse of them—you're so lucky to have the chance, and so on. You can start by being skeptical—are they really dinosaurs? Are they *sure?* Let's pick a survey team today, and brief them—you can introduce them as fellow hobbyists tomorrow. They'll probably accept two or three, and if they go for that maybe another two or three later. How's that sound?"

"Right. Makes sense." Ford, faced with a problem, tackled it wholly, absorbed and alert at once. She watched as he scrolled through the personnel files, with a search on secondary specialties. "We'll have to pick those who *do* have a real interest—they'd catch on to something faked, and I can't teach someone all about dinosaurs in one night—" He stopped, and fed an entry to her screen. "How about Borander? He's taken twelve hours of paleontology."

"No, not Borander. Did you see how he interacted with Varian?"

"No, I was with Currald then."

"Well, take a look at the tape later. Young trout let her dominate him. Admittedly, she's a Disciple, and she's declared herself planetary governor, but I don't like my officers buckling that easily. He needs a bit of seasoning. Who else?"

"Segendi—no, he's a heavyworlder and I doubt you want to complicate things that way—"

"Right."

"What about Maxnil, in supply? His secondary specialty is cartography, and he's listed as having an associate degree in xenobio." Sass nodded, and Ford went on, quickly turning up a short list of three crew members who could be considered "dinosaur buffs." It was even easier to come up with a list of those who knew a reasonable amount of geology, although harder to cut the list to three. All had excellent records, and all had worked with non-Fleet personnel.

Sass nodded, at last. "Good selection. You brief them, Ford, and be sure they understand that they did *not* know dinosaurs were here until tomorrow. We didn't see anything on the way down: we came too fast. I had seen the information stripped from the beacon, but no one else had. Once you see the beasts, I imagine you won't have to fake your reactions. But keep in mind that I need information on more than large, noisy, dangerous reptiloids."

Ford nodded. "Do you still want to speak to Major Currald before lunch?"

"If he feels he has things well in hand with the transport. What's that captain's name—Cruss? Foul-mouthed creature, that one. I want Wefts and heavyworlders, round the clock—"

"Here's the roster." As usual, Ford had anticipated her request. She thought again how lucky she was to have Ford this time, and not Huron. In a situation like this, Huron's initiative and drive could have been disastrous. She could trust Ford to back her tactics, not go off and do something harebrained on his own.

She glanced at the roster of Fleet personnel stationed inside the transport to ensure that personnel in coldsleep were not revived. She didn't want to face a thousand or more heavyworlders: the *Zaid-Dayan* would have no trouble killing them all, but Fleet commanders were supposed to avoid the necessity of a massacre. Each shift combined Wefts and heavyworlders: she trusted her heavyworlders, but with Wefts to witness, no one could later claim that they'd betrayed her trust. "Get Currald on the line, would you?"

A few moments later, Currald's face filled one of the screens, and he confirmed that the situation remained stable.

"I've told the native-born survivors that I'll supply some of their needs, too," Sassinak told him. "I don't want them to think that all good comes from Diplo. I've got some things on order, that'll be delivered to the perimeter. But if you can turn surveillance and supervision over to someone, I'd appreciate your company at lunch."

"You're not giving them weapons—"

"No, certainly not."

"Give me about half an hour, if you can, captain; I'm still arranging the flank coverage."

"That's fine. I'll order a meal for half an hour from now—and if you're held up along the way, just give me a call." She cleared the circuit, and turned to Ford. "See if Mayerd can meet with us, too—and you, of course, after you've notified your short lists that you'll brief them this afternoon. I'll be on the bridge, but we'll eat in here."

On the bridge, she told the duty officer to carry on, and came up behind Arly. Although most of the ship had been released from battle stations, the weapons systems were powered up and fully operational. It would be disastrous if someone erred at this range—no doubt the transport would be destroyed (with great loss of life she'd have to account for) but the resultant backlash could endanger the *Zaid-Dayan*. Arly acknowledged her without taking her gaze from the screens.

"I'm just running a test on quadrant two—" she said over her shoulder. "Interlock systems—making sure no one can pull the same trick again—"

Sass had more sense than to bother her at that moment, and waited, watching the screens closely, although she could not interpret some of the scanning traces. Finally Arly sighed, and locked her board down.

"Safe. I hope." She smiled a bit wearily. "*Are* you going to explain, or is this a great security mystery?"

"Both," said Sass. "How about lunch in my office?"

Arly's eyes slid back to her screens. "I should stay—"

"You've got a perfectly competent second officer, and it's my considered opinion that nothing's going to break loose right now. That Cruss may be up to something, but we've interrupted his plans, and this is our safe period. Relax—or at least get out of that seat and eat something,"

Currald brought the stench of the Iretan atmosphere back into Sassinak's office, just as the filters had finally cleared it out after the morning's visit. He apologized profusely, but she waved his apology aside.

"We're going to be here awhile, and we might as well adapt. Or learn to wear noseplugs."

Arly was trying not to wrinkle her nose, but positioned herself a seat away from Currald. "It's not you," she said to him, "but I simply can't handle the sulfur smell. Not with a meal on the table. It makes everything taste terrible."

Currald actually chuckled, a sign of unusual trust. "Maybe that's what drove the mutineers to eating meat—I've heard it ruins the sense of smell."

"Meat?" Mayerd looked up sharply from a sheaf of lab reports. "It makes the person who eats it stink of sulfur derivatives, but it doesn't confuse the eater's own nose."

"I don't know..." Sass paused with a lump of standard green vegetable in white sauce halfway to her mouth. "If things taste different in a sulfurous atmosphere—and they do—" She eyed the lump of green with distaste. "Then maybe meat would taste good."

"I never thought of that." Mayerd's brow wrinkled. Ford grinned at the table generally.

"Here comes another scientific paper... 'The Effect of Ireta's Atmosphere on the Perception of Protein Flavorings'... 'Sulfur and the Taste of Blood.'"

"Don't say that in front of Co-leader Varian," Sass warned. "She seems to be very sensitive where the prohibition is concerned. She wouldn't think it was funny."

"It's *not* funny," Mayerd said thoughtfully. "It's an idea... I never thought of it before, but perhaps an atmospheric stench would affect the kinds of foods people would prefer, and if someone were already tempted to consider the flesh of living beings an acceptable food, the smell might increase the probability—" The others groaned loudly, in discordant tones, and Mayerd glared at them. Before she could retort, Sassinak brought them to order, and explained why she'd wanted them to meet.

"Co-leader Varian is perfectly correct that the Iretans are not responsible for the mutiny or its effects. At the same time, it's in the interests of FSP to see that this planet is not opened to exploitation, and that the Iretans assimilate into the Federation with as little friction as possible. They've been told a pack of lies, as near as we can tell: they think that the original team was made up of heavyworlders, and abandoned unfairly. They expected help from heavyworlders only, and apparently think heavyworlders and lightweights cannot cooperate.

"We have the chance to show them that heavyworlders *are*

assimilated, and welcome, in our society. We all know about the problems—Major Currald has had to put up with harassment, as have most if not all heavyworlders in Fleet—but he and the others in Fleet believe that the two types of humans are more alike than different. If we can drive a friendly wedge between those young people and that heavyworlder colony ship—if we can make it clear that they have a chance to belong to a larger universe—perhaps they'll agree to compensation for their claims on Ireta, and withdraw. That would be a peaceful solution, quite possible for such a small group, and with compensation they could gain the education they'd need to live well elsewhere. Even if they don't give up all their claims, they might be more willing to live within the limits a tribunal is almost certain to impose... especially if Varian is right, and there's a sentient native species."

Currald said, "Do you want active recruitment? The ones I've seen would probably pass the interim tests."

Sass nodded. "If you find some you want for the marine contingent, let me know. I'd approve a few, but we'd have to be sure we could contain them. I don't believe any have been groomed as agents, but that's a danger I can't ignore."

Mayerd frowned, tapping the lab reports on the table beside her tray. "These kids were brought up on natural foods, not to mention meat. Do you think they could adjust to shipboard diets right away?"

"I'm not sure, and that's why I want you in on this from the beginning. We're going to need to know everything about their physiology. They're apparently heavyworlder-bred, but growing up on a normal-G planet hasn't brought out the full adaptation. Major Currald may have some insights into the differences, or perhaps they'd be willing to talk to other heavyworlders more freely. But you're the research expert on the medical staff: you figure out what you need to know and how to find out. Keep me informed on what you need."

"I've always thought," said Mayerd, with a sidelong glance at Currald, "that it's possible heavyworlders *do* require a blend of nutrients delivered most efficiently in meat. Particularly those on cold worlds. But you can't do research on that in the Federation—it's simply unmentionable. Not fair, really. Scientific research shouldn't be hampered by religious notions."

A tiny smile had twitched Currald's lips. "Research has been done, clandestinely of course, on two heavy-G worlds I know of. It's not just flesh, doctor, but certain kinds, and yes, it's the most efficient source of the special requirements we have. But I don't think you want to hear this at table."

"Another consideration," said Sassinak into the silence that followed, "is that of crew solidarity. It will do the heavyworlder critics in our crew good to see what heavyworlder genes look like when not stressed by high-G: with all respect, Currald, the Iretans look like normals more than heavyworlders." He nodded, sober but apparently not insulted. "But as you know, we've had trouble with a saboteur before. If anything happened now, to heighten tensions between heavyworlders and lightweights—" She paused, and glanced at every face. They all nodded, clearly understanding the implications. "Arly, I know you've made every possible safety check of the weapons systems, but it's going to be hard to keep your crews fully alert in the coming days. Yet you must: we must not have any accidental weapons discharges."

"Speaking of that," said Hollister. "I presume we're screened. . . ?" Sass pressed the controls and nodded. "I hadn't had a chance to tell you, and since the crisis appeared to be over—" He pulled a small gray box from his pocket and laid it on the table. "I found *this* in the number two power center just as we landed. Disabled it, of course, but I think it was intended to interfere with the tractor controls."

Sass picked up the featureless box and turned it over in her hands. "Induction control?"

"Right. It could be used for all sorts of things, including setting off weapons—"

"Where, precisely, did you find it?"

"Next to a box of circuit breakers, where it looked like it might be part of that assembly—some boxes have another switchbox wired in next to them. Same shade of gray, same type of coating. But I've been looking every day for anything new, anything different—that's how I spotted it. At first I wasn't even sure, but when I touched it, it came off clean—no wires. Nela cracked it and read the chips for me; that's how I know it was intended to mess up the tractor beam."

"Dupaynil?" She looked down the table at him. His expression was neutral.

"I'd wish to have seen it in place, yet clearly it had to be disabled in that situation, with the possibility of hostile fire. Did you consider physical traces?"

Hollister nodded. "Of course. I held it with gloves, and Nela dusted it, but we didn't find any prints. Med or you, sir, might find other traces."

"The point is," said Sassinak, "that we've finally found physical evidence of our saboteur. Still aboard, since I'm sure Hollister can say that wasn't in place yesterday, and still active."

"If we find a suspect," Dupaynil said, "we might look inside this for traces of the person who programmed it."

"If we find a suspect," said Sassinak. "And we'd better." On that note, the meeting adjourned.

Chapter Seventeen

Sassinak had made extensive preparations for her meeting the next morning with Captain Cruss. Unless he had illegal Fleet-manufactured detectors, he could not know that a full audio-video hookup linked her office to Ford's quarters and the bridge. Currald had furnished his most impressive heavyworld marines for an escort through the ship, although Sassinak had chosen Weft guards for her personal safety. She wanted to see if Cruss would overreach himself.

When Currald signalled that Cruss was on his way, she watched on the monitor. The five men and women that sauntered across the grid between ships were unpleasant-looking, even for heavyworlders. They had not bothered to put on clean uniforms, Sassinak noticed; even Cruss looked rumpled and smudged. She glanced briefly at her white upholstered chairs, and muttered a brief curse to rudeness... no doubt they would do their best to soil her things, and smirk to themselves about it. She knew too many fastidious heavyworlders to believe that they were innately dirty.

By the time they reached Main Deck, Sassinak had heard comments from observers she'd stationed along their path. They had argued about leaving their hand weapons with the guards; Captain Cruss carried a small, roughly globular object which he insisted he must hand-carry to Sassinak himself. She signalled an assent. They had made snide remarks to Currald and the heavyworlder escort, and pointedly turned away from the Wefts. They had lounged insolently on the grabbar in the cargo lift, and commented on the grooming of ship's crew in terms that had the reporting ensign red-faced. And of course they were late ... a studied discourtesy which Sassinak met with her own. When Gelory ushered them in with cool precision, Sassinak glanced up from a desk covered with datacards.

"Oh! Dear me, I lost track of time." She could see, behind the heavyworlders, Currald's flick of a grin: she *never* lost track of time. But she went on, smoothly and sweetly. "I'm so sorry, Captain Cruss—if you'll just take a seat—anywhere will do—and give me a moment to clear this." She turned back to her work, quickly organizing the apparent disarray, and tapping the screen before her with a control wand. Arly, by prearrangement, appeared in the doorway with a hardcopy file, and apologized profusely for interrupting.

"It's all right, Commander," said Sass. Arly's eyes widened at this sudden promotion in rank, but she had the good sense to ride with it. "Are those the current status reports? Good—if you'll relay these to Com, and tell them to use the Blue codebook—and then ask the Chief Engineer to clear these variations, that will be all." She handed Arly a stack of datacards and the hardcopy that had just spit from her console. With a quick glance at the file Arly had handed her, she thumbed a control that opened a desk drawer, deposited it therein, and returned her attention to Cruss and his crew. "There, now. We've had so much message traffic, it's taken me this long to sort things out. Captain, I've spoken to you—and this is your crew—?"

Cruss introduced his crew with none of the overused, but filthy, epithets of the day before. They glowered, uniformly, and stank of more than Ireta. Sassinak wondered if their ship were really that short of sanitary facilities, or if they preferred to smell bad.

"May I see your ship's papers—" It was not really a request, not with the *Zaid-Dayan*'s weaponry trained on the transport, and her marines on board. Cruss took a crumpled, stained folder out of the chest pocket of his shipsuit, and tossed it across the room. One of the marines turned to glare at him, and then glanced to Sassinak for guidance, but she did not react, merely picking up the distasteful object and opening it to read. "I'll also need your personal identification papers," she said. "Crew ratings—union memberships— if you'll hand those to Gelory—" They knew Gelory was a Weft; she could tell by the subtle withdrawal, as if they were afraid a Weft could harm them by skin touch. Sassinak went on reading.

According to the much-smudged (and probably faked) papers, transport and crew were on lease to Newholme, one of the shabbier commercial companies licensed by the Federation Colonial Service to set up colonies. Stamps from a dozen systems blotched the pages. Entry and exit from Sorrell-III, entry and exit from Bay Hill, entry and exit from Cabachon, Drissa, Zaduc, Porss... and Diplo. Destination a heavyworld colony two systems away, which Sassinak thought she recalled had reached its startup quota.

With hardly a sound, Gelory deposited the crew's individual papers on Sass's desk, murmuring "Captain," and drifting back to her place. Sassinak made no comment, and turned to these next, ignoring the squeaks and grunts of her furniture as the heavyworlders shifted in bored insolence, as well as their sighs and muttered curses. With the heavyworlders safely installed in her office, Ford should soon have Varian and Kai—the co-leader she hadn't met—in his quarters nearby, where they could see the interview without being seen. Until then, she intended to pore over these papers as if they were rare gems.

Luckily they were about as she'd expected, justifying a long examination. Captain Cruss, it turned out, had no master's license— just a temporary permit from Diplo. He had been a master mate (and what kind of rank was *that*, Sassinak wondered... she'd not seen that before) on an ore-hauler for eight years, and second mate on an asteroid-mining shuttle before that. Newholme had granted a temporary waiver of its usual requirements on the basis of Diplo's permit—that looked like a bribe.

First-mate, senior pilot Zansa, on the other hand, had had a master's license and once worked for Cobai Chemicals—which implied that her master's license had been legitimate. But it was stamped "rescinded" in the odd orange ink that nothing could eradicate completely—and with a notation that Zansa had become addicted to bellefleur, a particularly dangerous drug for a ship captain. Sassinak looked up and found Zansa, who bore the characteristic facial scars of a bellefleur addict, though they were all pale and dry.

"I'm clean," the woman growled. "Been clean five years, and next year I can retake the exams—"

"Shut *up*," said Cruss, savagely, and Zansa shrugged, clearly not intimidated. Sassinak went back to the papers. So . . . Zansa was the expert, and Cruss the cover—though she wondered why they hadn't found a legitimate master. Surely they could have done better than a recovering bellefleur addict.

Second pilot Hargit had had a checkered career, with rescinded visa stamps all over his records: charges and some convictions for petty theft, assault and battery, and "disturbance." That was from Charade, which usually had a pretty tolerant attitude towards disturbances. For the past five years, he'd piloted a cargo hauler between two heavyworlder planets, apparently without incident.

Lifesystems engineer Po was the largest of the five, a gross mass of flesh that escaped his shipsuit where the fastenings had strained from the cloth. He had a toothy grin that made Sassinak want to reach for a stunner—the kind of grin she remembered too well from her days as a slave. He had also been cashiered from the Diplo insystem space militia. She wondered how many of the hopeful colonists in coldsleep on the transport would have a chance to wake up with this . . . person . . . watching over their safety. He'd given up the fight to maintain traditional heavyworlder fitness on shipboard, but Sassinak did not doubt his strength.

And last was the "helper," Roella. Her papers listed a variety of occupations, in space and on planet, including "entertainer"— which, for someone of her appearance, meant only one thing. She'd also been jailed twice, for "disrespect"—but that was on Courance, where unlike Charade they were very picky indeed.

Plenty of questions to ask, but nothing she wanted to pursue too far, not now. A light came up on her console; she ignored it, and went on reading, rolling the control wand in her fingers. If they were clever, these heavyworlders, they would realize what it was—a stun-wand, as well as a link to her computers, With their backgrounds, they'd all had intimate experience with a stun-wand, somewhere. She finished turning through Roella's ID packet, and sighed, as if deeply pained by all this. Then she looked up at the tense, angry faces across from her.

"Yes, yes, Captain Cruss," she said, pouring all the smoothness she could into her voice. "Your papers do seem to be in order, and one cannot fault your chivalry in diverting to investigate a distress call . . ." What distress call? For they'd have had to receive it many light years away, the way they'd come. Of course they didn't know they'd been followed.

But Cruss was explaining, or trying to, that it had not been a normal distress call. Sassinak pushed her own thoughts aside to listen. A homing capsule, intended for the EEC compound ship which had dropped both the Ryxi colony and the exploration team. It had gone astray, somehow been damaged, and been found just beyond the orbit of the outermost planet of this system.

Not bloody likely, Sassinak thought grimly . . . it would be like someone in an aircraft happening to notice a single small bead on the end of the runway as they landed. Nothing that size could be detected in FTL flight, and it was more than a little unlikely that they'd come out of FTL on top of it by accident. She was surprised when Cruss stood up, and deposited the battered hunk of metal on her desk with insolent precision. So—that was his surprise—and he *had* a homing capsule, or part of it. Stripped of its propulsion unit and power pack, it was hardly recognizable. She refrained from touching it, noting only that engraved ID numbers were just visible along one pitted side.

She was not convinced of his story, even when he generously offered to let her extract the capsule's message from his computer, but she had no intention of arguing with him at this point. She doubted he knew that the Fleet computers had their own way with such capsules—and could extract more than a faked message implanted therein. But all that would come out at the trial. Now she smiled, graciously, and explained her reasons for confining them all to their ship, but with permission to trade for fresh foodstuffs with the locals. Cruss surged to his feet with another stale curse, and his companions followed. Sassinak sat quietly, relaxed: behind them the two Wefts had shifted to their own form, and clung to the angle of bulkhead and overhead. The marine escort was poised, hands hovering over weapons.

"I hope your water supplies are adequate," she said in the same conversational tone. "The local water is foul-tasting and smells." Cruss actually growled, a rumble of furious denial that he needed *anything* from her or anyone else. "Very well, then," she went on. "I'm positive you'll wish to continue on your way as soon as we have received clearance for you. The indigenes will have all the help we can give them. You may be sure of that." She stood, tapping the wand against her left palm, to watch them leave. Cruss made a motion toward the capsule, but Sassinak lowered the wand to forestall him.

"I think that had better remain," she said calmly. "Sector will wish to examine it—" His eyes shifted angrily. Guilty, she thought. What had they done to that thing? And where had it been sent? Surely not all the way to Diplo—at the sublight speed a capsule traveled, that would take years. His muscles bunched; Sassinak flicked a finger signal and the Wefts reassembled themselves beside him. He flinched, his expression shifting from barely controlled fury and contempt to alarm.

"Good day, Captain," she said easily, despite a mouth suddenly dry as the crisis passed. Of the others, only Zansa looked longingly toward the pile of personal documents on her desk—Sassinak avoided her eyes until she'd turned to leave.

As soon as the door slid shut, Sassinak relaxed back into her chair and turned it to face the video pickup. Ford quickly hooked their video into her screen, so that she could see them. Varian looked much better today: a vividly alive young woman who reminded Sassinak of herself, with those thick dark curls. But Varian's eyes were a clear gray, today untinged by the pain or stress that had clouded them the day before. Kai, on the other hand, looked nothing like an expedition leader. Slumped in his seat, pale, a padded suit protecting vulnerable skin . . . and his voice, when he spoke, revealed the strain even this much activity placed on him. He seemed harried, nervous—in a way more normal than Varian, for someone who'd been through a mutiny and forty-three years of coldsleep. Plus whatever had attacked him. She chatted with them, trying to assess Kai's condition and Varian's wits. Neither of them had any idea what the Thek presence meant, although Kai told her about the existing cores, found before the mutiny. She was still digesting that when Kai turned formal, and asked if she considered her presence to be the relief of the expeditionary team.

"How could it?" she asked, meanwhile wondering why he'd give her such an opening. Did he *want* to be removed from command? Did he distrust his co-leader? Varian seemed as surprised by his question as Sassinak. Sassinak filled out her quick answer, explaining her understanding of their entirely legitimate position, and reminding them again of her willingness to give them any assistance. Varian accepted this happily, but Kai still seemed constrained. Either he was very sick still, from all that had happened, or something else was wrong. After she'd turned them over to Ford, who would take Kai down to sickbay for Mayerd's diagnostic unit to work on, and Varian to supply, she sat for awhile, frowning thoughtfully at the screen that had held their image.

She put the ID papers of both transport and crew in a sealed pouch, and stored it safely away for later examination. Dupaynil came in, with two Com specialists, to take the homing capsule away. He asked if she wanted to watch them extract the message, but she shook her head. At the moment, she'd take a break from the day's craziness, and discuss the evening's menu with her favorite cook.

When the call came in from the survivors' geologist, one Dimenon, relayed through Com, she collected the Iretan heavyworlders and the expedition co-leaders. Mayerd shepherded Kai, clearly unwilling to let such an interesting case out of her sight, and Ford brought Varian. Dimenon had had a good reason for contacting the cruiser—not only a video of twenty-three small Thek, but an interaction between them and the creature that had attacked Kai. Sassinak had already viewed the tape once, and now in the re-run watched Kai's reaction to these odd creatures—fringes, they called them. The man was positively terrorstruck as the fringes advanced on the Thek, his breathing labored and his skin color poor. He had not moved well, coming into her office, but she thought if a fringe appeared in real life he would somehow manage to run. Pity and disgust contended in her mind. Had he always been like this, or had events overcome him? What did Varian think? Sassinak glanced at her, and realized that she, too, was covertly watching him, her expression guarded.

Sassinak distracted Varian with a question about the fringes, and Mayerd, bless her perception, kept the conversation going thereafter ... although Kai's answers, when he spoke, tended to cause a sudden rift. Then the Iretans began to ask their own questions, about the Thek, and their place in the Federation. Sass's opinion of Aygar's intelligence climbed another notch. He could think—and, it seemed in the next exchange, he even had a sense of humor. For when Sassinak asked him what weapon his people used against the fringes, he said, "We run," in a tone of rich irony.

A slight easing of tension, and the conversation continued: fringes and their habits, the aquatic fringes the expedition had observed before the mutiny. Aygar was surprised by that . . . and Sassinak was just wondering how she could shift the conversation to the reptiloids when Varian, answering a question, mentioned the word. Dinosaurs. Fordeliton leaped on it with such eagerness that Sassinak half-expected Varian to recoil suspiciously. But apparently she thought it was natural for a grown man, a Fleet cruiser Executive Officer, to leap into an argument about whether anything resembling a true Old Earth dinosaur could have evolved in such a different world. Varian reeled off a string of names, Ford gaped, and then brought Aygar into it.

Sassinak let the excited exchange continue a minute or so, then put a halt to it with such pointed lack of interest for anything but the political situation that she knew they'd erupt again when her back was turned. So much the better. By the time she ushered the Iretans out, Varian and Kai had practically adopted Ford. She had no trouble persuading them to take all six of the short-listed specialists . . . Varian, in fact, was openly gleeful.

She wondered if Mayerd had found out anything from Kai, besides the nature of his injuries and illness, but the medic had spent all her time on physical symptoms.

"It's no use asking why he's depressed and nervous until he's no longer in pain, feverish, and numb in places."

"I should think numbness preferable to pain," said Sassinak tartly. "How can he be both?"

Mayerd gave her a look which reminded her she hadn't eaten on time, and suggested they take a short break. "Eat a bit of that chocolate you keep hidden around here," she said, "and I'll have a cup of tea, and we'll all keep from biting our heads off, shall we?"

"Don't mother me, Mayerd. I'm not old and decrepit."

"No," said Mayerd shrewdly, "but you're about to meet a fourth-generation ancestor who's years younger than you are, and for all you know a raving beauty who'll steal Ford's heart away and leave you withering in the blast of dead passion."

Sassinak whooped, and her tension dissolved in an instant. "You—That's ridiculous!"

"True, O Captain. So are some other people. Done grieving for Huron yet, or are you still feeling so guilty you can't enjoy your many admirers?"

"You're making me blush. None of your business, I'd say, except it is, since you're my physician. Well, yes, I have enjoyed normal—or at least pleasurable—involvement in the last few weeks."

"Good. About time. That boy Tim's in awe of you, by the way, so I hope you're going to let him back into your good graces sometime."

"Already done, fairy godmother, so let me be."

"Back to Kai, then. The toxin destroyed nerve tissue, so he's got sensory deprivation on some areas of skin—nasty, because he doesn't know when he's hurt himself. Where the tissue's not destroyed, it's stimulated—just like pain, but the brain can't register constant stimulus like that, so he just gets these odd stabs and twinges, and a general feeling of something very wrong, very deep. His blood count's off, which probably causes the exhaustion you noticed, and he's not sleeping well, which doesn't help. I offered to slap him in one of the big tanks, and let him sleep it off until we got him to Sector, but he refused. Which, in this case, took considerable guts, despite that display while you ran the tape."

"Umm. It bothered me, particularly in someone in his position."

"That Varian's got enough bounce for two," said Mayerd; Sassinak could detect the faintest trace of distaste, and knew that Mayerd would always prefer a patient to a patient's healthy friend. With that in mind, she suggested that Mayerd visit the survivors that afternoon, when the diagnostic unit had finished meditating over Kai's condition.

"I'd already thought of that. They'll need clothes...you *were* planning a formal dinner, weren't you?"

"To show off, yes." Sassinak chuckled. "You mind-reader: people will think you're a Weft if you keep that up. Raid my closet, if you need anything I've got—there's a red dress that might suit Varian."

"I've got a green that will be perfect for Lunzie," said Mayerd smugly. "And all Kai's measurements, so I've already located something for him."

By the time Mayerd stopped by to show Sassinak what she'd chosen, on her way to the sled, the stewards were giving Sassinak sideways looks that meant they'd like her to clear out so they could set up for dinner. She had elected to serve in her office, a more intimate setting than the officers' mess.

"I'm going, I'm going," she said, grinning at the cook as he came to survey the room's layout, with an eye to planning service. She stopped by the bridge, where everything seemed to be under control, and discovered that most of them knew about her ancestress . . . after all, she hadn't told Ford or the others to keep it a secret. She worked through the day's reports, noting replies to some queries back to Sector, and some pending—she'd hoped to have more information for Kai and Varian tonight, but apparently not. Something might come in any time, of course. Finally Arly caught her attention and pointed to the clock. Time to be getting ready—but she'd cleared most of her work, and would start the morrow only slightly behind.

As she went to her cabin to clean up, she found she could not quite analyze her emotions. Lunzie . . . another Lunzie. No, not another Lunzie, but *the* Lunzie. That hardly seemed fair to her little sister—but then nothing had been. She wouldn't think about that, she told herself, and poured another dollop of shampoo on her hair. Thank the gods that the cruiser didn't have to use Iretan water!

But what would she be like? What *could* she be like? More like someone her elapsed age, or more like an old lady . . . a very, *very* old lady? She had the file holo . . . but that told her little. Her own file holo, the still one, didn't tell a viewer that much. Movement was so much of a person—she thought of this, wringing out her hair, and flipping it into a towel with easy practiced gestures. No two people even bathed alike, dried themselves alike . . . and what if her ancestress turned out to be prudish about sex? That thought brought a blush to her cheeks. She looked at herself in the mirror, thinking of Mayerd's teasing remarks. What if she *wasn't* . . . what if she had Sass's own casual attitude . . . and after all Ford *was* very good looking. No. Ridiculous. Here she hadn't even met her, and already she was thinking of *that* kind of rivalry with her great-great-great-grandmother?

Besides, Mayerd would be back before then, and could tell her—if she would, because doctors did stick together—and would it be worse, Sassinak asked herself suddenly, to lose a family because of long coldsleep, as Lunzie had certainly done, or gain one because someone down the line was alive when you awoke? She eased into the long black slip that fit under her formal evening dress uniform, and began assembling it: the black gown, skirt glittering with tiny stars, and the formal honors winking on the left breast of the bodice. Somehow the formals, jeweled as they were, seemed more remote from the events that earned them than the full-size medals that jingled softly on a white-dress suit. This was the first time she'd pinned the formal rank jewels of Commander on the shoulders; the last time she'd worn this outfit, she'd been a Lieutenant Commander at Sector Headquarters, on duty at a diplomatic ball. The long, close-fitting black sleeves were ringed with gold: the captain of the ship, even in evening dress.

A last look—the merest touch of color on her lips—and she was ready. The proper twenty minutes before the guests would arrive, and there was Mayerd, also ready, and Ford. They grinned at each other, and Sassinak resisted the temptation to check on her office. Ford would have done it. She congratulated Ford on the increased "coverage" of his chest... he had picked up more than a few impressive medals, in the years since she'd seen him last. Mayerd wore her Science Union badge, and the little gold pin that meant honor graduate of the best medical school in the human worlds. They chatted idly, waiting at the head of the ramp, and Sassinak was very aware that both were watching her closely, to catch her reaction to Lunzie. They'd said nothing except that her relative would "suit" her.

"There it is—" Ford gestured, and Sassinak caught a moving gleam in the darkness. Hard to see which was which, with so many bits of light shifting around, but Ford, as usual, was right. A four-seater airsled settled gently near the foot of the ramp, and the honor guard jogged out into place. Sassinak wondered, suddenly, if she should have gone quite this far without warning them... civilians, after all... but they seemed to understand what the shrill piping whistle meant. And the crisp ruffle of drums.

Varian and Lunzie, long skirts swirling in the wind, led the way up the ramp past a rigid honor guard. Sassinak could tell they were impressed, though she had trouble keeping her eyes off Lunzie's face: she hadn't wanted to stare like that since she was a first-year cadet.

Instead, she pulled herself up and saluted: appropriate to the planetary governor and her staff, but they'd all know it was for Lunzie. Varian gave a quick dip of the head, like a nervous bird, but Lunzie drawled a response to her greeting and offered a firm handshake.

For a long moment they stood almost motionless, then Lunzie retrieved her hand, and Sassinak felt a bubble of delight overcoming the last bit of concern. She would have liked this woman even if she hadn't been a triple great-grandmother—and she'd *have* to find an easier way to say all that. They had too much to say to each other! She grinned, cocking her head, and Lunzie's response was too quick to be an attempt to mimic—it was *her* natural gesture, too.

From there, the evening went quickly from delight to legend. Whatever chemistry went into the food, the drink, and the companionship combined into a heady brew that had Lunzie making puns, and Sassinak reciting long sequences of Kipling's verse. She noticed, as she finished a rousing version of "L'Envoi" that Lunzie had a speculative expression, almost wary. On reflection, perhaps she shouldn't have accented "They travel fastest who travel *alone*" quite so heavily, not when meeting the only member of her family she'd seen since Myriad. She grinned at Lunzie, and raised her glass.

"It's kind of a Fleet motto," she said. "Convince the youngsters that they have to cut free from home if they want to wander the stars..."

Lunzie's answering smile didn't cover the sadness in her eyes. "And your family, Sassinak? Where were you brought up?"

It had never occurred to her that Lunzie wouldn't know the story. She felt rather than saw Ford's sudden stiffness, Mayerd's abrupt pause in lifting a forkful to her mouth. No one had asked in years, now: Fleet knew, and Fleet was her family. Sassinak regained control of her breathing, but Lunzie had noticed; the eyes showed it.

"My family were killed," she said, in as neutral a voice as she could manage. "In a slaver raid. I...was captured."

Varian opened her mouth, but Kai laid a hand on hers and she said nothing. Lunzie nodded without breaking their gaze.

"They'd be proud of you," she said, in a voice with no edges. "I am."

Sassinak almost lost control again . . . the audacity of it, the gall . . . and then the love that shone so steadfastly from those quiet eyes.

"Thank you, great-great-great-grandmother," she said. A pause followed, then Ford leaped in with an outrageous story about Sassinak as a young officer on the prize vessel. The others followed with their own wild tales, obviously intent on covering up the awkwardness while Sassinak regained her equanimity. Mayerd and Lunzie knew the same hilarious dirty rhyme from medical school, and rendered it in a nasal accent that had them all in stitches. Varian brought up incidents from veterinary school, equally raunchy, and Kai let them know that geologists had their own brand of humor.

As they lingered over their liqueurs, the talk turned to the reports Kai and Varian had filed on the mutiny. Sassinak noticed that Kai had not only moved better, coming up the ramp, but seemed much less tense, much more capable, during dinner. Now he described the details of the mutiny in crisp, concise sentences. Mayerd had said she'd begun a specific treatment for him, but had it really worked this fast? Or had something else happened to restore his confidence?

They were interrupted by Lieutenant Borander, who was still, to Sass's eyes, far too nervous in the presence of high rank. But his news was riveting: the heavyworlder transport had tried to open communications with the Iretan settlement, and had not received an answer. Sassinak's party mood evaporated faster than alcohol in sunlight, and she noticed that the others were as sober-faced as she was. Lunzie pointed out that they had nothing to answer with—no comunits could last forty-three years in the open in this climate. But Aygar, Ford said, had not asked for communication equipment. Yet, when they all thought about it, the Iretans had been in contact with the transport before it landed. How?

"On what frequency was Cruss broadcasting?" asked Kai. Sassinak looked at him: whatever had happened, he was clearheaded and alert now. Borander answered him, and Kai gave a wicked grin. "That was our frequency, Commander Sassinak . . . the one we used before the mutiny."

"Interesting. How could he have learned that from the supposed message in the damaged homing capsule? It doesn't mention any frequencies. He's well and truly used enough rope . . ." She called in

Dupaynil, after a little more discussion, and the party broke up. Sassinak wished they'd had just a little longer to enjoy the festive occasion. But the time for long dresses and fancy honors was over— an hour later she was back in working uniform.

Chapter Eighteen

The next morning, after several hours in conference with her supply officers, she began allocating spares and replacement supplies to the Iretans and the expedition survivors. Surely Sector would order them back to report, rather than expecting them to finish the usual cruise—and that meant they could spare all this. She put her code on the requisitions, and went back to lean on Com again. Better than brooding about Lunzie—the more she thought about that, the more unsettled she felt. The woman was younger, not older—apparently a fine doctor, certainly an interesting dinner companion, but she could not feel the awe she wanted to feel. Lunzie might have been one of her younger officers, someone she could tease gently. And yet this "youngster" had a right to ask things that Sassinak didn't want to recall. She knew, by the look in Lunzie's eyes, that she would ask: she would want to know about Sassinak's childhood, what had happened.

She saw a crewman flinch from her expression, and realized her thoughts had control of her face again. This would never do. She wondered if Lunzie felt the same tangle of feelings. If she thought her ancestress should somehow be older, in experience, perhaps Lunzie felt that Sassinak should be younger. And yet she'd had that jolt of sympathy, that instant feeling of recognition, of kinship. They'd be able to work their way through the tangle somehow. They had to. For the first time since her capture, Sassinak felt a longing for something outside Fleet. Perhaps she shouldn't have avoided her family all these years. It might not have been so bad, and certainly Lunzie wasn't the stuff of nightmares.

She caught herself grinning as she remembered Mayerd's tart comments. No, Lunzie wasn't a raving beauty—though she wasn't exactly plain either, at least not in that green dress, and she had the warm personality which could draw attention when she wanted it. And Lunzie approved of her, at least so far. *It will work out*, she thought again, fiercely. *I'm not going to lose her without at least trying.* Trying what, she could hardly have said.

From this musing, the alarm roused her to instant alertness. Now what? Now, it seemed, the Thek were appearing, and demanding that the expedition leaders be brought to the landing site.

"Ford, take the pinnace," said Sassinak, ignoring Timran's eager upward glance. She had finally let him take an airsled on one of the supply runs, and he'd managed to drop one crate on its corner and spew the contents all over the landing area. One disk-reader landed on an Iretan's foot, creating another diplomatic crisis (fortunately brief: they were barely willing to acknowledge pain, which made it hard to claim injury), and Tim was grounded again.

While the pinnace was on its way, she tried to guess what the Thek were up to this time. They'd been acting like ephemerals in the past few days, whizzing from place to place, digging up cores, and, unusual for Thek, chattering with humans. Then the Thek appeared above the landing grid.

"Large targets," said Arly, her fingers nervously flicking the edges of her control panel. They were, in fact, the largest Thek Sassinak had ever seen.

"They're friendly," she said, wishing she was entirely sure of that. She had enough to explain to the admiral now, without a Thek/human row.

"Are they coming to see us, or that co-leader fellow?"

"Or them?" Sassinak pointed to the main screen, showing two of the largest Thek descending near the heavyworlder transport. "Umm. Let's treat it as diplomatic: Major Currald, let's have a formal reception out there, and," she turned, quickly pointing at officers with the most experience in working with aliens, "you, and you, and—yes, you. We'll assume a delegation's coming, and since we represent FSP here, they'll come to us."

By the time she reached Troop Deck and the landing ramp, two of the smallest Thek had planted themselves on the grid nearby.

Around the bulge of the *Zaid-Dayan*, she could see a section of the pinnace as Ford landed it.

But the Thek appeared to be far more interested in Kai than in the cruiser's welcoming committee. One of them actually greeted him, in recognizable if strained speech. Sassinak motioned her officers to silence and did not interrupt. Whatever was going on, she'd find out more by going along with the Thek plan.

The Thek offered a core to Kai for examination; he gave the coordinates of its original location. Thunder rumbled underfoot: Sassinak noticed nothing in the sky. Theks talking to Theks? Sassinak glanced at each of them in turn: the immense ones and a medium-huge one near the heavyworlder colony ship, the medium-large and relatively smaller ones nearby. After a moment's silence, Sassinak leaned forward.

"Kai, ask if this planet is claimed by Thek." Although she spoke as softly as she could, the Thek answered her instantly.

"Verifying." Then, a moment later, "Dismiss. Will contact."

Kai turned to Sassinak, a look between respect, frustration, and annoyance. Well, she had intruded on his private conversation. She shrugged, and tried to lighten the mood.

"Dismissed, are we?"

Apparently that worked, for she could see his lips twitching with controlled laughter. Ford gave her a fast wink, then smoothed his face into utter blandness as Kai looked at him. What had Ford been up to with the co-leader? The wink told her only that he'd have a good story to tell later . . . and she'd have to wait to hear it. In the meantime, she dismissed the honor guard, who departed cursing quietly at having been put into the tight-collared formal uniform in this heat if it wasn't really necessary, and invited Kai up for a visit.

He certainly looked better today, far more the sort of vigorous, outgoing young geologist who had been chosen co-leader with Varian. For a moment she wondered if he and Varian had ever paired up—and if so, why they weren't paired now.

But the real question was what the Thek were doing on Ireta. So many Thek on one supposedly unclaimed planet was as great a mystery as anything else. Kai ventured hardly any explanation, beyond saying that perhaps the Thek were "worried." Sassinak wondered if that was really all he thought, or all he thought he should say. She had no reason to hide her chain of logic from him, and went on to explain, watching closely for his reaction.

"A convocation of such size surely suggests a high degree of interest, Kai. And that old core—that was the same core which brought Tor?" He nodded, and she went on. "All those little Thek sucking up old cores—when they weren't frying fringes...you see my point, surely. Your EEC ship's records, and Fleet records, both list Ireta as unexplored. Yet you found Thek relics and the first Thek on scene appeared surprised at them. Doesn't that suggest a missing link in the famous Thek chain of information? Something happened, here on Ireta, to one or more Theks, which somehow did not transmit to the others?"

Kai followed her argument but his expression settled on anxiety rather than relief. "The old core is of Thek manufacture," he said, almost reluctantly. "Unquestionably it's generated Thek interest. But I can't see why..."

Sassinak felt a moment's impatience. The scientists always wanted to know why, before they halfway understood exactly what had happened. Or so it seemed to her. She was glad enough to put events in order, sure she had all the relevant parts, before worrying about why and what if. She let Kai and her officers go on talking, wandering their own logical or illogical paths through Thek behavior, the geology of Ireta, and the probable age of the core in question.

A light flashed on her console: message from the bridge. She thumbed the control on her earplug. "Sir, all those little Thek have landed near the original expedition campsite..."

With two key punches, she had that up on one of the screens and the scene stopped Kai in mid-sentence.

"Every fringe on Ireta is homing in on our campsite," he said, his expression anxious.

It took her a moment to realize what he meant: the heat exuded by so many Thek would inevitably attract fringes, just as one Thek had attracted the fringe that had attacked Kai. Before she could think of something to reassure him, the screen showed new Thek activity as a score or more spun away crazily into the sky and offscreen. Now what were they doing? Kai looked as confused as she felt.

By this time, Sassinak felt the need of refreshment and, noticing that Kai looked a little wan, she invited him into the officers' mess. A few deft comments from her and Kai, and Anstel and Pendelman were into a lively discussion of Iretan geology with excursions into evolutionary biology. Sassinak listened politely enough, but with the internal feeling of the adult listening to eight-year-olds discussing the merits of competing toys. At least they were busy and happy, and if they stayed out of trouble, she might get some work done.

Varian's arrival added another bit of fizz to the meeting, so that Sassinak had no need to keep up any corner of the conversation. Relaxed, she let herself think about the Thek from a Fleet perspective. If the data relays had all worked correctly—and she knew whose heads would roll if they hadn't—they'd gathered more information about Thek in flight and landing today than Fleet had anywhere in its files.

Her technical specialists, now busily talking hyracotheriums and golden fliers with Varian, had already taken discreet samples of the landing grid and the plateau face. Those data, along with the observations of the large Thek sinking into the landing grid, should reveal more about the way Thek handled heat dispersion.

Varian broke into her musings with the kind of questions a planetary governor ought to ask, Sassinak noted. Were the Thek known to be interested in planet piracy? Were they indeed? She wished she knew.

The meeting broke up shortly after that, with Anstel now in the role of one of the "science officers" accompanying Varian and Kai. The rest of that day, Sassinak spent composing messages for Sector Headquarters, and poring over the first, incomplete replies to her queries. Fleet had to be informed that the Thek were there, and rather than be bombarded by stupid questions when she was likely to be busy, better that they be supplied with some sort of explanation . . . but the admiral would want all the data. In order.

Her original signals, asking for clarification of Mazer Star's status, the Ryxi colony's status, and so on, had of necessity been brief. The incoming stack in her official file had its own priorities. Only one item surprised her, and that was "predominant owner" of the company holding title to the heavyworlder transport: Paraden.

She thought of the pale-eyed, red-headed young man who had tried to get her in such trouble in the Academy, and of Luisa Paraden's connection (of sorts) to the slaver she and Huron had captured. This time it was Arisia Paraden Styles-Hobart, holding fifty three percent, and not on the board of directors at all... but Fleet had been able to discover that she was active in the company... or at least A. P. Hobart, whose ID for tax purposes was the same, was the "Assistant Director of Employee Assignment." Handy, if you wanted to hire a crooked man to captain your crooked ship.

She wondered where Randolph Neil Paraden had ended up: somewhere in Newholme? The treasurer or something? Surely not; Fleet would have noticed that, too. The good news was that the ARCT-10 had shown up—or at least its message to Sector HQ had arrived. Severe damage from a cosmic storm (Sassinak quirked her lips: "investigating a cosmic storm" was a stupid sort of civilian idea. Space had enough hazards when you tried to play it safe), some (unlisted) casualties, but "no great loss of life." Whatever that meant to a ship the size of most moons, with a normal shipboard population in the thousands in a variety of races.

They'd lost their FTL capability, and most of their communications, and spent nearly all the elapsed time hobbling toward a nearby system at well below lightspeed. No real hardship for those who lived their lifetimes on board anyway, but it must have been tough on the "temporary" specialists who'd expected to be home in six months.

And, of course, for the ones left behind on Ireta. Sassinak's hand hesitated on the console. Should she call Kai now, or wait until tomorrow? She glanced at the time, and decided to wait. They'd be getting ready for that gathering she'd heard about, and perhaps by morning she'd have a list of casualties so that he could quit worrying (or start mourning) his family. And those children—their parents on the ship would be old, or dead, by now. She could and did call up *Mazer Star* to confirm that she'd received Fleet clearance for them.

"And you should receive some kind of official recognition," she told Godheir. "There's a category for civilian assistance. Depending on the tribunal outcome, it might even mean a cash bonus for you and your crew; certainly I'll recommend it."

"Ye don't have to do that, Commander Sassinak..." Captain Godheir's screen image looked appropriately embarrassed.

"No, but you deserve it. Not just for your quick response, although it's in everyone's interest to encourage honest citizens to respond to mayday calls, but for your continued willingness to help the expedition. I know you aren't designed to deal with youngsters recovering from that kind of trauma. And I know you and your crew have spent a lot of hours with them."

"Well, they're good kids, after all, and it's not their fault. And no family with them."

"Yes, well, I expect, with the Thek here, this will wrap up shortly, and you'll be free to go. But you have my gratitude for your help."

"I'm just glad you weren't the pirate I thought you at first," said Godheir, rubbing his head. "When you hailed us, that's all I could think of."

Sassinak grinned at him; she could imagine that having something like the *Zaid-Dayan* suddenly pop up behind him could have startled a peaceful transport captain. "I was just as glad to find that you weren't an armed slaver escort. Oh, by the way, do you have as many dinosaur buffs as I seem to have brought along?"

"A few, yes. They're convening at the main camp tonight, along with some of yours, I think."

"That's what I thought."

His expression asked if she had a problem with that, and she didn't, except to wonder if fanning the flames of the dinosaur enthusiasts had been such a good idea.

"I don't expect any trouble from Captain Cruss, with the Thek nearby, but still—"

"I'm taking precautions, Commander," he said quickly, not quite offended at her presumption. Sassinak nodded, glad he'd taken the hint, and willing to have him a little huffy with her. Better that than trouble in the night.

"I assumed you had, Captain Godheir," she said. "But so many things aren't going according to Regulations already . . ." He smiled, again relaxed.

"Right you are, and we'll be buttoned up tight. I'll tell my crew not to overdo the hospitality juice, whatever it is and wherever it comes from."

Dupaynil was waving at her from the corridor; Sassinak signed off, and turned to him.

"Captain, we got the homing capsule stripped," he said happily. "And a fine bit of imaginative writing that was, let me tell you.

Imaginative wiring, too. We're still doing forensics on it. We've got surface deposit/erosion scans going, another seven hours on that, and there's a new technique for analyzing biochemical residues, but basically we've got Cruss and Co. in a locked cell right now."

"In order?" suggested Sassinak. Dupaynil nodded, and laid it all out for her.

"A fake, of course; a clever one, but a fake. First the homing capsule itself, which clearly shows the pitting and scarring one would expect from some four decades of space travel. Except where the propulsion unit and so on were removed—not by natural causes, either, but by tools available to any civilized world. Then roughed up to a pretense of the distressed natural surface."

"Which tells you that the homing capsule went somewhere, then was broken apart, and returned—"

"Probably with Cruss in his ship, although not certainly. It might have been placed for him to find. Now the message . . . the message was clever, very clever. Ostensibly, it's the message Cruss told you, the one he let us 'copy' from his computer. It's not a long message, and it repeats six times."

Dupaynil cocked his head, giving Sassinak the clear impression that he wanted her to guess what followed. "And then another message?" she prompted. "On the loop behind those?"

"Precisely. I was sure the Commander would anticipate. Yes, after six boring repetitions, which any ordinary rescuer must have assumed would go on until the end, we found a sixty second delay—presumably the number of repetitions coded the length of the following delay—and then the real message. The location of Ireta; the genetic data of the surviving heavyworlders, including the planned breedings for several generations; a brief account of the local biology and geology; a list of special supplies needed; a recommendation for founding colony size. There are, as you would expect, no destination codes remaining. We cannot prove, from the message alone, who were its intended recipients. For that we await the physical evidence of the shell; it is just possible that its travels are, in a way, etched on its surface. But what they sent was an open invitation: this is who we are, where we are, and what we have. Come join us."

Sassinak could think of no adequate comment. Proof indeed that the mutineers were intentional planet pirates. She took a long breath and let it out. Then: "Are you sure they intended it for heavyworlders exclusively?"

"Oh yes. The genetic types they asked for all code that way. Besides, I've now got the old Security data on the mutineers. Look, Separationists, but not Purists. All of them, at one time or another, were in one of two political or religious movements."

"And no one spotted this beforehand?" She felt a rumble of anger that no one had noticed, and therefore people had died, and others had lost over forty years of their lives.

Dupaynil shrugged eloquently. "Exploration ships do not welcome Security, especially not Fleet Security. They insist that their specialists must have the freedom to investigate, to think for themselves. Of course I am not against that, but it makes it very hard to prevent the 'chance' connivance of those whose associations cause trouble."

"Umm. I expect that Kai and Varian will visit again tomorrow, Dupaynil, and I would prefer to withhold this until we have the physical data—or until something else happens. At the rate things are going wild, something else may indeed make disclosure necessary."

"I understand. When you're ready for me to arrive with the discovery, just let me know." He gave her a very Gallic wink, and withdrew to continue his investigations.

The next morning, Sassinak was glad that she had made it to bed at a reasonable hour: the Thek abruptly summoned her, Kai, Varian, and, to her surprise, the Iretans and Captain Cruss. She sent Ford with the pinnace to pick up the governors and Lunzie and recall any crew from the campsite.

Meanwhile, the outside pickups revealed that the Thek which had been positioned near cruiser and transport were now grouped at the far end of the landing grid. Sassinak studied the screen for a few moments, and turned away, baffled. What were they doing?

She ate breakfast and changed into a dress uniform without expressing any such confusion to the crew, though their bafflement was apparent to her. Halfway through a glass of porssfruit juice, something tickled her memory about Thek.

She'd seen something like this . . . it came back in a rush. The dead world, the time she had gone down with a landing party, and the Thek had come. First a few had clustered like that, and then others had come and clumped into some kind of structure. She'd forgotten about it for years, because of that mess with Achael, but... "cathedral" was what someone had termed it, the special conference mode of the Thek. To which she was bidden.

Despite herself, Sassinak shivered, remembering that folk involved in a Thek conference often found themselves extremely obedient servants of its determinations. She promptly initiated a Discipline procedure so that she would remember *all* that transpired during that unique experience. Then grinned to herself. This could make a riveting recital the next time she needed something to enliven a dull evening at the Sector HQ Officers' Club.

While she and most of the other "invited" guests went willingly through the one opening left by Theks fitting themselves into the immense structure, Captain Cruss did not. His boots dug grooves in the ground to show his unwillingness but inexorably he was brought into the cathedral and the last Thek clunked into place. Oddly enough, a curious ambient light provided illumination. Sassinak caught Aygar's contemptuous look and turned away, only then noticing the collection of porous shards, a dull dark charcoal grey rather than the usual Thek obsidian, but patently a nearly disassembled Thek.

"Your core evidently bore strange fruit," she said to Kai, keeping her voice low. "And if that is indeed a very ancient Thek, we ephemerals will have to revise some favorite theories... and some good jokes."

"Commander," Cruss cried, his heavy voice reverberating so loudly the others winced, "I demand an explanation of the outrageous treatment to which I have been subjected."

"Don't be stupid, Cruss," Sassinak said, pivoting to him. "You know perfectly well the Thek are a law unto themselves. And you are now subject to that law, and about to sample its justice."

"We have verified." The words, intoned in a non-directional voice, opened the conference. "Ireta is for Thek as it has been for hundreds of millions of years. It will remain Thek. For these reasons..."

✧   ✧   ✧

With no apparent passage of time, Sassinak found herself leaning against Aygar. She needed to: she felt every second of her age in the steamy Iretan midday with its blazing sun beating down on them. Aygar clung to her for a moment more, obviously experiencing a similar disorientation. In the touch of his strong hands, she sensed that his earlier contempt for her had lessened. When he came out of his current shock, she expected he'd be a much more pleasant fellow.

Someone groaned. Sassinak blinked her eyes clear and saw Varian holding Kai upright. Cruss crouched on the ground in such an attitude of dejection that she could almost pity him. Almost, not quite.

In the meantime, she had had her orders. She had to get her marines, Weft and human, off that transport before Cruss woke up and lifted it off-world. Innocent or not, anyone on board at lift-off would have only one destination. That, the Thek had made quite clear. Trying to shake off the aftereffects of that extraordinary experience and access the Discipline-retained memories, she let Ford and Lunzie shepherd them into the pinnace for the short hop back to the cruiser. But she couldn't organize her thoughts beyond responding to the implanted instructions.

Once in her quarters she gave the necessary orders and then paused to catch her breath. The Thek had somehow compressed the very air inside their cathedral, enervating to the humans, and what she'd really have liked was a long quiet stretch of solitary meditation, to regain her own sense of space.

Half-bemused, and half-annoyed, she noticed that Lunzie was not so patient. Her great-great-great prodded Ford into finding her liquor cabinet, poured drinks for everyone, and offered a toast "To the survivors!"

Sassinak drank, thinking to herself that Lunzie must have enjoyed that Sverulan brandy as much as it deserved, to be so eager to find more. Prior to the conference, Lunzie had buffered Kai and Varian and now she snapped them out of it. They burst into speech, and stopped as their voices clashed.

Sassinak chuckled. "Cruss took quite a beating." Gingerly she touched her temples where a massive headache was gathering. "We all did."

"Despite our clear consciences and pure hearts," Varian added with a sly grin at Lunzie.

Sassinak depressed the comunit button. "Pendelman, request Lieutenant Commander Dupaynil to join us. And didn't we just get exactly the information we needed. Cruss spilled his guts. Not that I blame him."

"Then you know who's behind the piracy?" Lunzie asked, excited.

"Oh, yes. I'll wait until Dupaynil gets here. Kai and Varian have been covered with glory, too. Which is only fair."

Kai took up the narrative then, explaining that they had rescued a Thek who had been trapped for eons and buried so deeply it had been unable to summon help. Originally Ireta had been earmarked as a feeding ground with its rich transuranics so satisfying to Thek appetites, hence the cores. The Thek Ger had been guardian, to make certain young Thek did not strip the planet of its riches and leave it a barren husk.

"The Thek are the *Others*," Lunzie gasped.

"That is the inescapable conclusion," Sassinak agreed. "Thek are nothing if not logical. We were also exposed to quite a hunk of Thek history. I'll joggle the rest out of my head later. The relevant fact is that it became apparent to the Thek after a millennium of gorging that, if they couldn't curtail their appetites, they ran the risk of eating themselves out of the galaxy."

"No wonder they had an affinity for dinosaurs," Fordeliton exclaimed with a whoop of laughter.

"We get to preserve them now," Varian said, rather proudly.

Kai grinned shyly. "Ireta is restricted, of course, as far as transuranics go but I, and my 'ilk,' as they put it, have the right to mine anything up to the transuranics for . . . is it as long as 'we' live? I'm not sure if the limit is just for *my* lifetime."

"No," said Lunzie. "By ilk, the Thek probably mean the ARCT-10, for as long as it survives. You deserve it, Kai. You really do."

"Curiously enough," Sassinak said into the respectful pause that followed, "the Thek did appreciate the fact that you all have lost irreplaceable time. Thek justice is unusual."

Thek had lumped all humans—the timelaggged, the survivors, and the descendants—in one group as survivors. They could remain or leave as they chose.

"I wonder if some of the Iretans might consider enlisting in the Fleet," Sassinak mused, thinking of Aygar. "Wefts are excellent guards but Ireta produced some superb physical types. Ford, do see if we can recruit a few."

"And the surviving member of the original heavyworlder contingent?" Lunzie asked.

"Mutiny cannot be excused, nor the mutineer exonerated," Sassinak answered, her expression stern. "He is to be taken back to Sector Headquarters to stand trial. The Thek were as adamant on that score as I am."

"And Cruss is being sent back?" Ford asked.

Sassinak steepled her fingers, permitting herself a satisfied smile. "Not only sent back but earthed for good. Neither he, his crew, nor any of the passengers will ever leave their planet. Nor will that transport lift again."

"The Thek do nothing by halves, do they?"

"They have been exercised, if you can imagine a Thek agitated," Sassinak went on, getting to the real meat of the cathedral's findings, "about the planetary piracies and patiently waiting for *us* to do something constructive about the problem. The intended rape of Ireta has forced them, with deep regret, to interfere." Just then, Dupaynil entered. "On cue, for I have good news for you, Commander. Names, only one of which was familiar to me." She beckoned the Intelligence officer to take a seat as she leaned forward to type information on the terminal. "Parchandri is so conveniently placed for this sort of operation ..."

"Inspector General Parchandri?" Fordeliton exclaimed, shocked.

"The same."

Lunzie chuckled cynically. "It makes sense to have a conspirator placed high in Exploratory, Evaluation, and Colonization. He'd know exactly which planetary plums were ready to be plucked."

Kai and Varian regarded her with stunned expressions.

"Who else, Sassinak?" Lunzie asked.

She looked up from the visual display with a smug smile. "The Sek of Formalhaut, Aidkisaga IX, is a Federation Councillor of Internal Affairs." She noticed Lunzie's startled reaction but went on when she saw Lunzie close her lips tightly. "One now understands just how his private fortune was accrued. Lutpostig appears to be the

Governor of Diplo, a heavyworlder planet. How convenient! Paraden, it will not surprise you to discover, owns the company which supplied the grounded transport ship."

"We could never have counted on uncovering duplicity at that level, Commander," was Dupaynil's quiet assessment. He frowned slightly. "It strikes me as highly unusual for a man at Cruss' level to know such names."

"He didn't," Sassinak replied equably. "He was only vaguely aware that Commissioner Paraden was involved. The Thek extrapolated from what he could tell them of recruitment procedures, suppliers, and what they evidently extracted from the transport's data banks."

"But how can we use the information they obtained?" Dupaynil asked.

"With great caution, equal duplicity and superior cunning, Commander, and undoubtedly some long and ardent discussions with the Sector Intelligence Bureau. Fortunately, for my hypersuspicious nature, I've known Admiral Coromell for years and trust him implicitly..."

"*You* know Admiral Coromell?" Lunzie asked, amazed.

"We are in the same fleet, dear ancestress. And knowing where to look for one's culprits is more than half the battle, even those so highly placed." Sassinak saw her thoughtful look and went on briskly. "I have been given sailing orders, too. So, Fordeliton, brush up on your eloquence and see whom you can recruit from among the Iretans. Kai, Varian, Lunzie, I'll have Borander return you to your camp with any supplies you might need to tide you over until the ARCT-10 arrives. Just one more thing..." and she swiveled her chair about, turning to the rank of cabinets behind her and opening one with a thumblock. She heard Lunzie's sigh of satisfaction as the squatty little brandy bottles came into view.

"Clean glasses, Ford—I've a toast to propose." And when all stood with their glasses ready, she expanded Lunzie's brief presentation: "To the brave, ingenious, and honored survivors of this planet...including the dinosaurs."

That got a smile from all of them, and a chuckle as the smooth brandy slid down. Revived by the brandy's kick, Kai and Varian rose, eager to get back to their camp. The Thek decision had given them both a lot to look forward to, and plenty of work.

"Kai, Varian, you go on without me," Lunzie said, surprising the co-leaders but not Sassinak. "I'd like a little while longer with this relative of mine." She turned to Sassinak, a bit shy and stiff suddenly.

In the flurry of parting, Sassinak rather hoped she knew what might be coming. After all, Varian would have her animals to study; Kai would have his minerals to mine... what would Lunzie have? Nothing. She'd be picked up by the ARCT-10; she'd try to find a recertification course to bring her up to date in medicine, and then she'd hire out for something else. Not the sort of life Sassinak would want. Even if she'd been a doctor.

"Let's eat here," she said, as Kai and Varian, escorted by Ford, went off down the corridor. "It's an awkward time for them in the messhall, right between shifts."

"Oh. Fine." Lunzie wandered around the office as Sassinak ordered the meal, looking at the pictures and the crystal fish.

"That's my favorite," said Sassinak of the fish. "After the desk. This thing is my great hunk of self-indulgence."

"Doesn't seem to have hurt you much," said Lunzie, with a bite to it.

Sassinak laughed. "I saw it fifteen years ago, saved for seven years. The place makes them one at a time and won't start one on credit. They spent two years building it, and then for five years it sat in storage until I had a place to put it."

"Umm." Lunzie's eyes slid across hers, then came back.

"As near as I can make it, that Thek conference lasted four and a half hours," Sassinak said, running her finger around her damp collar. She'd loosen it once lunch had been served. Right now she had to loosen up Lunzie. She held up the bottle. "Wouldn't you recommend another shot, Doctor Mespil? Purely medicinal, of course."

"If this old fool can prescribe a similar dose for herself?" Lunzie's smile was little more natural as Sassinak filled both their glasses with a generous tot.

"Thanks."

Before they'd finished savoring the brandy, two stewards brought trays heaped with food: thinly sliced sandwiches, two bowls of soup, bowls of fried delicacies, fresh fruit obviously bartered from the Iretans.

Lunzie shook her head. "You Fleet people! And I always thought a military life in space was austere!"

"It can be." Sassinak tasted her soup and nodded. Another one of her favorite cook's creative successes. The stewards smiled and withdrew. Now Sassinak loosened her tunic. "There are certain... mmm...perks that come with rank and age."

"Mostly rank, I'd guess. I'm happy for you, Sass, you seem to have earned a lot of respect, and you're clearly suited to your life."

For some reason this made Sassinak vaguely uneasy. "Well...I like it. Always have. It's not all this pleasant, of course."

"No? Have you seen combat often?"

"Often enough. Cruise before this one, we were boarded. Someone even took a potshot at me."

That caught Lunzie with her spoon stopped halfway to her mouth, and she put it down safely in the soup before asking more.

"Boarded? I didn't know that happened in...I mean, a Fleet cruiser?"

"That's exactly the reaction of the Board of Inquiry. It seemed like a good idea at the time, though, Lunzie." Far from being upset by her great-great-great as a listener, Sassinak discovered a certain catharsis easing tension, almost as beneficial as medication. And just the thread of a new thought, bearing on the information the Thek had extracted. "My Exec had a shipload of slaves to get out of that system asap." She told Lunzie the whole story, backing and filling as necessary.

"And you'd been a slave...you knew..." Lunzie murmured softly.

There was more understanding in that tone than Sassinak could well stand; she changed the subject again, surprised to find herself mentioning another problem.

"Yes, and as for crew loyalty, by and large you're right. But not entirely. For instance," and Sassinak leaned back in her chair, regarding her guest with a measuring glance, "right now, I'm fairly sure that we have an informer aboard: someone in the pay of any one of those prestigious names we've been made privy to. Dupaynil and I have scanned and dissected the records of everyone on board and it hasn't done us a bit of good. We can't find tampering or inconsistencies or service lapses. But we have got a saboteur. My crew're all starting to suspect each other. You can imagine what that does to morale!" Lunzie nodded, eyes sharpening. "The timid ones came to me, wanting me, of all things, to arrest our heavyworlders. As if heavyworlders were the Jonahs." She noticed Lunzie's startled expression. "And the next thing will be some political movement or other. There has to be a way to find the rotter, but I confess I'm stymied. And I particularly want the bugger found before any hint of what we've discovered here on Ireta can possibly leak."

Lunzie began peeling a fruit, letting the rind curl below her fingers. "Would you like me to look through the files—the unclassified stuff, I mean? Maybe an outside eye? Sort of singing for my lunch, as it were?"

"Singing for your lunch?"

"Never mind. If you don't trust an outsider..."

"Oh, I trust you—gods below, my own great-great-great-grandmother. " Sassinak caught herself on the rim of a hiccup, and decided that she was the least bit cozy from the brandy. "You could look through my bottom drawers if you wanted. But what can you find that Dupaynil and I haven't found?"

"I dunno. But being older ought to do some good, if being younger can't."

At this, they locked glances and giggled. Fresh eyes, Lunzie's eyes, made no sense, and very good sense, and they were both more relaxed than necessary. Two hours later, poring over the personnel files, they had sobered but were no nearer solving Sassinak's problem.

"I didn't think you needed this many people to run a cruiser," said Lunzie severely. "It would be easier to check a smaller crew."

"Part of that great life I have as a cruiser captain."

"Right. One more engineering technician, grade E-4, and I'm going to..." Suddenly she paused, and frowned. "Hold it! Who's this?"

Sassinak called up the same record on her own screen. "Prosser, V. Tagin. He's all right; I've checked him out, and so has Dupaynil." She glanced again at the now-familiar file. Planet of origin: Colony Makstein-VII, somatotype: height range 1.7-2 meters, weight range 60-100 kg, eye color: blue/gray, skin: red/yellow/black ratio 1:1:1, type fair, hair type: straight, fine, light-brown to yellow to gray.

Longheaded, narrow pelvis, 80% chance missing upper outer incisors. She screened Prosser's holo, and saw a 1.9 meter, 75-kilogram male with gray eyes in a longish pale face under straight fine, fair hair. By his dental chart, he was missing the upper outer incisors, and his blood type matched. "There's nothing off in his file, and he's well-within the genetic index description. His eyes are too close together, but that's not a breach of Security. What's wrong with him?"

"He's impossible, that's what."

"Why?"

Lunzie looked across at her, a completely serious look. "Did you ever hear of clone colonies?"

"Clone colonies?" Sassinak stared at her blankly. She had neither heard of such a thing nor seen a reference to it. "What's a clone colony?"

"What databases do you have onboard? Medical, I mean? I want to check something." Lunzie had gone tense suddenly, alert, almost vibrating with what she wouldn't explain—yet.

"Medical? Ask Mayerd. If that's not enough, I can even get you access to Fleet HQ by FTL link."

"I'll ask Mayerd. They were talking about covering it up, and if they did—" Lunzie didn't go on; Sassinak didn't push her. Time enough.

Lunzie was on the internal com, talking to Mayerd about medical databases, literature searches, and specific medical journals, in a slang Sassinak could hardly follow. "What do you mean, *Essentials of Cell Reference* isn't publishing? Oh—well, that's a stupid reason to change titles...Well, try *Bioethics Quarterly*, out of Amperan University Press, probably volume 73 to 77...nothing? Ceiver and Petruss were the authors...Old Mackelsey was the editor then, a real demon on stuff like this. Of course I'm sure of my reference: as far as I'm concerned it was maybe two years ago." Finally she clicked off and looked at Sass, a combination of smugness and concern. "You've got a big problem, great-great-great-granddaughter, bigger than you thought."

"Oh? I need any more?"

"Worse than one saboteur. Someone's been wiping files. Not just your files. All files."

"What exactly do you mean?" It was the first time she'd used her command voice in Lunzie's presence and she was glad to see that it was effective. It didn't, she noticed, scare Lunzie, but it did get a straight answer out of her.

"You never heard of clone colonies, nor has Mayerd who ought to have. I was a student on an Ethics Board concerning such a colony." Lunzie paused just a moment before continuing. "Some bright researchers had decided that it would be a possibility to have an entire colony sharing one genome: one colony made up exclusively of clones."

"But that can't work," Sassinak said, recalling what she knew of human genetics. "They'd inbreed, and besides you need different abilities, mixtures..."

Lunzie nodded. "Humans are generalists. Early human societies had no specialization except sexual. You can't build a large, complicated society that way, but a specialized colony, maybe. They thought they could. Anyway, in terms of the genetic engineering needed for certain environments, it would be a lot cheaper to engineer one, and then clone, even given the expense of cloning. And once they'd cleared the generation-limit problem, and figured out how to insert the other sex without changing *anything* else, it would be stable. If you know there are no dangerous recessives, then inbreeding won't cause trouble. Inbreeding merely raises the probability that, if such harmful genes exist, they will combine. If they don't exist, they can't combine."

"I see. But I'm not sure I believe."

"Wise. The Ethics team didn't either. Because I'd been around, so to speak, when that first colony was set up and because I'd worked in occupational fields, I had the chance to give an opinion on the ethical and practical implications. One of a panel of two hundred or so. We saw the clones, well, holos of them, and the research reports. I thought the project was dangerous, to both the clones and to everyone else. For one thing, in the kind of environment the clones were designed for, I thought random mutations would be for more frequent than the project suggested. Others thought the clones should be protected: the project had a fierce security rating anyway, but apparently it went a step further and all references were wiped."

"What does that have to do with Prosser, V. Tagin?"

Lunzie looked almost disgusted, then relented. "Sassinak, that colony was on Makstein VII. Everyone in it—*everyone* had the same genome and the same appearance. Exactly the same appearance. I saw holos of members of that colony. Your Mr. Prosser is *not* one of the clones, though he's been given the somatypes."

"Given?"

"The Index entries were written to cover the appearance of the clones should any of them travel, while indicating a range of values as if they were from a limited but normal colonial gene pool. His somatype has been faked, Sassinak. That's why you didn't catch it. No one would, who didn't know about clone colonies in general and Makstein VII in particular. And you couldn't find out because it's not in the files anymore."

"But someone knows," said Sassinak, hardly breathing for the thought of it. "Someone knew to fake his ID that way...."

"I wonder if your clever Lieutenant Commander Dupaynil could ask Mr. Prosser where he actually does come from?" Lunzie said in a drawl as she examined her fingertips, a mannerism which made Sassinak blink for it was much her own.

She keyed in Dupaynil's office and when he acknowledged, she sent him the spurious ID they'd uncovered. "Detain," was all she said but she knew Dupaynil would understand. "Great-great-great-grandmother," she said silkily, well pleased, "you're far too smart to stay in civilian medicine."

"Are you offering me a job?" The tone was meek, but the sharp glance belied it.

"Not a job exactly," Sassinak began. "A new career, a mid-life change, just right for fresh eyes that see with old knowledge that has somehow got lost for us who need it." Lunzie raised an inquiring eyebrow but her expression was alert, not skeptical. Sassinak went on with mounting enthusiasm, building on that little inkling she'd had before lunch. "Listen up, great-great. Do you realize what you have, to replace what you think you've lost? Files in your head, accessible facts that weren't wiped ... and who knows how many more than just references to a prohibited colony!"

"The old clone colony trick works only once, great-great."

"Let's not put arbitrary limits to what you have in your skull, revered ancestress. The old clone colony trick may not be all you've *saved* behind your fresh old eyes. You've got an immediate access to things forty-three and even a hundred and five years old which to me are either lost in datafiles or completely unknown. And this planetary piracy's been going on a long, long time by either of our standards." She saw the leap of interest in Lunzie's eyes and then the filming of old, sadder memories before the new hope replaced them. "I'm not offering you a job, old dear, I'm declaring you a team member, a refined intelligence that those planet-hungry moneygrubbing ratguts could never expect to have ranged against them. How could they? A family team with almost the same time-in-service of say, the Paradens..."

"Yes, the Paradens," and Lunzie sounded very grim. Then her thin lips curved into a smile that lit up her eyes. "A team? A planet pirate breaking team. I probably do know more than one useful thing. You're a commander, with a ship at your disposal..."

"Which is supposed to be hunting these planet pirates..."

"You're Fleet and you can ask certain questions and get certain information. But I'm," and Lunzie swelled with self-pride, "a nobody, no big family, no fortune, no connections—bar my present elegant company—and they don't need to know that. Yes, esteemed descendant, I accept your offer of a team action."

Sassinak had just picked up the brandy bottle to charge their glasses when a loud thump on the bulkhead and raised voices indicated some disturbance. Sassinak rolled her eyes at Lunzie and went to see what it was.

Aygar was poised on the balls of his feet just outside her office, with two marines denying him entry.

"Sorry about the noise, captain," said one of them. "He wants to speak to you and we told him..."

"You said," Aygar burst out to Sassinak, "that as members of FSP, we had privileges..."

"Interrupting my work isn't one of them," said Sassinak crisply. She felt a discreet tug on her sleeve. "However, I've a few moments to spare right now," and she dismissed the marines.

Aygar came into her office with slightly less swagger than usual. If he ever dropped that half-sulk of his, Sassinak thought he'd be extremely presentable. He didn't have the gross heavyworlder appearance. He could, in fact, if he mended his attitude, be taken as just a very well developed normal human type. He'd fill out a marine uniform very well indeed. And fill in other places.

"Did Major Currald recruit you?"

"He's trying," and that unexpected humor of Aygar flashed through again.

"I thought you intended to remain on Ireta, to protect all your hard work," Lunzie said in the mild sort of voice that Sassinak would use to elicit information. But she had a gleam in her eye as she regarded the handsome young Iretan that Sassinak also instantly recognized. It surprised her for a moment.

"I . . . I thought I wanted to stay," he said slowly, "if Ireta was going to remain our world. But it's not. And there are hundreds of worlds out there . . ."

"Which you could certainly visit as a marine." Sassinak sweetened her tone and added a smile. Two could play this game and she wasn't about to let her great-great-great-grandmother outmaneuver her in her own office.

Aygar regarded her through narrowed eyes. "I've also had an earful of the sort of prejudice heavyworlders face."

"My friend, if you act friendly and well behaved, people will like a young man as well favored as you," Sassinak said, ignoring Lunzie. "Life on Ireta and out of high-g environment has done you a favor. You look normal, although I'd wager that you'd withstand high-g stress better than most. Act friendly and most people will accept you with no qualms. Swagger around threatening them with your strength or size, and people will react with fear and hatred." Sassinak shrugged. "You're smart enough to catch on to that. You'd make an admirable marine."

Aygar cocked an eyebrow in challenge. "I think I can do better than that, Commander. I'm not about to settle for second best. Not again. I want the chance to learn. That's a privilege in the FSP, too, I understand. I want to learn what they didn't and wouldn't teach us. They consistently lied to us." Anger flashed in his eyes, a carefully contained anger that fascinated Sassinak for she hadn't expected such depths to this young man. "And they kept us ignorant!" That rankled the deepest. Sassinak could almost bless the cautious, paranoid mutineers for that blunder. "Because we," and when Aygar jabbed his thumb into his chest he meant all of his generations, "were not meant to have a part of this planet at all!"

"No," Sassinak said, suddenly recalling another snippet of

information gleaned from the cathedral's Thekian homily, "you weren't."

"In fact," Lunzie began, in a voice as sweet as her descendant's, "you've a score to settle with the planet pirates, too. With the heavyworlders who sent Cruss and that transport ship."

Aygar shot the medic such a keen look that Sassinak damned her own lapse—that'd teach her to look at the exterior of a man and forget what made him tick.

"You might say I do at that," he replied in much too mild a tone.

"In that case," Sassinak said, glancing for approval at Lunzie, "I think we could actually take you on as a...mmm...special advisor?"

"I've just signed on in a similar capacity," Lunzie said when she saw Aygar hesitate. "Special duties. Special training."

"Not in the usual chain of command," Sassinak gave him a look that had melted scores of junior officers.

"And who do I have to take orders from?" he asked, looking from Sassinak to Lunzie with the blandest of expressions on his handsome face.

"I'm still the captain," Sassinak said firmly, with a glare for her great-great-great-grandmother, who only grinned.

"You may be a lightweight, captain, but I think I can endure it," he said in a drawl, holding her gaze with his twinkling eyes.

"Welcome aboard, specialist Aygar!" And Sassinak extended her hand to take his in a firm shake of commitment.

Lunzie chuckled wickedly. "I think this is going to be a most..." her pause was pregnant "...instructive voyage, granddaughter. Shall we toss for it?"

Just for a moment, Aygar looked from one to the other, with the expression of someone who suspects he hasn't quite caught a hidden meaning.

"We specialists should stick together," she added, offering him a glass of the amber brandy. "You'll drink to that, won't you, Commander?"

"That, and other things! Like 'down with planet piracy!'" She pinned Lunzie with a meaningful stare, wondering just what she'd got herself in for this trip.

"Hear, hear!" Lunzie lustily agreed.